the
Night and its
Moon

the Night and its Moon

PIPER CJ

Bloom books

Sourcebooks and the colophon are registered trademarks of
Sourcebooks. Bloom Books is a trademark of Sourcebooks.

Published by Bloom Books, an imprint of Sourcebooks
P.O. Box 4410, Naperville, Illinois 60567-4410
(630) 961-3900
sourcebooks.com

Originally self-published in 2022 by Piper CJ.

Cataloging-in-Publication Data is on file with the Library of Congress.

Manufactured in the UK by Clays and distributed by
Dorling Kindersley Limited, London
10 9 8 7 6 5 4 3
003-335280-September/22

Can my dedication read:

"To buttery chardonnay, manic episodes,
and every child who wished they were a fairy"?

*No, you can't thank alcohol, mental illness,
and encourage escapism in your dedication.*

Well fine, then. I don't want one.

Continent of Eyradin

Sulgrave
Mountains

the unclaimed wilds

the Frozen
Straits

Raascot

Gwydir

the
Etal Isles

the university

Uaimh
Reev

Stone

Raasay
Forest

Farleigh

Yelagin

Farehold

Priory

the Temple
of the All Mother

Aubade

Henares

Tarkhany
Desert

Pronunciation Guide

Characters

Amaris: ah-MAR-iss
Achard: A-kard
Ceres: SERE-iss
Gadriel: GA-dree-ell
Malik: MAL-ik

Moirai: moy-RAI
Samael: sam-eye-ELL
Odrin: OH-drin
Zaccai: za-KAI

Places

Aubade: obeyed
Farleigh: far-LAY
Gyrradin: GEER-a-din
Gwydir: gwih-DEER

Henares: hen-AIR-ess
Raascot: RA-scott
Yelagin: YELL-a-ghin
Uaimh Reev: OOM reev

Monsters

Ag'drurath: AG-drath
Ag'imni: ag-IM-nee
Beseul: beh-ZOOL

Sustron: SUS-trun
Vageth: VA-geth

Prologue

IT'S SELDOM THAT A SOUND DEFINES THE COURSE OF history. A cannon might blast through a ship, its splintering contact a declaration of the early sounds of war. A bell could ring through a city to alert its citizens to invading forces, or a king might wail into the quiet of the night at the passing of his wife as his grief begins to slowly steer his kingdom. But this night's course-altering sound was sharp knocks against wood as they reverberated off the stones just past midnight.

People weren't supposed to visit the orphanage at such an hour. Nox was only three, but she knew a few things for sure. The first: Running in the halls made the matrons terribly angry. The second: Swimming in the pond was a very bad idea. The third: There was never, ever a reason to leave your bed after dark.

Until there was.

Rain tapped on the windowpanes, broken only by intermittent rumbles of thunder. Nox sat up in the warm folds of her sheets, listening intently as the house matrons stirred from their beds. The rhythmic pounding must have woken them too. She huddled against the high, whistling noises of wind on the windows, conjuring visions of ghosts and dark fae with sharp teeth and long talons. She blinked at the sleeping children who lined the cots around her. The storm's haunting melody and the staccato percussion of knocking didn't seem to bother them.

A new sound joined the storm. Not just the waking sounds of the matrons, but the grumbling of angry words. Nox slipped from her bed and followed the noise. The muted sounds of sleeping children disappeared behind her as the banging continued. Perhaps she wouldn't be the only one awoken.

Nox wrapped her fingers around the edge of the door and peered into the hall.

Though she hadn't made a sound, the unfortunate orange of a candle hurt her eyes. She lifted her forearm to shield the pain as the shadow gave way to light. The Gray Matron stilled at the top of the stairs. The matron peered down at her. If she had been anyone else, Nox knew the woman would have yelled. Instead, the matron frowned and her voice softened ever so slightly. "You shouldn't be out of bed, Nox. It's time to sleep."

The Gray Matron walked away without waiting to see whether Nox obeyed.

No, she would not be going back to bed. She watched with wide eyes as the woman disappeared down the hall with only the candle's flicker to betray her place in the dark. Something was at the door, and if the matron wanted to know, then she wanted to know too.

Nox followed. Curiosity pulled her forward like a rope, the desire to know burning hotter than the chill of the night. Carpet muted her footsteps as she padded along the corridor, allowing her to move soundlessly down the hall. If it hadn't been for the distracting crack of thunder and ongoing banging at the door, the matron might have spotted her as she descended the stairs. Instead, Nox remained several feet behind the Gray Matron and the buttery glow of her candlelight, unnoticed.

Nox knew she was clever for her age, as the matrons had repeatedly told her as much. On more than one occasion they'd complimented her curiosity, her studiousness, and remarked on how peculiar it was to see such an old soul in someone so little. She spent hours watching the world unfurl around her, learning its games, rules, and players. Her small stature and quiet nature helped her remain undetected as she observed.

Her cleverness for shadows reassured her she wouldn't be spotted if she crouched behind a table in the foyer. The curtain of her hair fell around her, concealing her in the shadowy puddle of her hiding place. She curled her hands around her toes to warm them as she sat in darkened silence, watching, inhaling the scent of rain and wet earth and the cold, sharp smell of late seasons.

A visitor in the middle of the night was a new player. This was a game she'd never seen before.

The matron reached the large wooden front door and lifted the iron cover to the glass spyhole carved into its middle. She peered at whoever pounded on the door from their place on the landing. The matron appeared to consider her options briefly before lifting the wooden slot barricading the manor from trespassers. The knocking stopped the moment she began to pull the door open. Swirling raindrops blew over the threshold with windswept fury as if the storm itself spat in her face. A cloaked, rain-drenched man with wild eyes leered down at the woman in her wool shawl and nightclothes. He did not step into the manor, but the sight of him sent a shiver through Nox all the same.

"Agnes, I have something you'll want to see."

The Gray Matron started to shake her head with a disgruntled sound. She moved to push the door shut once more, ridding herself of the bother of the rain and the unwanted presence of the stranger.

The man flattened his palm against the door, refusing to let it close.

He pushed past her as he crossed the threshold. The Gray Matron let out an irritated protest, but the man didn't seem to care. He stopped on the landing and presented a large, covered bundle that he'd tucked carefully under his arm. He lifted the treasure into the space between the two of them. Wanting to know what the man held, Nox leaned forward as far as she could. She frowned, realizing she wouldn't be able to see his treasure without giving herself away.

Water droplets dripped from the blankets that shielded the bundle onto the rug below. The matron glared, whispering something in sharp, angry tones. Nox strained her ears but couldn't discern one verbal hiss from the other. The pounding rain and angry howls of wind drowned out whatever the two were saying. She wished they'd shut the door. The storm was wetting the carpet and drenching the matron's nightclothes, hair, and face. A few stray droplets carried in on the wind and pressed chilly kisses into Nox's face, hands, and knees.

The Gray Matron tried again to usher the man out of the hall, but he disregarded her efforts entirely.

The man began to uncover the bundle. Matron Agnes shook her head again, volume growing with her anger.

"I don't do that anymore," she said.

The man's eyes seemed to sparkle with a smile, though his mouth did not curve as it should. Nox's stomach twisted uncomfortably at the man's unsavory delight. He grinned. "You mean you *didn't* do this anymore. That was before you saw what I've brought you." He peeled off the sopping wet top layer of blankets, continuing to unwrap what appeared to be a wicker basket. He lifted the bundle, urging the matron to peer inside.

Matron Agnes lifted her candle close to the bundle and let out a small gasp as its glow illuminated whatever it contained. "Wait," she breathed.

Even from her puddle of shadow, Nox could feel the way the energy shifted.

The Gray Matron hurried to the door and closed it the rest of the way, shutting out the world beyond and the storms that raged. She ushered the man a few more steps inside the manor onto dry carpet. The new silence had a smothering effect. With the door latched once again, the wind, rain, and thunder were muted with unnatural intensity. The silence was so pressing that Nox wondered if they could hear her little heart as it thundered with curious anticipation.

She clutched herself more tightly, not only to protect herself from the cold but to hold herself back from the temptation to see what had caused the Gray Matron to gasp.

The Gray Matron walked away from the man to light the hall's fixtures. She held her candle to the lanterns on either side of the door, chasing the eerie gloom from the room as their oil-soaked rags caught fire. While the lanterns filled the foyer with light, Nox remained concealed. The woman returned to the basket, her face betraying a complex array of emotions. Wary curiosity bubbled to the forefront as she stared down at whatever had been smuggled into the manor.

The Gray Matron's fingers stayed against her mouth, stifling her sharp inhalation. She looked up at the man's degenerate grin. Nox's eyes flitted between them before fixating on the strange way the man's eyes and mouth failed to match as he smiled. The pair kept their voices low as they spoke, tones hushed with secrecy.

Nox scrunched her face in whatever unnamed frustration burbled within her. She hated that she couldn't hear. She wanted them to share what they'd found. She needed the tether that wrapped itself fully within her chest and pulled her toward the basket to relax its taut hold.

"Well, that does change things." The matron's words seemed painted with disbelief.

"What did I tell you?" the stranger asked.

She didn't look away from the bundle.

The man pushed on. "It's just past its first birthday. It won't be needing a wet nurse. Anything in the kitchen can be mushed up right fine. It's already made it through the hardest time. I've been traveling with it for nearly two weeks and had no trouble keeping it alive."

"Two weeks?" The matron's brows collected in the middle as calculations flitted behind her eyes. "Where did you find it? Why did you bring it here?"

"You know me," he said with too much familiarity. "I owed you one. You deserved first bid at the treasure."

Nox heard their words but couldn't fully understand their meaning.

The matron's face creased as her mind moved. She seemed to experience conflicting emotions that gathered in the twist of her mouth, the wrinkle of her forehead, and the parallel lines between her brows. She stared for a while longer before asking, "How much do you want for it?"

"Fifty crowns."

She made a sound between a cough and a laugh that shocked Nox from her pose in the stillness of the quiet manor. She jolted upright in a startle, but the shadows clung to her, keeping her safe from detection. The matron's bark mixed with the sounds of the storm outside. The shadows from the lanterns made her face look like an animal as she prolonged her disbelieving gape.

"Fifty crowns! There isn't nothing in the good goddess's lighted earth worth fifty!" The matron looked over her shoulder, her gaze roving up the stairs as if she could see through the stones and into the dormitories where the children rested on their cots. Nox curled more tightly into herself as the matron spoke. "I haven't paid a penny over five silvers for half the bastards in here. I have one girl worth ten crowns on a good day, and she's the rarest of them all. Ain't no one spending fifty crowns on your stolen babe."

The man's gaze no longer twinkled. His mouth tugged upward, revealing his teeth, cold smile glinting in the candlelight. He said nothing but remained holding the basket, unmoving.

The Gray Matron balked. "I'll give you fifteen."

He remained impassively rooted to the carpet.

"Twenty, and that's the highest I'll go."

Nox knew little of money, except that it was good to have some and that people always wanted more. She thought of the coppers, steel, and golds of the heavy coins she'd seen and what it might be like to have twenty metal circles in her tiny hands. Instead, she continued to clutch her toes against the cold. She wiggled them within her hands, knowing she had ten toes and ten fingers. That was twenty.

The Gray Matron's offer had already betrayed her. She wanted whatever the stranger possessed.

The man tilted his head ever so slightly, raising a brow. Rain dripped off his soaked cloak. Small puddles formed on the carpet around his wet boots. "Farleigh isn't the only mill on this side of the mountains, Agnes. It's a rainy night, and I don't particularly want to play games. I like you, and we've done business in the past, so I wanted to give you the first crack at the treasure. But you and I both know that no one's getting this pretty thing for a cent less than fifty crowns."

The matron shuffled her weight from one foot to the other for a moment. "Is it a boy?"

"It's a girl."

She chewed her lip, looking conflicted. She lowered her voice when she spoke again.

"Your stolen goods were fine when we were younger." She seemed to be arguing against herself. "We had a good thing back then. You'd take from the village. I told myself you were doing a favor to the parents, I did. You were taking away a mouth to feed. I've always preferred that parents come to me on their own, of course... I'm not that person anymore."

Nox was still listening intently as the matron spoke. Her eyes had adapted to the dark, but she strained them as she squinted up at the matron, hoping it might help her understand what was happening.

"I didn't feel guilty, you know? I always felt I was doing a good thing—we did a good thing. Give a poor mother a silver to feed the rest of the young ones at home. Perhaps even a few pennies to a peasant or a town whore so she could get boots for the winter or a warm blanket in exchange for the struggles of motherhood. It was a good thing, it was. Times were different then. But after..." She shook herself and met the man's eyes. "It's not like that. People are going to come searching for this one. Look at her."

His smile fell a bit as he spoke with seriousness. The hush of his voice sent a chill through the hall. "No one is going to come looking for her."

The matron's brows puckered. She let the silence

between them stretch. The window and rain beyond the closed door had a soothing, stifling effect on the room. Torches flickered, rain droplets continued to drip onto the floor from soaked clothes, thunder rumbled in the distance, and yet the matron stared.

"Will she be any trouble? With her lineage, I mean?"

"You're asking me if she's one of them?"

The matron said nothing.

He didn't seem perturbed by the question. "Raise her however you want, and don't let her give you trouble. When the time comes, sell her for a hundred."

She reached a hand in close to touch whatever was within the bundle. Her fingers stroked a slow line along the unseen package. Nox's fingers twitched from where she hid, aching to feel whatever it was for herself. "One hundred?"

The man's wordless stare seemed to be the only negotiation tactic he required.

"I said I was done," she repeated. Despite her words, it was clear she had already decided. Her fingers lingered on whatever or whoever was inside the basket. Her words came out nearly as a purr: "Turn fifty crowns into one hundred...or one thousand." She finally lifted her eyes to the man, speaking with certainty. "Never again. After this, you don't come back."

He dipped his chin once in solemn acknowledgment.

The Gray Matron sent him a final, telling look before giving him a hushed command and pattering away from the large landing room. She headed up the stone stairs and down the corridor lined with doors to the children's rooms. A moment stretched when the man watched after her, shifting his weight on the threshold.

The tether tugged Nox once more, and she obeyed its call.

From her hiding space several paces away, she straightened her legs and stepped out from where she'd been crouching. The man noticed her immediately. He smiled, his face a bit soft, a bit sad. For the first time that night, Nox thought his expression held no wickedness. Now that the matron was absent, he was able to drop whatever hardness he'd needed for negotiations. Nox saw how droplets of water caught in his beard and reflected in the torchlight, giving him something of a shimmer. The sparkle seemed reassuring somehow.

The man knelt on one knee and placed the wicker basket on the floor between them.

"Do you want to see?" he asked. His voice lowered with a paternal gentleness, though he framed his question like a conspiratorial temptation.

She did indeed. Nox had no desire to draw closer to a strange man, but the basket called to her. She took a few careful steps across the cold stones of the corridor onto the carpet of the threshold. Her bare feet paused on the fibers of the scratchy rug. Her eyes felt too large as she gazed at the man and his treasure. A renewed rush of rain and earth greeted her with every step she took.

He looked at her expectantly. She remained several cautious arms' lengths away from him. He chuckled quietly, as though he knew she wasn't permitted to be awake past bed and had no interest in getting her in trouble.

He motioned her toward the basket. Nox took the opening. She moved forward on the tips of her toes, hands extended. She folded her fingers around the wicker edge of the basket and looked. She stared down at the baby inside, her glossy hair creating a shadowed curtain around them while she peered. A rush of something other than rain—something more like cold and pine—drifted up from the swaddled little one. Nox peered at the infant wrapped in furs, sleeping soundly despite the turmoil raging outside.

"It's a baby," she whispered. She did not look back up to the man. For all she cared, he had ceased existing. She was transfixed.

Nox had seen babies before. The matrons let all the children play together, often with the older ones looking after the younger ones. Infants never lasted long in the manor, sometimes for good reasons, sometimes for bad. The orphans who survived their first year of life were taken off the matrons' hands more quickly than the rest of the children. Babies came and went, creating fairy tales amongst the children built on hopes of escape and wishful thinking.

Nox had sat excitedly at the feet of the older children who'd woven tales of orphans adopted by knights, by fae, by kings and queens, or by leagues of assassins who guarded the continent. Her favorite story was that of a princess who'd come to their orphanage in search of an infant boy to match her husband's golden-brown hair. The princess had traded her daughter—one with the traitorous features of a love outside of marriage—for a golden-haired boy who could inherit the throne. It was a story she and the others had asked to hear time and time again, all of them hoping that one day it might be they who were swept away from the dingy cots and cold floors and bland food for life in a castle.

As Nox looked at the baby in the basket, she wondered what kind of story they'd tell about her. This babe was unlike any she'd ever seen.

Nox took a small, tanned hand and brushed a silver-white strand of hair out of the baby's face. The motion revealed a tuft of white brows and thick white eyelashes.

The baby stirred slightly at the movement, eyes fluttering open. It didn't cry when it looked at her. Instead, it seemed to wiggle within its blankets, blinking happily at her with lavender-colored eyes flecked with silver and cooing slightly before drifting back to sleep.

"She's made of snow," Nox said quietly.

"That she is."

PART ONE

Alone, Together

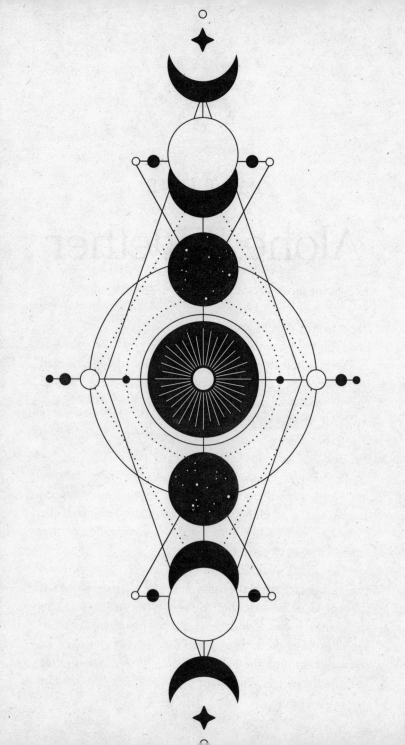

One

FEW OF LIFE'S JOYS ARE AS PURE AS A PRETTY ROCK.
Nox's eyes twinkled with amusement as she took the odd shape from Amaris's outstretched hand. Glittery bits crumbled from Amaris's palm like powdered stardust as she brushed her hands together. Nox dragged a nail over the rock, curious at how the shimmery surface flaked at her touch.

"Where did you find it?" she asked.

"There are a whole bunch by the pond. They look like jewels. Come look!"

There was no such thing as a day without chores, but occasionally the goddess smiled down on the children and allowed a break from the toils of life in Farleigh. The list of dos and don'ts before enjoying the pleasure of a free afternoon was exhausting.

Do all of your chores. Don't enter the rooms or offices beholden to the matrons. Do ask your peers if they need help with their duties, ensure everything in the manor is clean, and check on the younger children. Don't go into the kitchen, get stains on your clothes, or track dirt through the halls. Do thank the All Mother for your free time by saying your prayers. Don't yell, run, or leave the grounds. And whatever you do, don't disturb Matron Agnes.

Today, Nox and Amaris had been separated. It was her least favorite kind of day.

Nox's hands had pickled and pruned from her hours scrubbing in the laundry while Amaris was tasked with the gentler chore of dusting the furniture. When she'd finished with the soap and bubbles and linens, Nox stumbled up the stairs to lie down. She'd rather stare at the ceiling and trace the crown molding in silence than interact with peers.

She'd been surprised, but always happy, when Amaris had entered with a handful of natural magic.

"You went to the pond? Already?" Nox asked, attempting to bury whatever small hurt at the idea that Amaris had gone without her.

Amaris made a face. She crossed her arms defensively. "Just for a minute," she said. "I was already outside when I helped shake the dust from the curtains, and it's really nice out. There are no matrons there yet. Don't be mad! Now, are you going to come look or not?"

Two mosquito bites, four stumbles over exposed roots, and one pause for the distracted plucking of a flower later, they arrived at the pond's edge. Amaris was right—it was indeed a beautiful day. The bright, blue sky of early summer was neither too hot nor too cold. The air smelled faintly floral from the lavender bushes that clustered around the property. If it weren't for the numerous other children in and around the water, the day would have been perfect. One of her least favorite frogs, a boy named Achard, was splashing a pair of freck-led sisters rather obnoxiously from where they sat on the shore.

Her lip curled in irritation whenever she saw him.

Perhaps she was meant to be the bigger person. Achard had been punished more times than most in the house, the spankings, the time locked in isolation, and the thousands of lines of contrition that would stoke the fire of his hateful heart. Anytime a matron took out her anger on him, he turned around and unleashed his fists on one of his peers. Misery may love company, but Nox's sympathy ran dry whenever Achard forced others to join his suffering.

Nox couldn't make out what the older sister said to the boy as she sheltered the ginger toddler from the water, but apparently, it had irritated him. The squelching sounds of mud filled the air as he stomped from the pond.

"Leech!" someone screamed.

A boy with britches rolled up to his knees looked down at his toes in horror at the swollen parasite suckling on his ankles. The children around him shrieked as he pulled it off his leg and began to chase them with the disgusting aquatic worm. Nox nearly gagged in horror, disgusted by the water and its murky terrors. She was equally agitated by the presence of other people, but there was little she could do about that.

She turned to Amaris, angling her body away from the chaos as she asked, "Where are these secret jewels?"

While one side of the pond offered shallow, muddy shores, the rest was rimmed with scattered pines, boxelder trees, and a cluster of enormous, gray boulders. The rocks were tall enough that the older children would sometimes jump from them into the water below, though Nox could imagine few fates more horrifying than plunging into its brackish, brown depths. Amaris led Nox around the pond's rim, scaling tenaciously up the side of one of the boulders farthest from the water.

Nox scrambled up the edge with less grace. She examined her reddened palms for loose pine needles and scrapes as she approached the place where Amaris crouched. Toward the middle, a white-gold cluster of strange rocks seemed to grow from the boulder itself, almost like mushrooms from a rotting log.

"Your jewels?"

"Aren't they pretty! They're too far from the water for jumping, so I don't think the others have found them."

Perhaps they'd found them, perhaps they hadn't. Clearly, no one had cared enough about the scaly, sparkly rock to chip it from its boulder and bring it into the manor. Nox picked at it curiously, wondering how a rock could flake like pastry dough.

"How many pretty rocks do you think Achard is worth?" Nox asked, jutting her chin to the obnoxious pack of boys.

"Oh! I've already done the math on this one," Amaris said. She scraped the rock against the boulder, dusting the resulting film onto her palm. She offered her handful of stardust to Nox, saying, "Here you are. Go buy yourself an Achard."

Nox's cheeks ached from smiling. It felt good to laugh. The sunshine tumbled from the sky, down her throat and into her belly.

Amaris sent the sparkling powder into the sky with a single puff. She giggled as the dust glittered around them, a sound that reminded Nox of the tinkling of silver bells that covered the manor during the yule holidays. Her wit was sharper than her genteel exterior made others believe. She was little but had the dry, sidelong humor jokes and quick responses that Nox had only heard in passing from the eldest children or the least pious matrons. It was one in a list of ten thousand things she loved about

Amaris. She couldn't imagine what life would be like if they weren't together.

"Oh, Amaris!" Nox gasped, looking up from the distant shores.

"What?" Amaris froze.

Nox grabbed the hem of her dress and immediately began to dab at a splotch of blood on Amaris's knee. Amaris made a frustrated sound but sank into the rock, allowing the small wound to be cleaned.

"You're lucky it doesn't look bad. But they won't be happy." Nox sighed.

"They're never happy."

Nox deflated, clutching her handful of flaky gems until they bit into her hands. Only moments prior they'd had hands full of stars and bellies full of sunshine. She hadn't meant to ruin it. She said, "They just want to keep you safe."

Amaris was quiet for a long time. A small breeze picked up the silvery strands of her hair. It fluttered around her like a cloud before she turned back to Nox. Her frosted lashes remained lowered over her eyes as she told Nox she was ready to go back to the manor, her voice as damp as her spirits. Nox kicked herself internally. She hadn't meant to spoil what little fun free time they had.

Amaris hadn't waited for a response before scaling back down the tall, gray boulders.

Nox followed, her frown absorbing into her skin. She kept her eyes on her feet as they rounded the trees that crowded the far shore until they came upon a familiar, obnoxious voice.

"Look who it is!" Achard put his hands on his hips. Nox found Achard irritating on the best of days and worthy of being drowned in the pond on the worst of days. She briefly debated whether it would be worth it to get in the vile pond water if it meant holding his head under the surface.

She was no stranger to her temper. Emotion roiled through her, heating her cheeks and forcing her hands into fists. She opened her mouth to snap back when Amaris beat her to the punch.

"I'm sorry," Amaris said. "It must be hard for you to see someone who has a friend who actually likes them."

Nox wanted to laugh, but her body spiked with adrenaline. If Achard retaliated, she'd at least have an excuse to give him a black eye. The moment lingered between them as Achard stood on the muddy shore, slack-jawed and seething. Amaris returned a proud, defiant glare. It was rare that a matron saved the day, but a voice calling from the manor cut their altercation short. The standoff simmered for a moment as a matron's voice called again, the children refusing to break eye contact.

"Knock it off" came the soft voice of the redheaded girl from over their shoulder.

Nox swallowed in surprise at who had spoken. It was rare to get a peep out of the sisters, and no one in Farleigh blamed them.

Their arrival had been memorable and traumatic for everyone.

The pair of strawberry-haired siblings had been dropped off together many years ago in the filthiest of rags. Emily and Ana's arrival had not been a clandestine event in the middle of the night but a very public, humiliating midday display while the children of Farleigh looked on from their seats in the dining hall. The girls' bedraggled mother had been desperate to give them a roof over their head and something to eat other than the cold water and the scraps from pitying strangers.

The peasant woman had stood in the foyer with smudged hands cupped to receive the coin for which she'd traded her only children. Agnes had paid her well, perhaps better than the girls had been worth, not only as compensation for the loss of the girls but also as a quiet charity for the woman to find a place to sleep for the night and a hot bath.

Nox's heart squeezed at the memory while she listened, not daring to breathe.

Achard rolled his eyes "From the sisters—"

Emily popped the freckled toddler onto her hip and pointed her scowl at Achard. "They don't have to be sisters to be friends," she said, squeezing her sibling against her chest. She began the walk back to the manor.

"Don't waste your time thinking about him," Nox said, grabbing for Amaris's hand.

"I never do," Amaris promised.

Two

NOX HADN'T GOTTEN TO ENJOY ANY OF HER PLANS FOR the morning. She normally had until lunchtime before the frenzied banshee wails of the matrons signaled the man's unwanted arrival. Month after month, they scrambled like headless chickens, acting as if it were the bishop's first time visiting. Generally, their exaggeration annoyed her. Today, she agreed. It was irritating that the man of the cloth had arrived so soon after breakfast.

There would be no sketching, no riffling through the maps she'd stashed, and no flipping through the stolen books she'd carefully tucked between the wall and the cabinet. The moment she heard Agnes's curses, Nox knew her window for joy had closed.

She stashed her books while the arguing continued from down the hall. She fixed the bed, tucking the sheets into neat lines within her cot until it matched all the perfectly empty rectangles surrounding her. Most of the orphans hated the first day of the month. She knew Amaris counted herself amongst those who found it to be one of the twelve worst days of the year, and yet, it had always been amongst Nox's favorites. She had time to herself. And when she wasn't alone, she was with Amaris.

The sharp sound of someone getting a tongue-lashing let her know that Agnes had broken free from the matron's rooms.

Feet slapped down the hall, and Nox knew she had exactly fifteen seconds before she would be called upon. She folded her hands in her lap, straightened her back, mimicked the most sanctimonious expression she could think of. It was a day intended to honor the All Mother, after all.

The door to her dormitory flew open. The wood banged against the stone wall behind it as it swung on its hinges. Agnes had brushed her peppered hair into a familiar bun, its muted grays matching her dull linens. The matron's temper more than made up for any subdued appearance.

"He's early," Matron Agnes hissed.

Nox nodded. "I'll be right there."

"Your hair isn't braided?" Agnes asked.

Nox blinked with genuine surprise. "He's early! You said it yourself. Do you want me to fix it first—"

"No." The woman gaped in horror at the suggestion. "Get downstairs now!"

Nox turned her temper inward, fueling an ever-burning irritation. She gathered the linens of her skirt into her fingers as she ran down the stairs, joining the matron in the foyer. Agnes pulled her shoulders back and released a long, slow exhale. She painted a reverent, placating smile onto her otherwise bitter features before she opened the door.

Agnes bowed as she ushered the man into Farleigh. "Your Excellency."

Through trial and error, Nox had learned better than to speak in the bishop's presence. She kept her eyes on her soft leather shoes but could see the steepled press of his fingers from her peripherals.

The bishop was the only adult male Nox had ever

officially met, and it had taken roughly thirty seconds upon their first encounter for her to know that she hated him. The man was impeccably dressed and appeared to be in his early fifties. He was always dressed in the whites and golds of his station. Agnes was of similar age and equally intimidating stature, but she was cunning enough to play whatever games of diplomacy were required of her.

Nox had learned more about games and how to play them from Matron Agnes than from anyone else. The Gray Matron had the sort of wicked cleverness that allowed her to see several moves ahead of her opponent at all times. Agnes acted accordingly, and Nox made an excellent student. The Gray Matron often won the game without the competition realizing they were playing at all.

Despite the smell of the road and the horses outside, the bishop was clouded by a choking perfume of white musk and lemons. There was a falseness to the lemon scent that made Nox's stomach turn, and she knew from the years of uncomfortable mutterings that she wasn't the only one who struggled to keep her breakfast down after the bishop had left his stench throughout the orphanage. The tangy smell and its link to the church drove the children to hate the presence of citrus if ever it was brought from the coast.

Nox parted her lips slightly, breathing through her mouth.

The bishop did not acknowledge Nox, but she'd expected as much. He never did, no matter how often he visited. At least the thin, balding man kept his visits brief—a small blessing.

Agnes accepted the bishop's traveling cloak. She looked fleetingly at Nox as she said, "Please hang this in my office, and be sure everything is in order."

Though the matron said "everything," only one thing was truly implied.

Nox nodded. She did exactly what was expected of her and nothing more. Her bronze skin was a showcase to the church of the holy nature of Farleigh and its reach beyond Farehold's borders. She served as a living advertisement of the matron's magnanimity and charity.

She accepted the bishop's cloak, fully aware how her very presence served as a display of tokenism as her tanned fingers contrasted against the white and gold of his fabric. It was more than a little insulting, but she didn't mind being trotted out like a show pony if it meant she could then disappear for the rest of the day. It was better than staying amidst the others and being subjected to their miserable monthly traditions. She dipped her chin slightly in obligatory respect. She caught the bishop's flicker of approval as she departed.

The bishop would be gone within an hour or two. The man typically breezed through the manor, made notes of any new additions to the population, inspected the premises, and dutifully inquired whether any of the small magics had manifested in any of the children. If everything went according to plan, the bishop would leave empty-handed once more.

It had been a long time since the manor had seen a faeling, as the last young boy with beautiful elfin features and a gentle disposition had one traitorous attribute betraying half of his heritage. He may not have inherited the pointed ears of the fair folk, but his forest-green irises had been nearly double the size of his human peers'. Any careful student would see his eyes as evidence of his lineage. She wondered if this was the fate the matrons feared for Amaris. Though she lacked the sharpened canines and slender point of her ears, everyone who laid eyes on Amaris suspected her to be fae around the edges.

Nox hadn't participated directly in the rumors, but

25

it was hard to miss what was said at dinnertime after the boy's departure. Some of the children swore he could speak to the trees. Others insisted they'd seen him move the wind. The child may have been utterly powerless, possessing little more than a single telltale feature of a fae lineage, but it hadn't mattered. The bishop had taken him from the manor, and the boy was never heard from again.

Nox had asked Matron Mable what use the bishop had of him. The matron said that some religious folk believed both the fae and those born with the small magics to be manifestations of the goddess's power. As such, Farehold's fae were often conscripted to work by the church or put in servitude to the crown. Whispered rumors circulated that the faeling was somewhere in a house of the goddesses, living in fine robes, worshipping the All Mother and eating as much fruit as he liked. Fae were so rare in Farehold that Nox felt with some certainty it had been her first and last opportunity to meet one, halfling though he might have been.

She decided that being born fae in such a world seemed like more of a curse than a blessing. Being different in any capacity was a threat. She had been separated from the others, given tasks and assignments and stations for years based largely on her looks. Even Amaris, with her moonlit hair and lilac eyes, was guarded like a secret to prevent the very same fate from happening to her.

It was attractive to think that the fae boy was living a beautiful life, but Nox didn't believe in happy endings. The others invented stories to help make sense of a chaotic world, but their daydreams made the world no less terrible. She wouldn't rob them of their doe-eyed dreams, but in a world so cold, she knew better than to let herself hope.

Cloak draped over her arm, she left the foyer and

headed for the stairs. She turned down the corridor and hurried along the line of dormitories, stopping at the third dorm on the right. Her face shifted the moment she opened the door. The heaviness she carried fell from her shoulders like rainwater off a roof. Nox beamed at her white-haired friend alone inside.

"Finally!"

"You ready, Snowflake?"

Amaris was on the bed closest to the door. Her smile glowed the moment Nox entered the room. Her feet dangled off the edge as her hands clutched either side of the mattress, feet kicking impatiently. She hopped up from the bed, her starlight hair hanging loosely down her back.

"I found a thing for you."

Nox smiled. "You always find things."

Amaris procured something green, offering it to Nox. "It's so pretty though. I knew you'd want to see it. Look at the pattern. It looks like writing in a distant language, doesn't it?"

Nox took the leaf and smiled, agreeing. "It's from a bug's language. A worm does this."

Amaris rolled her eyes. "I know it's from a worm. I'm just saying it *looks* like writing from a far-off land, like in those books. I thought you might like it."

"I do like it," she promised, tucking it into her pocket. Amaris had the sort of habit that Nox was quite certain she'd die without. Whenever Amaris found a particularly twisted stick, a pretty drawing, a new book, a spare pastry, or a pretty rock, she'd bring the object of tangible affection to the dorms and offer it to Nox. There wasn't a lot of room at Farleigh to keep odds and ends, but Nox had dedicated a sock to storing the treasures that could be effectively hidden from the matrons.

Amaris smiled with some degree of victory.

"Come on," Nox said. She led the way, and Amaris followed wordlessly along the length of the hall before they let themselves into the Gray Matron's study. Nox hung up the bishop's cloak but was nowhere near ready to leave the room. It was far from her first time in there, but every visit felt like a special adventure. There was something about forbidden spaces that gave them an added weight of importance.

Agnes's private study looked nothing like the rest of the orphanage. While Farleigh was a mundane mix of gray stone, simple linens, and cotton dresses, this was laminated with fleur-de-lis wallpaper and a plush carpet that existed only within the confines of her study. A gaudy painting of Farehold's royal family, an embroidered tapestry of Gyrradin, and several decorative objects were mounted on the wall. Each time Nox entered never failed to conjure a jarring sense of incongruity. It was a bit like traveling to a foreign land that remained hidden within the always locked study of their very orphanage.

"Where do you think all this stuff came from?" Amaris asked, wandering around the room. "I've never seen anything new added."

Nox shrugged. "Her past life as a dragon sitting atop a treasure hoard."

"Are dragons real?"

Nox shrugged again, answering, "I don't think so, but I know Agnes is real, and she's enough of a monster for the continent, don't you think?"

A large, mahogany desk rested at the study's center. There were ordinary things on it like neat stacks of papers, rows of books, and bottles of ink. Then there were more peculiar oddities: a crystal sphere on what appeared to be the body of a golden snail, a pen with a long, black embellished feather quill, and an ornamental carving of a stag. Some furnishings were enclosed in glass with delicate possessions hidden behind their frosted doors. Shelves were filled with books of various sizes and in various states of decay, a mix of old, leather, dusty things and small, new, bright bindings with jewel-covered backs and scarcely a sign of use.

"Look at this," Nox said from across the room.

Amaris looked up from where she had been tracing her pale finger along a map of the kingdom, finding Farleigh pinned with a star. The dry, scratchy parchment created a dragging noise beneath her finger as Amaris allowed her nail to trace their place in the world. Farleigh was just up and to the right of the center of the map, sitting before a sprawl of forest that was intercepted by an endless stretch of darkly shaded mountains. The dotted line that separated them from the northern kingdom loomed terribly close. It wouldn't do them much good to dwell on matters of geography, though.

Amaris stepped away from the map and joined Nox in front of the frosted cabinet doors. Inside, the black velvet head of a mannequin sat with a black-gem-studded silver tiara resting atop.

"Can you imagine Matron Agnes in such a thing?" Amaris asked, voice tinged with amusement.

"I like to think she puts it on after we've gone to bed." Nox giggled.

"Put it on," Amaris goaded.

"Are you trying to get me in trouble? You're the little princess—you put it on."

"Where do you think she got the money for all of these things?" Amaris asked, and Nox felt a small stab that the girl hadn't yet pieced together the answer. Maybe it was a blessing to still hold on to the scraps of innocence that allowed her to be spared from the harsh realities of their mill. She didn't want to be the one to shatter Amaris's world.

Nox shook her head, as she did whenever she couldn't find the right words for what needed to be said. She angled her body to signal that their time playing with forbidden treasures had come to an end.

Amaris sighed. "Where does she want me to go this time?"

Nox scrunched her face. "She didn't say, but I think we're safest in the kitchen. I'll stick you in with the potatoes." She smiled at her joke. "We probably shouldn't be in Agnes's room for much longer if we don't want to get caught, in case they come in here to talk business. Besides, even if the bishop visits the kitchen to see that it's clean, he never goes into the pantry."

"But the pantry is so dirty!"

"Then I guess you're getting a bath tonight."

Amaris shivered preemptively at the thought of the chilly bathwater. It was challenging enough for the matrons to keep the orphans clean. Heating the water between children would have been an impossible inconvenience.

"What if we hid in the clean laundry basket? It would smell much nicer."

"I bet it would," she said, deflecting, "but the potatoes are calling." Nox gave Amaris a gentle push out of the office and closed the door behind them.

Most days in Farleigh blurred together with monotony. The breaks in boredom and continuity were moments like these—days of stress, fear, and trepidation. The ability to find small, secret joys amidst stomach-churning anxiety was something Nox didn't take for granted. She knew they wouldn't have their privacy much longer.

Three

IF THEY WERE DOOMED TO SUFFER, THEY MIGHT AS WELL do it somewhere with the possibility of food. Hopelessness was less manageable on an empty stomach.

The girls avoided the front of the manor, knowing it was where the bishop monitored the students and their lessons. A set of narrow, curving stairs connected the corridor's end directly to the kitchen below before opening into the world and forest beyond. It had probably been intended for servants upon the manor's construction but had long since served as a functional convenience for the matrons to drift from the kitchens to the chambers as they monitored their wards.

Following the sizzling scents of meat and onion, the girls descended the steps. Nox pushed open the door, which led them into a large, sweltering room. Heat from the crackling fire beneath the pot of stew hit the girls immediately as they entered. Nox was comforted by the figure she saw in the kitchen. Matron Mable was the youngest matron in the house, and whenever she was on kitchen duty, her presence gave the children some hope for the edibility of the evening meal. Mable was one of the few matrons who believed in spices and seasoning, which made her meals a blessing compared to the bland porridges and dry meats prepared by the others.

Mable's face perked at the sight of the girls, and Nox waved a quiet hello. Mable, scarcely in her thirties, was an honest young woman with the kind of simple generosity that seemed to foster no dreams that reached beyond the walls of her life in Farleigh. Her hair had curled a bit against the heat of the kitchen, sweat and steam unraveling a few loose strands from the bun she'd gathered at the nape of her neck.

The girls smiled at the matron in her pressed gray linens and apron, kneading dough on the wooden block table where they opened the door to the room. Mable knew as well as anyone in the manor that it did no good to draw attention on days the bishop visited. She wordlessly jutted her chin upward and to the left, motioning the girls toward the pantry as she smiled in farewell. Nox offered a thankful gesture and led her friend into the dark, enclosed space, shutting the door behind them.

The air was slightly cooler behind the closed door. Earthy smells of dirt and root vegetables overpowered the stew that simmered just beyond the pantry door.

"Welcome to your kingdom for the day," Nox said dryly.

Amaris ran her finger along the shelf to collect dust. She made a face at the dirt.

"Careful. Don't get a splinter," Nox cautioned.

Amaris attempted to blow the dust off her finger, but it was caked on too heavily. She wiped it on her pants. "Goddess forbid I get a splinter. The world would end."

Nox's mouth quirked into a half smile as she answered, "They'd blame me if you got hurt, and you know it." She took a seat on the floor of the little room and reclined against a sack of flour. She raised one arm, allowing Amaris to tuck herself in tightly.

"I hate the first day of the month," Amaris said.

Nox pressed a kiss on the top of Amaris's head with a reassuring gentleness. "I don't think it's so bad."

While the kitchen smelled of what would undoubtedly be dinner and the pantry of roots, Amaris's hair had always smelled like juniper. It was the sweet, lingering scent of the forest and the melting snow that signaled the end of winter. The girls were roughly two years apart in age, and while some days it seemed like no time at all, in these protective moments, it felt like a lifetime.

"What if we just...didn't hide? Would it be so bad if we stopped running and let the bishop see me? Or"—Amaris reached her hand up to a shelf, threatening to touch it—"what if we just cut up my hands on splinters? Let's cover me in scars!" She smiled at the suggestion, but Nox didn't return the expression.

Her mouth turned down, knowing the many reasons it would be a very bad idea. It was useless to ask, but she couldn't blame Amaris for wanting a normal life.

Amaris was hardly the only stolen child at the manor, nor was she the only one for sale, but she was the only one Nox cared about. The boys and girls alike would be presented to hopeful parents as prospective heirs, farmers who needed labor, once or twice to a knight who needed a squire replaced for one reason or another. Occasionally a wealthy father who didn't need a dowry would come to purchase his son a young, virginal wife, or a duchess would find her way to the teenage girls and fetch a lady-in-waiting. Unlucky boys would be sold off to work under the bellies of ships once they were strong enough to hoist the sails and carry the barrels. Equally unlucky girls would be purchased for pleasure houses. The university occasionally picked up children who showed an aptitude for the small magics if the church didn't find them first, whether to study or be studied, no one knew.

Nox had seen them come and go. She'd heard the stories. She'd listened to the fetching prices. She'd tried to ignore the rumors.

While all of the children at Farleigh had a clock ticking above their heads to their eventual sale date, Amaris would be shown only to those with wallets deep enough to make it worth Matron Agnes's while. It had been pressed into the heads of the matrons that their ivory child was both a high-value asset and a target for theft should anyone lay eyes on what they wanted but could not afford. This was why they hid when the bishop visited. As if the children hadn't already spent years whispering behind Amaris's back, mocking her over what ghost, fae, or snow beast had sired her, her worth in crowns merely added to the laundry list of reasons she was alienated them from her peers. And it was precisely why Agnes didn't dare risk her investment being dragged off to the church without so much as a coin in compensation. Amaris was valuable, and history had proved time and time again that the world was not always kind to its treasures.

"Is there anything to eat in here?" Amaris asked, scanning the shelves.

Nox unraveled herself from Amaris's arms and stood, scanning the shelves. "Do you like raw turnips?" she asked, mouth quirking again.

"Are you sure there aren't boxes of chocolates up there?"

"I'm confident Agnes is hiding sweets somewhere in her office."

"Next month? Treasure hunting for candy?"

Nox wrapped her finger around a rather large radish and sat next to Amaris again, allowing them to slip into their familiar embrace. "You can close your eyes and pretend it's candy. Though raw radishes are a bit sour… and bitter… On second thought, this might be a challenging game of make-believe."

"I've never been good at pretending. Things are what they are," Amaris sighed.

"That they are. Sometimes it doesn't hurt to want something more."

Nox looked at the radish in her hand, turning it over as she examined the magentas and whites of the root. She thought of Amaris's earlier question and landed on an honest, simplified answer to why they needed to continue to hide. "You're worth more than the bishop would know how to handle," she said.

"What about you?" Amaris asked, looking up with her soft, lavender eyes.

Amaris's tone made it sound like she didn't care too much about the response—she'd simply been talking to make conversation. There'd been nothing malicious or insensitive in Amaris's question, but Nox didn't know how to answer it. Nox knew it wasn't her value that kept her away on market day, nor was it her need to avoid questions of the church that had her hiding in the pantry now. Agnes had favored Nox from childhood and trusted her to shield Amaris when prying eyes came to Farleigh. Perhaps being the dependable hand of the Gray Matron was her value, even if it was a title and set of duties that should have gone to one of the other matrons, not to an orphan.

Nox opened her mouth to answer when a sound came from the kitchen, stopping her response. It didn't sound like Matron Mable. The scraping of shoes and the disorderly noise of more than one body in the space jostled beyond the door.

"Did you hear something?" Amaris whispered.

"Shh," Nox said, her muscles tensing with a peculiar readiness. The girls stilled as they listened to the evidence of scuffling with wide eyes.

With a burst of light from the hearth and a wave of heat, the pantry door flung open. Three silhouetted shapes pressed into the doorway.

An angry, defensive jolt struck Nox like lightning. She was on her feet before the others had the chance to take a single step inward. Her face tightened, fists balling at her sides.

Amaris was slower to react, still scrambling to her feet as Nox positioned herself to defend.

Of all the nightmares at Farleigh, between the chores, the matrons, and the threat of being sold off to the highest bidders, it was insult upon injury to have to manage the fragile egos of Achard and his friends. Nox was no stranger to their tripping feet, their jeers, their sniggered words or their punches. Agnes's preferential treatment of Nox had been just another target on her back.

"What are you doing?" she demanded.

Achard sneered. He had picked on her and pulled her hair when they were children, then pushed his mouth against hers behind the stables after they'd crested thirteen, wanting more from her than she'd ever give. She had gagged, disgusted at his forced affection, and left him with a swollen, black eye. Nox would never forgive the type of person who took what they wanted, though the mentality was everywhere in Farleigh. After that day, Achard had brewed hatred for Nox known only to unbridled youth scorned from unwanted advances in the black cauldron of his bruised, childish heart.

"Why would you come here?" Nox asked angrily. Even in her darkest moments, she wouldn't have subjected a peer to the mercies of the bishop.

The way his sneering face snagged on Amaris was answer enough.

Nox had long been unbothered by the limp insults of the ignorant. She held her head high, their words unable to penetrate her diamond-tough skin. But targeting Amaris with their ugly jealousy was something Nox refused to tolerate. The snow-born girl whom the matrons shielded from labor, lest it mar her perfect skin, had no say in whether she chopped wood or clean the chimneys. Amaris was unable to live any sort of life, save for the gentlest of tasks, at the behest of the Gray Matron. Being hated by their peers was something Nox and Amaris had in common.

"Don't do this," Nox said firmly. She raised a hand to stop them.

"Get up!" barked one of the boys. He pointed an outstretched finger at Amaris.

"Leave!" Nox demanded again, but she may as well have been a turnip for all the mind they paid her. "What do you little wart-filled toads hope to do? Drag her by the hair to see the bishop? Get out!"

She punctuated her final command with a shove against the closest boy's chest, pushing him out of the pantry. The small slit of a window at the top of the pantry showcased the dust kicked up by the scuffling of their feet as if it were smoke. Over the shoulders of the intruders, Mable was nowhere to be seen. They were alone with the boys.

"Grab her!" Achard commanded, shoving past Nox.

Cries of protest rose from the brawl on either side.

She heard Amaris but couldn't discern what was being said as she scrapped with the boys.

Achard yanked painfully on a fistful of Nox's hair, immobilizing her. The fire of her rage exploded against the action. Nox threw her entire body weight into the oldest boy in protest. She made contact with a loud thump, sending him off his footing.

"Get *out*!"

A sack of flour overturned in his backward stumble. A bottle full of cooking oil shattered to the floor as his body smacked against the shelf, eliciting a pained groan as the wood bruised his skin. Achard's immediate reaction was one of feral intensity. He kicked Nox in the side and sent her flying to the ground. Her head bounced against the stones on the floor. Her ears popped against the pain of impact.

She scanned again for a matron—for anyone—but they were on their own.

Splayed in a half-crouched position, she grasped toward the destroyed bottle of oil. She was willing to spear the boy with its jagged edges if he touched them. Her hand clapped on the ground through the flour as she wriggled her fingers toward the bottle's neck, feeling a cutting sting as a glass shard bit into her palm. A small cloud of the powder muddied her vision, but her fingers found the neck of the bottle and she scrambled to her feet, brandishing the weapon in one hand. A paste of flour, blood, and oil had smeared itself against her.

"Why!" Amaris asked uselessly from over her shoulder. She could scarcely see what was happening through the cloud of flour.

There would be no response. They hadn't come to discuss the rationale of hateful idiots.

The boy slammed a fist into Nox's sternum, knocking the wind from her the moment she stood in defense. Nox absorbed the blow and bared her teeth, feeling her eyes glaze with fury as she tried to catch her breath. She poised herself to slash at him again when a shriek from Amaris turned her around. In the time it took to draw

Nox's attention, Achard closed the gap between them, grabbing her from behind. White flashed as the other boys hoisted Amaris to her feet, one successfully knotting his grubby fists through her starlit hair.

Nox felt the internal rage boil over her edges, an inner heat not born of flame but of poison and acid. She slammed the heel of her foot down into Achard's instep, thrusting her elbow up into his chest. As she turned on him, winding up to kick him between the legs, watching him cower beneath her, she heard Amaris behind her once more.

It was not a shriek or any cry of fear. She snapped with fury. "Get off me! Let me go!"

Perhaps out of shock that she'd spoken, grimy fingers unraveled from her hair, and their grip on the girl's arms seemed to slacken.

Amaris's eyes were as wide and white as saucers. Her voice, normally soft and gentle, rose to shrill desperation. She commanded, "Leave! *Now!*"

The commotion stopped with jarring immediacy. Feet stilled. Clutching hands fully released their grasp. A smothering, bewildering silence pressed down on the kitchen.

Nox blinked. She was confused, relieved, and disturbed all at once by the abruptness of the boys' halt. Her lips parted as if to speak, but she didn't know what to say. She didn't know what to ask. They'd stopped. The fight was over.

A beetroot rolled from its place on the wooden shelf to the floor with a soft thump, the only evidence of the ceased scuffle. Baffling stillness stretched for a long moment. The boys took one step back, then another.

Nox and Amaris exchanged uncertain looks. They were still tense, prepared for whatever horrible trick or ploy their attackers were plotting.

"What?" Nox asked, her single word barely a breath. Her back remained rigid, muscles flexed to run, eyes wild.

She wasn't sure what she was asking. What made them attack? What made them stop? What possessed them to be such horrid, hateful pigs that they'd make another discarded orphan's life any worse than it already was?

The bullies created space as they untangled themselves from the mess they'd made. Achard looked between his companions wordlessly. Still half feral, Nox continued to clutch the shattered bottle. She looked at Amaris, who continued to glare at the boys, fists clenched at her sides.

"Go, and don't come back," Amaris said. Her voice trembled as she called after them.

The only noise was that of Nox's blood dripping to the ground from where her hand had been cut by the bottle. Soon, the rhythmic sound of blood was joined by the scuffling of shoes as the boys turned and wordlessly left the kitchen. Once the door swung shut behind them, the sounds of infuriated accusations drifted from the hall through the door until there was nothing to hear.

"What was that?" Nox blinked rapidly at Amaris.

The younger girl shook violently, rippling fear and adrenaline clear on her face. Nox had never seen her make such a bold assertion. From the tremble of her chin, it looked like the very act of standing up for herself was about to make her cry.

"Are you—" Nox started.

A yelp from the hall beyond told them that either the boys or the flour-pasted footprints had been discovered by one of the orphanage's guardians. Within seconds, Matron Mable burst into the kitchen. From the wildness of her expression to every tense muscle of her body, Mable dripped with panic. Evidence of their brief fight littered the kitchen, spilling from the pantry to the flour-marked footprints leading out into the hall. There were only seconds between understanding the severity of what had just occurred contrasted against the impending doom that was approaching.

Mable locked eyes with Nox. Using two frantic words, she pleaded, "He's coming!"

Nox understood.

The fight didn't matter.

The boys were meaningless.

The bishop was coming, and he was going to see Amaris.

Nox moved without a second thought. She turned on her heels and gave the wide-eyed Amaris a quick shove back into the pantry. She closed the door behind her in one swift motion. What remained of the jagged bottle tumbled from her hand to the floor with a tinkling clatter. Barely four heartbeats passed in the time it took for the door to click shut and the robed man to enter. The bishop stepped into the space accompanied by Agnes. Nox leaned her back against the pantry door, attempting a face of contrition.

Agnes's face flashed from confusion to fury to horror. A three-act play painted itself across the older woman's face as she regarded the disaster that had befallen the kitchen. Nox stood alone as the sole object of blame.

The kitchen suddenly felt entirely too cramped. The way the bishop filled the doorway made Nox feel terribly small as the permeating smell of homey foods and the happy crackling of the fire mocked the grim occasion. Nox's linen clothes were covered in paste, splotches of cooking oil pressed into her knees where she'd been kneeling only moments prior. Droplets of blood continued to leak from her palm, dripping off her fingertips and joining the mess on the floor. Her dark eyes remained fixed on her shoes, unwilling to meet the judge and jury of the adults around her.

The holy man's eyebrows had arched with painful disapproval.

The Gray Matron spoke first, her words raspy and hurried. "What happened?"

What had happened, indeed?

Nox scarcely knew, though she had been present for all of it. Agnes wasn't really asking, as the answer didn't matter. Nox was at the epicenter of this disaster, and that's all the bishop would be permitted to see. Agnes's voice caught in the question as though it had been filtered through a sieve. Even as it left her lips, she'd known Nox wouldn't be able to respond. The Gray Matron understood precisely what treasure lay behind the closed pantry door, just as she knew why Nox now leaned against it.

The bishop turned to Agnes, his lip pulled up in a sneer. "Is this the kind of home you run for children?"

Agnes shook her head, reining in the emotions and willing her face into a quilted stillness. "No. Certainly not."

"And how will this be punished?"

Nox watched the exchange, knowing the end was a foregone conclusion.

The bishop's face portrayed little emotion. He sounded nothing more than curious as he examined Matron Agnes, looking down at her over the length of his nose. He struck a pose that was perhaps meant to emulate a vision of piety and patience.

Mable looked between Agnes and the young girl. As if she might protest, the matron's hands went to her apron, fists balling against the fabric in what may have been smothering her urge to defend Nox.

Nox's silence as she guarded the door had nothing to do with the fifty-crown value they'd used to label Amaris. She couldn't have cared less about whatever monetary value had been ascribed to the girl. She'd known from the moment she laid eyes on the vulnerable infant in the wicker basket that she'd never let anyone hurt her. If she had to betray the church and cut every matron in the house with the shards of the oil bottle, she'd do it without a second thought.

They would have to leave the kitchen to draw the bishop's attention away from the pantry. Amaris was the only friend, the only family, the only person in the world who mattered to Nox. She'd do what she needed to in order to get the man away from her snowflake.

Voice strained, Agnes gave a curt command. "Nox, come."

Nox pushed away from the door and leveled her chin, keeping her face blank. Her inky braid was in slight disarray, strands tugged out during the brawl floating around her as she moved. The cold drench of adrenaline pumped through her veins. Her heart rate increased in an arrhythmic thunder as she readied herself for punishment.

Nox followed Agnes and the bishop out of the kitchen. She resisted the urge to look over her shoulder, praying Amaris would stay put. Her feet led her through the corridor as if detached from her body, carrying her without the help of her conscious mind as they walked her past the dining hall, over the threshold, and into the courtyard in front of the manor.

She heard the patter of feet behind her but didn't see who'd joined them until they were in full view of the orphanage's exterior. They reached the center of the courtyard and turned to see the house. Mable had followed, shaking her head in a worthless, silent plea.

She thought the weather was rather mild, considering it felt like the end of the world.

The clouds overhead were a flat, depthless shade of gray. Wind moved the bishop's robes as he grazed the courtyard with speculative eyes. They landed on the Gray Matron, curiously examining her inaction. Her mouth remained pinched as she seemed to fight the urge to speak. His cool curiosity wandered to the still shaking head of Matron Mable. The only sound in the courtyard was that of the leaves rubbing together and the fine, loose gravel that wiggled against the stones. He scanned Nox, from her disheveled hair to the flour smudges on her hands and clothes.

"Where is your whip?" asked the bishop.

Nox heard the word, but a loud buzzing in her ears made it difficult to understand the ensuing conversation.

Agnes balked. Whipping had never been a punishment the matron allowed, though abstaining from corporal punishment had nothing to do with benevolence. The Gray Matron would never hurt her children in a way that would leave scars. Neither Nox nor the other children had cared much about her rationale. The fact was, the Gray Matron wouldn't risk their market value by marring them. Agnes was not a virtuous woman, but she was a shrewd merchant.

The bishop's eyebrow remained frozen expectantly.

"Your Grace, I thought perhaps public repentance would suffice. The girl will kneel here for the peers to see until this time tomorrow morning," the matron said woodenly. Agnes was not a woman easily won over by pity or begging, and this would be no different. "With the cold of the night and the long hours, it's a fitting, miserable punishment."

"This child destroyed property, did she not?"

The matron inhaled slowly. "She did, but—"

"Property that belongs not only to the bellies of orphans but to the All Mother herself, does it not?"

"Yes, but you see—"

"And she was out of bounds, in direct disobedience of the safety and virtues required of the children, was she not? Or are your children allowed to wander the private kitchens, to desecrate items meant for service to the All Mother, and to vandalize spaces forbidden to them?"

"No, Your Excellency," she said. Her answer was as stiff as her back. Tension stretched from the pepper of her bun to her very feet as they planted on the cobblestones.

He closed his eyes while reciting a text from the Blessed Obediences. "Though I've known suffering, I make all things new. In the absence of mercy, I create goodness. It is through my pain that I can rightly see."

Nox knew the text. It hadn't made sense to her then, and it didn't make sense to her now. While many matrons and devotees interpreted this passage as a call for clemency, empathy, and benevolence in the presence of cruelty, men of the cloth had used this verse to justify correction.

"Pain is purifying, is it not? To punish this disobedient child is to cleanse, so that she might rightly see, to be made new, and to create goodness," he stated. He steepled his fingers just as he'd done upon entry that morning. The indifference in his voice seemed crueler than if he'd been angry. He wished to see a child suffer for little more than semantic appeasement.

"Many interpret 'the absence of mercy' to mean that the All Mother is *calling* for mercy..." Mable's words flitted away on the breeze at the sharp, cutting glare from both Agnes and the bishop.

Nox knew that Mable's feelings mattered little against an important, more pressing truth: One should not bite the hands that feed them. Farleigh needed the church's provisions more than it needed to protect the innocence of the children within it.

45

Nox didn't want to see Agnes's expression or witness the woman's unwillingness to advocate for her. She didn't want to see the pain in Mable's eyes, as she didn't have the space to be sympathetic for another adult's failure to protect her. She most certainly would not meet the taciturn face of the stoic judge who had already decided her fate.

A detachment called to her, and she answered. Nox responded to the lure of the void and felt herself retreat into a small, protective space within the walls of her mind. Her body was in the courtyard, yes, but she was no longer present for what the powerful chose to do to the girl who stood before them.

She disassociated into the way the branches moved gently in the forest surrounding Farleigh. She absently watched a ladybug crawl in the grassy space where vegetation sprouted up between the cobblestones. Some part of her was conscious of the curious faces of the children who had ceased practicing their letters or reciting their prayers in order to press their faces against the windows of the manor. There were other bodies in her field of vision. Other people. Other things. A few other matrons clutched nervously at the front door, fretting as they watched after the commotion in the courtyard.

Agnes gestured for Mable to go around back to where the manor's lone whip hung in the stable for the few times animals had needed correcting. After all, what were the sinful to the church other than animals in need of correction.

"Kneel, girl," the bishop said.

Girl. He hadn't bothered to learn the name of the child he intended to harm. Her identity meant nothing. She was a pawn in the games of men, religion, and power. She had no moves. She had no chance at victory. Her defeat, as with the loss of all under the oppressive shoe of those in power, was predestined.

Nox knelt, though her mind remained drifting with the sparrows that fluttered somewhere near the roof. She faced the children and matrons of Farleigh with glazed, unseeing eyes. She'd stay with the leaves, the birds, the beetles.

Though she remained as far from her body as the clouds in the sky, she was distantly aware that the Gray Matron was touching her. With trembling hands, the matron untied the topcoat of Nox's dress and left her white underclothes exposed.

Her spirit found somewhere new, somewhere darker, somewhere farther away. She would not remain with the rustling leaves or the free things of the earth and sky. Instead, she fixated on emptiness. The doors to the orphanage remained open, revealing a blackened mouth of a monster made of stone and mortar. She lost herself in the indistinguishable void as she detached.

In her periphery, Nox witnessed the single, acknowledging dip of the chin from the bishop as he pressed for her correction to begin.

Her teeth set with readiness as she stared into the shadows until she was one with them. She was numb to the high-pitched crack that echoed through the courtyard. She was dead to the gasps, the blood, the twisted faces of the children and matrons. She fixed her eyes so tightly on the dark space between worlds that reality fractured, breaking free as it drifted into the emptiness, like a star into the night sky. Its sounds ceased to register as it broke through her underclothes, her skin, her back, over and over again.

Four

THERE IS A WORD FOR THE SPACE BETWEEN MOMENTS. It's a term for the quiet that echoes after each heartbeat, for the emptiness that exists betwixt things, though its name is one that's been forgotten. The nothingness is much like the gap while one sleeps—when time catches on your last breath of consciousness and releases on your first moment awake. This spell might be minutes or hours or months that stretch into years, everything blurring together as if nothing has happened at all. The word is for the time that passes when no time is passing at all, and yet everything changes.

Five

I'M READY."

"You don't have to be ready," Nox said, maybe as much for herself as for her snowflake. "We can wait."

"Wait for what? I'm as ready as I'm going to be."

This was the fourth time Amaris had reassured her that morning while Nox worked on her hair. It was spring market day, and Nox was thinly veiling that she had more anxiety over the day's arrival than Amaris. Nox had brushed and plaited the girl's pearly hair into a half-knot, leaving the bottom half of her white tendrils to spill down her back. Amaris was now tall and slender, with the early hourglass shape of a young woman. She wasn't old enough to have switched into the dresses that Nox was now forced to wear. If Amaris was lucky, she'd probably spend another year in the unisex britches and tunics worn by all children before the curse of adolescence. Where once a snowy baby had rested on Nox's threshold in a basket, now stood a young woman in a white tunic. At least, the tunic was white on most of the children. On Amaris, the purity of her hair and lashes made the shirt appear rather dull and yellowed.

The years had come and gone. Agnes had announced

to both Nox and Amaris that she was ready to call in the axe of a life debt that had hung over Amaris's head for thirteen years, though she'd used less descriptive language. This eventuality had loomed from the moment the babe had been "gifted to them by the goddess," as the matrons liked to cleverly word her unorthodox delivery.

Nox had felt it coming. Farleigh's children were spoken for at slower and slower rates as time marched on, which was one of the many reasons that Amaris could no longer remain set aside on market day. She had been trotted out only twice in her thirteen years in Farleigh. Once to a lordling and his wife as a prospective adopted daughter—a meeting that had ended disastrously. And another time to a duchess seeking a proper lady-in-waiting. The duchess had been genuinely offended that she had been presented with someone who would outshine her in her own court.

There were a few catalysts for the lack of consistent profits that the mill now faced, one that Nox understood and one that she didn't. The first cause of their ever-thinning purses was a result of Farleigh's increase in runners. After three young boys with promising fetching prices had escaped the mill following the altercation in the kitchen many years ago, more orphans were emboldened to try their hands at braving the forests rather than take their chances with the market. The second was the Gray Matron's own reluctance to replenish the beds as they emptied, as she seemed less and less willing to purchase incoming children as she aged, which was something of a curiosity to Nox. Why should the matron develop a conscience so late in life?

It was now time for Amaris to make herself present-able for buyers, though she would continue to hide once a month whenever a representative from the church would inspect the manor.

While they had once spent the first day of the month in smiles and conspiratorial whispers as they hid, the bishop's visits were now accompanied by ritualistic silence. Nox and Amaris had an unspoken agreement never to discuss the traumatic day the bishop had forced Nox to kneel, or the atrocities that had been committed at his command. Instead, it served as a sobering monthly reminder of how powerless they were at the hands of their overseers.

The nights that had followed her punishment had been the longest nights of Nox's life. She neither slept nor spoke. She'd tumbled so deeply into the detached void within herself that it had taken weeks to return. By some small mercy, Nox had been permitted to remain in monastic silence. No one forced her to rise, or eat, or participate in lessons. Agnes had shooed the other children and matrons away from the healing young woman in her own show of remorse, aside from Matron Flora, the nurse who was allowed in and out to change Nox's bandages and oversee her healing. While the Gray Matron hadn't wanted to perform such an inhumane punishment, intentions were dust in the face of inaction. Agnes was not blameless, and Nox would not forget.

Angry, ripping scars had been expected. There had been speculative whispers about torn, raised skin, discolored welts, and the jagged intersections that would forever mark her with the evidence of the church's intervention. Instead, Nox's wounds had healed somewhat miraculously. Flora had commented with no attempt at concealing her amazement that, where maiming had been expected, only a few nearly imperceptible lines remained. But there were scars. Not all wounds could be seen on one's surface. A hardness had been born in the darkness that day that never fully dissipated. The shadows had built a home within Nox, one that wrapped themselves around her heart, pushing away anyone and everyone who wasn't Amaris.

For the rest of that cruel day and the painful ones that followed, Amaris had knelt wordlessly at Nox's bedside. She'd been the only one permitted to stay near Nox in those solemn hours, curling up beside her in sleep and holding her hand during the daylight.

"Let me do your hair," Amaris insisted now, pulling Nox back from her memories. Nox obliged and sat on the bed, leaning into the touch as Amaris began to quietly weave her fingers through her hair. "I'm sorry. I'm not very good at it."

"That's okay. It feels nice," Nox said.

"Maybe they should have taught me how to style hair. It would have made me a better lady-in-waiting."

All children were obligated into the basics of education. It molded them into a state of competence, should they serve as the hands of shopkeepers in need of basic math or purchased as young penmen for wordsmiths whose fingers had tired with arthritis. Farleigh was not the most pious orphanage in Farehold; it was, however, the most determined for financial success.

The matrons overwhelmed Amaris with the sort of lessons expected in high society, burying her in books, in calligraphy, in sketching and song. The Gray Matron had already invested so much in her purchase, it only strengthened Agnes's resolve to ensure that Amaris could pass any social or proprietary test put forth and prove she was worth any asking price. Nox served as her tutorial counterpart, learning alongside her to supplement Amaris's education. Her lessons intensified as her years stretched on, her studies more thorough than most anyone else's at the orphanage. Agnes seemed to grow more and more determined to foster Amaris's value with every day that passed. The monetary fate of the mill rested on her moonlit shoulders.

Amaris commented that at least market day meant they'd get a break from lessons. But Nox's heart was as heavy as a stone sinking deep into her belly, as she understood the implications of attending market day. They'd both have to show face. Their time to be set apart had come to an end. She would take fifteen more years of sitting beside Amaris in reading, writing, and arithmetic before she'd choose to attend the spring market.

Amaris's fingers hadn't moved in several moments. Perhaps her reprieve from the day's realities had come to an end as well.

"Are you done?"

"I'm not as good at braiding as you are. Let me try again."

Nox combed her hair with her fingers, allowing her glossy tresses to cover any evidence of the small scar that peeked above the collar of her dress. She smiled. "It's fine. I think it looks better unbound."

"Then why did you braid mine!"

"So they can see that pretty face of yours."

Amaris made a face. They drifted past the dorm's cots to peer over the balcony onto the landing where prospective buyers were already filtering into the manor. The girls stood beneath one of the few decorations in the orphanage: a gaudy portrait of the royal family. A similar painting hung in the Gray Matron's office. Nox wondered if such displays of fealty garnered them any additional favors when bishops and patrons came calling.

Nox had seen this oil painting in its ugly, fake-gold frame for fifteen years. She looked to see Amaris regarding the overly regal portrait too. She knew this must be a very old painting, as it hadn't truly represented those in Farehold's seats of power for a long time. The portrait contained the king, queen, and princess—at least, he once was their king, and she once was their princess. Farehold's king had left the earth to be with the All Mother nearly twenty years before Amaris's birth. The golden-haired Princess Daphne had also passed rather tragically, presumably during childbirth, after giving the kingdom its crowned prince. Maybe someday Matron Agnes would update her oil painting to reflect Queen Moirai and the young prince. Perhaps she'd wait until Moirai departed and the prince took his rightful title as king. Perhaps she'd never change it at all.

Amaris looked away from the portrait. Her eyes returned to the foyer below. Without looking up, she asked, "What's expected of us?"

"Nothing." Nox shrugged. She had spent most of the markets at Amaris's side, though she'd occasionally had to help Matron Agnes with a thing or two in the middle of the day, giving her a bit more exposure to the process. "We're limited to the halls, dorms, and dining rooms so patrons can find us. I don't recommend wandering out of bounds on market day unless you want to be locked in the closet for the night. Want to stay here and watch? See if anyone gets swept off their feet by a handsome lord?"

"Does that happen often?" Amaris asked.

"Does what happen?"

"Being bought for marriage," she responded.

Nox looked away. Yes, of course it happened, though she didn't know how much of life's misfortunes she should put in Amaris's head. It was clear from the matrons' grooming that they were specifically preparing Amaris for the sorts of social circles that might allow for her to be wed into upscale society. There were worse fates than being married off to a lordling. There were probably better ones as well.

Nox glanced up at the painting of the royal family, then back to Amaris. "Maybe the crowned prince will find himself in need of a particularly pretty bride. Then Agnes can update her portraits to reflect Farleigh's favorite snowflake."

"I think you mean *Farehold's* favorite snowflake," she responded dryly. Her tone made it clear she neither believed nor entertained such an idea.

"Look," Nox said quietly.

They'd barely relaxed against their perch on the balcony before a captain, black coat stained with remnants of splashed salt, picked a boy near sixteen. The seafaring man toted him away just as soon as the doors to Farleigh had opened. The orphanage was nowhere near any sea. Nox hadn't minded the boy and stared after him wondering what a life at sea would be like. His whole world was about to change from the stone walls of the orphanage to the open, endless expanse of the blue horizon. It was a world she couldn't fathom.

Spring market tended to be the busy time for ranchers needing helping hands in the field in calving season. As a result, the boys were under a bit more pressure than the girls, which had been a relief to Nox. A farmer, hands and knees still covered in dirt from his freshly tilled soil, had arrived to inquire as to whether any of the children had shown an aptitude for growing things. The matrons had chastised him for pursuing the use of magic and attempted to get the man to settle on a young farmhand, but the man wasn't interested in any of the orphanage's perfectly ordinary children.

"Can you imagine yourself as a farmer?" Amaris asked.

"I'm too pretty to get dirty," Nox whispered back.

"Would you prefer to have gone with the sailor?"

Nox attempted to twist her face into a look of revulsion, but her eyes sparkled as she answered, "I already said I was too pretty to get dirty! Now you want to hide me in the hull of a ship? Honestly, Snowflake, it's insulting. What about you? Where would you like to go?"

They both spotted Amaris's answer.

A girl of about four with a muddy brown halo of ringlets was plucked up by a plump woman and a docile-looking husband who followed along in his wife's wake. The woman had a permanent blush about her cheeks and joy in her eyes that made the unselected girls bite back snarls of jealousy. What sort of happy life was the mousy-haired girl about to go live with her new jolly mother and father? What sort of pies and toys and dresses awaited her? Only the small children had a hope of finding families and being raised as natural-born heirs. After a certain age, only horrors awaited.

"With them," Amaris answered, eyes watching the newly stitched together family of three. "She looks like she'd make a good mother."

They weren't the only children who had gathered near the balcony. Over their shoulder, the reclusive pair of sisters murmured similar commentary as they watched the foyer below.

"What about you?" Amaris asked them.

Emily raised her coppery brows as if she were surprised she'd been spoken to. The girls were occasionally assigned the same chores and tasks around the orphanage, which always resulted in friendly pleasantries, but neither considered the other a friend.

"Where would I like to live?"

"Yes," Amaris prodded. "Don't you two talk about it?"

The siblings exchanged a telling look. They clearly

didn't want to go anywhere with anyone. The looks on their faces told her everything she needed to know. If given the chance, they'd run. Nox couldn't blame them. Knowing when to stay silent was a weapon in and of itself.

On market day the children often muttered about what it would be like to flee as Achard and his friends had done long ago. The sisters had more than likely been amongst those exchanging such whispers. Had those boys found nice homes in warm cottages where their bellies were always full of breads, meats, and pies? Had they been swept up by the fae of the forest, or trained to be warriors from distant lands, hunting in the spaces between things? Those were some of the favorite tales the children told, that of Achard the Shadow Warrior, an invention born of the boredom, wanderlust, and hope of their little minds.

"Good luck," Emily said quietly as she and her sister departed for lunch. Nox and Amaris followed suit, picking through sliced ham and stale bread before returning to their perch on the balcony.

Nox didn't blame the siblings for their dreams of running away. Rumors and wishes flitted amongst the residents of Farleigh, but she felt with some certainty that the fate of running was as bad as that of staying. More than likely, the very boys the orphans had turned into folk heroes had made it twenty steps into the forest before being torn to shreds by wolves or pulled under the earth by wicked creatures of the night. She'd sooner believe she'd find their polished skeletons than hope to see Achard and his friends gathering straw outside of a farmer's cottage one day.

Families, merchants, and prospective buyers of all sorts were given free rein of the orphanage's grounds on market day while children stayed within its walls.

Unfamiliar faces with odd clothes and off-kilter accents wandered in and out of their rooms, examining the merchandise. Some adults would ask questions of the orphans. Some would sit a child on their lap; some would tower above, barking down with breath stinking of sour ale as they examined the young charges. Usually enough children were purchased to line Agnes's pockets until the following solstice's market.

"I'm going to be honest," Amaris said quietly. "I thought market day would be more exciting." She relaxed her back against the cool stones, enjoying her precarious seat overhanging the foyer.

"Exciting?" Nox smiled, amused. She leaned her elbows on the banister and propped her face in her chin, eyeing her friend. "I'm sorry there was no handsome prince this time around."

"I'm not saying I want to be somebody's wife! But the matrons made such a big deal of hiding me. Now that I'm here, I thought someone would look at me at the very least."

Nox sighed at the very thought, looking deeply into the lilac eyes staring back at her. "Count yourself lucky, Snowflake. You made it through your first market without being dragged off to live in the belly of a ship. But we did it. We made it through the day unscathed."

Reds and oranges glowed through the open door and the polished windows of the manor as the sun began to set, showcasing the end of spring market. Nox smiled gratefully at the sky, glad for the sign that the day had come to an end, when something caught her eye. A glossy, black carriage pulled by two chestnut horses pulled up in front of the manor. Most of the buyers had come on broken-in quarter horses with flat-bed wagons. Some of the farmers had come on foot. It was a rare sight to see a fully covered carriage at Farleigh, save for the bishop and his visits. The arrival of this dark coach and its owner was as much a source of curiosity as it was something vaguely ominous.

Nox couldn't explain the coal she felt in her stomach as she watched the carriage. She had no reason to feel any emotion toward the stranger, but a sinking heaviness filled her with inexplicable dread.

"We should go," Nox warned.

"Why?" Amaris whispered back, rising to her tiptoes to peer through the window that overlooked the courtyard. "I want to see who owns such a carriage!"

Nox wanted to grab Amaris's hand and drag her away but couldn't summon the strength. The coal in her belly spread, creating a lead in her feet that weighed her to the ground.

The sunset had been so beautiful only moments before. Now the bloodred sky sang its ominous warning as it backlit the newcomer.

The carriage belonged to a woman in her late thirties. She was dressed in deep-blue finery with green, jeweled accents, resembling the noblest aspects of a peacock. Her attire contrasted starkly with the black gloss of her carriage. Her curled yellow hair had been elaborately pinned atop her head. The season was still chilled enough that she had a black fur around her shoulders held together with a gem-covered clasp, and long, dark gloves stretching up beyond her elbows. The stranger glided over the courtyard. She stepped over the threshold and immediately began tutting under her breath, waiting for a matron to attend to her.

"Have you seen her before?" Amaris asked quietly.

"No, I'm always with you on market day," Nox murmured, a chill snaking down her spine. She tried again. "Please, let's go."

"Who do you think she is?" Amaris asked, ignoring her.

Matron Agnes greeted the peacocking woman with some familiarity. Whoever she was, she'd visited before. Set against the gray and white cottons of the matrons and the children, her lavish outfit was absurd. Nox's anxiety continued to bubble as she watched the women chat on the landing. After thirty seconds of pleasantries, Agnes turned to escort the stranger up the stairs. Nox repositioned herself to block Amaris from the woman's view as they floated over the stairs and into the dormitories.

"What are—"

"Don't speak," Nox breathed. She kept her eyes trained on the door to the oldest girl's dormitory until the moving shadows betrayed their departure. Nox turned to face Amaris, keeping her back to the women. She hoped that from behind she was little more than a gray dress and black hair.

The threat passed nearly as soon as it had arrived. In under thirty minutes, the strange, jewel-toned woman was in the foyer once more with two young women in tow, exchanging a purse full of coins with Matron Agnes. The tightness in Nox's chest relaxed slightly as the danger began to pass. The girls she led out of the orphanage shifted their weight uncomfortably behind her, clutching their own arms in sorrowful attempts to self-soothe. Nox and Amaris may have avoided whatever misery the woman held, but for the other two, the dread was just beginning.

Cici, nearly seventeen, had short-cropped hair and a waifish build. Beside her stood Emily. Perhaps their names would no longer matter in Farleigh and would become as forgotten as the stones beneath them. Once they left, who would remember them?

Emily's face twisted anxiously as she scanned the balcony. She was looking up the stairs at the vacant space beyond Nox and Amaris. Emily's stress was both unmissable and tragic. Amaris's eyes widened at Nox in a silent question, but Nox only shook her head. She had no answers. She knew nothing about the opulent woman on the landing or where Cici and Emily might be taken.

"Always a pleasure, Madame Millicent," Agnes said, escorting the stranger out of the mill. The woman called Millicent said something indiscernible in a preening voice that was appropriate for her birdlike features. She angled her body toward the door, ushering the silhouettes of the two girls into the salmons and yellows of the setting sun of the courtyard. Emily resisted the push to depart, continuing to look up the stairs.

Millicent reached as if to physically pull her to the carriage when a voice broke the moment's tension.

"Em!" called a distressed voice from somewhere down the hall. Ana bounded down the corridor toward the front doors to the manor.

The younger sister pushed past Nox and Amaris and ran down the stairs to hug her only family in this world. She crashed into Emily with an intensity that nearly knocked the older sister off her feet. The child's thin, dotted arms wrapped around her sister's hips as she cried. Hot tears spilled over her face, clinging to her jaw and smudging against Emily's dress.

"Please," Ana begged. "You can't leave me!"

Emily scooped her up, shushing her. She wiped at the tears spilling over. She played the reassuring role of comfort and confidence despite the turmoil that had been painted on her face only moments prior. Nox's heart cracked as she watched the pair, knowing precisely what Emily was doing. She didn't want her sister to see her afraid.

"Be good now, okay?" Emily said with gentleness. "You listen. You mind your manners," she continued. She kissed the young girl on the head, muttering the love into her pale reddish hair. "You'll go to a good home someday. I'll write to you when I get the chance. I love you." She scanned her sibling's face, waiting for a nod in acknowledgment. She kissed her again. "I'll always love you."

The energy shifted as Nox's eyes left the sisters and saw that Madame Millicent had turned in response to the commotion. Her peacock eyes froze as she spotted something far more interesting than the grief of a shattered family. Millicent ignored the display of affection unfolding beside her.

On the floor above, just out of Matron Agnes's eyesight, Nox and Amaris were still glued to the balcony, watching.

Nox's hand slipped to Amaris, grabbing her wrist as if to tug her away. Amaris looked at her with quizzical brows.

Millicent did a full-faced turn, no longer interested in departure. She gestured. "And what have we here?"

Agnes shifted her body to follow the jeweled woman's gaze. A lifetime of emotions flashed in the Gray Matron's face as she landed on exactly what it was that had caught Millicent's eye, from surprise to anger to opportunity. Agnes cleared her throat.

"Yes, yes, Madame. I have several beauties still kept in the younger girls' quarters, as neither of them has bled."

Nox swallowed at the words. Agnes was talking about them.

The matron's assertion wasn't entirely true. Nox had

had her first blood several years prior. She wasn't sure why Agnes would lie for her. She was confident that it wasn't believable to anyone that she was not yet a young woman, but the lie hung between them, as the Madame's true query was the white-haired girl.

Nox's eyes brimmed with tears as she looked at Amaris, understanding precisely what was coming next.

The peacock took one step forward, then another, sight locked onto the girls.

Six

AMARIS FROZE. SPRING HAD SHIFTED INTO THE DEEPEST, coldest day of winter within her. Nox's eyes were as wide as teacups, pain and panic clear on her face as she continued to clutch Amaris's wrist with bruising strength. She wasn't sure if she'd ever seen Nox cry, but the water rimming her eyes was as prominent as a warning bell.

Amaris wanted to run, but there was nowhere to go. The Gray Matron and the Madame had not only seen her but were coming for her.

Millicent used two fingers of her gloved hand to motion for the head matron to stand behind her. She led the way, high heels clacking on the stone stairway. A cloud of vanilla preceded her arrival. The heavy perfume wafted up the stairs, choking Amaris. Millicent stopped in front of the girls and stared with cool calculation.

The Madame paused and looked at the Gray Matron to explain herself.

"Nox is my personal servant girl. Come here, Nox." Agnes waved her hand quickly, ushering the young woman to stand behind her and away from the prying inspection of the Madame.

Amaris watched with panic as Nox hesitated. She

recognized the reluctance in Nox's step. Her friend didn't know how to intervene. She twitched her hands, almost as if fighting the urge to throw her arms around Amaris. Nox was powerless, and Amaris knew it. Instead, she held Amaris's gaze, conveying a sense of calm and reassurance onto her. The look told her Nox was there for her, even if there was nothing to be said.

"But this one." Millicent stretched a hand to touch Amaris's face, cooing absently as she drew her fingers over her features. "My, what a pretty shade of purple. Milk and cream and moonlight, you are.… Such angelic features, this one."

"Have you ever seen anything like her?" Agnes prodded.

"Truly, I haven't," the woman purred. She stared into Amaris's eyes for a long moment.

Amaris resisted the impulse to flinch, showing whatever strength she could conjure as she held the Madame's evaluating stare.

"Come," she commanded. Millicent herded Amaris into the dorm room behind her with a shooing sound. The lavish woman acted as though she were the true matron of the house, clearing the other children from the room and its many cots in a demand for privacy. Two younger girls scattered, leaving their things in disarray as they hurried from the space.

"Shut the door," Millicent said curtly to no one in particular.

Nox and Agnes trailed behind Millicent's formidable presence. Agnes complied, closing the door to the dorm room.

"Disrobe," Millicent commanded. Her face was cold as she watched Amaris impatiently.

Amaris gaped, looking from Madame Millicent to

Agnes. Her lips parted in appalled speechlessness. She clutched at the edges of her tunic as she looked to the matron, silently begging the woman to help.

"What?" Amaris croaked weakly.

"I need to see if you are unmarked," the woman said, annoyed.

Agnes gestured for Amaris to hurry up.

Nox started toward Amaris in a wordless protest. The Gray Matron lifted a hand to keep Nox behind her. It was as if Agnes knew that one plea from Amaris would be all it took for Nox to interrupt. The Gray Matron addressed the Madame directly, saying, "We have taken extreme precautions. She's a rarity. She's been spared from any activities that would mark her."

Millicent didn't look at Agnes. Her beady, birdlike eyes remained fixed on Amaris. "Forgive me if I'm unwilling to take your word for it. Disrobe, girl."

Her hands did the opposite. Amaris crossed her arms in front of her. The room was too cold. The request was too vile. Her head swam as she shrank under Millicent's withering stare.

"Nox?" she asked, eyes welling with tears as she looked at her friend.

She saw the answer on Nox's face. Pain lined her every feature. Her posture wilted, her brows scrunched, her lip quivered as she returned Amaris's helpless look. Nox's skin was turning a pale shade of bloodless green as if she were going to be sick. Amaris knew from the ragged hitch of Nox's breath and the fists balled at her sides that this was the single, worst moment of Nox's life.

They had no power.

When it became clear she would not be rescued, Amaris began the quiet, humiliating process of taking off her clothes. Her face, neck, and chest burned red with her shame. She moved with glacial slowness, slipping her tunic off, shuffling her pants down around her ankles. Angry tears threatened to spill, but she fought them with every drop of strength. One arm draped over her small breasts while the other hand hid her womanhood.

Millicent took two unceremonious steps toward her and pulled her hands away, looking positively delighted at what she saw. Amaris's face remained hot with humiliation. She fixed her sight on the ground as eyes roamed over her, evaluating her as though she were little more than cattle. The Madame put her hands lightly on Amaris's shoulders, spinning her slightly to ensure there were no scars or deformities anywhere on her.

"Such perfect, milky skin," Millicent said, speaking of Amaris as if she weren't in the room. "She is starlight personified, isn't she?"

The comment made Amaris snap to attention, looking to the Gray Matron for her response. Nox turned her face away, trembling with her anger.

Agnes was practically vibrating. The confidence in her posture grew with every passing moment. "We have many inquiries about this one," she said proudly.

The lie was said quickly and believably. There was no point in correcting the woman. Amaris knew damned well that no one had offered to purchase her, only as no one's pockets had been deep enough to have afforded her.

Agnes continued. "Lords have stopped by to see this rare beauty for their sons. The church has examined her as an excellent ambassador for the All Mother for the sacred temple. She truly is brimming with opportunity."

"I assume she is also intact?"

Acidic bile burned the back of Amaris's throat at the question. It was as soulless and abhorrent as the woman asking it.

"She's never been touched by a man. We've kept her very protected—set apart from the others. Nox has been something of a personal attendant to ensure she was always escorted by a female peer for safekeeping. We know what a treasure we have in her."

"Men would pay a small fortune to take the maiden-hood of winter in its human form," Millicent said, voice cool and emotionless. She continued speaking to no one in particular, marveling over every inch of the stripped girl.

Amaris could almost hear the tinkling sounds of crowns rubbing together as they tumbled into the purses of the women before her.

"Mmm," Millicent continued, turning Amaris around with the evaluating eye of a rancher eyeing its livestock. She brought her hand to Amaris's mouth. "Let me see your teeth."

"Like I said," Agnes reiterated, stopping the process, "she hasn't bled. She is too young to leave our guardian-ship now. But if you put down a deposit, I'd be willing to hold her for you and send word to the Selkie once she reaches her womanhood."

Amaris took the opportunity to redress.

The women ignored Amaris as they began discussing business.

She'd refused to cry, but silver tears continued rimming her eyes. She knew if Nox met her gaze, she'd lose her resolve, though out of the corner of her eyes she spied the tight fists of Nox's anger. As if Agnes could sense the impending exchange between the two, the matron reached around and placed her hand in front of Nox's path once more. She treated Nox like an antago-nized bull pinned behind a gate.

Millicent clucked her tongue. "Many of my clients

would be thrilled that she hasn't bled. There is quite the market for—"

Amaris found her voice. She choked on a single, infuriated word. "No."

The women in the room turned to her, giving her their attention. Millicent tilted her head curiously.

Amaris swallowed, feeling as though dry bread were caught in her throat. She could scarcely breathe through the obstructing emotion that threatened her. Still refusing to cry, she leveled her voice. She summoned a resolve beyond her years as she said, "Matron Agnes has already said she will send word when I'm ready. Today, I'm not going anywhere."

A flood of tension filled the room. Like the ocean's tide, it rushed in and rushed back out, leaving a strangled sense of nothingness behind it. Agnes was rigid, perhaps worried that Amaris's disregard for authority would ruin her business dealings. The matron failed to stop Nox as the young woman finally bypassed her and went to Amaris's side. She wanted to feel relief at Nox's presence, but the pain of her humiliation ran too deep. Nox tied the back of Amaris's tunic, murmuring a stream of unintelligible somethings that may have been rushed, quiet apologies. Nox's hands shook as she tied the knots once more.

Millicent seemed to consider the two for a long while before dipping her chin slightly in acknowledgment. "Fine," she said with cold amusement. "I will respect your spirit, girl."

It was over.

Millicent turned to Agnes, leaving the girls behind her as she went out the door, discussing something about timelines and deposits. They headed down the corridor, their footsteps quieting as they walked away. Talks of coin and crowns faded into the distance. The girls were left alone in the dorm. Tears won the battle at long last, breaking through Amaris's barrier as they began to spill. Hot, salty water tumbled down her cheeks.

"I'm so sorry," Nox said, choking her. She pulled Amaris into the sort of crushing hug that communicated everything she failed to say. She stroked Amaris's hair in a frenzied attempt at comfort. "I should have done something. I should have stopped her. I—"

"I'm not going with her," Amaris said, her voice quivering. She used the cloth of both sleeves to mop up the buckets of free-flowing tears.

"I know," Nox said, voice wavering. "I know."

"No," Amaris clarified, hiccuping against her suppressed sobs. "I'll never go with that woman. I'll never go with her."

✦

Nox crushed Amaris against her with a primal sense of protection. She'd fight, she'd die, she'd kill until no one stood before she let Amaris go with that woman. The charge between them was something more profound than the ties of family. There was a ferocity and bond between the girls that held no logic, no reason. Nox squeezed her more tightly before loosening her hold. She took Amaris's face in her hands, dark eyes burning with intensity as she begged Amaris to see her sincerity.

"And I will never let her take you," she swore, her words a solemn oath.

Nox's life had never meant much to her or anyone around her. She'd been discarded before she was old enough to remember such horrors. She'd always been glad she couldn't recall being sold to the orphanage the way that Emily and Ana must. Nox couldn't imagine what her own mother had been like, though there had always been a sickening pity that the matrons had when they looked at Nox that made her feel like her arrival had not been the tear-filled loving regret of a mother making the right choice for their child.

Her first memory was of Amaris.

In her twisted upbringing, she had found purpose. It had been planted as a tiny silver seed. It sprouted into starlit connection with the snow-white baby whom the other children hated with their jealousy. Amaris had loved her back, and their moonlit plant grew into a metallic wildflower with roots so deep that they bore themselves into her very core. For years she had called it friendship, and for years that had been what it was. The two stayed cast off from the others, defending their inseparable bond. To one another, they were the world.

As she held Amaris's face in her hands, guilt gnawed in her gut. What she now felt was an intimate love that she couldn't bring herself to understand. Maybe she didn't need to understand it. It didn't make it any less real.

"What just happened—"

"It will never happen again. I can't tell you how sorry I am." Her voice broke with the pain of helplessness, of regret, of anger. When Amaris had needed her most, she had failed her. Nox vowed, "I promise with my life: you won't go with her."

✦

The rumors were inescapable. They'd barely sat down to push their steamed yams and boiled chicken around their plates when a boy no more than ten asked Amaris what she was worth. She'd stared despondently into the mush of her orange vegetable. Nox glared at him until he went away, apologizing under his breath.

Whether it was the matrons or the other orphans generating the rumors, who was to tell. Farleigh was aflutter with their fixation on Amaris's fetching price. Some whispered twenty crowns had been put down as deposit, while others claimed they'd heard it was a song to the tune of fifty. One matron cursed quietly to another that one hundred crowns were locked in the office as she dished out slimy, stewed okra onto the children's plates.

The girls shrank into silence, allowing the talking and scraping of forks and knives to become a white noise around them. No one else seemed bothered by the inedible meal, too excited by the day's events to scowl at the slop on their plates. There would be no murmuring from the ghostly silent girls. The food tasted like ash on Nox's lips, settling into her stomach with the coal-heavy weight of certainty that everything she knew was drawing to an end.

Seven

"ARE YOU AWAKE?"

"I'm looking at you, aren't I?" Nox whispered back, voice nearly inaudible. She'd always struggled with insomnia, but after the day's events, she knew she'd have no chance of falling asleep. She'd watched the door for an hour as the tossing and turning of her peers had faded into the steady, rhythmic noises of their slumber. She'd spotted Amaris the moment the door eased open, and she watched her silhouette as her friend tiptoed toward her bed. The matrons had moved Nox into the older girls' dormitory two years prior, which had been miserable for them both. Night was the only time the two were truly separated.

"Can we talk?"

Nox emerged from beneath her covers before Amaris had finished her question.

It was a warm enough spring evening that she didn't bother with socks or sweaters. Her thin nightdress clung to her, betraying evidence of chill as they headed for the back door. It was dangerous to get caught after bedtime. Even if the matrons wouldn't leave lasting marks on the children, the threat of closets one could be locked in, darkened spaces in which one could be shut, or forced skipping meals, served as adequate punishments.

On a night like this, the crime was more than worth the risk of consequence.

Nox and Amaris slipped down the stairs that led from the second floor to the exit just off the kitchen. The door seemed to approve of their plan as its well-oiled hinges opened and closed silently behind them. Fresh air and privacy greeted them the moment they stepped beyond the listening walls of the manor.

The full moon guided them as the girls headed for the stables. They scampered on bare feet, knowing the sooner they could round the corner out of view of anyone who might peer through a window, the safer they'd be. A horse whinnied softly from within the stable, but the silence reassured them that no one else was out.

They positioned the walls of the stables between themselves and the windows of Farleigh, sandwiching themselves between the wooded structure and the looming shadows of the forest that encircled the property. The silver moonlight bathed them, illuminating the pair where they stood.

"Goddess damn it!" Amaris panted. After hours of simmering in the blackened cauldron of what had transpired, her anger had its chance to truly boil over. She fumed, "How did this happen? How can this be my fate?"

Nox slumped to the ground with her back to the stable wall, eyes glazed as she faced the dark forest beyond. It had been hours, and she still had no words for what had occurred. The shock she felt had seeped into her like wet tights freezing within one's boots.

Amaris didn't sit. Nox tracked her movements as her friend paced in tight, anxious repetitions. The moon painted curves and lines against her lithe figure, her hair, the tilt of her nose, her hips, her legs. It was hard to tell where the silky white of her nightdress ended and her skin began, as her entire body was painted from the same shade of dipped silver. Nox watched the way the moonlight reflected off the girl, so pale she might have been carved from chips of its surface.

Nox frowned, averting her gaze. Her friend was in pain. That was the only thought that mattered. She allowed Amaris her space, not interrupting her rhythmic march. Nox felt her chest tighten against the deep, terrible wound. She closed her eyes, allowing the throb of the unseen injury to consume her.

"I've been kept away for years for what—to be sold to a pleasure house?" Amaris demanded, incredulous. She barely kept her voice low enough to prevent detection. Her question had been rhetorical, but Nox answered anyway.

"Their pockets must be far deeper than the matrons had ever considered."

Amaris was furious. Her hands flew upward, reflecting white in the moonlight. "What am I supposed to do?"

Nox shrugged. Her tone did not match the intensity of the situation, but that was for the simple reason that she did not feel afraid. She felt only calm defiance. Her sentences were resolute. "The world is big. We will leave."

Amaris took seven steps to the left, spun, then made another seven steps to the right. She couldn't stop walking. Her arms were wrapped in front of her chest, but she raised her thumb and forefinger to pinch her chin anxiously.

Nox stood, cutting Amaris off in her pacing, extending her hands, hoping her grip would offer some source of comfort and stability. Her heart soared at the way Amaris visibly melted against her pent-up stress as their fingers interlaced.

Nox asked solemnly, "What do you want to do?"

The pause stretched between them, but Nox knew the answer long before it came from Amaris's lips.

"I want to run," she said at last.

"We will," Nox promised. "And we'll do it soon."

Amaris tightened her grip, squeezing Nox's hands as she asked, "Both of us, right?"

Nox almost choked on a laugh at the absurdity of the question. She echoed the squeeze, saying, "As if you could get rid of me."

Nox was sure she didn't imagine it as she slipped her arms around Amaris. The glow between them was nearly palpable enough to possess both shape and color. She felt the blue glimmer of life and soul and love between them as she clutched her snowflake. She would have to be pried apart from Amaris. She'd never willingly allow them to be separated.

If they were going to make it more than twenty steps into the forest before being picked clean by demons, they needed to be smart.

She slipped her arm around Amaris and began to steer them away from the forest. Tonight had just been an effort to escape the oppression of the manor. They'd needed to state their proclamation to leave. They needed to accomplish what the freckled sisters hadn't in their plans to run.

They would plan, they would wait, and they would prepare until there would be no question as to their success. Amaris would not go with Millicent to the place the matron had called the Selkie. The girls would not follow whatever fate Nox was sure had befallen Achard and his cronies, cleanly picked bones lining the forest floor, dead leaves burying them unceremoniously as their forgotten bodies joined the earth.

Eight

TIME PASSED AS IT DID. LESSONS, SHAMS OF CHURCH processionals whenever the bishop visited, prayers to the All Mother, reading, cleaning, chores, and so forth filled their days. The girls found ways to ask the matrons questions outside of their lessons and spent their time cherry-picking knowledge of geography, terrain, and the sorts of animals that roamed the forest near Farleigh. Every day was a new opportunity for covert reconnaissance. If they kept their questions spread out between the matrons and dispersed over time, no one would think to ask why Nox and Amaris were collecting mental layouts of their surroundings, of foods that grew naturally in the forest, of poisons or animals or towns.

Gathering provisions was a different story. Theft required both patience and caution.

They held their breath, hoping no one would question when things went missing as long as it happened gradually, with the plausibility of time and the forgetfulness of others. A spare sock here, a clean tunic there, a blanket, a wool hat, the odds and ends of their needs were slowly stashed in hiding places that could be easily retrieved in their moment of need.

Matron Mable proved to be the most conversational when they caught her in a good mood, though they'd expected as much from the friendly matron. They learned Mable was from a village two days' ride from Farleigh called Stone. While the children had been led to believe that Farleigh was on the northeastern-most edge of the kingdom, it seemed Stone was so named as it was backed up against a sheer cliff, drawing a firm, unquestionable barrier between the kingdoms. Mable missed Stone, she'd said, but she was happy to be of use to the All Mother.

Amidst the tales she told was the story of how, when Mable was sixteen, her deeply religious parents had dedicated her to servitude at Farleigh. Her life was to be spent in service of both the goddess and disenfranchised children. Mable had left it unsaid that Farleigh was neither a religious sanctuary nor a place that helped children, though her love for the goddess hadn't permitted her to leave. Nox wondered if it was the mill's very immorality that pressed her to stay. The All Mother needed Mable's small light of goodness in the shadowed depravity of a mill more than any pious institution.

Nox had asked why anyone would live in Stone, given its proximity to the Dark Kingdom. Mable waxed poetic about a league of guardians in the mountain who served neither the north nor the south. Nox and Amaris had exchanged looks at that, confident that Mable was more naive than they'd initially understood. It would be a lovely tale for parents to tell as they tucked their child into bed, allowing them to imagine guardians watching them in their poor peasant village. Certainly, such a legend would prove useful to keep the night terrors away when signs of demons filtered down from the northern kingdom.

Nox hoped Mable was too distracted as she skinned

vegetables and discarded the peels to pay much mind as to why the girls cared.

Nox kept her questions focused on the warmth of the southwestern coast.

"You've asked about the south a lot, little Nox. Do you have big dreams of living in the southern part of the kingdom?" Mable's hands continued working on the potato, thumb edging the knife deftly around its skin.

"I've always dreamt of the sea," Nox claimed. "It would be lovely to work for someone along the coast. I've thought about the water even more after the sailor visited on the last market day. Have you ever been? To the sea, I mean?"

The lie was pretty enough that Mable was happy to tell them about a time when she and a few of the devout matrons had taken their horses on pilgrimage to the Temple of the All Mother. From there, they'd gone onward another day to Priory. The coastal town was just outside the royal city of Aubade, where Her Majesty resided. It had been more than two weeks of hard travel, Mable said. Still, it remained a joyous memory, as she had been able to worship with other matrons who had come from surrounding territories throughout the southern kingdom, all sharing in the sacred pilgrimage to visit the All Mother in her earthly form. Her stories of the temple were otherworldly, surely colored by a combination of time and wishful thinking.

Lost to her thoughts, she continued to work absently on her chore as her eyes glazed over. Perhaps her mind drifted to the holier path her parents had wanted for her and to the thinly veiled slave trade masquerading as a church-run orphanage that her life had become.

"You'll get to see it, though, little Amaris," Mable said, her voice distant.

Amaris cocked her head curiously.

Mable nodded, not really speaking to either of them. "You'll have to make the trek to the Temple and say a prayer for me when you go off to live in Priory. It's only a day or two away. I'm sure she'll let you visit the All Mother."

Mable continued discarding skins into one bin and placing the peeled potatoes into a pot as the girls left the kitchen. She'd bid them a rather absent good night, presumably still lost to her memories. She'd unwittingly shared where the Madame was to be taking Amaris. The menagerie of exotic women, of special treasures from around the world, was just outside of the royal city. Her virtue, her body, her life were to be sold in the seaside town of Priory.

Nine

SOMETHING WAS WRONG.

Pain lanced through her side. A light sweat clung to her brow. Amaris jolted awake, curling into herself as she brought her knees to her chest with a gasp. She couldn't fully stretch herself into a seated position as she moved her legs over the edge of the bed, bare feet chilling against the cold floor.

The summer's heat had cooled into nipping autumn. Leaves tumbled to the ground in shades of brown, yellow, and orange somewhere beyond the darkened windows. It was a moonless night, leaving her concealed in the dark with a swirling, gripping pain.

Cold continued to work its way from her feet into her calves as she stumbled out of the dormitory, down the hall, and toward the bathing room. Amaris didn't light a candle but felt her way through the dormitory on memory alone. She bumped into a bed as she gripped at her abdomen, waking someone. One of the other girls stirred in her beds and called softly after her, but she ignored the child as she continued to stumble through the dark.

Amaris was almost to the bathing room when she

doubled over, a fresh pain twisting its fist deep inside her. She muffled the sound that threatened to tear from her mouth, not wanting to alert the matrons. She had been sick before from food, or when a bout of flu had swept through the house and stricken nearly all of its residents, but this felt like a hot, angry poker in her lowermost belly. This nauseating brand of pain was something she'd never felt before.

Amaris made it to the bathing room, instantly regretting not bringing a candle. She gripped at her nightdress as she searched for the source of her pain. It felt as though she'd wet herself, which stirred a renewed sense of panic. How sick must she be if she'd wet the bed? She dabbed at the mess with the towels on the wall, barely seeing through the gray-black gloom of the window. From the next room, a sharp yelp cut through the night. Amaris clutched her abdomen and padded back down the hall to see who was in trouble, only to find a candle had been lit in her dorm. Two of the younger girls looked up at her.

"Amaris is hurt!" one cried.

Amaris had barely registered their upset before a new shape shot into the hall from the older girls' dorm. Ever the light sleeper, Nox was through the door in a heartbeat. She shushed the girls frantically, eyes wide with an alarm Amaris couldn't comprehend. Amaris moved toward Nox, but Nox didn't look at her. She focused all of her attention on the crying girls as low, hurried commands burbled over her lips.

"Shut up! Shut *up*! Go back to bed!" she begged, her voice strangled urgency.

The youngest of them had taken to pitiful sobbing.

"Stop it! Be quiet!" Nox pleaded. Amaris continued to blink at her in confusion. She didn't understand why, but it sounded like Nox might cry herself.

The other young girls began to stir, lighting the candles by their beds as they woke. The younger ones were fussing louder and louder, and the more Nox urged them to quiet, the more distressed their murmurs became.

As the yellow glow of candles filled the room, one of the girls closest to the door pointed at Amaris, face pale with terror.

"She's dying!"

✦

Minutes before, Nox had been staring sleeplessly at the ceiling, tracing the crown molding with her eyes while the peers around her slumbered. It was as if some quiet part of her mind had known she would be needed. The sound had pierced through the night, and she'd tripped on her twisted sheets in an adrenaline-fueled sprint to the younger dorm.

Of course, Nox understood exactly what had happened the moment she'd entered the room. It had proven impossible to silence the idiot children with no education about their bodies. Amaris was the oldest in their room, and as such, this was the first time they'd borne witness to the curse of womanhood. While her exact birthday was unknown, her moonlit friend was between her fourteenth and fifteenth year. Amaris's curse had been blessedly belated, as these things went. While some of the women and girls suffered relatively little during their moon time, this had been an especially crimson sight for Amaris. The horror was appropriate, as this was the moment that officially marked her as a sacrificial lamb.

Amaris's time had come.

The bed linens would be scrubbed and boiled of the telltale blood. Amaris's nightdress would be soaked, salted, and washed until it shined once more as if this gruesome event had never happened. Letters would be sent and the Madame alerted. Amaris's first blood had come, and it was too late to hide it.

She looked at Nox and shook her head slightly, and Nox knew what it meant.

Amaris was not going.

No matter what.

Ten

T HEY WERE OUT OF TIME.

The girls had physical provisions stored through-out the manor. They had knowledge of the continent, where to go, and how to survive. They knew from Mable's tales of travel that Priory was at least two weeks on the road—assuming they'd find access to horses. They could taste their freedom.

While neither girl had stepped foot beyond the grounds of Farleigh, they both knew enough of the land to know that if they went north, they'd reach the forests at the base of the mountains. Raascot wasn't just the kingdom of dark fae, nor was it only the birthplace of monster lore. It was also terribly cold, densely wooded, and filled with icy, treacherous terrain. All hushed manner of things mentioned about the mountains filled Amaris's and Nox's veins with enough ice that they knew their safest bet was to angle themselves southwest toward the coast. Even if they were to end up unloved and homeless, it was a fate best served in conditions that wouldn't chew their fingers and toes with frostbite.

Amaris had pulled her weight in their efforts. She'd reported that her chores in the laundry the day before had gone well, though she'd only found one new cloak and wasn't sure that their thin, leather shoes would be sufficient for their travels. Nox had smiled sadly at the pretty mittens Amaris had pocketed for her. Even in their haste to get away, Amaris was still looking for lovely stitching, warm gifts, and small ways to make her smile. Still, they'd need more if they had any chance of surviving beyond the walls.

"Mable said that Priory was more than two weeks away," Nox said.

Amaris was resolute. "It has to be tonight."

"It doesn't," Nox cautioned. "Even if Millicent left the Selkie the very moment she received the raven, there'd still be two weeks of travel ahead of her. That was one week ago. It's a large continent. We have seven days. If we aren't ready…"

"We're ready. We'll go after you finish your chores in the kitchens. Tonight."

Nox bit her lip as she eyed Amaris's unwavering intensity. She recognized the look of a trapped animal and knew that if they stayed for a moment longer, Amaris would chew her leg off like the proverbial fox in a snare.

"Okay," she conceded. "Go see what you can do about a second cloak. I'll get us what we need. We'll leave tonight."

Her shifts in the kitchen had always been pleasant. It was Nox's favorite chore, as it meant the ability to spend time with Mable. Being amidst food and the friendliest matron was significantly better than scrubbing the floors, pressing linens, or doing yard work. Tonight, she brimmed with tense anxiety. She desperately hoped it couldn't be sensed by the matron. Nox would need to sweet-talk Mable if she hoped to have any time alone with the food.

Nox's greatest asset was her general aura of likability. It was the quality that had caused Agnes to single her out as Amaris's chaperone. It was the character trait that soothed the staff into giving her things like mugs of warm milk before bed or a pastry when she wanted to sneak dessert. Time and time again, it spared her from the worst chores or punishments Farleigh had to offer—save for one.

Her charm, like most things, had infuriated the other children.

"Matron Mable?"

"Hmm? Yes, little Nox?"

Nox hadn't been little for more than ten years, but it was a term of endearment Mable had tacked on to all their names. The woman smiled up from the kitchen's washbasin.

"Are there extra apples? I'd love to be able to bring one to the horses."

She smiled. "Remember to keep your palms flat! Don't be getting your fingers nibbled off."

"Yes, of course," Nox agreed, using what she hoped was her most innocent, disarming show of appreciation. She couldn't spend more than a few moments rummaging around in the pantry if she was to avoid suspicion. While Nox pillaged the kitchen, Amaris's task had been to go through the laundry again and find another pair of mittens and warm clothes.

If they were successful, they'd be able to leave as soon as everyone in the manor fell asleep.

Nox had never traveled, but she knew enough of food to understand what would spoil and what would keep. She reached for things that would last them long enough to get to a village and plan their next steps. She stuffed as much white, hard cheese, dried venison, and whole-grain bread into the pockets of her clothes that she could possibly conceal and then emerged from the pantry with an armful of apples. The fruit excused her awkward angles and lumps. Mable laughed dismissively and shooed her away, too distracted by her kitchen duties to pay Nox much mind.

Nox hurried up to the dorms while the rest of the children were eating dinner. She stripped her pillow and used a pillowcase to create a makeshift satchel. It wasn't the best time of the year to be running from the grounds, as late fall was just starting to threaten them with frost. She eyed her bed and wondered whether she could risk taking the entire scratchy comforter from her cot without being detected. Her mind drifted to how long it would take for the climate to become milder. Surely, people used the regency's road to venture to the royal city all the time. They could be on a cart and bound for warmer weather before they knew it.

A jarring noise shook her from her thoughts.

The manor erupted in a confused flurry as the sounds of banging, followed by the commotion of an argument floated up from the foyer. Nox looked over her shoulder to ensure no one had spotted her. She felt her heart catch in her throat, somehow convinced she'd been thwarted. She shoved the pillowcase full of food under her bed, tucking away evidence of her plan for escape. She sidled around the corner to peer over the balcony and see what was causing the excitement.

She blinked against the sight, struggling to comprehend. It was a man.

The sight of him was as rattling as if there had been a troll on the landing. She'd sooner believe her eyes were betraying her. There were never visitors to Farleigh. The only people who came and went were the bishop, the sellers, and the buyers. This man was unaccompanied, and it didn't look as though he was here to purchase.

The stranger was the size of a mountain and covered to the gills with more weapons than even the heroes of stories. He spoke with a loud frustration to a defensive Matron Agnes. The Gray Matron made no secret of her loud displeasure as she confronted him. Other children peeked their heads from the dining room, down the hall, out of their dorms, and over the balcony, all drawn by curiosity to witness the disturbance. The front door to the manor remained wide open as if it had been flung on its hinges and left where it stuck itself to the innermost wall, letting in the cold autumn air. The night behind him pressed in, with the lanterns and fires in the manor barely making a dent in the gloom beyond.

"You can't stay here." Agnes raised her hands to herd him out as if he were a feral animal. There was no kindness in her voice as she motioned the man from the manor.

The grizzly, dark-haired man took a half step back but made no move to leave. The steel of his weapons jangled against his armor, drawing further attention to just how outfitted for danger the stranger was. Nox scanned him with intense curiosity, soaking in everything from the hilt of his swords to the hardened leather of his armor. The bearded man had a fatherliness to his features, belying his years. His face and neck were etched with the pink lines of battle. Her eyes locked onto where his hand clutched his abdomen. The man was injured.

"Your temple has the sign of the All Mother out front," he argued.

The stranger's gravelly voice referred to the iron that had been welded to the manor's doors. The goddess's sigil consisted of only three simple components: two straight, vertical lines, and one half-circle. It was the same emblem that the bishop had embroidered onto his finery and painted on his carriage.

"This is no church." Agnes shook her head, still pushing him backward.

"I am in need of a healer," he said. His tone was firm but held an underlying hint of something akin to resignation.

Agnes held no compassion as she said, "The closest healer is in Stone. That's about a two-day ride. We wish you well."

Nox knew the matrons were not kind, but turning away a wounded stranger in need of help was a new level of cruelty. From somewhere behind the commotion, she heard Mable's quiet voice chime, "Matron Flora was trained as a nurse."

Agnes shot a fuming look over her shoulder. Nox immediately witnessed the meek matron's face melt into regret over speaking. Mable would surely be punished later. Perhaps no marks could be left on the children, but the same was not true of the matrons who defied Farleigh's Gray Matron.

With resolute chill, Agnes said, "This is a haven for children. No weaponry is permitted in this house."

Nox pressed herself into the cool wall of the overlook, her eyes darting between the matrons and the newcomer.

The man looked neither angry nor threatening. His deep voice remained steady as he answered, "Any establishment with the sign of the All Mother is bound to the Law of Sanctuary. I call on that law now and seek sanctuary in your establishment. I will leave my weapons in your care and pay whatever coin you see fit in exchange for a night's stay. I'd also like to buy any tonics you may have. Please show me to Matron Flora for bandaging. Thank you."

His negotiation tactic was one Nox tucked into the back of her mind—the firm way he offered no alternative while still providing the matron with something she wanted and making it sound like a win for all parties involved. Agnes was no holy woman, and the Law of Sanctuary was probably as important to her as any other prayer she faked or formality she navigated. Coin, however, was a language she knew how to speak.

Agnes's face twitched against the need to argue. The man took several steps to ground himself more deeply into Farleigh. Logically speaking, Nox supposed she should have been afraid at the presence of a strange man in the night. Yet something about him didn't seem frightening. She was instead somewhat pleased that he'd bested Agnes in an argument.

Clearly unhappy, Agnes turned and led the man to her office, where she would presumably lock up his weapons and accept his compensation for lodging. Nox took several quick steps away from the balcony, slipping into the dormitory as Agnes guided the man down the hall before they could spot her. Nox's eyes widened from her place in the shadows at the small, ruddy droplets that fell onto the stones as the stranger trudged down the corridor, the wound in his abdomen spreading with every passing second. The moment the door to the office closed, she took off into the hall.

She needed to find Amaris.

The din of chatter and sounds of eating resumed, perhaps with more excitement as the children pressed each other about the stranger in the manor. Dinner was almost over. Amaris and Nox would soon lose their distracted opportunity to gather supplies.

Maybe the chaos of this man's arrival would provide additional diversions, securing their escape from the orphanage. Nox pricked with an idea as her eyes floated over her shoulder and down the hall to where she knew Agnes's office would be locked. The stranger had been relieved of his weapons. Perhaps she could steal a knife or two. If the man had truly paid the Gray Matron, his coin purse may very well be sitting on her office floor amidst his pile of blades. Nox's mind was buzzing with the ideas as her thoughts began to slow. A fear-filled doubt crept in to replace her excitement.

What had injured him? Was whatever caused the wound still out there?

Nox pressed herself into another dormitory doorway just in time for one of the matrons to move quickly past.

Matron Flora padded past the entrance to the dorm, headed hastily down the corridor. It sounded as though the man was being helped down the servants' stairs in the back to be kept on the kitchen level overnight. It made sense that the matrons wouldn't want him slumbering near the children.

Nox popped into the younger girls' dorm and spotted Amaris's pearly hair immediately. She stood on a chair, collecting her stolen items from where they'd been hidden out of sight on top of a tall cabinet. She jumped off the chair, blanket bundled under her arms. She took three steps toward Nox, when they stopped to listen. The sounds of matrons hissing instructions snaked into the room from the hall.

"We're to take guard in shifts," one said, tone urgent.

"Do we just roam the halls? Do we not get to sleep?"

"We shouldn't be alone. We'll need to remain stationed throughout the manor to protect the children and guard the office. Agnes would be wary of having any man under our roof, let alone an assassin. This is meant to be a holy place."

One laughed. "It's no more a holy place with or without an assassin."

An assassin.

Nox tasted the word. She rolled it around on her tongue. Assassin. She made eye contact with Amaris and knew her friend had heard it too. Nox noiselessly returned the chair to where it belonged. Amaris lowered herself to her belly to procure mittens, wool socks, and a rolled cotton tunic from beneath a cot.

Quietly Nox said, "The one night we chose to escape is the night all the matrons will be patrolling in shifts and an armed killer is just down the hall."

Amaris exhaled humorlessly, saying, "Technically I think he's unarmed and in the basement."

She rose from her stomach and joined Nox on the bed. Their gazes touched, dissolving into a long, sad look. Nox put her arm up in that familiar way, and Amaris nestled in.

"This can't be happening," Amaris said.

Invisible hands wrung Nox's heart. This wasn't what they'd wanted. Their plans unraveled on the spool. She chewed her lip as she considered the path before them. She was afraid of so much more than a stranger's arrival or the disruption in their escape.

"I—" Nox began. Her mind raced, matching the hummingbird's flutter of her heart. She had to say it. She needed Amaris to know. She screwed up her courage like a tightly wound cork, allowing the seal to pop as she said the words.

Amaris relaxed against her, seemingly unaware of the bottled emotions raging mere inches away.

"I need you to know that I love you." Nox breathed into the silver tufts. A jolt of electricity spiked through her as the declaration escaped her, tightening her squeeze.

Tears threatened her once more—not from sadness but from fear of rejection, and dread that her snowflake wouldn't feel the same.

"I love you more," Amaris replied, disappearing more fully into the hug.

Nox pulled back a bit and shook her head slightly, but her courage had waxed and waned. Love had many names and faces, and this love stuck within her like dry medicine swallowed without water. It burned in the center of her throat, refusing to dissipate.

She couldn't do it.

Not now.

Not tonight.

Her stomach was twisted with the nerves of her adrenaline. She had wanted to speak her heart for so long but never knew how. Nox closed her eyes and allowed herself the coward's out. It was the assassin she feared. It was getting caught. It was the commotion. It was the cold. That was all.

Amaris's brows knit ever so slightly, a gentle question on her lavender eyes.

If she didn't get out of here, the tears would win. Nox stood, stifled her emotions, and asked, "Tomorrow?"

Amaris's eyes widened. Even in the dark of the night, her purple irises caught on the moonlight filtering in through the windows. Her question came out in a dismayed choke. "Not tonight?"

"Farleigh is more guarded tonight than it has ever been before or will ever be again. I'm so sorry, Snowflake. There has never been a worse night to run."

Amaris bit her lip and closed her eyes. Nox recognized the face the girl was trying to conceal. It was the same caged animal expression she'd seen before. Amaris needed to run, but she would not go alone.

"Amaris, I'm sorry…"

"You're right." She looked away.

Nox felt as though she were failing spectacularly once more. The broken pain in Amaris's heart was transparent through her every subtle expression, from the slump of her shoulders to the wilt of her face. She parted her lips just enough to exhale slowly, calming herself. Her frosted white lashes fluttered open as she looked up into Nox's and agreed with one final parting word.

"Tomorrow."

The girls separated. Across the hall, Amaris would surely be hugging her pillow and drifting off to sleep. Nox closed her eyes, but her mind would not rest. Behind her lids, she saw the pieces, the players, the possibilities that played out before them. She watched it all behind the dark curtain of her lids, anticipating one hundred outcomes. Every move had a countermove, as each risk required a contingency. She knew they could do it.

Tomorrow, they would run.

Tomorrow, at long last, they would be together.

Eleven

I T WAS AN HOUR TOO EARLY FOR EVEN THE CHATTERING OF birds as the purple-gray light of morning colored the room. Amaris saw the silhouettes of the other children in their beds, unmoving. The other girls in the dorm were still asleep. It took her a moment to understand why she'd awoken.

"Time to get up, little one," Mable whispered, squeezing Amaris's shoulder gently from where it rested beneath the covers.

Mable smiled down at her, a cup of tea in her hand. Amaris rubbed at her eyes, uncomprehending. The matron extended the warm teacup. Amaris sat up slowly, accepting the teacup. She looked around the graying morning light of the room for an explanation as to why Mable was there.

No one had ever brought her tea in bed.

"Today is your big day."

The porcelain cup was hot in her hands but felt nice against the cool morning air. She was still too groggy to understand what was being said. She blinked repeatedly at Mable, willing something about the matron's words to click into place.

Amaris frowned at the matron. Mable responded by tucking a tuft of hair behind Amaris's ear and allowing her lips to twist into a light, sad smile. The matron kept her voice hushed as she spoke.

"You get to move on to your next adventure today," Mable said, feigning quiet cheerfulness. Her words were bright, but her face was tightly controlled against thinly veiled pity. "We were so lucky to have you in Farleigh for so long, little moon. The Madame is downstairs in the dining room. She and Matron Agnes are having tea as we speak. The Madame would like to share breakfast with you before you leave. It's a long journey to the coast, after all, and you shouldn't go on an empty stomach. Get dressed and wash your face. I'll see you downstairs soon."

"Matron Mable—"

"Yes, little one?"

Adrenaline flooded her into a fully alerted state. Her breathing came out in rapid, shallow questions. She asked, "How can she be here? How can she in Farleigh already? Priory is two weeks away."

Mable made a sympathetic face. "She must have been close by when she received the raven, little one. Enjoy your tea. Wash your face. We'll see you downstairs in a moment."

No. This was impossible.

It had scarcely been one week since the raven had gone out. The bird shouldn't have been able to reach Priory that quickly, let alone a carriage to make the trek this far north. This couldn't be happening. It wasn't even first light. Nox wouldn't have woken yet. They were going to leave tonight. They had planned to run. Now she was being told they'd never have the chance to flee.

Amaris swallowed, working through her dread. She set her tea to the side without taking a sip. First, she needed to get up, but she couldn't stand while her head was spinning. Amaris closed her eyes and forced herself to breathe in the cold morning air slowly through her nose, then exhaled slowly through her mouth until she could think clearly. She would not be a helpless damsel. She would be strong. She would be capable. She would not be taken.

There could be no contingency plan. She had to escape at any cost. Amaris savored the cold as her feet hit the chilly stone floor. The discomfort helped to focus her mind, any remaining cobwebs falling away as she articulated her next steps.

Fetch supplies. Wake Nox. Run.

In less than three minutes she had silently dressed and gathered the bundle of the boys' clothes she'd stolen from the laundry. She peeked out of the doorway before committing to the sprint across the hall. The matrons who had been protectively patrolling the hall must be in the neighboring wing surveying the boys, as the older women were nowhere to be seen. Good.

Amaris carried her bundles with her as she crept across the corridor to the older girls' dorm. She knew Nox was awake before she even reached her bed. Two large, coal-dark eyes looked up at her from where she was still tucked between the sheets.

Amaris didn't need to say anything. The earliness of the hour and look on her face communicated enough.

Nox began wordlessly dressing into the offered tunic and pants without a moment's hesitation. A girl in a neighboring cot rolled over in her bed, and they froze, still as statues while they waited to ensure they would not be thwarted by a peer. But no one else so much as moved as Nox gathered the sheet filled with food for the road and held her shoes in one hand, lest the soft leather soles make noise on the stones.

It had been mere minutes since Mable had awoken Amaris with tea, and they were already well on their way, ready to disappear into the chilled, early purples of dawn without a moment to spare.

The girls snuck from the dorm and crept toward the back stairs that would allow them to escape through the kitchen, when Nox paused outside of Agnes's office.

"Why are we stopping?" Amaris asked. A tremor bled into her question. She looked over her shoulder and down the hall, staring into the shadowed gloom of the empty hall. Any second, the others would wake.

"Trust me," Nox said as she fished in her hair for a pin. Her fingers clasped successfully around the object, and within a moment she had begun picking the lock.

Nox had told Amaris that she'd slipped behind locked doors a time or two, but Amaris had never seen the skill in action. Gratitude and urgency competed for her attention as she squirmed impatiently. Nox's face relaxed into satisfied relief as the door yielded. She eased it open and began to search.

Amaris waited at the door. She continued to dance noiselessly at the threshold as she darted looks between Nox and the empty hall behind them.

Nox seemed to know exactly what she was looking for.

Disrupting the typical stateliness of Agnes's office, the assassin's weapons were strewn about the space. A long sword lay unceremoniously on the floor, a crossbow and accompanying quiver beside it. Amidst the blades, daggers, and arrows, she found the man's bloodied cloak. Nox plunged her hands into the fabric, patting it for the bulges of pockets.

She let out the tiniest of victorious gasps as her hand stopped searching.

"What?" Amaris whispered, keeping her question as quiet as possible. She took a few silent steps into the office to kneel beside Nox.

"Here." Nox pushed a small pouch into her hands.

"You found money?" Amaris breathed appreciatively at its weight, hearing the gentle scrape of metal as pennies, crowns, and silvers rubbed against one another in the pouch. Despite their planning and provisions, she had never hoped to escape with coin. Nox may have been good with locks, but Matron Agnes kept her silvers and crowns fastened and padlocked in a box within a box within a box. The All Mother seemed to smile on them this morning. Given the confusion of the assassin's arrival, this had been more good fortune than they could have hoped for.

"Hide it," Nox commanded in a whisper.

"Let's go," Amaris urged.

"One more thing."

Nox grabbed a thin knife from the man's numerous weapons and slipped it into the band of her pants. She palmed the second one and handed it to Amaris. Her eyes flared when she took the blade from Nox, but she asked no questions. She may have been too fragile to learn much by way of self-defense, but she'd need all the help she could get on the road. Amaris tucked the extra weapon inside her shirt and draped the winter cloak she'd grabbed from the laundry over her arm.

They slipped from the office and eased the lock back into place with a gentle click.

They were ready.

The tight corner from the office at the end of the corridor to the back staircase wound into the kitchen. If they aimed for the back entrance, they could be gone before anyone came looking for Amaris. The girls began their quiet descent down the manor's back stairs. They picked their careful steps by feeling the curvature of the stones, when they were brought to an abrupt halt.

Amaris inhaled sharply but resisted the impulse to cry out in surprise. Nox stiffened beside her. It took everything in them to remain silent as they skidded to a stop.

An unfamiliar figure blocked their path.

The man's eyebrows raised in surprise, but the stranger made no effort to chat.

"Ladies," he acknowledged. His voice wasn't loud, but the deep male grumble still startled them in the stillness of the morning light.

Amaris began backing away immediately. She took a step up the stairs, practically shoving against Nox in the tight hall.

"I'm sorry. We—"

"Amaris?" called a voice from the hallway.

"Shit," Nox cursed.

Clearly a matron had been alerted by the brief exchange. The sound of their detection was the single most horrible noise in the world. Amaris's stomach plummeted into her feet as if made of iron. The matrons must have come looking to see what was causing her delay.

The man grunted something akin to annoyance, but she didn't have time to care for his emotions. Perhaps he'd also been hoping to get up to the office and gather his things without being seen. Amaris handed the rest of the belongings to Nox with a shove.

"Go," she pleaded. "Wait for me out back."

"Amaris—" Nox clutched the cloaks and items to her chest.

"Tell me later," Amaris begged, face twisting with desperation. She would deal with this setback and meet her in a few moments. Nox could not risk getting caught with her now if they had any hope of escape. First, she would do what she must in order to rid herself of Millicent. Then they would run.

She stared into the stormy conflict that roiled across Nox's face, pain etched into her features until she finally tore herself from Amaris. The man raised a curious eyebrow but took a polite step to the side. He allowed her to push past him in a cloud of inky shadowy hair as she ran down the stairs toward the kitchen.

"Amaris?" the voice came again.

Her chest tightened as she struggled to remain calm. She began walking up the stairs and returned to the landing. Early morning light illuminated enough of the corridor to reveal Mable's face, painted with fear and surprise as she spotted the girl and the assassin ascending the shadowy stairs together.

Bewildered, Mable asked, "What on earth are the two of you—"

"I was just going down to meet the Madame in the kitchen," Amaris said, words a rushed, dry apology. "I ran into him on his way up. I'm sorry, Matron."

The man shrugged in agreement, further emphasizing his unwillingness to intervene in whatever the girls had been doing. He went from the staircase directly to the office, avoiding addressing them altogether.

It seemed as though Mable didn't know which issue to deal with first. She looked between the stranger and Amaris before leaving her eyes trained on the assassin.

"I said we were to meet in the dining room. Not the kitchen," she said. Though her words were to Amaris, her cautious gaze remained fixed on the man.

"Oh," Amaris said, attempting what she hoped was an apologetic smile. She moved past Mable toward the primary staircase that descended from the front of the manor toward the dining room, forcing her feet to walk at a normal, unbothered pace.

"What ever are you wearing?" Mable called after her, horrified as the pants and tunic unbecoming of a lady colored her vision. As a young woman, she'd been expected to be presentable in the dresses for maidens, not the children's attire she wore.

"Traveling clothes—for the road!" Amaris responded. She attempted to sound cheerful, throwing the response over her shoulder. Her stomach filled with rocks, and her knees felt wobbly as she continued her forward steps. Over her shoulder, Matron Mable exchanged words with the man, followed by the distinct noise of an unsuccessfully twisted doorknob. He jangled the knob in his attempt to get at his cloak and weapons as Amaris disappeared down the stairs. She was glad they'd remembered to lock it as they left. It seemed everyone was ready to make a hasty departure from this place.

She descended the stairs. Her foot hit the final stone on the landing with the resounding toll of a funeral bell. Amaris entered the dining room. Her frenzied pulse no longer seemed interested in keeping her conscious. She fought the urge to press her hand against her chest to still her erratic heart.

This meeting was never supposed to happen. She had intended to be long gone before this day ever arrived. Amaris had firmly believed that by the time Madame Millicent returned to Farleigh, she'd be a week's travel from this goddess-forsaken place. The Madame wasn't alone. Amaris made no attempt to show respect to either of the women sharing breakfast tea near the window.

Matron Agnes's worn features etched into deep disapproval upon seeing Amaris, doubtless irritated that she had chosen to arrive in boy's clothes.

The Gray Matron had barely opened her mouth to address Amaris's entrance when Mable hurried into the dining room, bending to whisper something into Agnes's ear. Agnes's frown deepened the carved lines of her age and she excused herself from the table, presumably to address the man's need to access his belongings in the first hours of dawn. While Agnes had been a vision of displeasure, Millicent's expression was the picture of delight. She radiated her catlike joy as she eyed Amaris, the little mouse who'd wandered in to play.

Her voice was bright, like the ringing of a silver bell. It was too pleasant, too musical for such a dark woman.

"My, what a flawless treasure you are. I'd nearly forgotten just how radiant. Come, dear; sit," she purred. Millicent motioned to join her across the table, sweeping a gloved hand in a graceful gesture.

Amaris made no move to sit, but the refusal didn't bother the Madame. Millicent shrugged and sipped her tea with proper, delicate movements. She acted as though she were performing for court rather than drinking from an orphanage's cup.

Amaris's breaths came out rapid and shallow as she scanned the dining room for any help, any plan. She saw only the wooden tables and chairs, the floor-to-ceiling windows, a cup of tea that had been presumably left out for her, and the dark, smiling face of a woman clad in finery.

Today Millicent was in a deep amethyst dress with black gems, her golden hair pinned half up in elaborate curls. Her elbow-length gloves stayed on while she used a fork to pick at her breakfast with birdlike delicacy. Her lips had been painted a shade of night to match her dark jewels. Although Amaris had never seen one, something in her gut distinctly shouted to her that this woman looked like a witch.

Amaris asked numbly, "How did you get here so fast? It's supposed to be at least two weeks' travel to Priory."

Millicent eyed Amaris's position from across the room. Her feline smile grew even more wicked. She said, presumably to herself, "Oh, it is fun when they have spirit."

Amaris looked over her shoulder as if the Madame had been addressing someone else, but they were alone. She took a single step closer to the table.

"What is your plan for me?"

The Madame let a frown flicker across her features. Millicent chose her words carefully, gesturing again for Amaris to sit, though Amaris was sure they both knew it was fruitless. She didn't have time to play Millicent's coy game of pleasantries. She needed to leave. Amaris wondered how much time had passed. How much longer would Agnes be upstairs? Was Nox already waiting outside? Would Millicent chase her if she turned on her heel and attempted to flee?

"You are a rare beauty," Millicent said finally.

"And if I weren't beautiful?"

Millicent clucked her tongue. "What's the point of such a useless question? The truth remains: you are. Short of being mauled by a beast, you're still the most marvelous diamond I've seen in my ages. You'd be amazed what men will pay to possess something unique, even if only for a moment. Everyone wants a piece of something special. Now, to be the first to have you…well, that will be worth your weight in crowns, my dear."

The Madame rose and began making her way slowly around the table. Amaris matched her steps, backing away in the opposite direction to keep the space between them equidistant. A voice within screamed at her to run.

"Your friends are already in Priory waiting for you. They're very excited to see you," Millicent lied.

Amaris knew the woman was referring to Cici and Emily, but she hadn't been friends with either of them. She wasn't friends with anyone. No one would be happy to see her at the pleasure house, aside from the hungry faces of patrons and the greedy coin purse of its Madame.

"They're both lovely," Amaris remarked flatly of the girls who'd been taken before her.

"Oh yes, they are," Millicent agreed. Nothing about her voice was kind. She had a bored tone, sinking her weight into one hip as she looked off into the distance. "They have the common, virginal beauty that fetches a high enough price on their first night, and then the steadfast price of a workhorse from then on. But you, Amaris, are no workhorse. The life that awaits you is quite spectacular indeed. The matrons tell me your name means 'gift from the goddess.' Believe me when I tell you that you will be marketed as such. You are a treasure. You can have a very pleasant life if you allow us to work as a team, dear. I'd like that very much."

Millicent took another step toward her. The clack of the Madame's heels on the stones mingled with the commotion of the matrons coming down the stairs with the stranger. The man's footsteps were heavy enough to indicate he had redressed in his armor, intent on departure. Amaris dared to take her eyes off the Madame long enough to glance behind her, peering beyond the dining room into the foyer. She saw the matrons clucking after the stranger like chickens after a fox in their henhouse. The man looked unbothered by their pecking as he sauntered after his horse. He was no longer clutching his stomach. Amaris hadn't been able to catch more in the brief moments her eyes grazed the stranger. Perhaps his wounds had been shallow enough that the nurse was able to stop the bleeding with bandages, if not by the manor's limited supply of tonics. It would doubtlessly be another scar to add to his collection.

Once the stranger and the matrons left her line of sight, Amaris was wholly alone with the Madame. Millicent made another move toward her.

"I'm rather eager to get on the road, if you don't mind."

"Stop," Amaris cautioned, and Millicent stilled in her steps.

She had nothing. She had no one. She had... That was it. A vision of the scarred assassin popped into her mind, striking her with inspiration. Amaris reached into her shirt and wrapped her hand around the hilt of the small dagger Nox had handed her only fifteen minutes prior.

The Madame let out a sharp, dark laugh, shaking her golden curls slightly to emphasize her surprised delight. Her black lips peeled back into a predatory smile, teeth glinting in the early morning light.

"You mean to hurt me, girl? Oh my, I wish you would try."

As the Madame began to peel off her gloves, Amaris shook her head. Her voice was stronger than she'd ever heard it before as she spoke her resolution.

"No," and her words did not waiver as she finished, "I mean to hurt me."

Amaris struck fast and hard with the dagger, closing her eyes and jerking her face up and to the side as she slashed the knife down in countering motion. A blood-curdling shriek filled the room as the merchandise mutilated itself, dragging a deep line from her forehead, across her brow bone, and down her left cheek. The acute pain was a sharp, sweet sensation of relief as she knew her dagger hit its mark. A hot rain of her own blood spilled over her face, soaking her tunic.

She was no longer perfect.

The Madame's horrified screams sounded as though she was the one who'd been stabbed. The pain, the blood—it had set Amaris free. She was no longer glued to the floor. Feeling as though a millstone had been cut free from her neck, she ran with the weightlessness of liberation.

Millicent took off in pursuit, but Amaris was already out of the dining room, over the threshold and out the door. She ran into the open, spinning amidst the bright, clear indigo morning of the courtyard to see how close the Madame was on her heels. It was not the clean break she'd wanted. She couldn't disappear into the forest. The courtyard was crowded with matrons and the assassin. Amaris spun to face the door to Farleigh, her back to the man and his horse, her eyes trained on the Madame while the matrons gaped in horror.

Amaris held her dagger aloft, and she swung again, this time cutting a line from her collarbone down nearly across her right breast, shredding and bloodying the tunic she wore. The matrons were realizing precisely what was transpiring as the crimson evidence poured down around their starlight girl. Agnes made a lunging move for her, but Amaris prayed to the goddess on the only wild card in the courtyard. She ran to the assassin. The man had already mounted his horse and had begun to nudge it off the premises when the pandemonium spilled from the manor into the courtyard.

"Please, take me with you!" she pleaded, reaching his horse.

The women advanced as if cornering a wild animal, triangulating Amaris between the Gray Matron, the Madame, and the assassin.

The man's face tensed with surprise, his mouth parted in speechlessness.

He spat out a bewildered stammer. "I—"

Amaris stared up at him with her frenzied plea. Her back remained to the women as she silently implored the stranger. As she looked into his face, her second good idea for the morning came to her. She took the risk and pulled a familiar coin purse from her shirt. She swung around, holding it firmly against the middle of her back so only the man could see it.

Amaris presented the assassin with his own money as bribery.

She wasn't sure if the stranger would be impressed or irritated with her boldness. She'd attacked herself with his dagger, begged him to help her, and offered him his own coin. Amaris was certain this wasn't the best way to forge new alliances, but she was out of options.

"Take me with you," she said again, her voice heavy with desperation.

His answering grunt seemed to be filled with conflicting emotions.

"I'll buy her off you," he finally said to the advancing women. His gravelly voice had an upsetting effect on the matrons and the Madame alike. They stirred like snakes disturbed into writhing.

Millicent was horrified. She cried out, "There was a down payment made!"

He nodded. "I will reimburse whatever down payment. I'm in need of a"—he searched for a word before, settling on—"squire."

Millicent shook her head so hard that her curls nearly freed themselves from her elaborate pins. Every step she took brought her farther from the open door of the manor and closer to the man and his horse. Her voice was shrill and cruel as she raised her gloved fist.

"I own you, girl," she declared.

If they did nothing, Millicent would be at her side in fewer than ten paces. The Madame began once more to yank at the black fabric on her forearms and stopped just short of pulling off her gloves.

They had an audience.

The moon-faced waking children pressed into the windows from the dorms up above. The matrons watched in open-mouthed horror, aghast at the mutilated young girl in the courtyard, fresh blood soaking her hair and tunic, plastering it to her body. More children poured from the halls and clutched the doorframes. A crowd had gathered both within and without Farleigh to witness the bedlam caused by the girl who would rather disfigure herself than go with this woman.

"Amaris," Agnes said sadly.

Amaris met the Gray Matron's mournful look, but the woman said nothing more. The matron truly did look sorry. Amaris's choice to slice her face and body rather than be sold to the Madame appeared to have broken something in Agnes.

"You can't make me go," Amaris said with a feral intensity. She took another step back until her shoulders pressed into the tall, dappled horse.

With a prayer to the All Mother, she reached her hand up and—praise be to the goddess—the man gripped her elbow, swinging her up behind him. Amaris passed him the pouch in a seamless exchange, and the man tossed his coin purse to Matron Agnes. He instructed the matron to keep the change before urging his horse into a trot away from the courtyard, down the road. The clatter of hooves against the cobbles clashed with the cacophony of angry shouts, shrill accusations, clustering children, and the incongruously happy chirping of early morning birds. The pandemonium had just begun.

Amaris looked back one last time and said a prayer that Nox had made it safely to the forest, hoping she was well on her way to the coast to start a new life. She prayed that the All Mother would bless their journeys and that the goddess's will would reunite them soon.

Twelve

A MARIS DIDN'T KNOW WHAT TO DO WITH HER HANDS. She had never been alone with a man, let alone touched one. Now she was supposed to wrap her arms around a stranger as their horse plodded onward. She was quite sure that she was only seated behind him since he'd already been in the saddle when she'd been swung to her rescue, and she wasn't sure if that made things more or less uncomfortable between them. It required her to use entirely too much muscle power in her thighs as she clutched the horse. Too many thoughts clashed against each other like mismatched music, angry sounds, and the counter-harmonies of voices. She couldn't make sense of the thoughts that overlapped so ignored them all entirely, focusing instead on the autumnal breeze that dried her blood against her shirt and skin.

She studied what she could of the strange man. He was broader than two bishops side by side. His hardened leathers were covered in the sorts of nicks and scratches that informed her they'd done their protective job quite well. His slicked-back hair hung just above his shoulders, revealing a slim band of age-weathered leather—something that may have been a necklace—on his otherwise unadorned features. She wasn't sure what to make of him. She didn't know how to talk to him, or even if she wanted to.

Morning gave way to a quiet, awkward afternoon before they finally dismounted for mealtime. The man tethered the dapple-gray horse to a tree and set to work building a fire. He allowed Amaris to sit silently in her blood and thoughts, numb from the events of the day. Soon, she was staring mutely into the campfire that crackled between them. Though it was still afternoon, the fire's glow felt nice against the crisp bite of autumn. Amaris stared into the flames, watching them twist and pop and dance in a mesmerizing tangle of reds, oranges, yellows, and blues. The sparks and embers helped her mind to detach fully, lost to her silence. The smell of smoke, the dying leaves, and the chill of oncoming winter would have been pleasant under any other occasion. An owl sounded from the trees, though she thought it too early in the afternoon for the great, nocturnal bird to hoot.

She raised her eyes to the trees to search for it, though she wasn't sure why. She didn't care about the owl, or the temperature, or the fire. Her world had unraveled, and she had no idea what to do.

The man wordlessly disappeared into the woods, and Amaris didn't bother to watch him leave. She wouldn't have known how much time had passed had it not been for the elongating shadows. He'd been absent for nearly an hour before reappearing with a rabbit. The bearded stranger sat across from her and began to quietly skin the creature.

She continued ignoring the assassin altogether, her pupils burning against her unbroken stare into the fire. She caught the man's occasional glances in her peripherals, each time wearing an expression that may have been concern. Perhaps he was right to be worried. Soaked as she was in dried blood after having screamed like a banshee just that morning in her grand escape, he probably thought she'd gone mad.

She studied him from the corner of her eye. Though she didn't look at him directly, she absorbed his dark beard, thick brows, and broad shoulders; the man appeared to be in his fifth decade of life. His hair had remained slicked back from his morning wash and hung roughly as long as his cropped beard, down the back of his neck. He appeared as though he would be an intimidating foe in battle, to be sure, but the man did not seem threatening in a way that had stirred her to run as she had from Millicent.

After he'd discarded the hare's bloodied fur, he skewered the rabbit and stuck it across the campfire to cook. While the meat roasted, he offered her a flask of his water.

"No, thank you," she said. Amaris was surprised at how her voice croaked. She hadn't used it since she'd cried in desperation that morning.

"It's for your face," he said. They were the first words he'd spoken since their exchange in the courtyard.

She blinked rapidly, wondering what she must look like through his eyes. A distant part of her felt quite certain he was staring at the gore of a girl's reanimated corpse. She took the canteen. The man tore a length of clean cloth from inside his satchel that seemed to be for just this purpose.

"Clean your cuts as best as you can, and I'll give you a healing tonic. I'll bill you later."

She wasn't sure if he was trying to be funny or if he genuinely wanted payment. Amaris was almost positive he'd purchased healing tonics from the orphanage and that whatever money he'd used to buy the tonics had been stolen by Nox and then swiftly regifted in exchange for her life.

It had been quite the deal. The assassin had received shelter for the night, healing tonics, bandaging by Matron Flora, and the life of a particularly valuable girl for one coin purse.

As the hours wore on, Amaris grew increasingly lucid about the weight of her decisions and the consequences that may result from following an assassin into the woods. She shifted uncomfortably at the thought. She had spent no time around men. She'd known boys at the manor—both cruel and stupid. She knew the bishop—pious and crooked. She believed little of men, save for the certainty that the lesser sex had never given her a reason to trust them.

When Amaris didn't respond, he tried again. "There's a village not too far from here. It's not big, but I need to meet a bishop about settling a debt. You should be able to catch a ride from there."

"A bishop?" she asked, paling. The fear in her voice must have been clear.

"It's not about you, girl," he clarified. His thick brows furrowed curiously. "We help the kingdoms with… Well, I suppose it doesn't matter. When I speak with him, feel free to find yourself a ride. I'll make sure you're safely on the road to wherever you're going before I leave you."

"Wherever I'm going?" she repeated. Amaris hadn't considered it. She had never planned to go anywhere without Nox.

The man's frown deepened as he asked, "Where are your people?"

She shook her head slowly. "I don't have any people."

He considered this. "And the woman at the orphanage?"

"She was buying me for her brothel," Amaris responded. She kept her eyes on the fire, her tone quiet and monotonous as if she didn't dare attach feeling to her words.

He blinked. It had undoubtedly been clear that he wasn't in a holy place, but this particular piece of information appeared to rattle him.

"Is there anywhere you'd like to go?"

She let her lashes flutter to a close as her mind wandered to the only plans she and her friend—her partner, her person, her missing piece in this world—had ever made. She thought of the blue expanse of the sea and how it was said to meet the horizon in an endless, salty sense of openness.

"I suppose I want to go to the southern coast, where it's warm."

He nodded at that. They didn't attempt further conversation.

Amaris took the time to wash the blood from her face as best as she could. She used the clean cloth as a compression against the gash that had skipped her eye but had otherwise marred her from her forehead to her cheek. Once she began washing the wound, she found even the simple tug of the cloth had reopened it to a fresh flow of blood.

"Good. Now that it's clean, press some of the tonic directly into the wound."

"But it's still bleeding," she argued.

"That's a good thing. It's more effective without the risk of dirt or infection."

Amaris dipped her finger into the bottle and watched her pale finger come up with a sticky, brown liquid. It matched the color of the bottle. She felt along her face for the gash, smearing the tonic into her cut.

She thought of the times she or her peers had fallen ill in the orphanage and how Matron Flora had busied herself with the small, brown bottles, feeding the orphans spoonfuls of the liquid.

"Do I drink what's left?"

He nodded. "That you do. It helps knit your insides and outsides."

"It's magic?"

He considered that, saying, "It's an old magic. Tonics like that are one of the first inventions that healers and manufacturers came together to create. Tonics have been around since…well…long before the lines between kingdoms were drawn."

She eyed the bottle, asking, "When was that?"

He raised a brow. "What do you know of history?"

She shook her head.

"Geography?"

Feeling a little defensive, she answered, "I know how to read and write. I've memorized prayers, practiced court decorum, and know all about the royal family. I'm not stupid."

"Stupidity and ignorance are not one and the same. Drink up."

Amaris didn't understand half of what he'd said. She didn't know what he'd meant by "old magic." Regardless, she drank half of the bottle. She dipped her finger into the bottle once more to wet it with the brown, honey-stick liquid as she attempted to rub the tonic over the gashes on her face and across her chest with what remained, wincing against the sting.

She stared intently into the crackling flames while the man finished cooking the rabbit. He tore into it, offering her half. She chewed on it sullenly, thinking of Nox and the meal of pale cheese and Matron Mable's bread that her friend was sure to be eating somewhere in the forest. Had they run in the same direction? How far would Nox be from Farleigh by now? That was, of course, unless she'd gone back inside to live amongst the matrons. Amaris hadn't considered the possibility that Nox might want to stay in the orphanage without her.

The stranger smothered the fire and began to untether the horse.

"Shall we?"

"We're leaving?"

"Like I said, I have a bishop to meet with."

She stood and considered the scarred, fatherly assassin from a ways off. He'd fed her, offered her healing tonics, allowed her silence, and most importantly, he'd aided her escape from a life of unimaginable horrors. She hadn't even asked him who he was.

Amaris felt a stab of shame at her ingratitude as she asked, "What's your name?"

He didn't look up from his horse, continuing to repack the satchel and prepare for departure.

"Odrin."

It was a nice name. A friendly name. She hoped he was kind.

"I'm Amaris."

He chuckled lightly. "That makes sense. Come here, Amaris," Odrin said, gesturing toward the horse. "You can take the saddle this time. It'll be easier on those jelly legs of yours." He helped her up with ease before swinging himself into the space behind her.

"Why do you say that?" she asked.

"About your jelly legs?" He did his best not to look patronizing. "It's clear you're no rider. You'll need the saddle's help more than I will."

"No." Her brows furrowed from where she sat in

front of him, knowing he couldn't see her perplexed expression. "Why do you say that about my name?"

He clicked his tongue to urge the horse forward. The dappled mount began plodding away from the campfire as Odrin asked, "Do you know what it means? Your name, that is?"

She nodded. She did know.

"The matrons gave it to me. Since I was a gift left on their doorstep, they said it meant 'gift from the goddess.'"

He held the reins, steering the horse from the woods as he considered the piece of information.

"Did they now?" He chewed on that for a moment. "Perhaps in a dialect deeper in the south of the continent it means something to that effect. But that's not what people in the north will hear."

"What does it mean in the north?"

She could hear the smile in his voice as he said, "Child of the moon."

✦

The two unlikely travel companions arrived in a small village by the last coppery lights of sundown. At least, Amaris assumed it was a village. She'd never been anywhere and had no basis for comparison.

The horse lumbered down the grassy center of the village, carrying them amidst the row of homes and shops. Amaris wasn't sure if there were establishments or cottages behind trees or around bends out of view, but the village seemed to have fewer than ten buildings. Wilted, gray-brown straw thickly topped the roof of nearly every home. A steepled church with the iron sign of the All Mother decorating its cathedral sat proudly in the center. The structure at the heart of the village looked just as she'd imagined an inn might.

They dismounted and Odrin waved her away, instructing her to ask around to see if anyone in town was headed to the coast. He didn't need her there while he chatted with the village's bishop. Odrin disappeared inside one of the only homes with clay shingles in an otherwise thatch-roofed village. Amaris idled nervously about the horse for a minute. She was nearly fifteen, but her whole life had consisted of the grounds of Farleigh. The world felt too big. Every face was new and strange. Every building was crushingly unfamiliar. Given that two strangers—one a towering man and the other a girl bloodied beyond recognition—had entered the quiet town, they were drawing some stares. It didn't help her ever-growing sense of crushing discomfort.

Amaris fidgeted before heading nervously toward the inn.

She stopped short of the door, unsure whether she was supposed to knock. Visitors and sellers at the doors of Farleigh always knocked. Buyers entered freely on market day. After a long moment, she decided that she was more of a buyer than a seller, and she eased the door open with extreme trepidation.

The woman within—whether a barmaid or the innkeeper herself—nearly dropped her pitcher of ale when Amaris entered.

Amaris stopped on the landing, unsure from the woman's reaction if she'd done something terribly wrong. Warmth and the sour smells of beer, sourdough, and smoke hit her, overwhelming her senses and gluing her to the doorway. She shrank, not knowing if she should retreat. Perhaps she should have knocked. This was one of the first decisions she'd ever had to make for herself, and clearly, she'd done it wrong.

"Oh my, dear" came the woman's gasp.

She approached Amaris with a friendly face creased with worry and extended two maternal hands as she examined the young girl's injuries.

"It's not that bad," Amaris said, lifting a hand self-consciously to the wound on her face. She nearly pressed her back into the door, flinching away from the woman's advances.

The middle-aged woman put her hands on her hip, one still clutching the dirty rag that she'd been using to wipe the tables around her.

"Do you have coin?"

"How much do you need?"

The woman shook her head, tugging Amaris forward. "I won't charge a wretched thing like you more than two pennies. Come now."

"I think my traveling partner might—"

The woman clucked her tongue and ushered Amaris into the back. Soon closed doors separated them from the tavern beyond for privacy as they sat beside a washbasin. The woman helped her scrub off the wound on her chest and bandaged it properly, blinding Amaris completely in one eye with bandages, covering half of her face with gauze. The other straps of clean cloth wrapped around where Amaris had nearly mutilated one of her small breasts, tightly binding half of her chest to her shoulder in a crisscross of bandaging. While wrapping her, the woman marveled at how she'd managed to keep so much blood on her face given the age of her wounds.

Amaris intended to correct that it had happened nearly that very morning, when she caught sight of the scarcely scabbed, grimy-looking wounds in the mirror above the washbasin. The violent lines did indeed look weeks old. Amaris had never heard of a healing tonic before she drank the one Odrin had given her. A memory of Matron Flora administering medicine in a brown bottle tugged at her, but she'd never been educated on its contents.

The woman filled the washbasin with warm, soapy water. She had Amaris flip her blood-stained hair into the basin and scrubbed at her scalp.

Once the crusted, crimson stains were cleaned from her strands and she had been fitted with a fresh tunic, the kindly woman was finally able to see precisely how strange Amaris looked. She could no longer hide behind the excuse of wounds or blood or dirty clothes. She flinched, feeling dreadfully self-conscious.

"So," the woman started, attempting to sound casual while Amaris looked at her bandages in the mirror, "was it your mother or your father?"

"Excuse me?"

The woman asked again. "Who was fae? Was it your mother?"

Amaris shook her head, comprehension eluding her. Her brows pinched in the center as she waited for the woman to explain.

The woman scoffed. "This village may be small, but we're not so backwater that we don't get our share of the fair folk from time to time, at least, some with distant lineage... Though I will say, it's been ages...I do know how to spot a faeling. I'll be damned, I've never seen one who looked like you... I haven't seen a purple like that since the lilac bushes blossomed last spring! Then with your hair... Well..." Her voice trailed off with each peculiar sentence, growing quieter with each passing word.

Amaris wasn't sure what to make of the stranger's speech. She involuntarily began with honesty, finding herself responding before she thought better of it.

"I never knew my parents. I grew up in—" She bit her tongue.

Amaris blinked at her own stupidity. She'd nearly told a perfect stranger that she'd come from Farleigh. She couldn't risk word of which direction she'd headed getting back to the orphanage. Amaris didn't know how far Millicent's talons reached. She pursed her lips to silence herself and offered a sad shrug. The gesture would have to suffice.

"No family, then?" The woman frowned apologetically, then added, "Come, let's get you something to drink. You look pale. Well—pale even for your complexion."

The maternal innkeeper led them from the bathing room and busied herself fetching a glass of water from behind the bar. She set a glass of water down in front of Amaris before tending to her other customers. Amaris looked around nervously and took in the two dark patrons skulking in the corner. A conciliatory hand went to her hair.

"Say." Amaris twisted her lips. "Since I'm already buying the tunic from you, would you also be able to find me a scarf for my hair?"

The innkeeper searched Amaris's features before nodding. "It might help a bit to wrap up those pearly locks of yours, but you'll want to be keeping your cloak on and hood up if you want any hope of people not catching those eyes of yours. They are…" She allowed her eyes to roam with more concern than Amaris understood. "They're really unlike anything I've seen."

Amaris knew her features were rare, but she hadn't understood just how unusual until this stranger had cast her evaluating gaze upon her. She'd been kept away from prying eyes for years. She'd had little to no exposure to outsiders responding to her traits.

Amaris caught a glimpse of Odrin through the window just as the woman returned with a scarf.

"Oh! One moment! Two pennies, right? I'll be right back."

Before the woman could stop her, Amaris was out the door. She ran up to the assassin as the man reached his horse. The gray mount nickered as it stepped to the side, wary of her rushed approach.

Her question tumbled out as she asked, "May I steal two pennies off you?"

"Haven't you already stolen enough of my money?"

He continued saddling the horse without looking her way.

"I stole it back from Agnes, so technically, she was paid twice with the same coin."

"That she was, but my purse is still empty nonetheless."

Amaris frowned impatiently. "Didn't your bishop—"

Odrin fished two pennies from a pouch in his vest. Offering them to her, he said, "I hope you found a ride, girl."

"Don't leave the village without me," she yelled as she took off.

Amaris dashed inside the inn and hugged the innkeeper, bewilderment clear on the woman's face. Amaris wouldn't forget this act of kindness, even if it had been in exchange for compensation. One heartbeat later she was through the door and jogging to catch up to where Odrin was already plodding away. He hadn't left the village. He also hadn't been willing to stand still.

"I want to come with you!"

He kept the horse at a walk. Odrin did not appear impressed with the breathless heaving that came just from her jogging to keep up with their pace. Without looking at her, he answered, "No you don't."

Dauntless, Amaris pressed on. She rebutted, "I know nothing of the world. I don't know anything about the villages. I don't know about people, about money, about customs. I don't know the first thing about getting to the coast. If I had known how to fight, I could have defended myself today."

The horse flicked its ears in irritation as it continued its forward motion. The beast was clearly uncomfortable with Amaris's invasion of its space.

"We all have to grow up sometime, girl. Why not start a new life here? Ask the inn if they're hiring."

She shook her head, short of breath. She panted, "Will you teach me how to fight?"

He looked down from his saddle. He chuckled. "Girls don't train where I'm from."

Amaris's tone was cheerful though short-winded as she said, "Well, that's rather sexist. Sounds like they had to grow up sometime."

He laughed appreciatively at her retort. Odrin shook his head, but she cut him off. He looked set to argue once more.

Amaris was resolute, arguing, "Look, I've never had a father. But if you'd have me, I promise I won't be a burden."

He pulled the horse to a stop then and she stopped running, still panting slightly at the exertion. The sun had set. Only the flickers of torches on buildings cast light and shadows against the sincerity of her plea. She knew her words had hit a chord with him. Something tugged his vision into the middle distance, perhaps a memory pulling his focus. Even the horse stilled as if respecting whatever reverie called to him. Odrin released a long, slow exhale and shook his head as if his body was willing him to say no. Instead, he looked her in the eye.

"I don't think you'll like what you're getting yourself into."

She put her hands on her hips, the inhalations coming in more easily now. Amaris challenged him, saying, "I won't like what? Getting strong? Learning how to defend myself? Take me with you."

He looked back at the town. It was clear from his face that part of him wanted her to leave, to start her new life. Amaris stared intently at Odrin for his response. She studied his features as he seemed to shake off whatever had invaded his thoughts. Odrin stared at her for a long moment.

The horse huffed impatiently as if urging them to make up their minds.

With a look that informed her he fully understood he was making a mistake, he extended his arm to her and swung her up behind him.

✦

Her tailbone had never felt such pain.

Amaris wanted to whine, but she knew she had to do everything within her power to prevent Odrin from regretting his decision. His reluctance had been clear, and if she griped about the ache of her legs or bruise of her lowermost spine, she was worried he'd make her walk back to Farleigh.

No one had told her that riding could be so grueling. Her legs throbbed painfully from gripping the saddle. Every muscle she possessed screamed at her as the pair dismounted for the night. She was as stiff as a corpse.

Odrin hadn't permitted them to start a fire that night. When she asked why, he explained that fires were fine during the day for cooking, but there were plenty of reasons a pair of humans—or a human and whatever she was—would not want to draw the attention of the things that lived in the dark.

Amaris curled on her side, listening to Odrin move about as he prepared himself for sleep. He'd disappeared into the forest, which wasn't unusual for their short time together. He'd gone to get rabbits and wood and taken care of goddess-knows-what whenever they'd stopped. This time he did not return empty-handed.

"Amaris," he said as he extended an object.

She sat up and looked at what was being offered. He'd cut a large bough of a soft conifer. Her brows puckered as she accepted the tree branch, staring at him with mixed confusion.

"Most of your body heat is lost through the ground. You shouldn't sleep directly on the earth, even with your cloak," he said. Odrin set down a few cut branches of his own and pulled his cloak up over his body, grunting what could have been a "Good night."

Amaris's heart tugged at the thoughtful gesture. She copied his actions, placing the branch beneath her to create a thin barrier between herself and the earth as she balled herself up for sleep. She curled her knees against her chest, huddling as tightly as she could. So much had happened between sunrise and sunset. That very morning she'd been with Nox. It was in the violet lights of dawn that Nox's dark eyes had opened and she had silently dressed as she prepared to run with her. But between Millicent, the dagger, the matrons, and the escape, it felt as though a lifetime had passed.

Sleeping on the forest floor, tucked into a tight ball under her cloak, made for the coldest, most miserable night of her young life. She couldn't imagine how much more frigid the night might have been if this cut of evergreen kept her any warmer than some bleak alternative. Amaris's mind thought of the frozen meats that were stored in the boxes chipped from ice in the winter and that rested in the snowbanks beyond Farleigh's doors. She was willing to bet that her thighs resembled the frostbitten slabs of beef that had been thawed and cooked in the orphanage's kitchens. Except, she had yet to defrost if something hoped to eat her.

Between the dull pulse of her healing wounds, the burn of her muscles, the maddening hurt of her tailbone, and the deeply bone-chilling temperatures, Amaris was quite certain she was in the most pathetic state she'd ever been.

There were no hooting owls to keep her company this time. Every so often, the moonlight revealed something as glossy shapes reflected against its silver beams. She would have sworn the yellow orbs of eyes stared right back at her.

She was scared. She was frozen. She hurt like no other.

None of it mattered.

She welcomed the pain like a new friend. She invited the chill to invade her muscles, her blood, her bones. Amaris didn't doubt her decision. She would rather freeze to death or be eaten by whatever unholy monster looked at her between the gaps in trees than have left with the jewel-toned Madame in her glossy, black carriage. Not a single stab of pain, twinge of fear, or dread of the future as she lay on the forest floor made her wish she were in Millicent's possession.

Somehow, she slept.

It hadn't been a long sleep, nor was it a restful one. However cold she'd been in the late hours of night was nothing compared to the frigid immobility she felt in the early morning. Her fingers were stiff. Her ears burned with the early signs of frostbite before she began chafing her cloak against them to get the blood flowing. It was not yet sunrise, and the pewter sky was all the light they needed to get going.

She hadn't frozen to death. She hadn't bled out. She wasn't in Farleigh. She wasn't with Millicent. She was alive. From one morning to the next, everything in her life had been made new.

Odrin wasn't chatty as they mounted the horse, and she didn't mind. She didn't feel like talking either. The only sound was the mount's hooves on the brittle, fallen leaves.

The gradient was beautiful as the sky transitioned from grays and blues to lavenders, soft peaches, and eventually a vibrant shade of orange. Still freezing, Amaris no longer feared touching the assassin. He'd given her the saddle again as he sat behind her. He'd draped his cloak to capture their body heat, a trick so effective that Amaris nearly cried from the small warmth. The trees thinned, giving way to great, rolling hills. Deep green, ruddy orange, and thick brown foliage that may have been mosses and lichens clung to huge stones spotting the hills. Now that the forest was no longer blocking the horizon, she was able to see the deeply violet mountains in the distance.

"Are we headed north?" she asked quietly.

"That we are. Well, northeast."

"To the Dark Kingdom?"

He laughed. "Who educated you, girl, folklorists? Only superstitious villagers who've never spent a day in a classroom call it such things...though I suppose you had little say over either the lessons or the ones teaching them," he amended. Then he said, "Call the northern kingdom by its right and proper name."

She felt a surge of bile rise in the back of her throat and tried the question again. "Are you taking me to Raascot?"

He seemed satisfied with her question this time but shook his head.

"No, girl; we're bound for the border, just past the village of Stone."

She perked, however dully, at the familiar name. She fixated on the purple mountains on the horizon as she summoned a memory. "One of the matrons was from Stone. She was nice, if a bit naive about the world. She said guardians lived in the cliff protecting their village."

Odrin smiled at that, which was rare from what she knew of the man. He'd had the lines and crinkles that vouched for a life of easy smiles, but during his time with Amaris he had remained guarded. Warmth now colored his voice as he answered her.

"That is a bit naive, I suppose. I don't think anyone outside of Stone would call us guardians."

So he was one of them.

She sat on the horse with one of the very assassins Mable had fondly referenced. She felt her body shrink away from the man, clutching her hands into the sleeves of her cloak. Amaris didn't mean to show cowardice, but she felt herself speak with a hollow, empty response.

"You're one of the assassins, aren't you?"

He shrugged. "We prefer to be called reevers."

If Mable's fairy tales were to be believed, Amaris realized they were headed into the mountain itself.

Thirteen

NOX'S MIND DRIFTED TO THE POND BEHIND FARLEIGH. The little lake had been a source of joy in the springs and summers, and an ominous threat come winter. The children weren't allowed to go near it in the final, chilly days of autumn for the insidious temptation of its clear, thin ice. If you stepped on before it was thick enough to hold your weight, it would fracture into ten thousand sharp slices, plunging you into the arctic waters below. Though the lake might appear clear and flowing beneath, the truth of its brokenness was plain on the surface. Nox thought of that pond as her hand went to her heart, clutching her palm against her chest as if to keep it from crumbling.

She had shattered. She held herself together with the only fragments she could grab with weak, listless fingers. Nox stared through the window of the black carriage as it bounced dully down the road, pulled by its powerful, chestnut horses. She'd kept her hand against her invisible, bleeding wound for hours.

Millicent attempted to talk to her many times after getting Nox into the carriage, but had long since given up, muttering something about how Nox wouldn't be very good at her job if she didn't know how to make conversation.

They were a few hours into their journey, yet everything out the window looked the same. Every naked, autumnal tree was the same tree. Every gray, broken rock was the same. The wind shuffled the branches around slightly overhead, blowing the same dead, brown leaves around the same stretch of bumpy road. The sounds of the hooves were the same, the too-sweet vanilla smell of the woman's perfume was choking her in cloud after cloud of sameness, her breathing was the same, but her heart... It had never been truly broken before.

Her eyes glazed as her mind fixed on the events of the morning.

Wait for me, Amaris had said.

Nox had. She'd gripped the pillowcase of dried foods and the spare cloak close to her body. She'd remained tensed and ready to run as the minutes grew achingly long. She'd waited until she heard a shriek coming from the front of the manor. She'd wanted to run, to see what was happening, but her feet were frozen to the ground. She didn't want to face the world without Amaris.

Wait for me.

She'd waited.

She could have fled without Amaris beside her, but her heart would not allow it. She wouldn't escape into the trees unless ivory fingers were interlaced with her own. She couldn't go. Not willingly.

And then something had gone terribly wrong. Though she didn't know what, the sensation had torn through her as if she'd been made of little more than paper. Now hours later, her body was in a carriage headed for the southwestern coast, but her mind stayed at Farleigh, listening to the screams that permeated her memories.

Her heart was somewhere far stranger as it continued to travel further and further from her, tugging the tether that bound them like a rope uncoiling as one end fell to the deepest bottom of a well. Nox had heard muffled cries, a protest, and the whinnying of a horse. The angry screams of women from somewhere beyond the court-yard punctured the air. She had felt them then—the hot tears that erupted from her carving salted lines down her cheeks. She hadn't known she was going to cry until it was already happening. Her face had contorted, her chest tightened, and she'd been unable to properly breathe.

Nox couldn't explain how she knew, but Amaris was gone.

The separation was a physical void, its presence a shadowy, terrible companion. The absence poured into her, flooding her as if she'd been little more than an empty glass before its black waters filled her.

Nox had willed her knees to bend. She begged her feet to take her into the woods, to break away from the mill. If she took off for the woods, it would be less than a three-minute run until she was out of the yard and into the forest. She could be between the browns and grays of their trunks and hidden within the underbrush in moments. She had the supplies she needed. She had the food, the clothes, and the provisions to run. She could do it. She could leave.

She'd pleaded with herself, begged herself, commanded her body to do *anything*. It could carry her back into her house, return her to her bed, sprint for the forest, it could do anything other than stand like a statue. It could transport her into the kitchen for seven-teen loaves of fresh bread. It could drown her in the cold waters of an early-winter river where the waves would wash her away, carry her on their icy rapids until she drifted into nothingness, her lovely corpse making it to the coast she had dreamed of one day seeing. How poetic would it be, to drift into the sea. Instead, she would bring the sea to her, as all the salt in her body poured out from its bottomless well in her eyes.

Then hands had been on her. Nox hadn't even heard the kitchen door open.

"Nox!"

Her eyes had snapped to see that it was Flora who had found her. The matron looked her over for wounds, searching for the source of Nox's tears. She found nothing.

Flora's face transformed from concern to anger in an instant. She grabbed Nox, dragging her into the manor. One hand flattened on her back, the other was wrapped firmly around her wrist as she restrained Nox against the ability to bolt.

She couldn't have fled even if she'd wanted to. She was stuck.

The moments following Flora's discovery passed in a blur.

The matron dragged Nox—empty husk though she was—down the hall and toward the main door. She knew without being told that she was being taken to be judged by Agnes. She was in trouble. The happy morning noises didn't match the severity of the situation. The sounds of breakfast were just starting up in the dining room from the other orphans and attending matrons. The smell of eggs wafted from the kitchen. She knew with some certainty she would not be joining her peers for breakfast.

Flora snatched the pillowcase of food and goods from her arms, lofting them in her own hand as evidence of the pending crime. It seemed quite clear that Nox had been ready to flee. Between her changes of clothes and bag of food, there was no hiding her intention. She'd been caught in a botched attempt at flight, making it no farther than the back door to the orphanage.

The moment they crossed into the courtyard, Flora started, "I caught her—"

Agnes registered Nox's disheveled state and immediately began to gesture for them to turn and leave. Her face twisted in incomprehensible anguish as she wordlessly urged Flora to turn around. While the nurse had only intended to drag Nox before Agnes's wrath, the Gray Matron was not alone in the courtyard.

Millicent cut Flora off, waving a hand. The Madame's temper staved slightly as her gaze explored Nox with cool examination.

Agnes shook her head with a strange intensity. Nox wasn't quite present enough to comprehend the Gray Matron's expression, though she knew it wasn't right. It didn't fit. There was a panic behind her eyes as if she was silently begging Flora to return Nox to the manor. The Gray Matron's wrinkles disappeared as her face tightened.

Nox said nothing. She was nothing.

"What have we here?"

"Oh, Madame Millicent, no, this girl—" Agnes began.

Millicent used her hand like a sword, slicing the sentence short with a single, quick gesture. "I won't be robbed of my down payment, Matron. But this substitute, albeit a disappointing consolation prize, will do."

Agnes made a strangled sound. She brought a hand to her mouth. The matron fought a peculiar, internal battle that Nox couldn't bother to dissect as the Madame made her determining proclamation.

"Millicent, she—"

"She is acceptable. Be grateful I don't pursue further action against your negligence and robbery."

Nox felt as though she watched the exchange from beyond herself. She registered that Agnes was acting quite unlike herself. The woman should have been glad for a sale, rather than suffer the demands of reimbursement. It was mildly interesting, but that was all. It was not stirring. It was not moving. It was vaguely curious.

The Gray Matron made a face to protest, but it was clear she had no right to do so. A debt remained to be settled. Nox looked uselessly from the Gray Matron to the Madame, then to the black carriage. She hadn't needed to inquire as to what was happening. She understood. Amaris was gone, and Millicent required someone to go in her stead.

Nox had promised Amaris that she would sooner die than let Millicent take her, and the All Mother was prepared to test that oath. The goddess offered Nox and her solemn vow on a silver platter.

Nox reached for an emotion but felt nothing. Invisible fingers grabbed for a hook within her body, trying to pull her back in, but she was too numb for emotions to touch her. She listened rather absently as the matron and Madame exchanged parting words. She remained loosely aware of Agnes's fretful gaze, but she did not bother to say farewell. Millicent opened the carriage door and ushered Nox in. She absently wondered if this was what it would feel like to climb into the black coffin of her own funeral procession.

That had been hours ago.

Her eyes remained glazed as they continued to see same after same after same.

The Madame sighed loudly enough that Nox felt something within her stir, eyes drifting to disinterested attention. She needed to face her reality: she was in a carriage bound for Priory.

Millicent allowed her to despondently refuse food at first, but by their second meal, the woman forced her to eat. When Nox finally drank, she realized her tongue stuck to the roof of her mouth like molasses. She hadn't realized how dehydrated she'd become. Awareness of her thirst brought her more sharply into herself, though the darkness stood nearby, ready for her retreat. Nox clutched the cup with two hands. She gulped the water down, and soon after heard a ringing in her ears. The ringing grew louder and louder into a deafening, constant sound. The Madame's smile drifted further away until Nox was asleep.

When she opened her eyes, the sameness had... ceased.

She blinked her eyes rapidly, straightening her stiff body as she pressed into the window.

Things were greener, somehow. Here, autumn had not yet consumed the land. How long had she been asleep?

"There she is," Millicent cooed.

Nox looked out the window and stared in open-mouthed awe at the city looming before them. The trees were unfamiliar. She saw tall, bare trunks, with leaves existing only in a collection at the very top. She brought her face closer to the window to peer at the buildings and colors beyond the glass. If she had to guess the distance, she'd say they were less than a mile away from polished white buildings, tall cathedrals, and bustling life. The smell of people, animals, salt, heat, and fish soaked the air.

They were near the sea.

Nox went from scarcely stirring to instant alertness. The young woman gaped at the Madame, shaking her head skeptically.

"Priory is two week's travel by horse," Nox stated numbly.

Millicent curved her black-painted lips into a smile. "She speaks."

Nox stiffened, fully aware of her body, the carriage, the horse, the Madame. The darkness vanished, her dissociative companion spooked as she was jarred to a state of full presence. Nox felt a new confusion prick through her.

"We haven't been traveling for two weeks."

"Well observed, girl," Millicent said, both bored with the conversation and seemingly disappointed that her lip-locked travel companion had loosed her words over something so mundane. Instead, she fancied herself to look out her window at her hometown, eyes sparkling with excitement.

PART TWO

Ownership

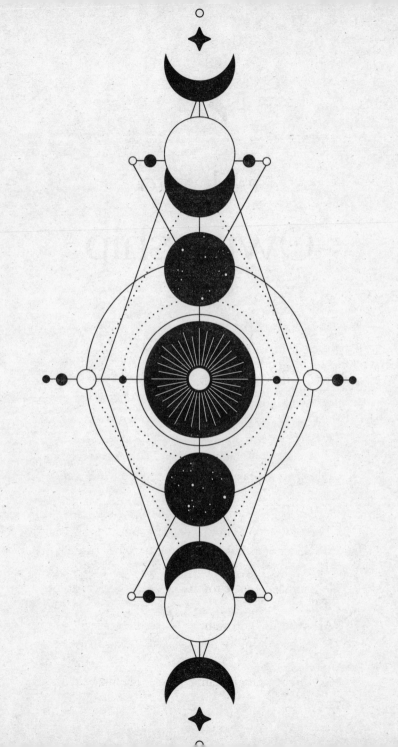

Fourteen

They stopped in the town of Stone, so named for both the suffocating presence of the mountain that loomed over it and the litter of discarded granite boulders its bluffs had released into the village below. The town clung to the perimeter of a sheer, vertical cliff. It had been positioned to limit the entrances and exits to the primary road, sheltering the village from comings and goings. It took Amaris roughly four minutes of shrinking against the long-cast shadows of the mountain to decide she hated being in Stone and hoped never to return.

"How can people live here?" She cringed as she eyed the town.

"What's wrong with it?" Odrin asked.

"The mountain! They're stuck against the mountain! How do they not feel like they're about to be crushed! I've never been anywhere that's made me feel so...suffocated."

He chuckled a little too heartily for the occasion.

"What?"

"Are you sure you want to become a reever?"

"Does becoming a reever mean being crushed by stones?"

His throaty laugh came again. He answered, "If

you have some trouble with mountains, you may want to reconsider your choices." Amaris wondered if Odrin was the first man she'd heard laugh. There had been the giggles of boys and smiles of orphans, but the rich, honest sound of Odrin's amusement came from somewhere deeper in his belly than she'd encountered.

Odrin dismounted the horse and helped Amaris down.

"Keep yourself busy for a bit. Don't go far," he instructed.

She didn't intend to wander away from her only means of escape from this wretched town. The sooner they could leave Stone and its ominous cliff, the better.

Odrin walked to what seemed to be a rather ordinary shopkeeper's stall and made idle chatter while refilling his waterskins, talking to the vendor as if he were an old friend. Odrin and his blades, bows, and armor weren't met with suspicion. The scarred, grizzly man drew no stares from the citizens. She wondered how often Odrin and his league of assassins made the trek to visit this village to have imprinted such a sense of ease in his presence. They hadn't been well received at the last village, and his appearance at Farleigh had caused outright chaos.

Amaris searched for signs of familiarity in the faces of its citizens as the people milled about the town square. She was curious if she would recognize Mable's family if she happened upon them in their hometown. Just yesterday morning, she'd looked into the gentle eyes of the friendly matron who'd handed her a cup of tea in the warmth of her bed. Now, she peered into the features of the woman selling goats, the man with crates overflowing with ears of corn, or the girl hanging shawls in the fabric stall, searching their qualities for the same slope of the nose, dimples, or traits that had been one of the few rays of kindness in Farleigh.

Odrin had told her not to wander, but she supposed a little nearby exploring wouldn't hurt.

The honeyed smell of something brewing drifted from Stone's inn, a lovely curiosity that required closer investigation. Her nose followed the sugar-sweet scent to the window. The inn in this small town was perhaps three times the size of the inn she had seen in the tiny village only one day prior. Merry sounds of a fiddle drifted through its open windows, an unfamiliar jig on its weathered strings. Honest, plump faces, loud belly laughs, and the thumping boots of uneven dancers too drunk to care about the tune or its steps colored the view beyond the glass. They seemed happy. Their lives looked so easy.

Amaris idled by the window but didn't enter. She didn't feel the joy the tavern's music intended to elicit. It had nothing to do with the traumatic changes she'd undergone in the past night and day. Those feelings were something she'd shoved into a small, wooden box deep within her. It was an airless, impenetrable container with no perceivable latches and mechanisms—one that she refused to touch. She wouldn't be able to function if she allowed herself to take them out, playing with her painful memories like toys from a treasure chest.

This morning's particular brand of joylessness was entirely the fault of the mountain and its ever-present shadow.

How did the people of Stone not wallow in the same claustrophobia Amaris felt? If the peak decided one day that it had become too tired to uphold its cliff, surely one tremble would be all it would take for the goatherd, the corn farmer, the seamstress, the fiddler, and all of the town's other laughing residents to be buried under its rubble.

Amaris had to keep her mind preoccupied to keep

anxiety at bay. She busied herself studying the characteristics of the village while Odrin finished conversing with the shopkeeper, a man who'd happily prattled on about this and that. She gave them their privacy, her feet carrying her around the nearby storefronts.

"Hey!" A child's musical call for attention floated above the sound of the fiddle.

A leather-stretched ball made from what looked like the skin of a deer hide rolled from the pressed muddy space between two homes and into the square, stopping just a few arm's lengths from Amaris. She bent to pick it up as two children, no older than seven, ran from the alley after their toy. A third stopped at the entrance to the alley, eager to restart their game. He paused when he saw Amaris holding their ball. The boy looked at her curiously, but he did not appear afraid. He tilted his head, undoubtedly waiting for her to return it.

"Well," he asked, somewhat impatiently, "are you going to throw it back?"

"Sorry." She blinked rapidly at the normalcy of the exchange.

A boy with matted hair, dirty hands, and mud-caked knees waved from behind him. His disheveled appearance seemed like one born out of a day's hard play rather than that of poverty, given his healthy, round face and the way he smiled at the others. He outstretched his arms for the ball, and Amaris tossed it gently into the air, satisfied when he caught it. He spun away, as if interacting with strangers was an everyday occurrence. The children ran off in the direction they'd come, shouting some instructions for their little sport. She marveled at what life must be like to grow up with friends, free to run, to roll in the wet earth, to see new faces, to live without fear of scrapes and scratches. She had nearly lost herself in a fantasy of what–ifs, forgetting to keep an eye on her companion.

She blinked in dismay when Odrin wasn't where she'd left him. It had been one single heartbeat of panic, convinced she'd been abandoned, before she spotted him a few feet away.

No, he had not left her. She was not alone.

Amaris jogged quickly after him to ensure he didn't change his mind and leave her altogether.

"Odrin!"

"I told you not to go far." He shrugged, not looking at her.

"I was right there!"

"I saw."

Odrin led his speckled steed away from the shop stall to the stable at the side of the inn. A large, stone tub rested near the edge of the stables, filled nearly to the brim with brackish–looking water. She'd never seen such a large object of solid stone before. She idly wondered if this had been one of the many uses for the boulders that had tumbled from the cliff and given the village its namesake. Rather than break the rocks down or roll the large boulders away, the citizens had chipped and chiseled them into functional fixtures throughout the town. While it had been innovative of the residents to find ways to use the rocks, their presence disconcerted her. Amaris wondered how often the cliff sloughed off its unwanted boulders onto the town below, and she itched with restlessness to get going.

"Are we leaving after this?" she asked.

"You wouldn't be so eager to get going if you knew what awaited you."

If she didn't stop thinking about the mountain, she was going to drive herself mad. Instead, she turned her attention to Odrin and his mount. Amaris rested a hand on its dappled neck, stroking it gently beneath her fingertips while it drank its fill.

"What do you call your horse?" she asked.

His eyebrows raised as he made a face to indicate this wasn't something that had crossed his mind. He gave the horse two quick pats on its side while he examined it.

"I don't rightly know. I took him as payment about four weeks back when a bishop couldn't settle his contribution."

"He owed you a debt? Are you a mercenary?"

Odrin laughed. "Hardly. We aren't swords-for-hire, girl. You'll learn soon enough."

"So, this is not your horse?"

A smile still crinkled the lines of his face as he petted the beast. "Well, he is now, isn't he?"

She continued to stroke the docile gelding's neck. It didn't seem to notice her existence while it kept its nose close to the water, lips gently parted while it drank. "Shouldn't we give your creature a name? Aren't horses meant to be like family?"

Odrin entertained the idea, asking, "What would you call it?"

"Maybe Cloud would suit him."

"That's a terrible name for a horse," Odrin said dismissively. He adjusted the saddle, letting the beast know they'd be moving soon. Water dripped from its nose as it raised its head from the trough.

She shook her head and continued stroking the creature. "You're right; that doesn't suit him. Hmm... He's not majestic enough to be a Twilight. I feel like Whisper would displease him."

"Does he have feelings about the process?" Odrin asked somewhat dryly.

As if in answer, the horse flared its nostrils.

Amaris inclined her head at that, listening to the horse. "Are you a Ghost?"

"You're not good at this."

She ignored him, stroking the horse's nose as she asked, "What shall we call you and your gray dots, my friend?"

"I had a dog named Cobb growing up," Odrin said. "He was a rambunctious little mongrel. After he died, I named the stray cat near our house Cobb too. I think it's a good name for a beast."

"Are you serious?"

Odrin mounted the horse and swung Amaris up with his scarred hand, giving his steed a small kick. He urged, "Come on, Cobb."

And so Amaris, Odrin, and Cobb plodded straight for the face of the mountain.

Fifteen

A MARIS RECALLED WEARING A PATIENT THOUGH somewhat patronizing face as she'd stood in the kitchen, listening to the sweet but naive Matron Mable describe the league of guardians who lived in the mountains just beyond her village. As Amaris drew nearer and nearer to the cliff, the All Mother's divine humor had her choking on the memory of the condescending look she'd given to the friendly matron. With Mable's words in mind, Amaris anticipated the open maw of a cave. She braced herself against the inevitability of being swallowed by the dark, horrible cavern. She silently chanted that she was no coward. Whether or not she believed the repetitious voice in her head was irrelevant.

They were only two hours from Stone before the last lights of the day faded to the slate and lavender glooms of dusk. The moon was already out, despite the day clinging to the purple light after sunset. Its nearly full, metallic light began to wash the space ahead of them. While she'd been afraid to lose the sun, every retreating moment of daylight allowed the moon to show Amaris what it could truly do.

Odrin, Amaris, and Cobb rounded corner after corner, following the foot of the mountain. Cobb carried them forward at a leisurely pace, hugging the base of the cliff until a thin trail began to rise. The narrow path was nearly imperceptible until they were upon it. The jagged trail switched back and forth as they climbed. When it became particularly tight, Odrin pulled back on the reins and had the two of them dismount. He led the way, handing the reins to Amaris. Odrin said that, while he trusted that most beasts would be sure-footed enough to find their purchase on the rocks, he didn't want to risk it after sunset.

She wasn't sure why. The air seemed every bit as resplendent as it might have in the full light of day. Now that the sun was a long-forgotten memory, the moon reveled in its chance to truly shine in its brightly waxing state. Its metallic beams glinted off the rock in ways Amaris had never imagined. The cliff reflected the pearly light, illuminating everything around them, giving the very air a shimmery, iridescent quality.

She wished sightseeing were all that was expected of her.

Instead, her legs burned from the ride. Her feet throbbed from walking. Her arms were as limp as wet noodles fresh from the pot. She opened her mouth to comment on her misery but thought better of it.

Amaris had learned that Odrin wasn't one for idle chatter and was satisfied whenever they managed to exchange a few words. She wasn't bothered by the silence. The quiet gave her an opportunity to release her tension, focusing on nothing but the way the stars burned, the sound of Cobb's steady breath, and the sharp, horrid feeling of the pebbles that poked through her thin, leather shoes.

Amaris opened her mouth and closed it repeatedly as the hours passed, fighting the urge to complain, or to comment on the pretty, pearly quality of the light, or the fresh smell of pine and crisp mountain air. She wanted to tell Odrin that she'd never seen such a star-soaked sky. She thought to comment on how high up they were. Then, she wanted to ask how much longer their trip would be and how often he made the trip. Instead, she asked only one question.

"If I fell off this trail, would I die? Or would I just be mangled and *wish* I had died?"

His silhouette pressed forward. She thought she saw his shoulders shake in a noiseless laugh as he said, "I was wondering when you were going to spit out your thoughts. You've been making gaping noises like a trout out of the pond."

"Well?" she pressed. "What would happen?"

He chuckled without turning toward her. Shrugging, he asked, "Are you planning on finding out?"

"No."

"Then I suppose it doesn't matter," he said. Ever amicable in their two days together, Odrin didn't seem the least bit annoyed by her question.

Cruel rocks continued to bite into her soft shoes. Amaris felt the passage of time acutely as blisters formed and popped within her shoes, scraping her raw. She fought the need to limp, to mount Cobb, to sit in the middle of the path and take off her shoes until the pain subsided. Stronger and louder than any of those needs was a single, potent desire: she refused to be treated like a special treasure, hidden away only for special occasions. It was a life she'd left behind. If she wanted acceptance, she was the only one responsible for its fruition.

She was on the trail to become an assassin. She didn't have the luxury of whining about her shoes or the blood from her own raw feet that soaked them. That being said, whenever she was sure Odrin couldn't see her, she allowed herself the grimaces, winces, and secret flinches of pain.

Amaris also learned something new about herself: she did not care for heights.

No one but the goddess should be this close to the sky. The birds scarcely dared to fly this far beyond the lines of trees. In the dark of the night, they were more daring than the bats and as lofted as clouds that scraped the mountain's granite peaks.

Whenever she dared a glance over the sheer drop-off, it was to note that the trees and homes dotting the countryside below were smudges no bigger than her thumb. The mountain had curved in such ways that the village of Stone would have had to be miles and miles wide for anyone this high up to spot it.

Amaris had lost track of the night, but her flair for the dramatic tended to count the passage of time a little differently. It had probably only been a few hours, though it felt like days. At one point, she knew in her soul that she had been climbing this cliff for her entire life. She had been born on this trail, and it was on this very trail that she'd grow old and die.

If she wasn't mistaken, the moon had moved low enough on the horizon to let her know it wouldn't be night much longer. Given the lateness of autumn, she was rather confident the sun had been down for at least twelve hours.

They walked and walked and walked and then, they didn't.

Odrin stopped in his tracks. He took Cobb's reins from Amaris, urging her alongside him, as there was now space on the trail for two.

"Is this it?" she whispered.

"Few more steps, unless you'd rather stay on the mountain."

The cliff had finally come to an end. They'd reached a stone bridge connecting the gap between two, terribly steep mountains of otherworldly sharpness and height. The singular stone bridge united the adjoining cliffs over the dramatic plummet of the valley below with what seemed to be little more than wishes and prayers. She squinted her eyes to the dizzying depths of the valley where the moonlight caught a tiny silver thread. The ribbon was that of a river—presumably the very one that had cut its path between these mountains many lifetimes ago.

"Is it safe?"

"The bridge? Probably not."

"But—"

"Like I said, you can stay on the mountain."

Her fear of heights had been a gnawing throb. The potent stab of arrival was a new, sharp terror. Odrin began to move forward, Cobb in tow, but she wasn't sure if she was ready to follow. It wasn't just the crossing of some bridge of nightmares that daunted her but the strange, obscure gloomy shape that awaited them once they crossed.

Amaris remained glued to the far end of the bridge as she squinted at the shape ahead.

It would have been difficult to understand what she was seeing in the sheer light of day even under the high-noon sun. By moonlight, it was damn near impossible. Just across the bridge, a few small lights seemed to have embedded themselves into the mountain itself, as if a few orange fragments of starlight had chipped from the heavens and landed on the side of a mountain.

Amaris strained her eyes as they shifted into focus. The orange flickers of light illuminated rectangles— candlelight in windows, she realized. Something rounded and smooth like columns or pillars loomed up ahead. A deeper, darker gloom seemed to cast an arch above the triangular roof of the structure, space between its ceilings and the rock above. She was staring at a fortress. This was no fortress built on a mountain but *into* it. Carved within the very cliff itself was an entire castle.

"It's in the mountain," she breathed.

She could see Odrin's appreciative nod as he answered, "I told you—if you were bothered by Stone, this might not be the place for you."

When her muscles had ached, she'd wanted her travels to end. When her feet had rubbed themselves raw within her leather shoes, she'd silently pleaded with the goddess to allow her to stop walking. Now that they'd arrived, she would have traded anything for another twelve hours to prepare for what she might face. She followed Odrin wordlessly, refusing to look down at the nauseatingly steep drop on either side. They crossed the final length of the bridge, leaving the dizzying valley below as they reached the last remaining steps of their journey. The bridge came to an end at a great door. Her heart thundered in a way that informed her she'd never be ready, no matter how long she delayed. The time had come. The door before her was made not of stone or wood but of iron.

Odrin banged on it a few times. Turning back to her, he broke his long traveler's silence.

"Welcome to Uaimh Reev."

Sixteen

IN THEORY, THE NEXT FEW DAYS SHOULD HAVE BEEN tumultuous, nerve-racking, and terrifying. In practice, they were exceptionally dull.

The fortress of Uaimh Reev was in an uproar over Amaris's arrival—or so she'd been told. As a result, she'd been sequestered in solitary quarters until the reevers decided what to do with her. She wasn't a prisoner, as she was free to wander back the mountain and return to the villages below should she please. That said, she'd been strongly advised to stay put if she hoped to win any favor.

As it stood, women did not live or train at Uaimh Reev. Whether it was an issue of permission, tradition, or coincidence was part of the three-day feud happening within the keep. The disputes, she was told, covered most of the subjects one might expect. Some arguments took on a medical or anatomical nature: women couldn't keep up in sparring, a woman's presence would slow down the pack on runs, women had special health needs the keep was not equipped to meet. Others bore a more misogynistic tone: women were too tender for the hardships of a reever's lifestyle, women required coddling and there was no place for pussyfooting in the ring, a woman couldn't be guaranteed safety in a castle filled with men. These were the rather unfortunate messages that had been relayed, anyway, when Odrin had visited Amaris in her rooms the first night.

"I'm to stay here by myself?" she had asked. Amaris didn't fully understand her anxiety, but the idea of being shut in her chamber with nothing but a stack of old books and piles of clean linens of furs gripped her with icy fingers.

"You're safe here. I'll come visit and let you know what's being said."

"I wouldn't be safe out there?" she asked. It was all she could do not to beg him to take her with him. Her fear of abandonment was a terrible, strangling thing.

Odrin frowned. "Let's just say that a few more conversations need to happen before you should be roaming about the keep."

"So they hate me," she clarified.

"They don't hate you. They might hate the idea of you, but they don't hate you."

"I'm sorry—is that better?"

It had taken her a full day to absorb the crushing isolation of being alone.

She had never had a bedchamber to herself. Her life had been spent in the dormitories, relying on the comfortable circadian rhythms of dozens of small bodies with their chests rising and falling in sleep. Her chores were with peers at the orphanage. Her free time was spent with Nox. She wasn't sure that she'd ever spent more than ten minutes alone in her life. Now as she paced the granite stones of the room, examining its nooks, bric-a-brac, and secrets, she wasn't sure if she enjoyed the solitude. This room was nicer than her dorm, and its bed far more comfortable than her cot, but a renewed desolation took her. The silence tempted her to open the box in which she'd tightly stored her unpleasant emotions. If she didn't find a way to distract herself, the lid would slip to the side, and everything she'd delayed feeling would spill into her chest.

She ran her fingers across the bobbles on the shelf and wrapped her hand around a roughly whittled bear perched upon the space. Her first impulse was to shove it in her pocket and bring it back to Nox. She loosened her hold on the figurine, realizing she had no one to give it to.

There was a quick, light knock in the door, followed by a pause to the count of five, before the door eased open as it had three times each day. A visitor was a welcome relief after she had endured suffocating loneliness. Despite her enthusiasm at his arrival, the boy, several years her junior, made it clear that they would not be speaking.

Three times a day he'd enter, and thrice daily she'd try to ask the child his name, ask of the weather, ask about the food, or ask his favorite color. He remained resolute in his polite silence. Every time the small boy came and vanished, she felt as if she had been abandoned again.

Eating was one of her few joys.

Amaris always had an appetite, but she refrained from devouring the food. Instead, she stretched her meals throughout the day, making each dish last for hours, just to give her something to do. The food was quite different from the porridges and stews commonly served at Farleigh. Everything she'd been served had been enjoyable. If she ate her split barley, corn cakes, meat pies, stewed apples, mushrooms, or whatever else he'd delivered too quickly, she'd have little else to entertain herself.

Amaris brought a small, coarse loaf of brown bread onto her bed and stretched across the fur coverings, slowly picking at the loaf while she paged through one of the dustier books. This one was a particularly dry text of histories of the continent's battles, heavily focusing on names of the deceased and locations of the conflicts. A few illustrations of weapons decorated the pages from time to time as a special treat. Boredom aside, it was a luxury to read something other than the limited selection filtered and permitted by the matrons.

The books, like the meals, were something with which she'd forced herself to pace her consumption. If she devoured everything too quickly, she'd be alone with nothing to read. Her first book had been a much more interesting choice, though poorly written and sickly sweet. It was some four-hundred-page ballad about a king of the night and the princess of the sun and the romance that had divided the world in its misguided attempt at unity. Their love story had been a tragedy, ending in murder. The sister of the slain princess had been offered as a replacement in marriage before the continent fell into anarchy. The prose was both sloppy and dreadfully unbelievable, but it was better than hours spent staring at the stones of an empty bedroom. Amaris vastly preferred the romantic nonsense to a list of the names of dead warriors and had already read the love tale three times.

Each night was spent in the bathtub in her en suite bathing room until her pale fingers shriveled into prunes, trying to see how far she could flick beads of water and making a competition with herself to see if any of the droplets would land on the ceiling.

Late into the second night, Amaris wrote *I'm bored* 652 times on a single piece of paper. She was just beginning to write it for the 653rd time when a loud thud sounded at her door. The only two knocks were those of the small boy at mealtime and the heavy fists of her lone ally. She perked as Odrin eased open the door.

"Anything?"

He nodded, dark brows lowered in seriousness. "They're going to meet with you."

Her heart skipped as she asked, "Tonight?"

He eyed her paper and how she'd perched against the desk but decided not to ask her about her very important written masterpiece.

"No, not yet. It's taken this long just to agree to give you an audience."

"When?"

Odrin hadn't fully entered the room, which made it clear he didn't intend to stay.

"Sometime tomorrow," he said. "I assumed you might have finished whatever books are in your room and brought you one on geography and another on the five kingdoms, given, you know..." He waved a hand in general reference to how she'd already managed to disappoint him regarding her knowledge of the continent. Before leaving, he said, "Keep your chin up. It's never the wrong time to study."

Odrin closed the door behind him.

Amaris was left staring up at the desk. She wished he hadn't said anything. Knowing was fruitless if there was nothing she could do about it.

Sleep didn't visit her that night. She took to staring at the ceiling with crippling anxiety, envisioning her life as a dirty, penniless street urchin scavenging the alleys of Stone. Nox had often spoken of her insomnia, and Amaris had never been able to relate. Now vivid images of the children who had kicked the leather ball burned her eyes. She wondered if they would let her join their group of friends, though she supposed it would mean she'd have to learn how to play their sport, and she'd never been interested in kicking a ball.

Amaris did eventually rest, though only for an hour or two. If one had asked her, she would have sworn she hadn't gotten a wink. She was up and dressed by the time the sky turned pink with dawn. Amaris tugged the fur from her bed and bundled it over her shoulders to stare out the window. The view was stunning, though its drop was too perilous to look beyond its panes for long before her stomach began to twist with the odd sensation of falling. She noticed that as she stared into the valley, the birds flew several hundred feet below. How high must they be in their fortress that even the hawks and crows wouldn't alight on the windowsills of this keep.

Knowing her fate awaited her caused the day to pass with excruciating slowness. Every minute took an hour. The sun taunted her with its lethargic crossing of the sky. Breakfast came and went as she studied another boring text about herbs with medicinal properties. If they didn't decide soon, she'd stay in these rooms forever and become the single most educated person on the names of dead warriors and the recitation of naturally growing healing plants.

Amaris scrunched her face in distaste as she looked through yet another book. This tome was a gruesome, anatomical text illustrating the inherent differences in a fae body and that of a human, from the fae's enhanced hearing and vision and regenerative cells to the predatory, deadly lure of their beauty. It had been morbidly fascinating, but the ghastly trail of scholarship had led the text's creator to recount every detail, whether for good or for evil. The morality of its author was called into serious question based on the nature of several of their entries.

She grimaced as she flipped through the text of autopsies. She landed on an image of something that might have been a man. It was a bipedal creature with arms, a torso, fingers and toes, but where humans had nails, the creature had talons. Where she had shoulder blades, it had membranous, batlike wings. Its lips were pulled back to reveal its elongated canines, and its irises were double the size of a human's. A faint memory of a boy with too-large irises flitted somewhere between her ears, and then the memory was gone.

Odrin's authoritative knock came at her door and her heart stopped.

She looked up from the book, heart in her throat.

Odrin eased the door open and slid inside. The man gave an apologetic smile as he closed the door behind him.

"I can't imagine this is easy for you," he offered by way of greeting.

Amaris shrugged. "I wouldn't say life has been easy, as a whole."

Her statement was neither wholly true nor entirely false. She imagined the other children at Farleigh would shake with fury to hear her call her cushioned life anything but easy.

"Are they going to kick me out?" Amaris asked. She didn't know how it was possible, but the question held no emotion. Her future would not change whether she worried, pleaded, or fretted. What would be, would be.

Odrin neither reassured nor confirmed her fear. He did his best to keep his message free of feeling, even if there were underlying notes of sympathy in his words.

"They want to hear from you directly, but we knew as much. You'll need to plead your case. You'll need to convince them that you deserve to be here."

"Is it the leader? Or a council? Or…what is your government here?"

He smiled sadly. "Perhaps I should have prepared you more for what you should expect—no, I definitely should have prepared you. I am sorry for that. This is no kingdom, girl. The reevers are as much of an orphanage as your shoddy home. We don't have a true hierarchy here, though Samael is as close to a leader as we have, as he's been here the longest. He issues our dispatches, and we trust his judgment." Odrin straightened before opening the door and making a sweeping gesture. "I'm to take you to meet with them. Just…be yourself. You convinced me, didn't you?"

It was a rather poor attempt at encouragement.

"Should I tie up my hair?" she asked, feeling stupid the moment the question parted her lips. It seemed a rather feminine worry for a fortress that demonized her femininity.

He responded, "Many of the men have uncut hair. They wear it tied back or unbound. Tying it is an issue of function, which you'll need to do if you spar. For now, your hair is of little concern, though, your hair, your brows, your lashes—they *are* silver. That may be a point of curiosity, but there isn't much you can do about that."

She tried to smile, as she knew Odrin was attempting to be comforting. He wasn't very good at it. She abandoned the book, ready to see what shape her fate was to take.

"I guess whatever's waiting for me in the dining room can't be too much worse than what's waiting for us in the woods."

"We can hope."

Amaris swallowed, glancing back to the page. She left the book open as she stood, the leather-bound tome displaying the horrid, unmistakable image of a demon.

Seventeen

AMARIS WASN'T SURE WHETHER THIS WAS THE SECOND or third most distressing moment of her life, but standing before one dozen judgmental assassins certainly contended for a prize in discomfort. The first, of course, was being separated from Nox. Battling for second place was meeting the woman who'd driven her to mar her skin and chase after a rogue life in the mountains.

In fifteen years, Amaris had seen only three dining rooms. The first was in Farleigh. It had been a well-lit room with a long, wooden table and high, arching windows to let in the sunlight. The table had been simple, lined with wooden benches and no decor to its name, save for a modest table runner that was easy to clean in the laundry.

The second dining room, made of wood and smelling of honest smoke from the hearth, she'd seen during her brief visit inside of the tavern of a nameless village the day before Stone, where the middle-aged woman had bandaged her wounds and found a scarf.

The third she stood in now.

She took one slow step into the room, then another, Odrin at her side.

Men of various sizes and ages sat at an oblong table carved from the mountain itself, though she couldn't bring herself to truly absorb any of their features. Looking directly at them would either intimidate or distract her, and she could risk neither. Amaris was unable to recognize which one of them had opened the iron door on her first night, though she scanned for a spark of familiarity in their faces before averting her gaze. She knew that obvious signs of hostility might further thwart her efforts for their acceptance, and the cards appeared to have already been stacked against her. She wouldn't require any additional obstacles in garnering their acceptance as she slowly walked into the space.

Odrin placed a fatherly hand on her back as he urged Amaris forward to the end of the table closest to the door. He left her to take a seat, joining the others while still saying as far from them as possible. As she stared at the distance between her and the others, she couldn't help but feel it was a bit like avoiding the snapping jaws of dogs on short leashes.

Her attention went to the table itself. Its legs did not end but rather melted into the stone below. It appeared as though the piece of granite had never moved from its place in the mountain's heart but simply been reshaped for a flat, polished surface. The table curved inward so the legs of those who sat here would find space beneath its lip before it rejoined the immovable rock below. She was unfamiliar with dining rooms, but even as someone with little exposure, she knew she was witnessing something peculiar.

No windows graced the innermost room of the fortress. A fireplace three times the size of the one in her room, accompanied by rows of vibrantly glowing torches running the length of the room, chased away any shadows and eliminated the need for the white light of day. The high, vaulted ceiling sparkled as its slate curved upward, making her think of a large, stone bell. She couldn't tell if she found this place beautiful or terrible. Perhaps her feelings toward the room would be contingent on the result of this meeting.

She felt completely alone.

Several empty seats ran on either side of her, isolating her at the far side of the stone table that was meant to sit thirty or forty. She wished she could have remained standing for the sake of her own comfort, but she knew enough of politics and courtliness to know it would win her no favors if she stayed poised to run. Amaris needed to prove herself strong enough to be in their presence. Surely, the first test would be their initial impressions of having a young woman at their dinner table.

She wasn't sure if they would speak first, or if she was meant to, but the silence must have been as uncomfortable for the men as it was for her.

In the spirit of first impressions, she could only imagine what a sight she was for them to take in. Not only was a young female in their keep but a silver-haired, purple-eyed anomaly with a scabbing slash marring her otherwise ghost-white face. Her clean tunic covered most of what she'd done to her chest, but the top of the wound she'd inflicted on her collarbone undoubtedly protruded above the neckline of her shirt. She was no ordinary child of the southern kingdom.

On the far end of the table directly across from her sat a too beautiful, dark-haired man in his late twenties. Though he wore the tactful face of a diplomat, she was surprised to see someone so young in the most prominent seat. Irrespective of her lack of exposure to men, this person did not seem like any natural-born male.

Something was strange, striking, and intimidating about his face all at once.

The seconds stretched like toffee. No time had passed, while still allowing her the ability to take in her surroundings. She searched the room, trying to guess which one was Samael. A disheveled man with an unkempt beard in thick fighting leathers looked to be pushing sixty years of age. He had the thick chest and broad shoulders of someone who looked like he could command a room. Odrin had said that Samael had been here the longest. If she were a betting woman, she'd guess him to be the oldest.

The acceptable moment for pause had come and gone, and it was time to speak.

The present snapped into reality. The deeply human rainbow of golds, reds, browns, and blacks tilted toward her as hair and eyes shifted expectantly in her direction. The men stared at her. The enormous fire popped and crackled, providing enough white noise to prevent the room from being as stiflingly quiet as it might have otherwise. She twinged with the recurrent sensation of unbelonging, wishing the fire would warm the chilly fear that had settled in her stomach.

She urged herself to begin. She begged herself to speak.

Goddess damn it all, she needed to say something, *anything*!

The matrons had wanted to raise a well-spoken girl— one who could fit in if she was purchased to live in the courts. They'd prepared her for a variety of positions, staking their time and combined intellects for their eventual return on investment upon her sale. The silver girl had no idea if the assassin's coin purse held anything close to the crowns they'd spent those years cultivating, nor did she care. Regardless, she was thankful for training in oration as she rallied her courage to introduce herself. She couldn't be afraid. She couldn't be self-conscious. She couldn't think of consequences, or danger, or anything but the words she had to spit out.

"I am Amaris, of Farleigh, though I do not call it my home."

Her treacherous heart thundered, but her voice did not shake.

The collection of assassins watched her attentively. The twentysomething man at the end of the table had one arm on the side of his chair, resting his chin on his hand. His face was impressively blank, though he paid close attention to every word.

Amaris's face had flushed earlier when she'd absorbed how disconcertingly beautiful the stranger was. Her eyes glided from the man to the table before them like droplets of water sliding off a glass surface. In the moments before she dropped her gaze, she'd taken note of the slender points of his ears.

He was fae.

Time had felt as though it had slowed once more while she'd taken in the features of the others. She'd managed to spy the faces, postures, and ages of the men at the table. While many were in the second half of their life, there appeared to be more than a few men in their teens and twenties at the table. Her eyes had snagged once more on the arch of fae ears as she looked away from a young, coppery man who may very well have been her age. That meant there were two fae at the table.

She shouldn't have looked. It had been a distraction, and one that cost her. Now she stammered as she attempted to pull her thoughts together.

Somehow, starting to speak and then stopping again made things worse than if she hadn't said anything at all.

She was butchering her first impression, and she knew it. Amaris didn't have the luxury of sounding like a child. She swallowed and willed authority into her voice as she spoke. She didn't truly know what she was saying, but she spoke from her heart, scarcely examining the words that left her lips.

"I have no people," she restated, voice wavering slightly. Insecurity would get her nowhere. If she didn't feel particularly bold, she'd need to fake it to survive. Her words swelled to a false confidence as she spoke. "But if you'll have me, you will be my people. You're worried I'm a woman? I have no interest in being a damsel. I want to train, to learn, and to fight alongside you. I know what you must see when you look at me. I don't blame you for your skepticism. Yes, today I am soft, but I wouldn't ask for softness. Treat me as you would any boy of my age who arrived at your doorstep. Put me through the same trials. If I fail, I will fail as an assassin, not as a woman."

"A reever," the fae at the end of the table corrected.

"I—" she stammered at the amendment, not sure if she should apologize. "If I fail, I fail as a reever."

His voice was almost as lovely as his face, though there was no question as to its strength. She'd tripped over the correction, feeling her courage unravel. She'd been on the edge of a rallying speech before stumbling over her words.

The eldest man grunted his disapproval, not looking at her as he spoke. "There's a reason we don't have women here. I won't be making lighter armor, making smaller weapons, creating dainty—"

"Grem." A golden young man in his early twenties cut off the older. So, the eldest man was not Samael. The bearded one called Grem stopped and glared, his bovine qualities distorted when set against the muscular young

167

man who opposed him. The one with the blond mop of hair continued speaking. "Her size is no different from the boys' in their teens. She wouldn't require new armor, clothing, or weapons. By the time she'd be ready for a real sword, she'd be strong enough to hold one."

"This is no place for your grandstanding, Malik—"

Was the golden young man arguing on her behalf, or just against the bearded older?

"There are no women here," the fae said, "because there is *no one* here. Look at our numbers. For hundreds of years I've served, as reevers from the corners of the continent overflowed these halls. Human and fae of all genders fought and lived side by side, and you know as much. Uaimh Reev has acted as the sword arm of the All Mother for a millennium. This reev was a keep for the honorable who believed in the protection of all peoples against magical imbalance long before it became today's band of society's discards." He eyed the men with some irritation before amending, "Though we seem to have become Farehold's discards."

"Say now," the bearded man grumbled, crossing his arms.

The fae arched a brow, but the bearded man lacked a rebuttal.

Amaris blinked slowly at the words the lovely man had spoken. The fae seated at the opposite end of the table was hundreds of years old. He didn't just have the delicate ears and beauty of some distant fae lineage; she was looking into the face of a full-blooded fae.

"That was then," Grem pushed back. "Womenfolk were different in your time, Samael. She's not a warrior at our doorstep. She's a stray cat who followed Odrin and his soft heart home. The reev is different now. Escort her back into Stone and be done with it."

Odrin spoke, tone both defensive and resolute as he said, "She's not a warrior by training, but she has the heart of a she-bear. The girl has no fear of the fight. See for yourself. Look at her face."

They did once more, considering her wounds more carefully.

While the other men studied Amaris and her scabbing injuries, she couldn't help but notice how Samael looked not at her but at Odrin. Something about Odrin's message struck a chord within the fae.

Odrin hadn't spoken the truth, whether or not he realized he was telling a lie. He hadn't witnessed what had occurred in the dining room at the mill. Amaris had accomplished what she had done at Farleigh not out of bravery but fear. She had been more terrified of a life with Millicent than of anything that could be found in an assassin's keep. The stolen knife—Odrin's knife—had been the quickest way to provide an exit. She would not be the pure, unmarked treasure, set aside like a delicate teacup for the finest of guests. She would take her life into her own hands. If she had gone with the Madame, she would have been bound and clipped, her spirit broken. With the kingdoms of men, she at least had a chance to become something more. She would sell her body to the fight of her own volition rather than to the highest bidder against her will.

"Shall we vote?" Grem pushed the men.

"No," Amaris objected, surprised at herself for speaking. Her voice was a mixture of confusion and impatience at their unwillingness to hear her story. She didn't have any follow-up plan, except knowing at her core that this hadn't been fair. They shouldn't be able to vote yet. They didn't understand. They didn't know what she'd been through. They didn't understand how far she was willing to go.

Several of the reevers shuffled in their seats, jarred by the firmness of the word. There was a tension, unsettled by how she'd disrupted Grem's petition for a decision.

Amaris shifted in her chair. She was confident that if it were put to a vote, the scowling faces would outnumber the open-minded ones significantly. The energy was not in her favor. Rather than allowing her feelings of discomfort to take root, she felt herself transition into anger. She would not have escaped Farleigh and cut her way out of the claws of Millicent just to be turned away by men and their prejudice. She did not leave Nox—the only person who had *ever* cared for her—just to be cast back into the world alone. She would not have begged an assassin to take her in, ridden for days, suffered mangled feet, aching muscles, bruised tailbones, and bright pink scars, only to be told her womanhood forbade her from training.

As she'd come to learn, passion often precludes wisdom.

Her body moved before her mind understood what she was doing. She was on her feet, slamming a fist onto the table. It was a childish outburst, and the flimsy impact of her balled fist made little sound on the stone table. Still, the confidence and command that surged from her hit their mark. She looked the men in the eye without a drop of doubt. The tumultuous curl of her fury burst out in a single demand.

"You *will* let me stay, and you *will* let me train!"

Her entire body hummed with adrenaline. Her fire burned into them for a moment until, in the quiet that followed, she realized what she'd done.

She blinked, horrified.

This had been far worse than not talking at all. Regret surged as bile in her throat. Her lips parted as if to apologize but shut quickly before she spoke another word.

She'd done enough damage. Her body remained rigid as the anger ebbed. Amaris wasn't sure what had come over her. She felt foolish standing before them, hand still planted against the stone table. A spasm of embarrassment clenched in her stomach.

The events that followed were...bizarre.

A hushing wave pressed down on the reevers as their faces drifted from an amalgamation of confusion to something accepting and contemplative as the men murmured amongst themselves. They appeared to be quietly nodding to each other.

The fae, Samael, glittered with near-wicked amusement. He lifted his head from where it had been resting, bored on his chin, and steepled his fingers together in a triangle.

"My, isn't that a talent."

Shame pushed her back down in her seat. She wished she could melt into the rock below her like the legs of the table. Amaris refused to meet the eyes of the men. She ignored the reevers and their mutters, horrified at what they must be saying about her.

Samael ignored the others, looking directly to Amaris.

"It appears it won't affect me, or Ash, for the most part." He gestured to the coppery teenage boy. "But I do applaud you. It's quite unlike any skill I've seen. Honestly, I'm relieved I'm spared from the onslaught of such a gift. Well done, Amaris."

Amaris lifted her eyes. Despite her crushing humiliation, confusion tugged her back to Samael's face. Her eyebrows pinched. "What?"

The men continued speaking to each other as if the conversation across the table weren't happening at all. Their mouths moved in quiet exchange as they discussed the situation at hand.

Samael sat up straighter, realization dancing amongst the entertained expression on his face. He pressed his fingers into the table, maintaining interested eye contact for a moment. The fae then stood and addressed the others.

"Well." He looked to the reevers. "Since it's clear you've all decided she's to stay and train, let's call this meeting adjourned." Samael made a sweeping gesture with his hands, and with no objection, the men began to push themselves away from the table. They rose from their seats and continued their chattering as they headed for the door. Samael continued, "Do carry on with your day. I need to have a word with our newest reever-in-training."

The disorientation was jarring.

Amaris's face twisted as if she were waiting for a slap that never came. Her brows lowered deeply. Her lips remained parted in an unclear objection. She looked to Odrin, but he appeared to be smiling with their success. She raised her eyes to meet Samael and felt her whole body cower at the realization that he was staring at her fully. His gaze was nothing predatory, but it was unquestioningly intimidating.

She had the disjointed sensation that she might be dreaming.

What had happened? After her tantrum, Samael had adjourned the meeting? Could this be some cruel form of sarcasm? Moments ago she had been certain they were about to vote her out.

Instead, they were filing out of the room.

Amaris stood as well, feeling too awkward to sit as they walked on either side of her to shuffle from the dining room. Odrin clapped her on the shoulder as he passed, and while his smile was relatively warm, hers was still a mask of confusion. It took fewer than three minutes for the room to clear and the boy to take the abandoned pints from the stone table. What on the All Mother's lighted earth had just happened?

She and the fae were alone.

Samael remained standing, backlit by the flames of their large fireplace. He made a sweeping motion as he returned to his chair, reclining in a way that was meant to be disarming.

"Amaris of No Home and No People, come take a seat by me, won't you?"

She twisted her mouth into discomfort but had few options. Odrin was gone. She hadn't understood the meeting's outcome. She didn't know whether or not she trusted this man and his invitations, but she politely abandoned her chair on the far side and walked closer to the fireplace. The idea of sitting directly beside him made her uneasy. She kept an empty chair between the two of them, taking a seat slightly off to his left.

Samael relaxed into his chair, waiting with impressive patience for her to talk.

She was quite sure he wouldn't have spoken at all if it hadn't been for the inarticulate, near-strangled sound she made as she shook her head. She was too confused to compose words.

He asked, "Are you to tell me you don't know of your gift?"

She stared at him stupidly.

"But surely, you've noticed this reaction before?"

She shook her head.

More to himself than her, he said, "Imagine going through life without bothering to consider the people in it or the implications of your actions? My, my, what a privilege that must be."

She wasn't sure whether she felt insulted or embarrassed, but nothing about this exchange assuaged her fears.

173

Samael frowned. "You do know you aren't fully human, correct?"

"I…" Her hand touched her ears. There were no points to them. What use had her years of schooling been if she was too unintelligent to find words when it mattered most? "It has been suggested that perhaps I was part something-or-other. But other than my hair and my eyes, I've never shown any traits…"

He smiled, though, not unkindly. His irises were the too large circles of the pure fae—eyes she'd seen only once in an unfortunate faeling who hadn't lasted long in Farleigh. There was a gentle consideration in them as he studied her. "Your hair and your eyes should have been giveaway enough. Odrin confided in me that you were in a mill when he met you. Isn't it interesting what humans commodify?"

She recoiled at the implication, even if she couldn't fully fathom its weight.

"I apologize," he said. "That was a poor choice of words. It's disappointing what humans commodify. And while I can't pretend to empathize with it, I'm not so unaware of the world around me that I don't recognize patterns. If I had to guess, I would say that your particular brand of otherness has laid a king's carpet at your feet. How interesting, then, that you'd seek a life of hardship at Uaimh Reev."

She narrowed her eyes. "It would have been a life of hardship either way. I'd rather a steel sword than a golden cage."

"Yes," he agreed, "but a luxury nonetheless to be able to pick one's metals. Now, do you truly not know of your ability?"

She shook her head. Not only did she not know of gifts, but she didn't even understand the nature of his question.

He relaxed again, the same amused expression returning to his face. He rested his chin in his hand as he had before, an entertained smile tugging at the corners of his mouth.

"What would you say happened just now? In the meeting?"

"I honestly don't know," she answered.

He nodded. "How interesting, Amaris of No People."

His eyes turned to hers with the gentleness of a teacher. He didn't seem to be chastising or agitated, merely instructional. He said, "Persuasion is a rare and dangerous gift. In my many centuries, I, myself, have never met one who demonstrated it—though those with the fabled silver tongue have been hunted and killed by humans for millennia. While other fae might find you compelling and charming, it's nothing like the absolute obedience you'll find when you give a command to a human. I didn't suspect such a gift of commanding crowds, but perhaps if they're engaged with you as you are with them… Well, given the results of the meeting, it would seem you can address a collective as well, so long as you address them directly. Fascinating. Do you know of persuasion? Any such tales?"

"Persuasion?" she repeated uselessly.

He didn't sigh as she might have expected. The matrons had never attempted to conceal disappointment if Amaris hadn't been ready with answers. This fae had the unruffled feathers of one who'd weathered lifetimes.

"Yes, persuasion," he continued. "You could tell a human man to leave his wife and marry you. You could tell a queen to hand over her crown. You could tell a mother to drown her newborn babe."

Amaris flinched. Her brows lowered. She shook her head against the absurdity of his words, but his face remained smooth. His conviction was both impassive and unrelenting. The men had shifted like the ocean's tide, their decision whirring with her outburst. Had she truly done that? Horror seeped into her features. What kind of monster did he think she was? What kind of witch would have such a horrible power? She shook her head more violently.

"What are you saying?" she asked. Amaris's voice escaped as a scratchy rasp.

"This can't be your first instance of exercising your gift, Amaris. Perhaps it's the first time you've been made aware of your ability, but think of a time—any time— when you've influenced those around you. Think of a time when you made a demand and your will was adhered to. Does anything come to mind?"

Even as her heart pushed against the information, a door in her mind opened to a memory. Something did come to mind. That day in the pantry, when the wretched, freckle-faced Achard and his friends had pushed through Nox and tried to drag her to see the bishop, she had told the boys to leave. They had. They had left the pantry. They had left the kitchen. They had left Farleigh, never to be heard from again. Had that been because of her? Because of one command ordering them to go? A gross, sickening understanding hit her, twisting her stomach into a pained knot.

He asked with a careful, quiet voice, "Did you ask Odrin to take you with him, or did you tell him to bring you?"

Repugnance filled her.

Samael seemed to understand her recognition as she worked through her past.

"While it has no impact on my feelings toward whether a woman trains in the reev, I do see its value on our team. Your gift is an asset," he said. He waved a hand toward where the redhead with arched ears had been sitting during their meeting. Samael continued. "Ash will also have a bit more resistance to your charm as a halfling, so it'd be pertinent to pair you two together. Don't mistake my words—he'll find any command you give to be immensely influential, but it won't be met with the same compulsory response, as he's only half-blooded. Gifts meant to work on the mind generally affect humans and halflings more acutely than the fae, though I acknowledge there are some powers of the mind to which even fae are utterly susceptible. That being said, I can't very well have you winning your fights by telling your opponents to drop their swords—at least, not while training. Your ability may be exceptionally useful in mortal battle, but what good will that do you if you come across a beseul?"

She knit her brows but was able to ascertain from context that a beseul was perhaps a creature that she did not want to stumble upon without the knowledge of how to wield her sword.

"It's evil," she said.

"The beseul? People think so, yes, but many of the dark creatures—"

"This power," she corrected. "It's evil."

Samael seemed finished with their conversation and stood. "As with all things," he said, "a gift is no more good or evil than the one wielding it."

She joined him on her feet.

"I think we've had enough of the dining room, don't you?"

Amaris nodded, though she wasn't sure why. She would have been fine remaining in the dining room. Anywhere other than her rooms had been a treat, and she wasn't entirely convinced she was in the frame of mind to see or do much more.

"Shall we tour the reev?" Samael motioned her to follow him, and she did.

As they walked, Samael disclosed that he had been living and serving at Uaimh Reev since before the kingdoms had drawn their jagged borders and divided the world. She couldn't call on any such dates that made sense to her. The borders between Raascot and Farehold had been drawn, disbanded, and redrawn nearly one thousand years before her birth. Surely, that hadn't been what he'd meant.

The reev—an old word for *fortress* in some fae dialect—was chosen for its neutralized location and hewn from the very mountain by someone with the magic to wield stone. The mountain had obeyed him, and the labor of love, Uaimh Reev, was ready. In those days, fae and humans found honor in defending the lands below from magical imbalance. Reevers were dispatched not just to fend off the dark creatures that filtered down from the Unclaimed Wilds but to unravel concentrations of unnatural power that might upset the harmony of the continent and its kingdoms. Reevers were the goddess's sword arm, fighting for no monarch but working in the shadows for the peace and stabilization of their world against the forces that warred men and fae alike, irrespective of territories or rulers or borders.

Every few lifetimes, a king or queen would rally his or her people for a territorial invasion, and as long as the battles were fought fairly and the magics untouched, the reevers would leave the ways of the monarchs to themselves. If magics were wielded that could level the lands or if the unnatural powers of blood magic were bound, the reevers would dispatch to intervene. Being a reever had been an honorable profession for centuries, he explained. Samael looked a bit sad as he told her that over the last two hundred years, the need for reevers had diminished in the public eye. Magic quieted as it had been slowly bred out of the southern kingdom, and the creatures of the land were content to roam their own territories. The fae populace in the northern kingdom of Raascot had asked little of the reevers. The Farehold's fae were far fewer, but they'd lived peaceably amongst humans for some time.

She wasn't sure why it was the first question that came to mind, but Amaris tilted her chin as she looked to Samael and asked, "What was Odrin doing near Farleigh?"

A nod. "There have been tales of beasts in Farehold that haven't been spotted south of the Unclaimed Wilds for centuries. There's no reason for this many monsters to have made their way onto the continent. The church called to us, and Odrin went to investigate the claims by a small town near—what did you say your home's name was? Farleigh? As it were, it seems he found a thing or two that the reevers will be discussing further."

They continued their tour of the keep. As this was her first opportunity to truly see the grounds, Amaris clung to Samael's every informative word. The fortress had the combined sense of decay and vitality. The structure was immobile and never to wither, as it had been made from the seamless pieces of the mountain. Other aspects of the keep revealed the centuries of their age. It was unnecessary to mind her step, as the floor was composed of the same clean, seamless granite she'd seen throughout the fortress, no threat of tripping or stumbling underfoot. Later elements composed by the handiworks and masonry of men and fae in the centuries that had followed would require slightly more upkeep than the unbreakable structure of the reev.

Samael continued to lead Amaris down a long, straight corridor lined with windows that showcased the plunge below lighting one side. They emerged on the far side of the keep and looked at what appeared to be something of a coliseum—she'd never seen one in person, but the rounded shape fit the descriptions from her books. Stadiums were generally meant for bloodsport, and that wasn't an issue she felt ready to discuss.

She changed her topic, her eyes flitting back to his pointed ears. "How many fae are left?"

He frowned before clarifying, "Here?"

Her forehead wrinkled, lower lip puckering slightly with her unspoken question. Before this day, the closest she'd come to a fae was a small boy with too large eyes. The matrons were human and entirely disinterested in discussions of magic. It stood to reason that the fae were few and far between.

Samael continued walking as he spoke. "You're a child of Farehold, aren't you," he said, not asking a question. "You were born at a time where the fae are almost a memory in the southern lands. Farehold is not a kind kingdom to the fae—it's not a kind kingdom to any human who doesn't display their pink undertones and colorless hair. It's no place I'd want to live, nor do I envy you for your upbringing. The fae are rather numerous in the north, though they haven't wanted to set foot in Farehold for decades. This is just speaking of two corners of Gyrradin, mind you. Your whole life has been limited to a rather narrow strip of the world. I suppose if you were to leave the continent behind, you would find magic still plentiful in the warmth of the Etal Isles or the Tarkhany Desert. If you were to cross the Frozen Straits, where humans haven't stepped foot in a millennium, the Sulgrave Mountains are a place where you won't find a rounded ear in sight. I've never had the privilege of crossing the Straits or been to the Isles myself. The descriptions of Sulgrave fae don't quite fit your coloration, but if you're going to find a fae people who resemble you, I suppose it would be there, as I've never seen such features on this side of the ice."

"Have you been to the other places?"

He nodded. "Tarkhany is magnificent, if you ever get the chance to visit. But as far as crossing the Frozen Straits is concerned…" Samael studied her, dragging his eyes with a scholarly question from the silvery tip of her hair down to her lilac eyes. There was a frown on his face as he considered her. "Those from Sulgrave would probably be horrified if they saw your poor, small ears on such a starlit face. For something not quite human, I'm sorry you weren't able to inherit fae hearing…though with those eyes, I'd love to see what gifts of sight you possess. You're not like any fae I've met, and I've been around for…some time."

Amaris didn't know what to say. He'd more or less welcomed her into the reev, and she'd been too tongue-tied to contribute. If this was their first lesson, she was already falling short.

Their brief introduction to history at a close, he gestured to the training arena beneath them. With an air of formality, he said, "Amaris, our newest reever, you've decided to stay and train, and so you shall. You'll arrive here each morning at first light. As Odrin has brought you to us, he's responsible for you. I'll inform Odrin that Ash is to be your sparring partner."

Amaris's mouth opened as if to speak, but once again, words failed her. The fae seemed level-headed enough not to judge her over the particularly overwhelming day, but he didn't let her off the hook entirely. Samael turned to leave. Glancing over his shoulder, he said, "Oh, and if I catch you using your persuasion again while in the reev, it will be your last night in this fortress. Is that understood?"

She almost choked, appalled with herself for the manipulation she'd wielded amidst the men, but nodded. Samael wandered off, disappearing into the keep. Amaris had spent so long locked up in her rooms that she had no interest in hurrying back to her chambers. She continued along the path he'd led, surrounded by the circular shape of their granite training arena. It had no roof and was fully exposed to the autumnal weather that rushed in from overhead. The air was cold both from the lateness of the season and from their elevation. The wind chafed her face and hands. The chill didn't bother her nearly as much as the idea of returning to her bedroom. Amaris picked her footing carefully down the stairs, sinking into the lower levels of the training ring.

The fresh air was a relief from the jarring meeting. She needed the crisp, bracing wind to shake her mind free of the cobwebs that had gathered, connecting her mind to her tongue as she'd remained speechless throughout the bewildering events of the day. Even if she hadn't just had a life-changing experience, the clean mountain air was a nice break from the days spent in her room, and she was not eager to return.

This was where she would train.

The arena was littered with objects meant for instruction, education, and honing one's craft. Wooden beams ran along one side. Spheres and disks of stone and iron intended for weight training were scattered on the opposite side near a rack of swords. Some blades were made of true steel, others composed of wood. A quiver of arrows hung from the rows of weapons. Hole-punched targets on the far end of the arena were evidence of the archery she was sure took place every day. She ran a cold, chilled finger along the blade of a sword on its stand and was surprised to see it draw blood. She'd expected practice weapons to be dulled.

"Don't you reckon you have enough scars?"

Amaris whirled and found the coppery boy of about sixteen, just barely older than herself, leaning against the opening to a dug-out pit in the arena. She wiped the droplet of blood on her pants. She blinked at the young man and shrugged, unsure of what to say. She recognized him from the meeting as the faeling Samael had mentioned.

He approached with a crooked smile, extending a hand. "I'm Ash."

She eyed his hand skeptically for a moment, then took it. His palm was warm and calloused in all the places that might indicate familiarity with a blade and its hilt.

"That was quite the performance back there."

She responded on instinct, attempting levity.

"What can I say?" She smiled. "I'm prone to theatrics."

He laughed in response. His teeth weren't pointed like that of the full fae, but his amber eyes, a swirl of honey, gold, and chipped bronze on their outermost lines, were slightly too large to belong to a human. His ears betrayed the fae half of his lineage.

"Won't the men be pleased to hear all their thoughts of women have been correct."

"Which thoughts, exactly? That women are dramatic? Or is it that we're remarkably persuasive?"

He seemed to be good-natured with his jest. He smirked. "A little of this, a little of that. I think a few of us are just excited to watch how much you'll irritate Grem."

"He seems like a joy to be around."

Ash grinned. "He's not that bad. At least, I don't think so. Malik doesn't like him—you'll meet him later, though I guess you got a fine enough impression of him in the meeting. He's a good egg—Malik, that is. Don't be surprised if Grem doesn't warm up to you anytime soon. He's not known for his warmth."

"What *is* he known for?"

Ash arched a brow. "He's our bladesmith. You can't be in Uaimh Reev without being useful." He looked her up and down before amending, "Clearly, Samael thinks you'll be useful, though you don't look like you're about to give Grem a run for his money in metalworking."

Amaris brushed it off, fully unwilling to engage in his line of questioning. Why Samael found her an asset to the team was a secret that would die with her and their fae leader. She eyed her would-be sparring partner.

Amaris changed the subject. "Samael mentioned we're supposed to train together."

He nodded. "I figured as much. I have fifty pounds on you, but better me than a warrior with thirty years of experience. I guess you could also fight Brel, but his training is pretty limited to the kitchen. He'll get there— he's just a bit young to go through the rite."

She almost repeated the name as a question, but through process of elimination, there was only one child in the keep younger than either Ash or Amaris. Brel must have been the child who had been responsible for delivering her meals. She made a note to use his name the next time the boy visited.

She did her best not to stare at Ash, but his fae lineage wasn't the only shocking thing about him. His reddish hair was the color of dark embers just as the fire died. His eyes were golden, ringed with the brown of the earth, and his golden skin reminded her ever so slightly of Nox, though perhaps she'd find a way for all things to remind her of Nox. He had an easy likability about him. Amaris's guard was up, cautious as they spoke, but she didn't feel threatened. He looked—and smelled, if she wasn't mistaken—distinctly of autumn. There was a spice about his relaxed energy.

"You're fae," she said. It wasn't a question. She had been told as much by Samael.

"Part fae."

"And part human."

"As are you, Snowflake."

"Please don't call me that." The pain in her heart hit suddenly, surprising her with its intensity. Had it merely been a week since she'd seen her friend? Her only family? Her tether to this world? Between the last few days locked in the keep and a number of days on the road, the math added up, though it felt as though she'd been away for several lifetimes.

Nox had gripped her arms roughly one week ago. The dark, bottomless eyes had quietly looked into hers, poised to escape with her in the twilight hours. Nox had held her in the pantry. Studied with her. Laughed with her. Grown with her. Plotted, shared, danced, and lived side by side with her throughout every moment of her life. The night-haired girl had taken an unspeakable beating from Agnes at the behest of the bishop to protect Amaris from the church's discovery. It had been the sort of memory that belonged in her tightly sealed box, too horrible for Amaris to unpack.

They'd been meant to run away together. Instead, Amaris had left her alone.

The morning Millicent had come, Amaris had told Nox to...

Oh goddess, no.

The sensation of a dagger pierced her gut, twisting deep within her. Goddess be damned, she understood the disgusting, treacherous moment all at once. As she called on the death of a thousand All Mothers, the sickening fear tore through her.

She had told Nox to wait for her.

At the time, it had been the hushed urgency of a girl who wanted them to run away together. Now she saw it for what it was: persuasion. A command, given and received. Her dreams of Nox running toward the coast were shattered. She pictured the dark-haired girl with her feet glued to the back of the manor. She wasn't sure if she was about to cry or be sick.

"Hey, I'm sorry," Ash said. His face contorted with confusion as he did his best to make amends, explaining, "Your coloration… I just thought—white, snow…" Ash searched uselessly for a defense, still unsure as to his misstep. "I wasn't…"

"Oh." Amaris shook her head, using the back of her hand to wipe away one treacherous tear before he could see it tumble. Of course, the first day they allowed a girl in the keep, she would blubber in the training ring. "It's nothing. It was someone…it's nothing. It's just not a nickname I like to be called."

Ash offered one quick nod, making an apparent mental note. She wished she hadn't made him uncomfortable. She would have to find better ways to seal off her emotions if she was going to succeed as a reever.

Amaris couldn't think of Nox right now. She pictured her emotion as the kraken of lore, battling it into a shell of space within her chest. She tackled the beast and locked it in a cage, forbidding it and its feelings for her friend to sweep its treacherous tentacles toward her.

The cage would be slapped with a lock, then wrapped in chains, then shoved into the same seamless chest where all traumatic feelings were kept.

She had told Nox to wait. Nox hadn't run after all. She'd still be in Farleigh, undoubtedly carrying out Agnes's personal chores. Amaris made a vow to herself. She would spend her life making amends to Nox for abandoning her. Amaris would not let her rot in that mill.

As soon as she had the skill, she would return to Farleigh and liberate Nox from the matrons. Perhaps she could earn enough to buy Nox's debt from Agnes. Unless, of course, seeing Amaris only enraged the Gray Matron. She shook the thought from her head, slamming the box on the kraken into place. Amaris resolved to train, to learn, and one day to rescue the one who had spent their childhood saving her.

Then, she refocused on the faeling in front of her. Attempting conversation, she ventured, "Did they buy you to fight?"

Ash blanched at the implication. He frowned. "What?"

Amaris gestured to the coliseum and the hewn keep around them. She reiterated, "The reevers—did they buy you for their cause?"

The offense was plain on his face, though Amaris wasn't sure what had provoked him. He pushed back, "What kind of question is that?"

She wasn't sure how she had managed to do so many things wrong in such a short amount of time. Everything she said, everything she did seemed to betray her ignorance of the world. What was the use of the books she'd read and the lessons she'd endured when everyone beyond the walls of Farleigh reacted to her as if she were a cave child?

Her face was a mixture of apology and defense as she pressed, "Some of the boys at the orphanage went to farmers, or sailors, but sometimes a knight would purchase them. It's not common. I just thought…" She let her words trail off, eyes on her shoes.

It took a few moments for her meaning to absorb. The red-haired young man softened a bit. She hated that pity in his eyes and hated what he had to say even more.

"I didn't realize," he said, his voice less playful than it had been before. "I'm sorry about your childhood. In much of the world, the buying and selling of others has been outlawed. It's easy to forget about the mills. And no, no one brought me here. My father serves the reev, and it was my mother's wish that I follow in his footsteps. She was human and passed away a few years ago from a common sickness. I didn't know much about healing then. It's not my gift. But when she left the earth, I had nothing left keeping me in her village. So, here I am."

She was grateful he'd so quickly changed the subject, as she wasn't sure if she'd be able to hold herself together if she'd been forced to reflect on the implications of her upbringing.

Once more, she had to deflect. Her box of emotions was growing too full for one day. She'd need time and space to grow the place within her until it could contain each new struggle and pain. For now, if she had any hope of maintaining a sense of normalcy, she'd need to convince the other reevers that she wasn't a wreck. Amaris shivered against the autumn chill, holding her arms to herself as she searched for a new question. She couldn't let Ash leave with this feeble impression of her.

"Does your father live?"

Seemingly unbothered by the weather, he nodded. "Yes, I believe as much, though I haven't seen the bastard in nearly ten years. He's still in service to the reevers. His work has taken him somewhere into the northernmost parts of Raascot. The north can keep him."

She didn't know what to say. Everything she'd heard of the northern kingdom had made it sound like a goddess-less hell. She opened her mouth to say she was sorry but pressed her lips into a tight line. There seemed to be no loss between the two, and if he'd done her the kindness of allowing her to sidestep questions of her childhood, then she should offer the same. The cold pushed down on her further. If she had known she would spend this much time outside, she would have brought her cloak.

Ash either hadn't noticed her growing physical discomfort or hadn't cared. Still entertained by the presence of the reev's newest member, he asked, "Do you have a nickname?"

She blinked, leaving her thoughts and coming back into her body. She chafed her arms for warmth. "No, not really," she answered.

"Come on," he pushed. "Everyone's friends give them a nickname."

"I didn't really have friends where I was," she said. And she definitely wasn't going to win any this way. Her awkward answers were garnering her no favors. She wished she could relax, but every gust of wind and chill of the weather only underlined how poor she was at communication. She couldn't even advocate for herself enough to tell her soon-to-be sparring partner that she was freezing. Amaris caught a glance at her fingers long enough to see the shades of red and pinks they were turning around the tips and knuckles.

Ash wasn't truly looking at her. He seemed to be eyeing the late-autumn sky as he chewed on an idea, unfazed. "Well, Amaris is a bit of a mouthful, but give me enough time and I'll think of something to shout at you while I'm crushing you in the ring."

"Ash?"

"Mmm?" He perked up at the use of his name.

"If we continue talking outside, you'll win all of our fights, because I'm about to lose my limbs. I'm freezing."

His smile sparkled at her frankness as he jerked his head toward the corridor. She returned the smile. The heat flooded into her the moment the door closed behind them. They parted ways as soon as they'd eased into the door to the keep, but she knew she wouldn't feel truly warm again until she had the chance to soak her bones in the hot bath of her quarters.

It took a while for her to find her way through the corridors, but Amaris returned to her rooms and took her dinner from the boy, Brel, in her chamber. Presumably, she would one day join the men where they ate, but she was grateful for the chance to be alone with her thoughts. She flipped through the books on her shelf and found one that was nothing but a genealogy of kings and their heirs, and she began to scratch in her own history with strokes of a quill. She wrote her name and an arrow from her to Nox, connecting them with a parallel line. She wrote the names she had learned from the reevers—Samael, Odrin, Ash, Malik, Grem, and somewhere below them she wrote Brel's name as well. She made a column for the matrons, one for her peers at the orphanage, one for Queen Moirai, and then, with a big black X to the side, she wrote Madame Millicent.

Eighteen

Torture took on a new name, and that name was training.

The road to becoming a reever was agonizing.

Every pain she thought she'd felt, every muscle ache, every embarrassment she'd experienced leading up to this moment had been a grain of sand on a frothy beach compared to the endless desert of daily misery that was exercise and practice with the reevers. True to her testimony, she would be offered no special treatment. She was given no grace as she was thrown into the ring.

Amaris woke at dawn for her first morning of training and followed the others as they walked up and over the many-tiered training ring to a trail she hadn't noticed on her tour the day before. It was just as thin as the one that had led up from Stone, though this particular pathway wound its way down the opposite mountain. The men took off in a pack, and her eyes widened.

"We're meant to run down?" she gasped. She hadn't meant for it to come with horror, but it didn't seem safe to sprint down such a steep trail. The one with the golden hair had patted her once on the back as he passed, responding with cheery levity.

"And back up again!" he said. The young man began his run, and she watched after the men as they began what would be a daily exercise in suffering.

For weeks, the distance between Amaris and the men was so great during their runs up and down the mountain that most of them would reach the base of the mountain, turn around, and pass her on their climb before she'd even completed her initial descent. If it weren't miserable enough to feel every muscle in her body scream in protest, the added humiliation of needing to avoid their eyes as they surpassed her was an entirely separate layer of excruciation. Even Grem, for his advanced age, never missed the morning run. The daily runs fostered community and maintained stamina essential to their survival on the job, or so the men had claimed.

The particularly agile reevers could finish the exercise in two hours. Others required three or four for their round trip. Amaris was lucky if she could finish her run in six.

The reevers kept this particular mountain to themselves. The mountains existed in neutral territory, belonging to no one but Uaimh Reev, a scattering of marmots, and the surrounding bighorn sheep. Precipitous trail running was as much about psychological torment and learning to control your fear and channel your adrenaline as it was a practice in stamina.

The steep switchbacks offered no forgiveness if a single foot slipped out of place.

It was not an entirely gray, lifeless run. The trail, like the keep, was dotted with tenacious little plants, including some scraggly pines that hung out of fissures in the stones, having found a way to survive high up in the mountains. Amaris had no time for sightseeing. She was too busy ensuring that she didn't make a wrong step, lest she tumble to her death and spare the reevers from the tribulations of having to raise a girl in their keep.

Running was the tip of the iceberg with these men.

After lunch came daily combat training, including weapons sparring, archery, and hand-to-hand fighting. If she wasn't exhausted enough to long for death after her run, they ensured she begged for a swift and merciful end within the first few minutes of combat.

When it came to weaponry, not only could Amaris not swing a metal sword, she could barely hold one. Her arms would have been too weak for the blade even before her runs, but the taxing exercise had turned her body into marmalade. They'd permitted Amaris the use of the wooden training swords intended for children, which, thank the All Mother, she still technically was. When she wasn't wielding her wooden weapon, much to her ever-growing humiliation, young Brel would lunge, slash, and advance on invisible opponents with triple the grace that she possessed.

Amaris was exceptionally disappointing as a new recruit, particularly as nothing came naturally to her. The singular quality she possessed was tenacity. If the goddess was good, an unwillingness to quit might just be enough to justify her presence.

The kindest reevers kept their comments to themselves. Others made no attempt to conceal their irritated groans, eye rolls, or overall displeasure as they continued to watch her flounder at every task. At least with running, she spent the majority of her time by herself. Sparring came with the shame of an audience.

She failed to parry time and time again. Amaris received blow after blow to the ribs, to the face, to the legs. She limped to bed each evening covered in purple bruises from neck to navel, refusing to whimper in front of the men, having never landed a single hit to Ash. Every night she'd test her bones for breaks in the bath and seemed to be single-handedly depleting the reev's supply of healing tonics in her desperation to stay on top of her injuries.

Ash was always kind but seemed relentlessly disappointed that his partner didn't put up more of a fight. Not only did it dampen his morale to thoroughly pummel his opponent each day, but it also meant he had to spend extra hours in the ring with Malik just to get in proper competition. Ash and Malik were a far better sparring match. Had she not arrived, they would have doubtlessly remained paired. She hated herself for holding Ash back in his training.

Malik had his own sparring partner of equal skill, but he didn't seem bothered by the additional opportunities for swordplay, shooting, and hand-to-hand combat. When he finished his own regime, he'd hang back and wait until Ash was ready to start their melee all over again. Fortunately, he was an eminently good-natured young man, whose kind smiles and dismissive shrugs had disarmed the apologies Amaris offered each time he had to train for extra hours.

"Move your feet, Ayla!" Ash shouted as he stood over her, cursing her in the southern dialect, insulting her as an oak tree. He'd knocked her to her back once again, just as he always did in swordplay. The shortened variation of her name—Ayla being the word for oak—had become his nickname for her. It was less of a mouthful than Amaris, and a more accurate representation of how her clumsy feet seemed to be rooted to the earth—her moves so slow and timbering that she might as well have been carved from wood. She didn't mind the nickname. Frankly, she deserved far worse.

Much to the chagrin of her and everyone around her, she did not seem to be improving.

As temperatures dropped with approaching winter, it became infinitely harder for Amaris to train. Her hands were red and chapped with the season. The extra weight of the warmer leathers and elbow-length fur cloak seemed to hinder her movements all the more. Was it possible that she was getting progressively worse? Between her beaten-down spirit, broken body, and the All Mother's forsaken weather on the mountain, it seemed she grew less impressive with every day that passed. Perhaps she truly was nothing more than an oak tree in a girl's body.

Still, she pressed on.

Wake up. Run. Train. Spar. Eat. Study. Sleep. Repeat.

After their lunches, most of the men went free for the day. Odrin, however, was responsible for teaching her about poisons, tonics, and the basics of being one's own combat medic. Reevers usually took on assignments throughout the kingdoms alone, independently dispatched on their missions throughout the territories. Should Amaris ever show a will to survive or the ability to hold her own in battle, she'd need to be able to avoid sabotage, spot healing plants, and know how to patch a wound. Odrin had her tying tourniquets, practicing the art of starting fires with nothing but a stone and one's weapon, and sniffing goblets of wine or water for signs of tampering. When they finished studying together, he sent her to her rooms each night with a stack of books up to her hip on what plants and creatures were safe to eat and which ones would paralyze, blind, or boil you from the intestines out.

"Isn't there a magic item or something I could use to do this for me?" she grumbled, pushing away her book on poisons and remedies.

"Probably," Odrin agreed, shoving the book back to her to force her to continue her studies, "but spelled objects are exceptionally difficult to make and even harder to come by. If you find one, hang on to it. In the meantime, why don't you focus on your studies rather than hoping you become the luckiest reever. Now, if you smell—"

"Roses in your beverage, don't drink it," she said, loudly banging her forehead against the wooden desk. Odrin chuckled as he abandoned her to her wallowing.

Time passed, but she would not give up.

While she excelled in little else, she'd discovered an aptitude for zoology. Amaris slept with her favorite bestiary tome beside her bed, reading it backward and forward. As winter melted into spring, she learned she could wound a vageth with a blade and use its blood to coat her weapons, as her opponents would be defenseless against the resulting infection. She studied the lore of the sustron and the ways one could steal its scent to hide in the shadows, though it would thirst for your blood in revenge. Odrin taught her of djinn, who could grant three favors to any who held it, but unless you were ready to recapture the beast, it would have your heart in its talons after your final wish. She skimmed over the more fictional beasts of lore like the icy aboriou or the collection of what were most certainly wishful sailor's tales of sirens and merfolk. She learned beseuls actively avoided the sizzling pain of sunlight and that if you met the ag'drurath alone in the wilderness, you'd best make your peace with the All Mother, as no method had been recorded to survive the winged dragon.

Demons, she'd learned, couldn't truly be killed. The knowledge had horrified her, but Odrin had reassured her that anything could be bested if you cut it into small enough pieces, whether or not those separated parts stayed alive.

"And if we don't?"

"If we don't what?" Odrin looked up from his papers to see what needed clarification.

"If we don't cut them into smaller pieces?"

He nodded. "Many things can reattach, given enough time. Bury the head separately and you'll be fine. We include a spade in your saddlebags to help with the digging."

"Oh joy."

It didn't sound like she'd be fine, but he said it with such nonchalance that it made her believe he'd dealt with such things a time or two.

Odrin was gentle but firm with his lessons. His relief had been no secret when he discovered her wit to be sharp, with an iron-clad memory. If he was going to break decades of tradition and bring a young woman into the castle, at least he'd brought a girl with a warrior's heart and a fox's mind.

Every few weeks, Samael would intercept her as she left training and educate her on politics, history, and strategy. She'd had numerous questions about the fae, and he'd been a willing vessel for her inquiries. Perhaps some part of him felt an obligation in his bones to help lost fair folk find their place in this world. Occasionally Ash would join them, sweat still clinging to his copper brows from the morning's practice, and listen while Samael spoke on Raascot or the Sulgrave Mountains. The older had smiled when he'd heard the girl called Ayla, but he hadn't expressly said why. He'd kept a knowing twinkle in his eye, teaching them of the empires. While kings and queens were titles in Gyrradin's kingdoms, *Imperator* had been the term amongst Sulgrave's fae until they'd dissolved to self-govern under a Comte for each of their seven territories.

There had been no Imperator in the mountain kingdom beyond the Straits for a thousand years, though on the other side of the world, the Etal Isles still had a long-beloved Imperatress sitting upon the fae throne.

"You said you've never been to Sulgrave, right?" Amaris had asked Samael.

"That's correct. It's a challenging pilgrimage, to say the least."

"How do we know, then? How do we know how their government is run and things like that?"

"I said it's challenging to visit. I didn't say it was impossible. Fae do cross the Frozen Straits, though usually only in one direction or the other, as it's too difficult to make the trek twice. It's rare, but visitors and ambassadors will come from Sulgrave once every few hundred years."

"And the Etal Isles?"

He'd shrugged rather nonchalantly and carried on with his lessons. It would take her years to learn all the things she should already know, but she was determined to make up for lost time.

She learned the kingdoms of Raascot and Farehold were the only known regions where human and fae lived together, though most fae who hoped for a quiet life migrated north.

"Why would any fae stay in Farehold?" she'd asked.

"They don't," Samael said. "Unless there's a loved one, familial ties, or ancestral land, most fae migrate to Raascot or Tarkhany. Would you want to stay where you weren't wanted?"

Amaris knew he hadn't asked the question pointedly, but it was hard for her not to take the question as a dry commentary on her own existence within the walls of Uaimh Reev. Yes, perhaps sometimes there was a compelling incentive to stay where one wasn't wanted.

Samael went on to justify that as the human lifetimes went on, many had intermarried with the fae, bringing generations of minor power to the continent. Magical blood thinned, years stretched, and fae failed to repopulate themselves at the speed at which the humans could reproduce, particularly throughout Farehold. Their numbers dwindled, and between the years and distance from exposure, the humans struggled to discern fact from fiction. As the relations between the north and south grew tense, the south had become especially distrustful of non-humans.

While they continued to help Raascot when needed, the reever presence in Farehold had felt eminently important to Samael, lest the people have nothing but insidious rumors on the fae and magic to educate themselves. The past fifty years had been particularly hard, Samael said. He felt uninspired to leave Uaimh Reev, preferring instead to dispatch his men from the fortress where he could best keep the continent safe.

"Samael?"

He arched a brow to acknowledge her question without looking up from his maps of the kingdoms, still intent on educating her about borders and disputes.

"I have a question about the All Mother."

He paused then, relaxing his weight into one hand as he turned his attention to her. "Ask it."

She swallowed. "We're a religious organization, aren't we? The reevers? Yet…"

He nodded. "Yet you'll find very few reevers who are practicing believers? Yes, our affiliation with the church is little more than the union of a common enemy. The All Mother is believed to want peace and balance above all else, and it's not the sort of thing priestesses and bishops can sully their hands in pursuing. You'll find friends in the church on our wish for neutrality. It's little more than that."

The more Amaris learned about reevers and the function they served in maintaining magical balance, the more astonished and offended she felt that she'd never even heard of this league of assassins before her fateful escape from Farleigh.

On several occasions over her first few weeks in the keep, Amaris had tried, and failed, to speak to Brel. Odrin caught her talking to the boy one day as he dropped her meal in her rooms, and as the child left, her surrogate father explained why the boy never spoke. She'd been horrified as he told one of the most terrible tales she'd ever heard.

As a babe, Brel had been discovered as someone with one of the small magics. He possessed the power to speak to fire. Some of Brel's first words aside from "mama" and "papa" had been the sort of magic that had caused the hearth in his home to spring to life under his crackling flame whenever he was hungry or cold. Brel's village had been superstitious, with little knowledge of the magics or how they manifested in human bloodlines. On the advice of their church, his human parents had cut out his tongue to keep him from casting spells on the town.

When magic chose humans, she learned, it revealed itself in unexpected ways. The small magics did not pass through lineages and heritages the way height and eye color might but instead emerged in long, thin blood-lines with distant magical heritage whenever the goddess saw fit. There had been no way for his parents to have expected power in their perfectly ordinary child.

It had been a coincidence that Brel was discovered by a member of Uaimh Reev when the reever had been on dispatch to the little boy's village. The reever had brought the young boy home to live in the keep, though he'd been scarcely older than four at the time, quickly becoming child, brother, and friend to all. Brel busied himself between lessons by helping in the kitchens. In the sanctuary of the reev, he could still train and grow in a place where his magic would be accepted, even if he would never again speak.

When Odrin had finished his story, Amaris had answered with the low, nauseated whisper that the world was a terrible place. Even as she said it, she couldn't bring herself to fully believe it. In the midst of pain, there was good. While there was dishonesty and jealousy and agony, there was also strength, beauty, and power. She had seen this goodness every day in Nox, and she saw it now amidst the men of Uaimh Reev.

Brel's parents had been afraid. His villagers had been ignorant. The man who had saved a mutilated child from a life of misunderstanding on society's fringes had certainly been good. She wanted to see goodness in herself as well.

It happened so gradually that she had no way to mark its progress.

Over the months, Amaris became a sponge. She absorbed knowledge, tactics, and skills every day. She would learn any ability, craft, trade, or technique from anyone at the reev who'd give her the time of day. Even Grem begrudgingly let her into his forge a time or two to show her how he hammered their weapons and made their blades from molten steel. She could have sworn she caught him smiling as he pounded away at the red-hot, unformed blade, but he stopped himself as soon as she saw the curvature of his lips. He chased her from his workrooms, remembering some old belief that blacksmithing—like Uaimh Reev—was not for women.

For months she trailed behind in their run, too proud to let herself stop no matter how pathetic her stride or how feeble her limping steps. Then one day, she kept pace with Grem. The older reever had been the slowest of the group, and it was to his extreme displeasure that she began to stay within arm's reach of him. The day after she surpassed him, he found a reason to excuse himself to an errand in the foothills and wouldn't return to the reev for a very long time.

✦

By her third year at Uaimh Reev, her muscles had hardened beneath her pants and under her tunic, turning her soft arms and legs into taut, sinewy appendages able to throw the iron balls on the field and hoist the disks above her head. As the months had stretched into seasons, she'd felt the sword become such a familiar part of her that she ceased to notice its weight, switching between left and right hands until neither could be encumbered by the blade. The steel was now an extension of her body.

The softness of her cheeks ebbed into the features of a woman. Any fat from her childhood was gone after her first winter in the fortress. She had acquired a few new scars from the ring. Perhaps the largest scar in her collection, apart from her self-inflicted dagger wounds, was a nasty scrape of skin from a time she had sprinted past Malik and Ash on the mountain in an attempt to show off and twisted her ankle on a loose rock, tumbling an arena's length down a drop-off before her bloodied arm and leg and caused enough friction to stop her fall. Odrin had watched over her as she washed and bandaged the wounds to ensure she wouldn't catch infection, eyeing the tonics she chose for her health, but he hadn't needed to intervene or correct her.

By the time Amaris was eighteen, she was ready to take the oath as a full-fledged reever.

Nineteen

I S IT ALWAYS AT SUNSET?" SHE WHISPERED.

Odrin smiled, though he kept his eyes forward.

Amaris had been waiting for this day for years, and now that it was finally here, she felt like she might be sick. Joy and nerves roiled through her stomach in a tangled, excited twist of nausea and emotion. After dinner, she'd washed, dressed, and plaited her hair with shaking fingers. She had no reason to be nervous. She also had no reason to be presentable, as most of these men didn't so much as own a comb. Still, staring at her reflection in the mirror gave her something to do with her nervous energy.

Now she swallowed once, then twice, as if the ceremony were little more than a hunk of dry bread caught in her throat. She continued staring at the rectangle at the end of the hall where the granite of Uaimh Reev sliced into the vibrant colors of sundown. As soon as they stepped out of the corridor, the rite would begin.

"It's tradition," Odrin whispered back, "plus, oaths require a certain sense of drama, don't you think?"

Amaris flexed her hands several times to get the blood flowing to her fingertips. She glanced at her palm, knowing it would be the last day her hand would exist without a deep, silvery scar. Her heart skidded as another thrill shot through her.

Odrin led her forward, exiting the keep to stand in the red light of dusk, joining the eleven other men. Everyone in the reev, save for Brel, was accounted for. The night was warm, with the lightest breeze to move the loose dust and sand of the ring in small swirls at their feet. The open-air fighting arena served many purposes, though this was the first time she'd seen it used for ritual. This was only the second swearing-in ceremony to take place since her arrival, but she hadn't been permitted to attend Ash's rite, as she had not yet been a reever. She'd pressed her face against the windows of her room throughout the ceremony but had seen nothing.

Now that her time had come, she had no idea what to expect. Every time she'd asked Ash about the rite, he'd merely winked and flashed the bright pink scar on his hand. She usually scowled, but she understood that taunting composed at least half of his personality.

The night was warm, with just enough of a breeze to make the torches flicker dramatically around the ring. Their flame joined the blazing oranges and crimsons of the dying sunset overhead. The smell of oil and smoke joined the otherwise crisp mountain air where they convened. The other men had gathered near the steps, sitting and chatting in a variety of positions. They pushed themselves to their feet, standing in a rough semicircle as Amaris approached.

"Ready to add to your collection of scars?" Odrin asked as he left her side to stand by the men.

Amaris did her best to remain solemn, but a grin escaped her. Odrin returned the smile.

Samael clapped his hands together little, more than a dark shape silhouetted against the sunset. He began,

"We're not much for liturgy, Amaris. Repeat the oath, and then shake hands with your brothers. Shall we?"

She nodded. They hadn't told her what to expect. Her surge of nerves seemed to set the sky on fire as the sunset bloomed into deeper shades of vibrant violet, gold, and crimson. The men looked at her expectantly as Samael began. He held a dagger loosely in one hand and looked to her as she repeated her vow.

"I am the sword of the All Mother. I will answer to no king, join no armies, and seek for myself neither power nor glory. I stand between magic and its imbalance as its sentry in this world. I will not flee, fail, or falter. I am a reever."

Samael finished, then looked at Amaris expectantly.

"Now, Amaris of No Home and No People: are you prepared to make Uaimh Reev your home and the reevers your people?"

Her heart squeezed with emotion. She nodded, slowly echoing the vow.

He raised the dagger to one hand, squeezing the blade to create a cut in his palm. His face betrayed nothing. He passed the knife to Grem, who did the same, though the man winced ever so slightly. Odrin traced a deep scar in his palm with the blade, exchanging the knife with the next man, then the next, until droplets of blood dangled from the fingertips of every man around her. Finally, the dagger was given to Amaris.

The knife was soaked with the reevers' blood from blade to hilt. She wrapped one hand around the handle, palm sticky against the hot, red life of one dozen men.

She stared at the knife for a moment, eyes examining the hand that clutched it, and the pale, open palm that remained ready for slicing. A vivid memory pulsed through her as she felt her hands wrap around a dagger years ago and the cut of a blade as she'd marred herself, becoming imperfect. It had been a morning of panic, of fear, of desperation and scrambling and hopelessness. The sting of a blade had set her free in Farleigh, unleashing her from the chains of the world. The same gash of a knife would now toss her a lifeline, a tether meant to bind her to a new life, a new family.

She smiled slowly as she lowered the knife to her palm, watching ruby mar the milky white of her flesh. Pride swelled within her as she finished the cut, ready to seal her vow.

Samael was the first to offer his hand, their blood exchanged in a solemn grasp. Odrin took her hand in a shake but clapped her opposite shoulder with pride, a smile on his face as she completed her ritual. The blood of every reever would pump through their veins, uniting them as brothers, sharing blood with the first true family she'd ever known. The process repeated with shakes, smiles, clasps, a wink from Ash, and a hug from Malik until she stood before them, pride, valor, and the unmistakable scarlet smear of blood radiating from the legacy that pumped through her veins as the thirteenth reever.

✦

Ash leaned his body weight to the side, drinking deeply from a waterskin while Malik and Amaris sparred in the ring. She occasionally heard him shouting encouragements to her over the reverberating clang of metal. They were long past dulled, wooden swords. The summer heat had them dressing lighter with every passing day, freeing their movements and enabling the reevers to navigate training in barely more than a tunic and pants.

"It's always your feet! Watch your feet, Ayla!"

"Shut it!" she chirped back without looking at him. "I know what I'm doing."

She caught the redhead from the corner of her eye, but her gaze stayed fixed on the exercise at hand. Malik was nearly a foot taller and markedly stronger, but Amaris knew she was only a few moves away from having him on his ass. A drenching of sweat caused his shirt to cling to his hardened body, betraying his exertion as he brought his sword up once more.

The other reevers finished up their morning routines and joined Ash, watching as Malik and Amaris exchanged blades. Amaris smirked as she watched a large bead of sweat trickle down Malik's brow. His features were normally relaxed in a smile, but his face was trained in concentration. His golden hair had been tied back in a knot, though a few stray curls had unraveled themselves as he moved. He lunged and she successfully blocked his blow and retreated, sword in the defensive position.

While both heaved from the effort of sparring, it was clear that Malik's stamina was waning. The hot pulse in her face as her body flushed suggested to her that she looked every bit as fatigued, but she would not give him the satisfaction of seeing her waver. She wet her lips, tasting the salt and heat and dust of the ring and the fight.

"When did you get this good?"

"I think you're just getting old." She winked.

He swung high and hard, but her spin had both her hands gripping simultaneously at her hilt, holding it with the rigid strength of her outstretched arms as she blocked again. She grunted from her belly as her weapon absorbed the hit. She took his blow and spun, swinging for his legs with another high sound. Amaris had hoped that his weight would slow him, but she should have known better than to catch him off guard.

Despite his size, Malik was quick. He leaped backward, successfully avoiding her sweep. His side- step may have helped him to dodge her initial swing, but it left his right side open. She faked to the left and came in hard for his right. His green eyes went wide with surprise as he registered her movements. Amaris barely had time to twist her sword and strike him with the broad side, sending him to the ground with a blow to his pride rather than a pierce through his ribs.

He groaned from where he'd fallen. She grinned, certain she'd won. She extended a hand to help him up, but Malik had some fight in him yet.

Dust kicked up between them as the golden-haired man bared his teeth. He was on his feet before she'd even realized that the fight was to continue. He twisted his full body weight into an arc, whirling from one side to the other, but what Amaris lacked in size and strength she made up for in deft, nimble speed. Her ground roll put her behind him before he could blink, now smiling with the thrill of the fight. She was on her feet with instantaneous grace before he could turn. With a hard kick, she shoved her foot into his back and had him on the ground. In one more leap, Amaris was atop him, beaming from ear to ear.

"Fuck!" he gasped as he stared up at the sky.

The older reevers unleashed a mix of cheers and good-natured boos as they watched.

Malik was momentarily conflicted between feeling proud of his friend and embarrassed at his own defeat, but he shoved her off him while she beamed her glee. The men around the camp barked their approving laughs. Malik dusted off both his tunic and his pride while Amaris made a show of bowing in faux humility.

"Fighting you is like battling a rabbit with a sword! You're so damn agile!"

"Yes," she panted happily, unbothered by his comparison. "I've always fancied myself a bunny with a blade. Thanks for that."

He clapped her on the back and grinned, heading for the water.

Ash stepped up. "Do you have another round in you?"

Malik took a break from the water he'd been guzzling. "Not fair," he gasped between swallows. "If you beat her, it will be because I wore her down."

Amaris jutted her chin slightly, arching a brow at the challenge. She remained baking in the heat, still tasting the chalky cloud of dust from her fight with Malik and the fine, powdery grime that it had scattered. She could use a water break, but rehydration would have to wait. She smiled. "And if I beat him even after you've worn me down, all the better I'll be proven."

A few annoying, fly-away pieces of hair had tugged loose from her braid during her fight, interfering with her vision. She raked her sweat-soaked strands backward, ready to spar once more.

Malik still wasn't pleased. He crossed his arms, arguing, "Look at her! Our snowman is as red as a strawberry. It's not a fair fight."

Amaris knew he was right about at least one thing. Her cheeks burned as though she'd set her face on a skillet on the hot, windless day. She knew she'd need to rub tonic all over her body once she left the ring to prevent sunburn.

She waved Malik off, saying, "We'll keep it simple. Hand-to-hand. I've got this."

Odrin had been sitting off to the side, pride on his face. He shouted into the ring, "Give our little tomato-colored rabbit a chance! If she says she can do it, my money's on Amaris."

He'd meant it as encouragement, but her heart

squeezed with emotion at his words. Odrin's pride was as rejuvenating as it was distracting. She wouldn't let him down. She shook the fatigue from her limbs, rolling her neck as she prepared for round two.

Ash took a few steps toward her, allowing the tension to build before entering the sandy space reserved for sparring. His red hair was fully tied up, not in a braid like Amaris's, but in a knot on top of his head in the same fashion as Malik's. The sweat clinging to Ash was from their morning run, and if she wasn't mistaken, Ash's sweat only underscored his distinct sweet smell of autumn's dying leaves. She'd always wondered if it was a fae quality—the lure of scent—though now wasn't the best time to ponder such attributes. She was quite confident she smelled of dirt and sweat and need of a bath.

Ash offered a foxlike grin, unable to keep the thrill from his eyes. Amaris had enjoyed the transformation of watching her sparring partner's daily opinion grow from disappointment to appreciation, to downright competitiveness. At long last, Amaris was a formidable force.

"You sure you can take me without your sword, Ayla?"

"My feet haven't been rooted in a long time, Ash!" she goaded. "Though I suppose imagining me as an oak tree will only make it easier for me to best you. You know as well as I do that underestimating your opponent will get you killed."

"I know exactly how you fight. I taught you half of what you know!"

She laughed, returning the sly smile.

She drew her right foot behind her left and lifted her fists.

"Are you stalling?" She arched a brow. "Afraid to hit a girl?"

Odrin started to shout something as the reevers

burst into excited applause as if at a sporting match. The cackles and amusement that erupted from the surrounding reevers egged her on. She hoped he could feel the twinkle in her eye as she challenged him. He slowly raised his own hands, curled to throw a punch. He tilted his head to one side.

"Fine. Dance with me," he tempted.

She unleashed the first blow—a kick to his chest. He caught her foot as it made purchase and twisted her leg, spinning her into the air. She stayed true to form as she swiveled, not fighting the movement. She flowed with the rotation and landed on both of her feet like a cat, one hand to the earth to balance her. Her land was graceful and as feline as every other element of her battle strategy.

Staying low, Amaris made a sweep for his shins that rolled into an uppercut. The red-haired faeling jumped over her sweep, but her fist made contact with his jaw. She felt the impact ripple through her arm, hurting her knuckles slightly as a slip of air escaped her lips against the pain.

She could tell Ash's vision danced as he stumbled backward, shaking stars from his eyes. Amaris didn't give him the time he needed to catch his breath. She went in for another swift kick. Ash dropped back and to one knee, opening up his side so her foot found only air. He grabbed her leg from beneath and had her on the ground, facing the wrong direction. She was quick to her feet in the cloud of dust, but from his advantageous position, he was faster.

Amaris attempted to grunt in a twist, voice pitched against impending panic, but he had her in a lock.

It took half a heartbeat for his arms to grip her. Holding her from behind in a split second, he had one arm around her neck in the crease between his bicep and forearm, the hand from his other arm grasping the elbow into the sleeper hold.

Her eyes went wild, and in a frenzied final attempt to free herself, she moved her hips to the side just enough to thrust the heel of her hand into his manhood. Ash gasped and released his grip in pain and shock. The watching male crowd either laughed or barked at the cheap shot as she kneed him again, sending him to the ground. She didn't waste a second as she crossed to him, kneeling over her kill.

Her knee stayed on his throat as he stared up at her from his place on his back.

She leaned in close, her mouth brushing his ear so only he could hear. She smiled as she said, "Sorry about hurting your favorite part."

He put both hands on either side of her knee to hold the pressure off his windpipe, but he had accepted defeat.

"I'm sure I'll think of a way for you to make it up to me," he said.

Amaris hopped to her feet, helping her sparring partner up with an outstretched hand. The reevers patted her on the back with heavy, calloused hands. At least two of them continued to cry foul about her cheap shot, but the others agreed that Ash would need to keep his vulnerable places guarded in battle to anticipate the enemy. She was the undisputed victor.

The time had come for pork, summer fruits, and ale. It was a little early in the day for the beer to flow as freely as it did, but between the dramatic retellings of the match, one would think that they hadn't all just been present at the same event. The men kept filling her mug, teasing Ash for leaving his manhood exposed. Malik defended him, pink in the face as the men ruffled his golden hair. The dining hall was thick with the smell of their sweat, their dirt, and their day. The food was hot, the laughs came easily, and their hearts were light. Here at the keep, Amaris knew she was with her blood, her family.

Twenty

NOX DRAGGED HER GAZE SLOWLY ACROSS HER TARGET. He hadn't seen her yet, and for at least a moment longer, she'd keep it that way.

The man was young and handsome in the rakish sort of way one rarely saw in Priory. She'd kept her eyes trained loosely on him while he made his way through the incense-laden haze of the lounge. Elegant tufts and silks lined the room, a few pillows with patrons already lounging on them as young women listened intently, feigning interest in crop yields or investments or politics. Aside from the boring chatter of patrons and the women who pretended to be enthralled, their in-house musician was a rather pretty woman whose fingers moved deftly and softly over her lute. The musician always knew what songs to play, picking up the tune when she read the room to encourage excitement, and selecting slow, sad ballads if the women needed to pander to emotional connections. Presently, the lutist plucked the pleasant cords of a song with no name, merely creating ambiance for the patrons and girls working the floor alike.

The room was thick with the same strong vanilla perfume she'd first detected on Millicent, accompanied by notes of sandalwood and the lush, smoky burn of the incense sticks themselves. After Nox's three years at the Selkie, the scented haze had begun to trigger the part of her mind that readied her for the hunt. The lush smell acted like a signal, tingling some imaginary talons.

Tonight was different, though. The Duke of Henares was of particular importance, and everyone under the Selkie's roof knew it.

Nox kept to a shadow behind a pillar until she was ready for him to see her; first impressions were vital. First, the man would need to swallow a gulp or two of burning liquor. She'd give him a chance to relax into the music. If she played the game correctly, he'd convince himself that he'd been the one who first spotted her—and she always won the game.

The duke made his way directly to the bar and ordered a drink, not bothering to look at any of the Selkie's girls. He had the arrogance of a lordling who was familiar with getting whatever he wanted. The bartender's gaze flitted briefly to where Nox leaned against the pillar, then he slid the duke his two fingers of whiskey.

Once he had his glass in hand, he turned to open himself up to the room, elbows behind him on the counter. This duke made it abundantly clear he was unimpressed. His posture informed the others that he'd been to brothels, and his expression declared to the world that the Selkie was nothing new. His golden-brown eyes began scanning for whatever life-changing encounter he'd heard whispers about, face slack with boredom. The young lordling took one, slow sip of his whiskey while he searched.

Nox's lips twitched in anticipation, but she fought down the smile. It would do no good to gloat before the victory. She glanced to where the Madame had remained engaged in conversation with a patron, though Millicent had kept her peripherals trained on Nox and the duke the entire time. She was a shrewd businesswoman, generous host, and an excellent multitasker.

With a nod of confirmation from Millicent, Nox was ready. The lutist across the salon knew the game as well as anyone else in the lounge. She transitioned her song into the soft melodies of a love ballad. Nox stepped into view wearing a paper-thin silk dress that clung to her curves, with a neckline so daring she may as well have been naked. Her gaze touched the duke's brown-gold eyes from across the lounge. Once he saw her, his face slackened. It was the distinct expression of someone experiencing the cacophony of the world fading away.

They made it too easy, she thought. Even from across the room, she knew he'd felt the world shift beneath him. The smug boredom had evaporated. The duke continued to hold his whiskey but didn't move as he watched her.

Feigning the unintentional brushing of gazes was merely her opening move. She looked away—not shyly, but as though she had more important things to do. She waited for his countermove.

Nox made a show of dangling the bait around the lounge for a few minutes. It was time for her to move her knight in their game of chess. She'd been given a helpful, though predictable tip, about what the duke might find engaging. This display of intrigue required her to chat with another girl, stroking a slow, idle hand down the bare skin of the girl's exposed back while casting sidelong looks at the lordling at the bar, heightening his anticipation with every moment that passed.

He'd respond in one of two ways. Either he'd remain passive and continue to push his pawns forward through hopeful looks, or he'd make a power play by buying her a drink.

The duke responded with the equivalent of his bishop.

He raked a hand through his loose, brown hair, eyes still trained on her. His body rotated toward the bartender, who'd been waiting for exactly such an event. The lordling ordered Nox a glass of red wine and held it aloft, beckoning her to him with the offer of the floral, gilded wine glass. It was bold, but not too daring—the perfect secondary play.

The next step was the most important. The opening had been performed flawlessly. The duke would need to feel as though he ran the match, confident in his victory long before she touched her queen.

With something of a wry smirk, Nox finally approached the bar and leaned into the space beside him. She mimicked his unimpressed boredom as if she were the one who needed convincing. It was a stalling move. She rested her elbow on the bar, arching a brow as she eyed the wine. Her curtain of dark hair tumbled over her shoulders. A common mistake game players made was showing too much enthusiasm. It was a faux pas she avoided by refusing to speak first. The highest-earning girls were those who prompted the men to do all the talking. And so, she waited. The duke lapped up the game, eager to catch her attention with each word.

"Would you do me the honor of having a drink with me?"

Her lips tugged upward, revealing a hint of teeth. She saw the pulse of hope and endorphins twinkle as if they were tangible stars in his eyes. She idly wondered what piece he thought he'd played and how far along he believed himself to be. She extended her hand for the stemware. She smelled the wine but didn't drink.

"What's your name?" he asked.

"You can call me Nox." She smiled, face relaxed in a posture meant to disarm the opponent.

"Aren't you going to ask mine?" He cocked a brow again.

"We'll see," she said, finally lifting the wine. She paused before drinking.

Her response hit its mark. They toasted the air before drinking. She smiled fully at the lordling, though the coy grin was as much for herself. His pretense had dropped, already enraptured. Once he'd begun talking, he hadn't stopped.

Yet, there were still moves to be made. Her eyes wandered away from the duke, landing on the lutist. She didn't need to signal the musician for the woman to understand her cue. The lutist picked an up-tempo drinking song. Priory was a coastal city, and there were several sea shanties known to excite the crowd. Many of the more intoxicated patrons jumped on the chance to sing along, which brought the perfect level of too loud rowdiness to the salon. The clients took over the tune with jovial energy.

Meanwhile, the duke's compliments burbled like water breaking over stones. After scarcely sipping half of her glass, Nox had heard enough. She tilted her head, as if struggling to listen to him speak over the happy chorus.

"It's a bit difficult to hear down here, don't you think?"

He agreed wholeheartedly. She felt as though the duke was practically glued to her as she led him away from the bar, far from the haze of vanilla and sandalwood, and beckoned him to follow her up the stairs, distancing themselves from the tufts and silks and prying eyes of patrons. Nox knew if she'd looked for Millicent's face, the Madame would be concealing a thin smirk.

There was something childlike about the way the duke smiled at Nox, his eyes wide and expectant as they entered a private room with a four-poster bed. The click of the lock behind them was heavy with implication. The lordling's eyes matched his hair, both golden brown and glittering. Nox lowered her lashes, offering an evocative, conciliatory smile. She knew enough of male eagerness to understand she'd have to temper his haste. She also knew enough of her own thirst to know she'd have to proceed carefully if she wanted to keep him alive. While greedy impatience colored his face, her returning gaze was positively bloodthirsty.

She gestured for him to find his way to the bed while she stepped behind an ornately carved wooden screen, the gaps in its pictures barely obscuring his view of her near-nakedness. Even through the lattice, she could feel the man eyeing her hungrily as she stripped off her black silk dress and let it dangle over the carved separation. The duke crawled onto the bed, breathing out with eager appreciation as she stepped out in a thigh-short, practically sheer dressing gown with nothing underneath.

Check.

The room, the bed, the silks, the scents, everything screamed of sex. This was not the quick, back-tavern draining of one's balls, or the chaste lovemaking of the marital bed, but the silks and perfumes and energy of wild, passionate affairs. There was no evidence of haze, smoke, vanilla, or sandalwood common to the salon here. This was Nox's room, and it radiated her scent. The air was thick with plums and dark spices. She watched his eyes for the telltale, dizzying glaze that betrayed his hunger over the prospect of their entanglement alone.

His hunger. How amusing.

She'd heard the report of his reluctance in the

debriefing. She knew the duke had been entirely sure the Selkie would be yet another event in his life that was overpromised and under-delivered. She hadn't been worried. Getting him in the door had been the hard part, though Emily never failed as the lure when fishing for new men. They made an unstoppable pair.

She still had one move left to play.

"Tell me why you want me," she purred.

His animated eyes widened a bit. She was done playing coy. It was time for power. She knew enough of his reputation to understand the bashful maiden would not impress him and enough of men to know what would thrill him. Nox was a force of nature, unlike any woman, or man, he'd come across, and it was time for him to see her as such.

"You're the most beautiful thing I've ever seen. Your hair, your eyes, your incredible body...what I can see of it, that is," he said. His words were heavy with implication. He wanted to see more. "You could be the goddess herself."

She enjoyed the answer, circling him a bit as her bare feet moved her slowly toward the bed. He lay on the tufted comforter, watching her very casually walk around the four-poster bed to one side. She'd ensured there was just enough dim, sensual light so that anyone in her room could see every detail of her mouth, her full breasts, her hips, and the way the sheer fabric left little to the imagination. She was nearly close enough to touch. The duke leaned forward, extending an eager hand to close the space between them.

Nox tutted her tongue in a playful, authoritative correction. She took a seat on the end of the bed, the weight of her hips compressing the duvet. She slid her dressing gown to the side in such a way to expose only her shoulder.

The cost of a night with her set expectations exceptionally high. The longing in his boyish eyes said he was ready to sink his teeth into the experience his money had bought. She dragged her eyes over him with a feline intensity, and every tremble in his face, from the throb of his jaw and the tension in his eyes to the twitch of his eager fingers conveyed this was lust more potent than he'd encountered before. She felt rather smug, knowing full well that the man before her would have paid the price three times over.

✦

Emily spotted him the moment she entered the tavern.

She hadn't even formally met him and was already annoyed. The Duke of Fucking Henares. What a prize.

Emily had been excellent at all facets of her job for years. It wasn't until she began venturing out into the surrounding cities as bait that Millicent saw her true potential. Nights on the road were a welcome adventure contrasted against the mundanity of everyday life within the salon. This particular adventure had taken a day's ride, and if she played her cards right, which she always did, she could be in and out in under an hour.

She fought the urge to glare at the lordling, dressed in his finery amidst the everyday folk of Henares. Despite the jovial music, the laughter, and the booze, the duke was anything but cheery. Bitter disinterest rolled off him. He'd sequestered himself to a far corner of the bar, angling his body to dissuade anyone who might approach.

This was fine. She had some work to do before wasting her time on the lord.

Emily sidled up to the bartender, a man who greeted her with a pitcher of ale in one hand and a damp rag in the other. He scanned her in the way a business owner might regard a paying customer, perhaps assessing her for her drink of choice and the depth of her wallets. Any man who didn't linger on her chest immediately gained a modicum of favor. It was fortunate that he didn't have an outright boorish personality, as the barkeep's looks were sure to win him no love from the ladies. His brows were entirely too thick for any man's face, two disconcertingly dark caterpillars that met in the center.

"What'll it be, miss?" he asked.

She made a show of considering the choices. Between the fiddle, the drunkenly sung shanties, and the patrons' chatter, the bar was too rowdy for the barkeep to hear her response. He leaned in close enough to understand her. The man smelled of garlic, sausage, and sweat. Despite her displeasure at his proximity, she knew he was close enough that no one would overhear their conversation.

"Maybe the mead, maybe the water, or maybe you'd spare a girl some stress and help her with a bit of information?"

The man leaned away. He frowned. "I'm not looking for any trouble."

She shook her head quickly. "Me either. In fact, I'm hoping you'll help me keep my cousin from undue suffering. You see that man over there?" Emily gestured vaguely toward the duke.

The bartender's lip wrinkled, pulled up as if he'd smelled something particularly unpleasant. "I do," he said.

The lie came to Emily quickly and easily. She nodded. "My aunt married well, much better than my mother did, anyway, and alas my cousin finds herself poised for an advantageous marriage. She's been set up for a match with your duke, and tomorrow they're to meet—"

"No," he said quickly.

Her heart sank. She'd find the necessary information

one way or another, but it would be so much easier if she could get the barkeep to share what she needed. Emily had become particularly skilled at her brand of espionage and had no intention of returning to Priory empty-handed. She wasn't particularly fond of referring to Nox as her family, even in the context of spying. She also wasn't particularly fond of sending men to Nox's room, or truly any of the dealings that Millicent had woven so tightly around the dark-haired beauty. Still, she was thrilled to have joined whatever twisted inner circle that had led to Nox's seeing her value. Even more, she enjoyed the pieces of her job that called upon her cunning.

Tonight was one of those nights.

"No you won't tell me of the duke?" Emily said, seeking clarification.

"No, I'm saying, tell your cousin to save herself the time. The boy's the worst kind of prick. I'll deny it if you go telling anyone I said so, but there are worse things than drinking in poppy dens and whoring with any man, woman, or the like who will tumble home from the bar with you. If your cousin is any sort of good lady, she ain't gonna want to be affiliated with his sort."

The bartender set down a glass indelicately and immediately began to fill it with frothy, amber liquid. He pushed it across the wooden bar top, and she wrapped her fingers around the pint, sipping politely while considering the information. She wasn't entirely sure whether his statement regarding ladies of the night was an outright insult or a backhanded compliment, so with a bit of dry wariness, she prompted, "And, pray tell, what's worse than being a whore?"

The bartender shook his head, setting down his rag emphatically.

"I don't want no trouble, miss. He is our duke after all."

"I promise," she sighed. "Whatever you say stays between us. I'll make something up to keep my cousin away from her match tomorrow, but it would be nice to know if there's reason for doing so. I'd hate to steal her chance at happiness."

He poured a glass for himself and lifted it in solidarity. The barkeep leaned in close once more, the scents of spending too much time in the kitchen filling her nose. He exhaled noisily. "It's my first pint of the night, and to be honest, I'm an hour past due. Here's to loose lips sinking ships."

They clinked their glasses.

"His father was a good man, he was," said the bartender. "He was fair. Henares did fine for itself for decades. But when our duchess died, well, the boy turned into the lecherous slob we can't seem to keep out of our taverns. Everyone should have their fun, right? And that's not the issue. I should mention, the lad doesn't pick fights; he settles his tabs. I shouldn't be complaining, but—"

"But?"

He used his free hand to rub at his temple, asking, "Would you want your cousin marrying the kind of man who wouldn't visit his father on his own deathbed? A boy too distracted by a party at another lord's estate? They sent word for him and everything, but he just couldn't be bothered. He told the servants to tell his father goodbye on his behalf. The man had been sick for so long, and now with him gone, and the taxes, and the military conscripts, and the politics…"

She drank deeply from her beer, smacking her lips against the bright, hoppy bubbles. "You're right," she said. "That's not the kind of man I'd want in the family. That's all I need to know."

Emily stood from the bar, sliding him five pennies.

"It's only worth two, miss," he said.

She smiled kindly. "It's worth a coin purse of pennies, believe me. If you'll excuse me, I need to go tell him that my cousin can't make their appointment, as she's fallen unexpectedly ill. I appreciate your help." She raised her glass again, saying, "My family thanks you."

She held her drink above the patrons to maneuver through the tightly packed crowd until she'd made it successfully to the duke's side. Emily slid onto the stool next to him—open only because his scowl frightened off anyone who dared approach—and set down her glass.

It took all of ten seconds to find him disgusting. He waved her away with a disinterested hand before she had a chance to open her mouth.

"Not tonight, my dear," he drawled, "though I'm sure whatever you have under that bodice is spectacular. Tell me, how far down do all those freckles go?"

No, Emily would feel no remorse for whatever fate the duke met. Ever the actress, she grinned dismissively, her eyes barely touching his.

"Oh, I'm not looking for companionship," she said. "I've already had the best there is."

The young Duke of Henares raised a half-amused, half-annoyed eyebrow.

"Trying to make me jealous?" he asked. "I'm glad a man keeps your bed mussed up. May we all be so lucky as to find someone to fuck until our days are done. Here, here."

He raised his mug to his own insincere cheer.

She laughed lightly, turning her body away from him as she murmured her own musings to the crowd, sipping on her beer as she said, "I don't much care for the company of men."

Clearly, this piqued his curiosity. She'd expected

as much. It was a particularly unevolved brand of male who fetishized the fantasy of two women together. She'd pegged him for exactly that sort of man and dragged a finger lightly along her collarbone, allowing it to trail down her neckline, pretending to be lost in absent thought as she drew his attention to her breasts.

Suddenly interested, the duke adjusted his posture. "Well," he prodded, "do share with a poor lad. Make my night a bit better, would you?"

She smirked. "Normally I'd say a lady shouldn't kiss and tell, but this…this changed my life. Have you been to Priory?"

The duke shook his head, leaning in. He clarified, "Your beloved is in Priory?"

"Oh, to call her mine," she sighed. Emily took another deep gulp of her beer. The raucous tavern noises drowned her thoughts for a moment, exacerbating the pleasant memories that stole her away. She continued dreamily, "This goddess belongs to no one. She is mine as much as she's anyone's who can afford her, if only for a moment. Though, I'll be damned, it's a once-in-a-lifetime price to pay. I will say, there aren't words for the night we shared. It ruined all men for me. And to think! I was once engaged to a merchant's son."

His interest dimmed once more.

"I've had whores," he said dismissively.

Twice in one night, she fumed within. No bother. As with all things, underestimation was their power. Emily kept her face serene as she said, "I'm sure you have."

He watched her with a bit of surprise as she stood to leave. Clearly he'd expected her to battle him for the pleasure of being in his company. He raked a hand through his golden-brown hair, loosening his locks as he examined her.

"And when you tire of your whores," she said, keeping the word as light as she could, "as all earthly things become tiresome, and if you find yourself seeking something transcendent, look for the Selkie."

That had been all.

She'd gone back to Priory that very night only to be met by a barrage of questions from Millicent. Exhausted, Emily didn't have time for Madame's line of questioning.

"And?" Millicent insisted. "Did you get any promises? Any guarantees?"

"No," Emily yawned. "But give it three days. He's a man who thinks without a drop of blood in his brain, as it's too busy pooling elsewhere. Three days, and I promise you, he'll be at our door."

✦

She nearly had him.

"Nox?" He repeated her name reverently.

"Mmm," she agreed, eyeing him half-curiously. The duke unbuttoned his shirt a bit hastily, and she chastised him with a wicked smile. Nox hiked her dressing gown up over her thighs and began to move toward him. Rather than mount him as he'd perhaps hoped, she slid into the space behind him, resting his golden-brown head against her chest and rubbing his neck and arms with her gentle hands. She could feel the slump of his disappointment, and it was all she could do to keep from rolling her eyes. Predictable. Surely, he'd entered her rooms expecting whips, wax, and knife play but instead found himself getting a massage.

He'd have to be patient for a moment longer.

"My Lord, you carry too much tension. I can't imagine the pressure you're under."

He agreed with her assessment, attempting to shake off his annoyance. "You don't know the half of it."

The banter in the lounge had been charming, but his eagerness would undo them if she couldn't keep him focused. He licked his lips and attempted to turn his body to make a move, but she held him to her, forcing him to stay in the massage. His impatience to touch her, taste her, see for himself if she was exceptional were little more than an annoyance to Nox.

She concurred, her voice a low, erotic drip of honey as each word stuck to the one before it. "And thank the goddess I don't have to!" she said. "The kind of responsibilities a lord of your stature must have…it's understandably too much to handle."

She ran a hand along his arm, her nails tracing soothing lines down his veins.

"I didn't say that it was too much," he protested. "I just don't see the point in it all. What does it matter what the queen wants to do with my men, or how much we owe the crown? Whatever Moirai wants, she gets. She can take them for all I care."

Nox reached a hand into his shirt, her fingers moving in lines along his chest. She felt the steady thud of his heart as she carved a path between the demarcation of his pectorals. His skin was too soft, almost as if it had been waxed and oiled before he arrived. "I agree," she soothed. "I wouldn't have the sense about me to deal with troops either."

The duke flushed with irritation. "I have plenty of sense. I just don't bother myself with her wars. I don't see why she needs me to strategize if she's on a witch hunt to find where Raascot has infiltrated. She clearly knows exactly where they're hiding. Why bother me at all if she's requesting a dispatch to Yelagin? Moirai knows I can't say a damned thing to the contrary, or I'm a traitor to the crown. Explain to me why I must have these consultations with ambassadors and feign my say in it when she's going to take however many she wants, wherever she wants."

Yelagin. There it was.

Their game of chess had ended. She was ready to finish the match.

Nox withdrew her hand and pulled herself on top of him, straddling the man, enjoying the gleam of his eyes as he admired her. She did love the way he looked at her. She was art, and his eyes worshipped her as such. His excitement was contagious. She was excited, herself, though for very different reasons. She brimmed with the full-figured body of a woman and the ethereal youth of something a bit more predatory than angelic. She appreciated the music of his moan as he watched her.

"By the All Mother, you are exquisite." He reached to cup her breast, but she stopped his hand, pressing it to her lips and kissing it gently. The duke made a slightly frustrated face once more but paused obediently. This was her game. He was here to play by her rules. As she reached under the pillow behind him, her breasts dangled dangerously near his mouth beneath the dressing gown that hid them. When she sat back up, she'd pulled out a long band of silk and smiled.

He beamed a tawdry, open smile at the new toy they'd put into place.

"Goddess, yes."

Nox winked and began to bind his right wrist to the bedpost, then his left, watching the duke tense in anticipation. Once his hands were secured, she approached him like a mountain cat from below, crawling toward him, drowning him in the plums and cinnamons and nutmegs and other spices of her scent. She tugged on his britches, pulling them down over his hips and unleashing him from the constrictive cage of his pants. His manhood throbbed, betraying his aching desire to be touched by her.

Nox began to lower her painted mouth, taunting him with her hot breath before she pulled back up and made a sound meant to say *not so fast*. The tension heightened his thrill. His desperation was so poignant, it had a flavor. It was a tangy, sticky want—no, a need. Goddess, she was lucky she'd tied his hands, or he'd have leapt for her. His reckless lust glinted wildly in his eyes.

This part was just for her.

"Tell me how badly you want me," she murmured. Nox moved to her knees, hovering slightly above him. He arched his hips, hoping to connect with her, to meet her, but it wasn't enough to bridge the gap.

"I want you."

"What would you do to have me?" she asked, sliding her dressing robe off the rest of the way, naked beneath the gauzy, silken scrap of clothing. Her skin was flushed with the heat of their arousal. She wished she had a mirror and idly considered putting one above the headboard just for this. Why should her men be the only ones able to appreciate her lean body and supple breasts?

"I'd do anything."

She bit her lip, following his gaze as he soaked her in.

"Would you bring me to your estate?"

"And fuck you every day," he answered confidently, ever the bastard.

"Would you give me a duchess's title?" she asked. She pushed her hands into his chest, her breasts pressed together to accentuate their fullness with the motion. She dug her fingers slightly into the muscles of his chest, and he made a sound at the bite of her sharp nails.

His words blurred together, hurried with his eagerness.

"I'd make the people worship you like I do."

She licked her palm and lowered her wetted hand to him, teasing him with the touch of her fingers. She encircled his shaft, allowing his appreciative moan to fill her as she made him slick and ready for her.

"Would you give me your lands?"

He groaned against her touch, closing his eyes as he answered, "All of them."

"And your men?"

"They're yours to command."

"And your soul?"

"It belongs to you," he whispered.

Checkmate.

Her hand remained upon his shaft, dangling his tip just at her entrance. She guided his length in as she eased herself down with tantalizing slowness. She slid the duke inside of her and watched the twinkle in his eye as every inch of him became soaked in the starlight and glitter and oceans that knit the very fabric of the universe. Nox moaned a true, wild sound of delight as the sensation within her exploded, the vibrancy of his life force coursing through him.

She inhaled sharply at the intense, perfect lightning that bound them.

Oxytocin flowed into her, a dam as pure and intoxicating as brandy erupting from the lake of the lordling's life force, now a river flowing from him to her. She arched her back, opening her mouth in a gasp, the delicious drug filling her veins, her capillaries, her lungs. Her hips thrust with the electricity, draining the river, sucking it dry. The hard, thick rod of dopamine and serotonin and heart and soul throbbed within her as she moved. Her back relaxed from his groan of ecstasy, and she saw the light in his eyes begin to dim. The lordling's body went limp as she rode him. His eyes remained open; his mouth slackened.

"Fuck."

She looked at him and frowned, doing little to conceal her disappointment. Controlling this part was more art than science. Her euphoria had felt a bit like a feeding frenzy each time she consumed the oxytocin, but she was learning to tame it.

"Goddess damn you, you're not even going to let me finish?" Nox glared at him, frustrated over the climax she'd been denied. She took several calming breaths and forced herself to stop. She wanted to continue. She wanted to drink deeply from this well until nothing was left, but she rarely got what she wanted. This mission was too important for her wants.

The duke looked back, unseeing.

"Well, you didn't last nearly as long as you promised. I thought I was supposed to be pleasured all night," she said, half-amused, still pulsing with the cocktail made solely of bliss, thirst, and chemistry. Her head vibrated pleasurably, but she'd need to clear her thoughts if she had any hope of getting things done tonight.

"Come on." She slapped him a few times on the face, then checked his pulse, the dying duke's semi-stiff manhood still inside her. He wasn't dead, but he was close.

Perhaps she had gone a bit too far, as was easy to do when she found herself drunk on the power. This part had gotten easier with time, but she still struggled. She needed him alive if her ownership was to mean anything. Even without the young duke, she'd still make her way to Yelagin, but it would be much easier to have a puppet titleholder carving a path for her. She needed to steady herself and think rationally. As much as she wanted to cling to every drop, it was worth sparing a spark or two for the mission.

She slipped from the wet grip within her, but her legs remained planted on each side of his hips in a straddle.

Nox leaned down to the young lord's mouth, planting her lips gently on his. She breathed a droplet of life back into the duke and watched the faintest spark of candle-light reignite behind his otherwise listless, caramel eyes.

"There you are," she purred, satisfied.

She dismounted and made her way to the bedpost to begin untying his wrists. Dazed, he was whisper-ing something about how sensational she was, and she agreed with the low murmurs of a lover. His compli-ments continued spilling over his lips. She was even more beautiful, even more magnificent than ever before. She sat him up and rebuttoned his shirt. Nox pulled the trans-lucent piece of fabric around her shoulders and tied it at the waist as she leaned into the duke.

"I need you to listen to what I'm about to tell you."

He nodded, entranced. "Anything you say."

Twenty–One

N OX RARELY THOUGHT OF HOW FAR SHE'D COME SINCE first seeing a corpse. She'd known since childhood that she had no taste for men, but her first true experience with one cast any doubts to the shadows.

With the duke, the reanimation process had been as simple as breathing, quite literally. She hadn't always been this lucky. The faces of the dead did haunt her.

The first time she'd seen the lifeless face of a man had been at the Selkie.

She had arrived in Priory to work, but not on the salon floor with the others.

Nox and Millicent had scarcely entered the vanilla-scented lounge on their first tour of the property when the Madame informed her that she'd begin her servitude as a barkeep. The piece of news had been more than some small stroke of good fortune. Nox had possessed a rather charming effect on adults throughout her life and couldn't help but feel that her gift had extended to Millicent. She didn't need to understand the Madame's rationale to be foolish enough to look a gift horse in the mouth. She milked her time as a barmaid, happy to run Millicent's errands, clean the rooms after the girls had finished with their clients, and flirt with the regulars who returned night after night, if it meant avoiding the salon and the duties of the private rooms.

That was, of course, until she met Theo.

Theo, All Mother rest his soul, had been a man of thirty with the clean, soft hands and baby face of someone who had never known labor. He was a barrister, which meant his entire life revolved around the paperwork and litigation of common law—all profoundly boring, in Nox's opinion. He had come to the Selkie four months before their fated night, intent on finding a woman to take his long-overdue virginity. He'd paid a girl handsomely, his coins damp with the sweat of his clammy hands. Once he'd gotten to her room, his nerves had overwhelmed him. He'd stammered a few things about what was decent and proper. He urged her to put her robe back on and insisted they talk about their childhoods. Despite feeling terribly awkward, the poor girl had politely obliged, fully clothed. She'd sat with Theo for his two prepaid hours while he asked her invasive questions about her siblings, her food allergies, her faith, and what had resulted in her life in a whorehouse—a term that she recalled definitively as her tipping point in patience. When his time was up, she'd firmly requested that Millicent pair him with another girl the next time he visited. She wouldn't allow his secondhand shame to sully her.

Theo returned the following night and tried to catch the same girl's eye, but she pointedly avoided him. Nox dutifully poured him a chilled pint and chatted with the downtrodden man. He finished his drink and thanked her for sharing her company and for listening to his woes on life and women.

Night after night Theo returned, usually guilting Nox into joining him for a glass of blackberry wine that she would cordially sip throughout the evening. Before long, she knew she was looking into the doe-eyed gaze of a man who fancied himself in love. While he did indeed ask her about herself, he preferred to do most of the talking, as was common with the Selkie's patrons. She listened, nodded, smiled, and always knew how to ask the polite follow-up questions to keep him drinking, tipping, and returning.

Soon, Theo was spending every evening at the Selkie. He had no family, he'd said, as his parents had passed, and he'd never married. He told Nox that she was his only family. Though he'd meant it as endearment, his proclamation tasted like sour mead. Theo had something of a knack for making women uncomfortable.

Before approaching Millicent, he asked Nox directly if she was available for the Selkie's private rooms. The expression he'd made when she said she'd never worked on the salon floor made his face shine like the sun itself. He glowed with romanticism as he painted a fanciful picture of the two of them, their bodies intertwined, deflowering one another in the most beautiful union. It was yet another soliloquy in the long line of reasons that made Theo nauseating. He didn't know her. He didn't care about *her*. He loved a fiction.

Nox did her best to find excuses to spend more of her time on the opposite sides of the bar, putting as much physical distance between the ever-growing feeling of distress that his awkward presence brought. Patrons chuckled at Theo's pitiful advances, often tipping Nox more generously to help ease her obvious discomfort.

When Theo asked Millicent for Nox's hand in marriage, the Madame calmly quoted him a bride price that was just astronomical enough to buy Queen Moirai's crown directly from atop her head, and he'd settled on inquiring about the cost of Nox's maidenhood. Theo's frequent visits had given the Madame plenty of time to investigate his estate, and she knew exactly how much the man could afford before it broke him. She asked that number plus a single crown more.

The flicker in his eyes between panic, desperation, lust, and love had amused the Madame greatly, but she knew all about the foolishness of men in love. The fortune Theo would pay to be the first to have Nox in his bed was more than enough to cover the Madame's long-forgotten hopes of having a silver-haired girl in the Selkie. Millicent informed her rather unceremoniously that she would not be bartending that night. The freckled Emily took her shift serving drinks. Her ginger colleague offered a sympathetic smile and comforting touch as Nox moved from behind the bar and walked numbly up the stairs. She was shown directly to one of the smaller rooms in the town house.

Her time to join the ranks of women of the night had come.

She'd numbly bathed, perfumed, and sat upon the bed waiting for the rotund man. He remained deeply in love with her while she fought nausea. She couldn't care less what he looked like. She'd grown to hate him for his refusal to see things for what they were. He'd painted a romanticized narrative onto Nox, viewing her as a concept of affection rather than a human. She couldn't bring herself to feel anything but annoyed and physically ill at the thought that he was to be her first.

Theo entered the room oozing with anxious energy, though that was nothing new. After fumbling with his hat, coat, and shoes, he sat beside her on the bed. His discomfort matched hers, if for entirely separate reasons. Still, Theo's misguided love emboldened him to make the first move. Doing her best to focus on the fact that he was a relatively good man—a sweet, foolish man—helped her abstain from cringing. He hadn't known what to do with his tongue when he kissed her; she recalled it feeling dreadfully like a worm as it pried her lips open. Save for Achard's single, nauseating attempt at forced affection in her youth, this had been her first kiss. She didn't like it then, and she didn't like it now.

"You taste like rich, ripe plums," he'd said with a poet's conviction.

She'd been told as much throughout her life. Even Amaris had commented a time or two on how her very skin had shimmered with the scent of plum. How pleasant for him, she thought. Through substantial willpower, she resisted the urge to respond by telling him that he tasted like stewed turnips.

Attempting a picture of heroism, he fumbled an attempt to scoop her onto her back. He failed, and she wriggled somewhat uncomfortably backward on her elbows to position herself toward the center of the bed. He kissed her on the mouth far too many times, which she found particularly repugnant, and desperately wished he'd go ahead and get whatever was supposed to happen over with. She shut her eyes, which he took as a sign of endearment. Let him think what he must. She had every intention to use this as an opportunity to visit the detached void where she could float when she couldn't exist within herself. She'd gone there while suffering the bishop's wrath. She'd gone there when she'd been left on the landing outside of the kitchen. And she would go there now.

Theo kissed the soft parts of her body gently. Perhaps if it had been someone else, the sensations might have been pleasant. She tried to imagine what it would be like if someone she loved were against her shoulder, her neck, her stomach.

She squeezed her eyes tightly and thought of another mouth, of other lips. She was glad Theo's face was too distracted with burrowing himself against her flesh to see how intently she scrunched up her face and eyes to block out his movements. She needed to relax if she was going to succeed at drifting off into the dark, shadowed nothingness.

She exhaled slowly through her nose and felt the darkness behind her eyes deepen as it accepted her.

Her mind left her body as she forced herself to think of something—anything—pleasant. She pictured a delicate, female touch. Her mind wandered to the scent of juniper and wet, winter days. She envisioned the face she loved so deeply in place of the one touching her neck, her arms, her inner thighs, the very center of her. Nox had spent so much time resisting her fantasies, but in this moment, there was only one person she wanted to share the bed with. Her first true kiss, her first sensual touch— they'd been reserved for someone special. At least in the escapism of her mind, they could stay that way.

No, she had never let herself think of Amaris in this way. Nox loved her deeply, but she hadn't permitted herself such daydreams. She wouldn't let herself want these things unless she knew that Amaris might want them too. But for now. Just for tonight. Just for this experience, behind the dark void of her floating emptiness, she needed to believe they were together.

When he entered her, she held on to the single, tender thought of the one she loved, hoping she was safe, hoping she was happy. Nox meditated on that love, holding it close to her heart, letting it fill her.

Her reverie was shattered in an instant as a thundering weight came down on her and pinned her to the bed.

She gasped, jolted from her reverie. She yelped. She nearly suffocated on the flesh of some part of his body that had pressed against her mouth involuntarily. Her eyes flashed open in surprise, shattering her quiet escape. Theo had fully collapsed. She was pinned beneath the unsupported weight of his limp, naked body.

"Theo!" Nox gasped angrily once more, trying to shove him off her. "Theo, get off! Get up!"

Her panic rose as she realized both that he was unresponsive and that she was still trapped with him inside of her. The sheer compression of his weight continued to force the air out of her lungs. She screamed and scrambled to get out from underneath the collapsed man, thrashing and twisting until she managed to remove herself from the crushing position. It was an effort that required more strength than she'd thought she possessed, as the dead weight of a lifeless body had smothered her. She cried again, jerking and shoving.

Nox could only imagine what it must sound like, but she was scarcely able to free herself and didn't care how many grunts of effort it took to writhe free from beneath a corpse.

A sound cut through the panic.

"Nox?" Millicent's voice was painted as professionalism, thinly veiling whatever underlying emotion she felt as she rushed to the girl's door. Nox's screams must have been heard throughout the Selkie if the Madame had come running. Nox clambered off the bed and opened the door, heaving for breath, tears spilling with abandon.

She stood naked and trembling, clutching the brass doorknob. She looked at the Madame with wild desperation.

"Did he hurt you?"

Nox shook her head wordlessly, still shaking. She covered her breasts with her arms as she melted into the wall, sinking slowly into a seated fetal position on the floor.

Millicent took one look at her, then over her shoulder to the man who remained facedown on the bed. The Madame pushed into the room and shut the door behind her. Millicent rolled Theo onto his side with a grunt of gargantuan effort. She lowered her ear to his mouth, checking for the telltale heat, sound, or moisture of breathing. The Madame lifted a hand to feel for the artery on his throat.

She shrugged slightly. "Don't worry, dear," she said. "He paid in advance. You can take the rest of the night off, of course. I'll handle things here."

Nox's eyes bulged. She felt like a fish snatched from the water as the calloused Madame brushed her hands, sniffing dismissively.

"He's dead," Nox said, her voice choking. "He's dead."

Millicent began to leave when her eyes fixed on Nox's huddled form. The stunned look that flashed across the Madame's face was an expression Nox had never seen. The woman looked as if she'd seen a true phantom, jaw dropping and eyes practically doubling as they widened. She remained frozen a moment, the same shock stuck to her features.

Nox raised a hand to her face to see if perhaps there was blood, or perhaps something horrible on her that she hadn't noticed, patting at her hair and cheeks before looking back at the Madame in confusion.

Millicent closed the space between them. She knelt on the ground in front of the young woman. The Madame grabbed Nox by the chin and tilted it up, peering down into her eyes at an unknown revelation. At first, she shook her head in amazement. Then, a slow, delectable smile spread across Millicent's lips.

"Well, well, well. What have we here?"

Twenty-Two

To her credit, Millicent handled the nightmarish events swiftly, quietly, and efficiently. The woman knew exactly which men of disrepute to summon to discard of the corpse of a middle-class barrister with no family or title. A perk of being the city's most elite Madame was doubtlessly the blackmail she had been able to compile against its patrons. The things she knew could topple kingdoms, and when she needed to call in favors, they were done without question.

"I killed him." Nox remained somewhere between her conscious attempt to detach and the numb horror of a corpse freshly dragged from her bed. "He's dead. I killed him. I killed him."

"Hush, dear," Millicent said. The Madame apparently didn't have time to deal with Nox's feelings at the moment. She was busy orchestrating extraction and disposal.

"Will the constabulary come for me?" Nox managed to ask.

Millicent laughed and proceeded to ignore her. Nox ascertained from the Madame's utter lack of concern that the law wouldn't bother getting involved, considering half of the constabulary frequented the Selkie.

Theo had been given no dignity in death.

Nox was a wreck. She paced the room, clutching her hands to her upper arms in an attempt to self-soothe. She was a barmaid at a brothel, this was true. A regular had fallen for her and paid to take her maidenhood, this was true. He had been inside her when he—

Her stomach roiled as her dinner bubbled up. Nox caught most of the acid and liquid in her hand as she spun for the chamber pot that the women kept in the rooms, should a patron be too tipsy to make it to the bathing room to piss. They'd made a number of contingencies for the disgusting tendencies of men. This pot was bliss-fully clean—goddess be praised—before she vomited the remaining contents of her stomach into it. Between the nightmarish events, the disgust with herself, and the texture of the half-digested food in her throat, her stomach churned again and again, forcing her to empty any last drop until she was left dry-heaving.

Her fingers clutched the cool edges of the chamber pot as her back continued to flex and convulse with the heaves.

She didn't even remember the soft, ginger girl enter-ing. Emily knelt at her side with a glass of water and a damp towel. Given Nox's year behind the bar, Emily had eighteen months of experience with patrons under her belt or, rather, atop her. Emily pulled Nox's hair away from her face, holding it as she finished dry-heaving. Her hands dropped from Nox's hair only when the threat had passed.

"It gets easier," Emily said, rubbing her back lightly in soft, circular motions.

"Has anyone ever died while inside you?" Nox spat into the pot, not lifting her eyes. She took a drink of the water, swirled it into her mouth, and spat again.

Emily kept her voice soft and compassionate, hands

still moving in comforting circles. She smiled. "Me? No, I can't say I'm so fortunate."

Nox glared up at the gentle joke from where she clutched the pot.

Emily continued rubbing her back. She let her eyes drift toward the wall as she looked into a memory. "When I was first here," she said, "a girl did tell me about an elderly gentleman who had dropped dead from the sight of her tits!" She smiled sadly, as it was one of their favorite stories to tell in their hellhole. "I do think she may have been embellishing, as he had been years overdue to go home to be with the goddess. His children were quite embarrassed to collect their father's body from a brothel."

Nox pressed her back against the wall and took another small sip of water. She used the damp towel to wipe her mouth and clean her hands before returning the soiled rag to Emily.

"Do you want me to stay with you?"

Nox eyed her freckled colleague. She shook her head.

"No," she said, her voice flat. "I'm sure the Madame will want to speak with me."

"Okay," Emily agreed quietly. She left her hand on Nox's back for a minute longer. "Please call on me, though. If you want to talk, or want company, or..." She didn't finish her thought. Slowly, she rose to her feet and left Nox where she remained near the pot. "I'll be right back," she promised.

Emily left the cup of water beside her reluctantly deflowered friend and disappeared for a few moments. She reappeared with Nox's nightgown, a pair of socks, and a robe made for warmth rather than the gauzy scrap of fabric intended for seduction. Emily cracked a window to allow fresh air to move into the space. The night was cool and damp, and always tinged with the coastal presence of salt. It was a welcome distraction.

Nox offered the ghost of a smile, and Emily departed, leaving her alone in the room with the memory of a dead man.

If Nox were honest, it was her heart, not her stomach, that recoiled at the night's events. As she checked in with her body, she felt a levity akin to the times she'd shot whiskey with patrons, enjoying the buzz beneath her skin. The sensation wasn't in her head the way alcohol blurred one's thoughts but, rather, in her tendons and her muscles, humming slightly in her limbs. She stretched her fingers and looked at them, almost expecting to see a change of some peculiar nature. She had nearly finished her glass of water and was feeling far better than she had any right to feel when Millicent entered the room.

"Well, you certainly managed to make your first night eventful."

Nox shook her head, dread and regret bubbling from her stomach into her words. She started, "I'm sorry, Madame. I have no idea—"

"How were you feeding before?"

"What?"

Millicent gestured for Nox to follow. They made their way down the now empty town house toward the Madame's office. Despite the fact that Nox had been under the Selkie's roof for over a year, it was only her third time in the space. It was precisely as ornate and gaudy as one might expect from a woman who wore jewel-toned gowns and black fur shawls. Millicent was too vain ever to remove her elbow-length gloves, lest she dirty her hands or expose them to sunspots. The woman covered nearly every inch of her walls with art, including a lavish oil portrait of herself commissioned in a rather flattering light. Statuettes, jewels, feathered quills, and even the taxidermied body of a snowcat with its exotic, speckled face forever frozen in a threatening snarl. The office would have been ridiculous had it belonged to anyone else. Millicent, however, fit right in like a dragon atop her hoard of treasure.

Nox wasn't sure what to do or why she was here. Still feeling the aching need to hold her knees to her chest, she sat near the desk and curled into a ball while Millicent continued scanning her shelves.

"Ah, here we are." The woman pulled a black-bound book embossed with gilded symbols from the wall. The Madame's elaborate ringlets bounced slightly as she sat in her high-backed chair across the desk from Nox. Millicent flipped through the pages until she found what she was looking for. Eyes twinkling triumphantly, she turned the book over and pushed it across the desk.

Nox looked at the Madame's feline grin, then down at the page. Her face twisted in confusion. She straightened her back and leaned closer to the book.

"What is this?"

Millicent shook her head as she said, "I think the question is, dear, what are *you*?"

Nox pulled the book closer to herself and read the entry in earnest. The passage started with a simple term, a definition, a territory, and a list of powers and ended with runes and wards for protection against and methods of defeat. Below that was a horrid illustration of a woman straddling a man, black wings outstretched, talons dug into the helpless flesh of the human male below as the creature arched in pleasure. The unmistakable drawing of the ghostly tendrils of his soul left his mouth as they were sucked out by the creature. It was a foul drawing.

"I'm not *this*!" Nox gasped.

Millicent rolled her eyes slightly. "Yes, the old tomes have a flair for the dramatic, don't they? However, I'm rather pleased to be the one to tell you: yes, you are."

Nox straightened further, slamming the book shut. Her eyes flashed with anger and disgust. She argued, "That's not possible! I'm not! I've never shown a single inclination toward this evil, this demonic—"

"Please, dear. 'Demon' is such a pejorative term. Such fae have been misunderstood for far too long. Don't let your ignorance betray you."

Nox's face twisted in disgust. Millicent couldn't be serious. This was absurd. It was appalling. It was blasphemous.

"You do know you're northern, yes?"

"I—"

"Do you possess a mirror, or did you think that you had the same pink, colorless cheeks of all of the other discarded orphans in Farehold?"

Nox blinked rapidly. She had known that she wasn't fully southern, but little else.

"The dark fae?"

"The northern kingdom and its fae are of Raascot, dear. My, my, how poor *was* your education?"

The air felt as though it had been sucked from the room.

Millicent pressed her fingertips together, repeating, "How were you feeding before tonight? I've been thinking it over while the men disposed of your handiwork. I have a theory or two, dear. Here at the house, I've considered that the validation and adoration of the men may have been sustaining you, however remedially. Their praise and affections, even from behind the bar, may have kept you going, though at a fraction of your potential. Even *I* didn't know why I found you so likable. I do wonder how much my own favoritism fed into your nourishment. Here I thought I'd just found a suitable protégée—not to say, dear, that you wouldn't make a splendid protégée, perhaps now more than ever."

Sickness struck Nox again. Just as before, it was a nausea of the heart manifesting in her stomach. Her physical body still hummed, insisting upon its contentment. Despite the fact she had just consumed a large glass of water, her mouth felt dry.

"I don't understand."

Millicent sighed impatiently. "Farleigh, dear. I'm asking about your orphanage. You didn't have men fawning over you, did you? Did you enjoy some puppy love with any such fellow? I'm just dreadfully curious how you've managed to stay in the shadows as a damned virgin! Think of it, a goddess-damned succubus under my own roof, the roof of a brothel no less, already twenty-one, and still a *virgin*! I don't know if I've ever heard anything as comical! Such a peculiar accomplishment, yours is, my dear."

Nox shook her head against the cruelties Millicent was saying. The ornate walls of the office swam. What sort of horrible lies were these to tell her in the wake of such trauma? What had she ever done to deserve this brand of emotional turmoil?

"I'm part demon?"

"Well, are you part demon or are you part stupid? We're a year in, dear, and I've never known you to be daft. I'm asking you a question. Do try to keep up."

Nox had no desire to speak, but her mouth moved of its own accord. She answered, "I guess the matrons always favored me? I was set apart from the others while the Gray Matron kept me for her personal errands? Is that what you mean?"

Millicent considered the answer but remained dissatisfied.

"You have an inherent ability to make people fall in love with you, Nox. Now that I think about it, even your name makes more sense. Who was it that called you 'Night'? Was it the matrons?"

"No." She shook her head, feeling her long, black hair as it moved against her chin, her shoulders, down the middle of her back like a thick, silken curtain. Her hair had always been her favorite feature. It made her look like the shadows themselves. "I'm told it was the only thing my mother ever gave me. It was her parting gift before she abandoned me."

"Well, I don't suppose she would have known what to do with you. A fae wouldn't have dropped you in Farehold, which means your father must have been the fae. It's lucky, really. You've been able to hide in plain sight. You would have been sired by a northern fae—"

"A dark fae."

"Pishposh, dear. You'll come to find the world isn't so black and white. Whatever it was that kept you nourished, I'm glad for the love in your life that sustained you for the seventeen years before meeting me. We wasted a year behind the bar, but no more time lost, dear! I don't know if the matrons could truly have achieved such a feat, but you kept yourself alive long enough to bring you here to me. Believe me, dear, you've been running at a tenth of your potential. Now that we know what you are and what you're capable of…oh, the world is just opening up for you."

Nox swirled within herself, fingers of her mind gripping like oil against metal. Nothing about Millicent's office was grounding. The colors and sparkles and sheen on the woman's gilded bobbles only added to the kaleidoscope Nox felt, as though the floor were rocking, as if she'd been stashed in the belly of a ship without her consent. She didn't know what to do, what to think, what to feel.

Nox didn't know where to go, but she didn't want to stay here. She didn't know if she could truly leave, but at the very least, she had to get out of this office. She stood, holding her robe closer to her sides.

She found her voice again, utterly disgusted.

"What is the point of this—of a creature like this? Why would I do this? Why would something be created to murder?"

Millicent nodded thoughtfully, still looking down at the book. "Yes, the murder is something we can work on. But that's barely half of it! You're missing the point! Look, my dear." The vanilla-scented woman rounded her desk.

Goddess, how Nox had grown to hate that smell.

Millicent rested two hands on each of Nox's shoulders and guided her to an ornate glass oval on the wall painted with two figures—one sporting an embellished updo of yellow curls and jewels, standing beside a truly stunning girl young woman with shimmering bronze skin and hair as inky as night. She looked at the metallic sheen of the painting for a moment. One was clearly the Madame, but the other...

Nox gasped audibly at the face that stared back at her, watching the berry-dark lips of the reflection part in synchronized surprise. It was not a painting but a mirror. The dark-haired woman within it was utterly alien. She hadn't recognized herself at all. Nox had never been plain, per se. Her features had always been pleasant—likable, to be sure. People had never lost their breath when they looked at her. No one had flung a hand to cover their mouth the way they had when they saw Amaris's frosted features. But this...

Could this truly be her?

The young woman who looked back at her in the mirror vibrated with a terrifying beauty. Her long, black hair came alive, as glossy and dazzling as the star-drenched sky. One could trip into her eyes, tumbling into the coal-dark trenches at the bottom of the ocean. Her lips, her breasts, her hips all seemed fuller somehow. Her skin glowed with a secret fire burning just beneath its layers, setting her aflame.

She was breathless. "It makes me beautiful?"

"Oh, my dear." Millicent's voice was barely a whisper. "It makes you powerful."

Twenty-Three

DELICIOUSLY BUZZED, A DAY-DRUNK AMARIS STUMBLED her way from the dining room up toward her chambers. She felt the bright pop of the bubbles as they continued to warm her belly, body tingling from the ale. Ash had seen her leave and chased after her, waving off the good-natured reprimands of his friends and fellow reevers as they scolded him to leave her alone. He'd downed just as many pints as his sparring partner, even if he hadn't earned them the way she had.

She'd heard him get up from the table and rolled her eyes good-naturedly, not bothering to look over her shoulder at him as she wandered off. She enjoyed the taunting from the other reevers, appreciating that they had her back, even if she didn't mind Ash's company. All of the reevers were uniquely bonded to their sparring partners, although their relationship their particular relationship had taken on an unusual flavor.

The coppery young man's feet were quiet as he padded out of the dining room and trotted down the hall. They both knew she was headed to her room. While the rest of the reevers had relatively small accommodations in the keep, hers was big enough that she never felt like leaving her sacred space.

"M'lady." He jogged up to her, offering his bent elbow. She smiled and accepted it. His muscles were firm beneath her hands. She always enjoyed his presence.

"Any bruises?"

"These days? Always. If you don't stop kicking my ass, I'm going to have to find a new sparring partner."

"But then how will you ever get better?" She winked.

Amaris rested her head on his shoulder briefly as they walked, her vision swimming from the alcohol in the afternoon sun that lit the hallway. He beamed down at her, his bright, ember features glowing from the beer in his belly. The high from the morning's exercise hadn't hurt either.

"Are you studying today?" he asked, his question heavy with ulterior motives.

She lifted her head and looked at him suspiciously. She didn't miss a beat. "Are you asking if I'm looking for lessons on the male anatomy?"

He grinned, delighted. "As always, I'd submit myself as your subject for experimentation."

She gave him a shove, releasing his arm. She bit down a laugh, refusing to give him the satisfaction.

"You're something of a bastard."

"That I am, but one of these days you might just say yes."

"A man can dream, I suppose."

He feigned a bow. "I live to fight another day." Hands in his pockets, jolly from the drinks and the exchange, Ash sauntered off down the hall. She could have sworn he was whistling.

Amaris shut the door behind her and giggled. His jovial energy was contagious. She loved that his spirits remained as she knocked him to the ground time after time. In their years at the keep, she'd watched Ash grow from months of disappointment in pummeling a weakling to the pride and respect of watching his partner blossom into one of the reev's deadliest champions.

He'd been an excellent sport.

She peeled off her clothes and walked to the bathing room, leaving a trail of sweat-damp things on the floor. While she was treated exactly like a male reever in nearly every way that mattered, they had allowed her to keep one of the only chambers with an adjoining bathing room, just as she had her first few nights in the keep. She sank into the waters of her bath, soaking away any aches from the day's practice. She kneaded her tender muscles under the warm, soapy water.

Amaris dipped her head below the bath's surface and submerged herself entirely, running her fingers through her hair as the bathwater washed off the sweat, dirt, and grime. When she broke the bath's surface, she looked into the mirror she had mounted on the opposite wall. She'd found the reflective piece in the fortress in a stock room nearly two years ago, and though she'd inquired, none of the men claimed to have needed it. She smiled at the young woman who looked at her in the mirror, loving the muscles, the bruises, and the prominent pink scars that tattooed her stance for freedom.

She would never be able to thank the goddess for the way Odrin had been like the divine intervention of holy lore. The father figure may as well have been the All Mother, arriving in the flesh when needed most. Thanks in large part to Odrin and the swift intervention of his healing tonics, the scars from her fateful morning at Farleigh had healed as beautiful, clean lines. They were little more than pink tattoos to mark her otherwise frosted features.

She blew a few bubbles in the water and thought

absently of Ash, their exchange still fresh on her mind. Her sparring partner was dauntless with his endless, teasing offers to take her to bed. He'd had no trouble bedding many of the enthusiastic young women of Stone in his treks down the mountain for nights in the tavern. He'd become a good-natured, albeit incorrigible flirt. His amiable advances had made beating him in the ring all the more delectable. Nothing was quite as satisfying as rejecting a man and then kicking his ass.

Why not take him to bed?

She blew disinterested bubbles in the soap water, continuing to scrub at her body. She wasn't saving herself—not as the matrons had hidden her away, keeping her safe and untouched like the finest of decorative, porcelain teacups. Perhaps a roll in the sheets would be something worth experiencing just to be done with it. It would be the final straw in breaking the efforts the matrons had taken to trap her behind tempered glass.

Whether or not to take Ash up on his offers one of these days was a question she had asked herself on more than one occasion. He was impishly handsome, roughly her age, and her physical match in nearly every way. She was extremely fond of him and struggled to imagine life without his steady, lovable presence.

Amaris understood why she would continue to rebuff his advances, as amusing as they were. It stemmed from a deep, unspoken agreement between herself and the keep. They shared blood in their oath for a reason. They were family.

Amaris was a young woman brought into Uaimh Reev under the expectation that she would behave and compose herself like any other reever. They were meant to see her as a brother-in-arms. The men of all ages had grown to respect her skill, and she knew that they would fight beside one another in an unbroken trust, holding each other's backs to the death if ever the situation arose.

They appreciated her for her tenacity, her stamina, her skill, her memory, her wit, and her unwavering spirit—none of which implied she possessed any gender or sexuality whatsoever, as any family member should embody those. Her first year had been filled with bets over whether or not she'd give up and run off in the night. She'd never given them the satisfaction. Not only had she stuck it out but she'd lived and thrived long enough in the reev to watch their hearts fully open to her as one of their own.

Perhaps she also struggled with what it would mean to Ash if they were to truly tangle, even if the thought was secondary. Would it impact the way he saw her, or the way they trained? Could sex just for the hell of it be worth its complications?

Unlike the old gods in some of the other religions, the All Mother expected nothing by way of celibacy, and as such, the reevers were no saints. Many had taken lovers whom they saw in their travels. Some had married and started families, living out their service and keeping up with their training on the ground, away from the reev. Amaris was quite certain that one of her brothers had a male lover in Stone whom he spoke fondly of, carefully avoiding pronouns when speaking of the man around Grem the bladesmith's backwater beliefs. But her brother's identity and proclivities hadn't made him look for sex within the keep's walls amongst his reever brethren any more than hers should. Maybe that was why Ash found it fun to flirt, as he, too, knew the unspoken agreements to keep the hewn reev as an escape from the world below with its entanglements. Knowing they shouldn't, knowing they couldn't… Well, maybe that was half of the fun.

The bubbles had popped and the water had started to

cool, telling her she'd been in the bath for long enough. Whatever questions she had could be dealt with on the bed, amidst a midafternoon catnap.

She toweled off from the soapy water and changed into loose-fitting clothing. Amaris braided her damp, silvery hair with deft fingers. She hadn't truly intended to sleep, but the alcohol convinced her that lying down was for the best, if only for a moment. Between the pleasant hum of the ale, the exhaustion of the afternoon's exercises, the joy of the victory, and the glowing, internal chemistry of the exchange that had gone unrealized between her and her sparring partner, she was tugged beneath the dark waves of rest before she realized what was happening.

✦

Cinnamons and plums filled her nose. Without opening her eyes, some piece of her knew she must be asleep. This was no perfume. The decadent smell was all-encompassing. Forbidden. A memory she'd hidden away. This scent was the sort of trigger that tugged at the box she kept locked within herself, a pain and past that she refused to open in the light of day.

Amaris struggled against the urge to open her eyes, knowing it couldn't be real. The internal debate raged within her as she felt the press of skin, the sweet scent of familiarity—a cloud of love and hope surrounding her. Her eyes fluttered open as she decided she didn't care. It felt real. Goddess, it felt so achingly real.

She wasn't resting on the cotton pillows of the keep. Instead, her cheek was pressed into soft, tanned skin as the anticipatory titillation from the way her fingers had wandered in the bath carried her on its waves into a pleasantly charged dream. She allowed her eyes to remain closed even in sleep as she inhaled, breathing in the scent that had been too painful to remember. She hadn't allowed herself to think of its owner. She'd done her best to cage all memories of the girl who had held her, enveloping her in the spices that swirled around her now.

"I've missed you," the one who owned the plum scent said. Her voice was low. It was a dark, sweet sound that Amaris hadn't heard in years anywhere but her sleep, though even the dreams were painful. The sentence was punctuated with the gentle kiss of soft lips into her hair, nearly against her temple. Amaris exhaled slowly as she absorbed the sensation. This was not a friendly kiss. This was not the familial kiss of a childhood companion.

There was something distinct, new, and intimate about the way these lips brushed against her.

"Nox," she murmured.

Amaris's breath hitched. Her heart skipped at the press of Nox's mouth against her hair. A silvery spike of nervous excitement tingled down her spine, rousing her from her dreamlike state. Amaris inhaled again, allowing the dark spices to consume her as she nuzzled against the exposed skin of Nox's collarbones and sternum and the pillow of her chest.

Amaris's eyes fluttered open. She turned to look at the owner of the lovely voice. Part of her wished she hadn't.

Amaris knew what Nox looked like. She had been her best friend for years. She had been the source material for many of the portrait drawings Amaris had done under the supervision of the matrons. She'd seen her face more times than she could count. Even still, she'd done her best to quiet her gaze when it had wandered in the orphanage. Amaris had regarded Nox's features, pausing her treacherous heart when it had suggested a want for more. She quieted the voice, damning it for its thoughts.

Her heart cracked. She knew for the second time that she must be dreaming, for everything was different. Nox looked more beautiful, more powerful, more ethereal. It was all evidence of a dream.

"You look different" was all Amaris said. She felt sad at the thought. Had it really been that long? Could she have possibly forgotten Nox's features? She knew this young woman. She knew her better than anyone in the world, and everything she saw was off somehow. Too pretty. Too glowing. Too different. Her mind must be filling in gaps with new qualities, forgetting the friend who'd loved her altogether.

Nox smiled, but the twitch of her lips did not reach her eyes. Her hand moved tenderly amongst Amaris's hair.

"Time will do that."

Amaris's eyes flitted around the room, but she felt no urgency to leave. They appeared to be in Farleigh, but they were not in the familiar multi-cot dormitories. They reclined together in one lone, large bed that rested against the far wall of the dorm room. There were no noises of children or echoes of company in the hall. They seemed to be utterly alone, the privacy as nerve-racking as it was intimate. The sheets were not the scratchy, cheap starchy linens of the orphanage but a soft, organic cotton that felt extravagant against her legs. Her nightdress was lovelier than anything she'd had the pleasure of owning. Its straps were barely more than threads as it seemed to hold itself together on mere prayers rather than fabric.

Misremembering Nox felt like a betrayal. It was painful. Dreams were meant to be a reprieve, but in a way, this was too lovely to be more than a nightmare. The hurt she felt threatened to unleash everything she worked hard to keep under lock and key.

"I don't want to miss you anymore," Amaris said, voice thick with emotion.

Nox arched her brow curiously. "There are two ways you can stop missing me."

"How?"

Her voice was soft, almost cooing as she closed her large, dark eyes slowly, then opened them again. "You can forget about me, though I hope you won't, because I could never let you go. Or you can wait, and I will come find you. I'm going to find you, Amaris," she promised. Her fingers moved from where they'd been in Amaris's hair and gently cupped the side of her face, one thumb tracing softly down the length of her most prominent scar. "You look different too, you know."

She swallowed, echoing the sentiment. "Time will do that."

Amaris raised her body from where it had rested comfortably against the soft curves of Nox's soft curves. The young woman before her was nothing like the childhood friend she remembered. She was fifteen the last time she'd truly curled against Nox. She had been weak, unmarred, and naive. Now she was a scarred, war-ready adult. She felt a knife through her heart as she eyed the dark-haired girl beside her, thinking of all that had changed. Amaris twisted her torso to truly soak in Nox's features.

Her eyes grazed over the edge of Nox's jaw, following the curve that drew a line from her ears to her bare shoulders. She shouldn't let her eyes dip, she told herself, but she did it anyway. Amaris's gaze dropped to the sharp collarbone and the thin collar of the silken nightdress that rested just barely covering the peaks of her breasts. Her gentle lines curved in an hourglass as her waist released its arc in lovely, wide hips. Nox's lips were parted against her quiet breath.

Amaris leaned her body toward her beautiful counterpart, but she was not closing the distance between them for an embrace. An ache in her belly clutched at her, lower and more primal than hunger. It was like thirst. It was curiosity and questions and yearning tingling against her lips and tongue. She felt an unfamiliar need tug at her as she looked at Nox. Maybe it was because she'd fallen asleep after Ash's invitation to come to bed and the unrealized anticipation she'd built alone in the warm waters of her bath. Maybe it was something else entirely. All she knew was that she wanted to be closer.

"I've missed you too" was all Amaris could say.

It was true. She'd missed her more than she allowed herself to believe. She could never let it go, or forget, or move on. It was a memory too painful to explore. Nox's face was one that conjured too much hurt, too much confusion. In the real world, Amaris had needed to seal the suction-cupped tentacles of her vicious emotions, clamping them into a locked safe inside of her in order to function. In some other, imagined world, the girls had successfully run away together and escaped into the forest. In that world, the Madame had never found them. There'd been no reevers, no matrons, and no distance to part them. In another world, they'd be in the same bed tonight instead of Amaris's dreams.

Nox dragged a slow finger from Amaris's forearm to her elbow, up her arm. The gentle scrape of her fingernail was hot and cold all at once, raising goose flesh on her arm and sending shivers down Amaris's back. It caused her stomach to clench and her throat to constrict. Her breathing trembled, staggering as she exhaled. She was conflicted. Part of her wished Nox would stop, wished that she wouldn't stoke the fire and exacerbate this unrequited want. The other part of her silently pleaded with her to continue.

The finger drew its path over her shoulder, tracing the figure along the lines of her neck, her jaw, and landing on her chin. Amaris's heart rate increased as she stopped breathing. She'd watched Nox's finger with a shy, confused anxiety at first as it had navigated between her wrist and elbow, but as it crept along the lines of her throat, she'd felt her eyes drift to a close and a soft sound, almost a moan, escape her lips. When the finger made it to the space beneath her chin, Nox had flexed her index finger inward, tucking a single knuckle beneath Amaris's chin.

Amaris understood the intent and obeyed, opening her eyes once more. How could she feel so deliciously powerless in her own dream? Vulnerability and uncertainty consumed her with incomprehensible craving. Maybe it was that her subconscious knew that between the two of them, Nox would always be their leader. She knew the steps to the dance, and all Amaris wanted was to follow the music that only they heard.

Amaris looked up at Nox through hooded lashes. She willed herself to breathe as Nox lowered her body closer, but the reever couldn't seem to remember how to summon air to her lungs. She'd forgotten how to inhale. Her lips parted as adrenaline surged through her. Her heart flitted like the pitter-patter of rain falling in one thousand places all at once as anticipation coursed through her.

Nox paused barely an inch above her mouth, allowing their breath to intermingle. As one breathed out, the other breathed in, junipers melding into plums, fresh winter into cardamom, cinnamon, and saffron as tense, warm air exchanged between them. The electric charge that coursed through them was as intoxicating as any drink that had ever entered her system. Her eyes closed again as she felt herself lean forward with longing. She wanted Nox to close the hair-thin gap. She felt with the sharp inhalation of her breath that if it didn't happen soon, she'd suffocate under her own craving. Nox's mouth was so near, she could taste every spice. Her scent, her hair, her soft, supple frame pressed into Amaris as the space between them closed.

The rapping of knuckles drew her attention from her dream as if she had been held under water, only now yanked above the surface by her hair. The air caught in her throat as her eyes drifted over Nox's shoulder to the door beyond. She wanted the knocking to go away. She wanted the room to belong only to them. The sound grew sharper and sharper as Nox began to ripple. The ripple increased as the fabric of the dream tore at the seams.

✦

The door opened before she could answer. The entrance to the room in Farleigh bled into that of her bedchamber in the keep. Amaris blinked awake, struggling to distinguish imagination from reality as she jolted into an upright position. Her heart thundered from a flood of emotions. Her body felt strange, and her mind raced.

Amaris cursed violently in both surprise and confusion. She pressed herself up and determined that she was, in fact, in Uaimh Reev and not at the orphanage. She felt the indentations of fabric that carved red, telltale grooves from her nap. She swallowed hard against the lump in her throat but found herself in need of water, the same way her body felt in need of a different brand of quenching.

She glared at the door as it swung on its hinges. This was precisely why she never loitered in her room in various states of undress. The boys knew nothing of privacy.

"Sorry! Were you sleeping?" Malik asked. Such a friendly, harmless question.

Malik and Brel let themselves in, Brel with a pastry

in each hand and Malik with a glass of water and a smile. Brel offered her a pastry and climbed up onto her bed, intending the other freshly baked good for himself. The child was almost thirteen now and had finally grown comfortable spending time with her. They'd become pals in their time together, and she was quite confident that she was the child's very best friend. She wanted to yell at them but knew nothing was their fault. It had only been a dream, after all.

Amaris did her best to smile at them. She wiped the sleep from her eyes and blinked at her friends.

Malik set the water on her desk. "Still drunk?"

She shrugged. It was a nonanswer, but he didn't seem to mind.

"I thought as much! We can't have you hungover for our rematch tomorrow. When I beat you, it must be fair and square. I didn't see you drinking any water between your beers. As for the kid here," Malik said, ruffling the boy's hair, "Brel needed an extra hand. One for you and the other for himself. It would have been *nice* if someone had brought *me* a pastry."

She shook any remnants of her dream from her mind. Nox was not in Uaimh Reev. Amaris was not in Farleigh. Two of her reever brethren were in her room, and they needed her attention far more than any demand of her sleeping mind, no matter how alluring its pull. Amaris smiled sleepily at the boys, rolling her eyes at their fussing, and selected the pastry in favor of the glass of water. Malik saw himself out with a happy parting gesture.

Amaris had kept a bestiary tome by her bed, as studying the dark creatures of the world had become a favorite fascination of hers since her arrival at the reev. There was a baseline knowledge required of all reevers regarding monsters and demons, but she'd developed a rather particular obsession with a favorite zoologist, digesting everything written by the fastidious fae, learning everything there was to know about the continent's beasts.

Brel sat on her bed to spend his time in companionable silence. She'd adapted, learning how to talk to him and hold daily conversations, despite his parents' actions preventing him from verbally responding.

Amaris grabbed the tome and turned her book to Brel. She did what she could to involve him in friendly exchanges. She slid a small, mostly blank notebook that she'd kept on her desk to the space beside him on the bed.

"Have you ever seen any of the creatures in the zoology book?" she asked. Amaris held the bestiary up, showing the boy some of the more frightening pictures.

Brel wiped the pastry crumbs on his pants. She'd offered it to him to flip through, but he didn't need to look at the pictures.

Without hesitating, he wrote, *Yes.*

Her eyes widened. He'd been so young when he'd arrived, and she didn't think he ever left the reev. She spoke her questions, and he penned his answers. She flipped through pages and began to gesture while asking, "Which one?"

He took the book from her and flipped to a picture of a vageth. It was a canine with amphibious features, the smooth skin of a salamander.

Amaris stared at the jutting shoulders and sharpened talons of the creature. It had the typical, large eyes of a predator on the front, then three, smaller beady eyes decorating the outside.

Amaris asked, "Can you tell me the story?"

Brel considered it for a moment. He took the quill and wrote his response.

When Corsoran took me from my village to this keep, we saw three vageth in the woods.

Amaris frowned at the brevity of his story. She knew two things to be true. The first was that she had never met a man named Corsoran. The second was that the blood of the vageth contained a poison that made infected wounds impossible to heal, with or without healing tonic.

"Do you know what happened to him?" she asked quietly, not sure she wanted the boy to relive his traumas.

Brel scribbled in the notebook for a moment, then turned the page so Amaris could see.

He beheaded and buried all three vageth but was scratched in the fight. By the time he got us back to Uaimh Reev, the injury was too bad to fix.

A reever could have survived a bite or scratch from a vageth if they'd avoided contact with its blood. As any good reever, he'd undoubtedly separated and buried the severed parts to prevent the demon from reanimation. She wondered if it had been Corsoran's thoroughness that had gotten him killed.

Her heart held so much heaviness for the boy. "I'm so sorry, Brel."

I'm not.

At her confused expression, he continued his penmanship in the space below his initial sentence.

He brought me here to be with my real family. I only knew Corsoran for three days. I barely have any memories of my parents or village before he showed up. I've known everyone at the reev for nine years. I will forever be grateful to him, but I will never be sorry that I was brought here. I'll be a reever someday. I'll have more brothers than anyone in my village might have had.

"And a sister." She smiled.

He shook his head.

You'll be my brother too.

Amaris had learned that sometimes when she was at a loss for words, it was best not to speak at all. She hugged him, and he tightened his arms around her in return. He was not yet old enough to feel embarrassed by her displays of familial love, and she hoped he'd always stay that way. She wondered how often the young boy received parental affection in the castle. It wasn't right for a child to grow up without hugs or gentleness. While everyone in the keep was exceedingly kind to the boy, she hoped he was getting the full and happy life he deserved.

After all, every child deserved unconditional love from their family for exactly who they were, not for who they hoped their child might be.

PART THREE

The Many Faces of Demons

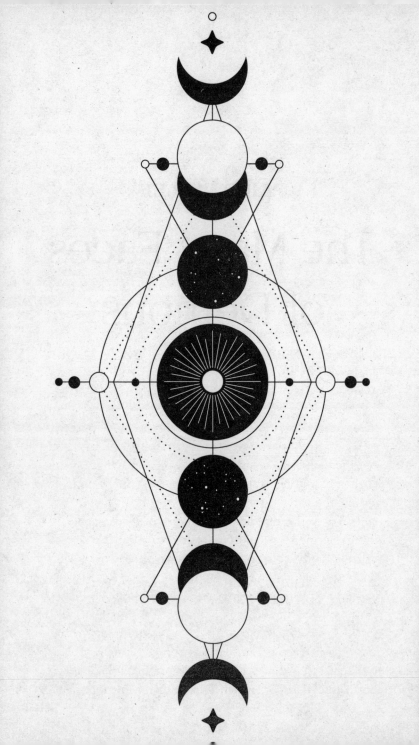

Twenty-Four

A MARIS ARRIVED AT THE RING THE FOLLOWING DAY, ready to start their run. She was already stretching her arms above her head and loosening her legs as she approached a small, seated group of reevers. She frowned as she drew closer, realizing it was not a running party at all.

Samael was the only reever who didn't participate in the morning exercise in torture. He claimed that after the others lived for over a thousand years, they could also sit out the daily run. His presence alerted her to the abrupt change in routine. Instead, Samael was holding a meeting against the early colors of morning. Odrin, Malik, Ash, and two of the middle-aged reevers had beaten her to the gathering. It would be a warm day, but the air was still pleasantly cool in the first hours of dawn. A light breeze moved her hair around her shoulders. She reached behind her head to begin tying it into a low, loose knot as she took a seat.

"I'm sending five of you down the mountain today," Samael was saying, "and I'd like you to leave as soon as you've had breakfast. I'll need Grem and Odrin to go north into Raascot, which I can explain in more detail once Grem arrives. Malik, Ash, and Amaris, you'll be going to Aubade. I need you to take an audience with the southern queen."

"We're traveling together?" Amaris asked. "Aren't reevers normally dispatched alone?"

Samael nodded, saying, "Sending you out in teams has just as much to do with the distance as it does the task at hand. You're all needed to meet with the continent's regencies, and I think Amaris might be particularly silver-tongued in getting the queen to listen to our cause."

Samael barely let his eyes linger long enough to convey the gravity of his meaning.

No one knew what she was, or what she could do. She wasn't even sure she knew herself. For years, Samael had kept her secret. No one in the keep had learned of her gift, and she had been careful never to wield it. Even Ash only knew he had been paired with her for their ages—not for any influences of persuasion to which he might be less susceptible than a full-blooded human. Perhaps that was why all three of them needed to go to Aubade. Ash could keep her in check should she need to begin barking orders to the humans around her. Similarly, Malik and his open, honest features would provide an excellent human buffer for any suspicion two nonhumans might draw.

"The south has been accusing the north of sending their forces into its lands for years, but now we've gathered enough intelligence to learn that the queen plans to act. There's a very good chance that Moirai is one bad day away from genocide."

"And Grem and I are to go to the king to see if he is indeed intentionally sending his forces southward?" Odrin asked, his gruff voice matching his raised brows as he clarified. His gaze flashed briefly to Amaris, and she wondered if he wished they were traveling together. He'd been her rescuer, her teacher, and the only father she'd ever known for years. They hadn't spent any time away since he rescued her from Farleigh.

"Indeed," Samael confirmed. "As you know, one of our men has been on an intelligence mission in Raascot, just outside of Gwydir, for the last decade. He has acted as an ambassador and held the peace in the north for a long time, checking in semi-regularly with his letters. He sent a message by raven insisting on an in-person meeting to explain his findings."

Malik looked between them before suggesting, "As Ash's father is in Gwydir, perhaps he should be on dispatch north?"

"I have no desire to visit those northern bastards."

"Don't be so narrow-minded as to conflate the north with your displeasure for your father," Samael said. It was one of the few times Amaris had seen him show no patience or sympathy. Unwavering, he continued, "I need you on this southbound mission. I also need you to have confidence in my reasons for entrusting you to accompany this party to the queen's city."

Ash looked profoundly unhappy with Samael's response but said nothing more. Malik was too excited for the somber occasion, but she knew he'd been on relatively few missions and was eager to wet his sword again.

"We are the stronghold for the continent."

Ash laughed. "There's twelve of us."

"Thirteen, now," Amaris amended, smiling.

So she was to get to Aubade and—what—command the queen not to kill people? It wasn't a particularly elegant plan, especially when her comrades didn't even comprehend the bare bones of it, but she trusted that Samael had known when he met her that she might be needed for just such a time. Her gift was needed to fix the world, but Amaris thought that even if the mission went awry, she could always use the curse of persuasion to have Moirai hand over the crown and begin her life of luxury.

✦

Odrin had done his best to allow her full independence, particularly seeing as how Amaris was a full reever and more than capable of handling whatever responsibilities the title required. Still, in their moments before departure, he'd run through the list of items with her like a father might for his daughter. How many healing tonics had she packed? What was her weapon count? Did she remember that most body heat was lost through the ground overnight? Had the kitchen given them enough dried foods that traveled well? Did she remember that the church was obligated both to fund and to shelter the reevers whenever they saw them, as they'd long been the firm sword of what was right and good, keeping peace through a constructive hand in a way that was free of the politics of the land? Finally, Odrin had insisted that she take Cobb. The dappled gelding hadn't really been his horse, after all.

Grem and Odrin saddled two of the broken-in pack horses that had served the keep for many years. Malik and Ash chose the mounts more for riding than for supplies, as the three of them had farther to go and a shorter window of time to get there if the queen was coiled to strike at any given moment. While Samael and the others bade them farewell from the keep, the two traveling parties wouldn't split until they reached the bottom of the mountain.

Descending the mountain took on an entirely new flavor when she knew she wasn't about to turn around and run back up again. Every pebble, every step, every gust of wind from the valley below seemed to echo nervous, excited energy. Grem grumbled about his headache for half of the trip down their mountain's steep slopes and how the summer sun was a hangover's worst enemy. Amaris recalled her first time walking up the mountain, shoes filled with blood, picking her footing in the dead of night long ago. The trip down the mountain in the morning light was much quicker than her climb up by moonlight had been.

The steep trail began to level as they rejoined the tree line and made their way onto the continent. The path that had connected them to the fortress let off just outside of Stone, stopping near a crop of pine trees and concealed by the backside of a hill from the prying eyes of nearby people.

The groups said their parting words at the trail's base, with Odrin hemming a bit as they meant to leave. Amaris decided to close the gap for the both of them and threw her arms around the wonderful, good-hearted, bearded man. She tightened her arms around his neck.

"Thank you," she said, chest tight with emotion, "for everything."

He seemed caught off guard and eventually lowered one arm into an awkward half hug. He smelled of tobacco and freedom. They were scents she would miss, not knowing when she'd see her father again. The crinkles in his eyes and calluses on his hands were the familiar features of the one who had saved her on the worst day of her life. The comfort of his presence felt like home. An embrace may not have been a natural instinct for the older reever, but when Amaris pulled away, she saw the fullness of his heart.

"You truly are a she-bear," he said, voice thick with an unrecognizable emotion.

The look of pride on Odrin's face was one she'd never forget.

Amaris had learned from her time at the keep that

Odrin had once had another family. They didn't speak of it, save for the knowledge that he'd had a wife he'd adored and a child he'd lost. She knew that it was a brief time in his life filled with love and sliced brutally short with the edge of a sword. She was his family now, and she hoped being in his life had played some small part in healing a wound too unspeakable to discuss, just as he had done for her.

The time had come. She was a true reever and ready for her first dispatch.

They didn't look over their shoulders as they mounted their horses. Amaris patted Cobb on the neck. Though she'd visited the docile horse in the stable now and again throughout the years, she hadn't had reason to ride him until now. Brel had attended to the horses, and other reevers had exercised them when they'd gone into villages or on missions. Amaris hadn't had cause to step foot outside of the keep for anything other than her daily runs in a long, long time.

As Cobb was a good, broken-in horse, he needed very little guidance or correction. This was fortunate, as she quickly revealed to Ash and Malik that, while Amaris had grown up in proximity to horses in their stable at Farleigh, she'd only learned how to ride sidesaddle as a proper lady. When she'd arrived at the fortress, her time with Odrin had been on the back of the saddle.

"Heels down, keep a straight line, shoulders back, stomach in—"

"Goddess damn it, Malik, I'm trying to ride a horse, not learn how to do a ballroom dance! I've got it!" she grumbled. In the midst of her insistence, her jerking motion made Cobb veer slightly from the path. He stumbled into the grass beyond the road, and she struggled to get her mount in line with the others. The boys did their best to conceal their smiles, but she saw the controlled twitches of their lips. She was glad they'd walked their horses down the mountain so Odrin hadn't been the one to watch her embarrass herself.

"Are you going to let me finish?" Malik asked.

She grumbled something hateful as he kept his horse straight, looking at her with a bemused expression.

"Soft hands. That's all I was going to say. Keep your hands relaxed as they hold the reins unless you actually want your horse to turn. And just be conscious of how you use your seat. Since you're armed, if you twist wrong, your sword might tap his hip and spook him. But mostly, the hands thing. Watch your hands."

She wasn't thrilled that she'd made a fool of herself, but the feeling subsided. It didn't take long for her to get the hang of it as they urged their horses between walking and trotting throughout most of the first day. After much trial and error, they were ready to stop for the night.

The ground beneath the road to the city of Aubade was pressed into parallel lines from the carriages that needed to make their way to and from the royal city to the villages of the continent. Despite the mild weather, they spotted no travelers on their day of riding. No matter how empty the route that connected the kingdoms may have seemed, they didn't dare risk being discovered in the night as they slept.

Perhaps it was just because it was her first dispatch, but Amaris thought she might be too excited to sleep. She hadn't wanted to stop for the night, but she conceded as the boys urged them from the road.

The three led their horses from the trail and into the woods, finding a clearing tightly enclosed with trees to shelter them from prying eyes. They tethered their mounts with long enough leads to allow the horses to graze and set off to scout the immediate area for any signs of animal habitation or creatures that they might not want to disturb. They'd been taught a pattern that they were to follow every night: brush your horse, ensure your weapons were cleaned and sharpened, set up camp, and secure the perimeter. They knew better than to light a fire after sundown, and fortunately, the warmth of the season was enough of a blanket as the three camped below the stars.

Having checked the perimeter, Amaris lay down for another uneventful evening. It would be another night with only the trees, the wind, and her thoughts.

Until it wasn't.

Twenty-Five

A MARIS OPENED HER EYES.
An eeriness soaked into her as she tried to understand what about the still, windless night felt so very wrong. The discomfort prodded her with unseen fingers, urging her to examine her surroundings. The night had cooled, and with it hung the fresh scents of the forest and its living vegetation. The slumbering shapes of Malik and Ash were scarcely discernible by the light of the moon. The horses were as still as statues. Had they heard something?

She strained her ears but couldn't discern any sounds. There was no nocturnal hooting of owls, no evidence of rodents foraging through the leaves, or even the flitting of insects. She didn't hear the trees, though she could see a slight breeze rub their leaves together. She'd been wrong. This was not a windless night. Why couldn't she hear the wind? Everything was far too quiet. Her heart quickened against the confusing realization, and she wondered if she'd fallen sick and lost the gift for hearing.

She brought her fingers to her ears, pressing her thumb and middle finger together to hear the gentle, papery sound of skin on skin. It was such a quiet gesture, one no one else would hear, but it was enough to let her know she had not gone deaf while she slept. Something else was happening. She hadn't been awoken by sound but by its sudden absence.

She reached for her weapons on instinct.

Amaris's dagger had never left the strap on her leg, not even in sleep. Her sword and bow were lying neatly beside her, both within arm's reach. Unwilling to break the pressing silence, she slowly rose to a crouch, fingers wrapping around the limb of her bow. She took one muted step away from the blanket on which she'd slept, then another. She followed an unknown sense as it angled her toward the trees, one silent motion at a time.

Like all reevers, she knew how to be stealthy. She'd been trained in the art of moving between breaths and keeping to the shadows. Their training exercises in ambush had ranged from fun games of hide-and-seek to the night-darkened slinking around the keep that had resulted in broken bones and the occasional light stabbing. Their covert nature of handling disruptions within the continent's kingdoms was part of what had led less-educated villagers into thinking of them as clandestine assassins rather than the silent peacekeepers of the realms they cunningly served. While nearly any reever would have known how to conceal the sound of their feet in the brush, Amaris's small size and lightweight agility had graced her with particularly feline movements.

She shot another glance at her slumbering companions and debated waking them. If she shook them from their sleep for the disturbance of a squirrel, she knew she'd never hear the end of it. She couldn't justify waking Ash or Malik just because it was too quiet. Similarly, if there was something more sinister in the forest, perhaps the sounds of them stirring would invite attack.

Reevers were typically dispatched alone, she told herself. She did not require their aid.

Silent as a shadow, she slipped from the clearing and into the trees. Though people had commented on her unique, lilac eyes for as long as she could remember, they'd proven relatively useless, in the practical sense. Despite Samael's insistence that she must possess some gifts of sight, they'd never offered her any ease when it came to seeing in the dark. While a supernatural edge would have been advantageous, she had spent years training to fight and stalk in the shade as well as in the sun. She'd reassured herself of this over and over, convincing herself she'd be fine. Whatever it was, she could handle it.

Amaris picked her steps carefully, moving through the thicket between the trees. She avoided fallen leaves, stepping around dried branches and avoiding the tugging fingers of thorny weeds to remain as imperceptible as what she currently sought. The pitter-patter of her heart was the loudest thing in the forest.

Her instincts insisted that she was headed in the right direction. She followed, trusting whatever unknown impulse guided her toward the night's disturbance. The tug told her not only that she was going in the right direction but also that she was closing in on whatever she'd sensed. If she didn't calm her nerves, she wouldn't be able to focus long enough to master whatever lay ahead. She cursed her thrumming heart yet again for betraying the anxiety she felt as she drew closer and closer to the unknown.

There was something brighter ahead. It was a break in the trees.

The moonlight washed the space ahead as if silver had been poured into a fishbowl and filled it to the brim. It was no grassy meadow but a clearing of bright, reflective water. The tree trunks encircling it were lit by the bright moon, acting as walls for the small bowl fishbowl of light in the otherwise darkened forest.

Her feet stopped of their own accord. Her senses spoke to her once more, and she listened.

Amaris paused as the tree line ended, several paces away from the pond. The silver light flooding the small clearing revealed everything, as the moonbeams didn't need to battle through a leafy canopy to illuminate what lay below. Her eyes scoured the small clearing from the hiding place where she'd stopped.

The smallest movement caught her eye.

The water of the pond was nearly still, but not quite. Something disturbed it, creating a ripple in the surface and preventing the glasslike reflection of the night sky that the body of water should have had for such a still night. She scanned the shores, following the tiny, silent waves to where a large, dark rock blotted out the light of the moon. The sphere of ripples seemingly emanated from the rock itself. Her eyes were focused on the rock as something—a branch?—extended from it.

The rock was strange, its offshoot even stranger.

Amaris stifled the urge to gasp as she realized she was seeing no rock but something living. The extension she saw was the thing's arm. She blinked, following the arm to its end as a hand filled a canteen with fresh water from the pond. The rock shifted to reveal that it was a wingspan, not a solid shape. The creature's wings had created the illusion of a solid figure while sheltering the form of a man beneath it. The glint of the moonlight was slowly revealing the enormous, crowlike feathered wings of whatever—or *whoever*—knelt at the pond.

Inhaling slowly to stifle her fear, Amaris reached for her weapon and, silent as death, nocked an arrow. She wished she'd spent more time on the archery range and less time on swordplay now that her life might very well depend on her ability to make her target. If she shot her arrow, she'd have only one chance. If she missed, the creature would be at her in a moment.

Amaris reached into her chest, willing her heart to still as she quietly stretched the bow's string, angling for the head of the demon before her. Her fingers shook, but she fought her tremble. She pressed the arrow's fletching against her cheek, keeping the string taut, as she took her aim for the creature's chest. The moment before release, she felt something cold on her neck.

The shape at the pond's edge moved slightly, but the distant creature was now the least of her worries. She was acutely aware of the precariousness of life as the sharp edge of steel pressed into her throat. Her throat bobbed against cold metal.

Amaris hadn't heard the second man approach. She hadn't heard anything at all. He moved too quickly for her to react. In a flash, one strong arm pinned her to his hardened body. She was rendered unable to twist free or grab for her weapons. He held her firmly with one arm while his free hand continued to clutch a knife to her jugular. One well-placed nick and she was dead.

Rage, confusion, and shock coursed through her as she begged for a plan, an instinct, a piece of training or knowledge that might help her, but no. Amaris had gone from ready to take down an enemy with an arrow to utterly powerless in the breadth of a second. She didn't even have the time necessary to experience panic. She was barely able to process the change as power shifted. She'd been rendered utterly helpless. She still held her bow aloft, but releasing her arrow would be assured destruction. The moment her hand let go, her throat would be slit.

"Put it down," the voice snarled into her ear with

low, dark authority. The sound of his voice flooded her with adrenaline while her other senses were assaulted by leather, pepper, and something like black cherries. His lips had nearly grazed her hair as he spoke. The assailant's breath on her ear sent a chill down her spine.

Amaris raced through her options. The stranger was too close for her to throw a punch, especially as both of her hands had been occupied with the bow. If she created the noise necessary to wrestle away, the demon who crouched at the pond would surely be upon them in a second, giving her not one enemy but two. She couldn't fight.

She had no choice. Her heart thundered under her breast as she slowly complied, lowering the bow.

The far-off demon continued filling his waterskin, completely unaware as to what transpired in the trees. He didn't look up from its place near the pond.

"There's a good girl," her assailant murmured somewhat dismissively, as if speaking to himself more than her in the same dark voice. He wrapped a large hand around the knife on her leg to pluck her remaining weapon from her grasp. He urged her forward with a step, forcing Amaris into the clearing. With the man still at her back, she became fully vulnerable as they abandoned the cover of the trees and moved toward the lip of the water. The demon looked up at them then, wingspan flaring behind him.

Amaris resisted the urge to close her eyes in fear. If she was going to die, she would die with pride. Her mouth dried, gooseflesh snaking up and down her spine as she winced in preparation for leathery skin, for jagged teeth, for a ridged spine, but instead she saw…a man. She blinked to ensure her vision was clear as she beheld a fae with dark hair dressed in hardened black leathers. She'd been expecting horrible, amphibious features, but instead she stood before a male who looked like he might as well have been a fallen angel. His darkened wings were not the membranous stretches of batlike skin from her bestiary tomes but resembled the tales of the seraphim and their unearthly beauty. The man who'd been kneeling at the water's edge folded his wings behind him cautiously as he approached Amaris and her unnamed captor. She still wasn't able to see who held her, but her chin remained defiantly lifted, and she arched her back away to keep from touching him.

One swift motion changed that.

The captor twisted her to look at him. Her hackles raised defensively as her back was now to the one she'd thought a demon, but she forced herself to look her captor in the eye. She was with not one fae but two. The only full-blooded fae she'd seen before this moment was Samael, and aside from the slender arch of his ears and too large eyes, this rugged fae looked nothing like him.

"I'll thank you not to hunt my men," he said, though once again, something about his voice sounded like he wasn't truly speaking to her. The assailant spoke to hear the sound of his own voice, grumbling with blackened agitation.

Amaris's lips parted slightly. She absorbed his features as she faced him in the moonlight. His black hair was darker than the night around them. His tanned skin and sharpened canines held a vague feeling of familiarity, though she couldn't name why. The shadow of his wings blotted out the view of the trees behind him, creating an obsidian halo around his face. He was beautiful. Truly, powerfully, extraordinarily beautiful.

She had never been more terrified in her life.

Amaris took a half step away from him, but the backward movement only brought her closer to the one who'd been at the water's edge. She pivoted sideways, a night-haired man now flanking her on either side. She raised her hands to create a barrier.

The one who'd held her still had her weapons. She was defenseless, save for her fists and borderline feral will to survive.

The demon with the waterskin spoke not to her but beyond her. His voice was gentle as he addressed the one who'd held the knife to her throat.

"I'm sure she was just afraid," he said.

The captor growled, "If I hadn't been there, you would have an arrow through your head."

"But I don't, do I?" the winged man replied, shouldering his canteen. He looked at Amaris and took a step. It wasn't a move to invade her space but one to put himself closer to his companion. She noticed with a somewhat furrowed brow that the positioning was meant to make her more comfortable. The closer they were to one another, the less trapped between the two of them she'd be.

The captor narrowed his eyes at his companion. "Does she look like an innocent village girl to you?"

They truly regarded her, eyeing her tunic with the supportive leather around her midsection meant to offer extra protection against blades. They saw her riding leathers, the holster where her dagger was sheathed, and the large scar tearing at an angle down her cheek and a second sliding down below the line where her shirt cut off, allowing the imagination to discern how deep the old wound descended.

"Who is she, and what is she doing stocked to the hilt with weapons in the middle of the night?" he asked. The captor gestured to the hand that still held the dagger he'd stolen. She wondered why they didn't ask her directly. It was rude, dismissive, and offensive. The longer they spoke, the more time she was granted for her fear to replace itself with anger. She didn't understand this particular brand of insult, but the fae were acting like she wasn't there. She could speak for herself.

Amaris burbled over with an infuriated question.

"Shouldn't I be asking you that? I protect the people from creatures of the dark that mean to sneak in and destroy them."

He smirked slightly, but it was barely one of amusement. His smile tugged as something else seemed to be flickering behind his eyes.

"Will you be doing any destroying tonight, Zaccai?"

"I hadn't planned on it, General, but I suppose we can see where the night takes us."

They were mocking her. He extended her stolen dagger back to her, hilt first. He was giving her the knife back? As he extended it to her, he paused, something akin to shock on his face. His body went rigid, peering at her—no, *into* her. She reached for the dagger, when the snap of a twig had them whirling. As he extended his hand, his expression changed.

"Wait," he breathed, eyes wide.

The one who'd been called general lifted a hand. He was choosing to ignore whatever approached to ask a pressing question. It was as if he was considering her for the first time that night, soaking in every stitch of her features.

"Can you—?"

"Drop!" someone shouted from the woods.

Ash's familiar voice barked the command from the tree line. He barely gave Amaris time to react before he loosed an arrow. Amaris flattened herself against the ground in a second, but she wasn't the only one who seized the warning. In the moment it took her to drop from the line of fire, Zaccai had grabbed for the general's attention. They were off with supernatural speed as they darted into the air. They dove back down into the trees with the inhuman speed of birds of prey. Ash sprinted out from the tree line to her, grabbing her by the arm and hoisting her to her feet. The pond was still once more. Her eyes remained fixed over Ash's shoulders on the space above the forest to where the fae had disappeared.

"Are you hurt?" he demanded.

She shook him off with growing irritation as she continued to stare at the sky where the fae had gone.

"I'm fine."

His face was still painted with contempt as he asked, "Did they take you?"

"No, I thought I sensed something in the woods. I followed that sense here."

Ash gaped. "Why didn't you wake me?"

His voice was breathless and angry. His flame-red hair, normally bound in a knot, was wild and loose from sleep. The sound of Malik's jogging crashed through the underbrush. He broke into the clearing to meet them. Amaris made no attempt to conceal her irritation. "I am just as competent a warrior as either of you. Reevers are meant to be perfectly capable alone," she defended. She looked to Ash, then to Malik from where he'd run into the clearing at the pond's edge. "I don't need your accompaniment when inspecting threats. Besides, if I had investigated the sound and found a mouse, you would have accused me of being a paranoid woman."

He scowled at her, lowering the bow he continued to angrily grip at the ready. Ash said, "I hope you don't seriously believe that of me."

The golden-haired Malik looked between his friends, his eyes bewildered.

"Is someone going to tell me what happened?" he asked.

"Amaris went off to confront a demon, apparently," Ash said, ripe with ire.

"It wasn't a demon!" she said, her tone climbing toward a yell. She held the dagger she'd been offered with one hand, the other open with emphasis. The moonlight glinted against the knife's steel, illuminating the pale intensity of her expression.

"Is now the best time to call the humanoid monsters by their right and proper name?" Ash asked, his temper flaring. "Are we fighting over semantics?"

"Listen! I woke up to…well, to a lack of sound," she said. She explained that the absence of noise was what had stirred her, and how she'd followed that sense to the clearing. Their faces had been skeptical at the beginning of her story, but it was decided that the winged men must have been using dampening magic to conceal themselves.

Malik considered this. He frowned. "You shouldn't be able to sense a dampener. That's the entire point of its power."

Ash shook his head. "Thank the goddess she did. What a sick magic. Ag'imni shouldn't be able to wield additional abilities. It would have to be stolen. Did they have any object? A ward? They're semi-intelligent, but I've never heard of them using tools.…" He shuddered violently. "Goddess damn it. For all we know, they were tracking us for just that purpose."

This didn't resonate as true with Amaris. She shook her head, saying, "I'm telling you, they weren't demons. I think they were just refilling their waterskins. If anything, I feel they were using their damper to avoid detection from people like us."

Malik smiled. "That's before they met Ayla. Who knew our oak tree could sense the forest of her namesake."

She was far from amused. Amaris's temper was little

more than an iron poker that had been left in the flame. It burned so hot, she was ready to let it scald anyone who touched her. Not only were they refusing to hear her, but doubling down on calling her the clumsy-footed nickname was an insult added to injury. Amaris uncrossed her arms and returned her dagger to its sheath. She forced herself into a semblance of calm, combing through the information.

"One of them was called Zaccai. Does that name mean anything to you?"

The men shook their heads.

"Ag'imni can speak, but I don't know of them having names. I suppose we don't know enough about them to consider their family structure, but I'm quite certain they're nameless," Malik said, face scrunched in a frown.

"I'm telling you what I heard," Amaris insisted.

The men asked her a few more questions about her encounter, but she offered only clipped, angry responses. They'd brushed her off with such entirety that she couldn't bring herself to say more. The depth to which they'd offended her with their dismissive refusal to believe continued to burn, an iron unwilling to leave the fire's coals. Her agitation wasn't the only peculiar sensation she felt. Something about the interaction with the winged fae had stirred in her, like a kernel stuck in her tooth that she couldn't get out no matter how much her tongue pushed. Something wasn't right.

She and her brethren knew of the night creatures and dark fae from their texts. They'd studied the ag'drurath and their hell-hewn wings, bodies slender and black like serpents, talons that could slice through armor, teeth that would shred and swallow your horse in one bite. What they'd seen were the humanoid counterparts to the snake-like dragon—the ag'imni—commanders of their serpent familiars. Reevers knew all of the descriptions regarding the unspeakable things they did to fill their stomachs on fae and men alike, their soulless bodies, and their blackened eyes.

But she knew what she'd seen.

The men fell into silence, allowing only the sound of their mounts, the saddlebags, the hooves, and the whinnying and chuffing of the horses to accompany them. The black sky lightened to the deep gray of a stormy sea, then indigo, then lavender, and soon the sun was up over the horizon, warming the land. While they continued their westward journey, her tongue kept pressing on the kernel, pushing her to understand the encounter. Her mind would not rest.

Twenty-Six

NOX WASN'T ABLE TO SLEEP, NOR WAS SHE REALLY trying. Her mind flitted rapidly from one thought to the next, an amalgamation of sounds and ideas and plans and memories. Legs wiggled restlessly as her finger thrummed against the mattress. Six musicians played different instruments and clashing songs simultaneously within her mind, their songs tumbling over one another, each vying for her attention. She tossed fitfully between her silken sheets, turning her pillow to find a cooler side.

Her eyes stayed open as they burned into the dark of the wall, thinking of what the duke had said. Yelagin. Forces were being dispatched to Yelagin. That was where she'd find information on the north. That was where she'd get her answers.

It had been two years since Millicent had lit the hateful torch within her for the northern kingdom. Two years of fitful nights, violent wishes, and dreams of vengeance. That's how long it had been since the Madame had told her everything, filling in so many gaps with vivid detail. A barmaid—an orphaned whore—hadn't been worth sharing the weight of her secrets, but someone groomed to lead beside her, on the other hand…

She tossed again, twisting the fabric between her fingers. One of the minstrels in her mind took the lead, the other sounds dying away as she focused her thoughts. The remaining song was that of the relationship that had dug its way into her life like a tick burrowing its head, the one between her and the lady of the Selkie.

Nox wouldn't forgive Millicent. She hadn't forgotten the loathing, the blame, the bitterness of chewed lemon rinds that filled her mouth whenever she thought of the Madame. Still, whether she liked it or not, she'd succumbed to the Law of Recency when it came to her feelings regarding the lady of the house. Perhaps it had been the familiarity of their now regular interactions. The informality of their relationship over the past two years had begun to smooth the edges of even her most awful memories of Millicent, leaving a begrudging companionship in its place.

A lot could change in two years.

Millicent had been mournful when she'd informed Nox of just how terrible the events had been in the courtyard. She'd hung the curled ringlets of her head in pity as she told the young girl that she had been standing on the cobblestones in front of Farleigh as the silver sprite had rushed from the house, intent on escaping to the woods. Nox had known Amaris had run. Nox had known that Amaris would do anything to avoid going to the brothel, and Millicent hadn't denied it. The Madame had paused sadly in her tale, murmuring over how Amaris had traded an unfamiliar devil for the one she could have known. The assassin had seen a vulnerable girl running for the woods and abducted her. The women in the courtyard had been helpless to stop it as the villain had swept her up amidst her cries.

Nox's memory pressed on, forcing her to relive every

detail. Millicent said she had shrieked for the matrons to do something, horrified that they had let such a man in their walls, but the agent of Raascot had urged his horse into a gallop and sprinted toward his northern borders. Millicent had sworn never to deal with Farleigh again after that, knowing now that they allowed men to take advantage of the young women they were sworn to protect. At the Selkie, she'd said, the women were empowered. It was a place where men and the blood of their bulges were merely a tool for money or, even more importantly, for information. The stupidity of the brutish sex was little more than a weapon for the cunnings of women.

The musician playing the song of Nox's memories took a bow, allowing another of the battling minstrels to take his place. Her restless mind shifted to her ever-evolving understanding of the world around her.

Nox saw life for what it was. She understood the divisions between the sexes and accepted places like the Selkie as the spy dens they really were. What better way to lure men in than to make them feel powerful, to lead them to a place where they thought they had the upper hand? How empty their heads, how blackened their hearts to think they were the ones with agency. The women who worked in the salon were underestimated, and the ability to hide in plain sight had been their truest strength, just as overlooking them was the patrons' greatest weakness.

Nox huffed against her sheets. She lit the bedside candle, giving up on the idea of sleep altogether. She left the comfort of her sheets, walking over to the desk that rested beneath her window. She had taken to sleeping naked, preferring the silk on her skin, but she wrapped a cashmere blanket around herself as she sank into the chair at the cluttered table.

The only thing that helped silence her thoughts was

pen and paper. The quill acted as a siphon, draining the chaos from her mind and channeling it into the manageable pages before her. She rested her elbows on the desk and let her fingers sink into her hair to let the funnel do its work, propping up her head as she stared at piles of loose-leaf pages all filled with cramped writing, diagrams, plots, drawings, and conspiracies.

Her desk was covered in notes and gathered information. Queen Moirai was demanding the duke's forces go northeast to the lakeside town of Yelagin. She briefly corrected the possessive pronoun in her mind—they had been his troops before tonight. They were her troops now. Nox a satisfied smirk curled her mouth when she thought of the lordling's slackened face and the puppet he'd become. Perhaps she was a demon, but she was a damn good one.

She returned her thoughts to the paper, scratching her questions in curling, slanted sentences.

Where else had the north been infiltrating, and what was their intent? How could she get her hands on someone high enough in their ranks to know where Amaris had been held for the past three years, and if she was even alive? She may not have known the best path forward, but she most definitely understood her end game.

Nox set down her pen, closing her eyes against the thought of a vulnerable snowflake living in the north. Because she was—living, that is. Somehow, despite going years without so much as a whisper of her silvery friend, Nox felt in her heart that she would know if Amaris's spirit had left the earth. The tug between them was a tethering bond. She knew it would snap her in two if it were severed by death.

Then she heard it. Something real. A sound that existed outside of discord within her mind. Something soft and gentle and comforting dragged her from her swirl of misery, bringing her into the present. Even before her knob began to turn, she knew who had come. The sound of her feet on the hall rug, the gentle way she twisted the handle, the ease with which she opened the door with every ounce of stealth were a sweet rush of relief.

Nox didn't need to look over her shoulder to know Emily was sliding into her room, clicking the door closed as quietly as she could. Five muted steps over carpet later, the supple, strawberry girl was at Nox's back. Emily put an arm around her loosely, brushing her lips against Nox's temple. Her full, soft breasts pressed into Nox's shoulder. The soft sweep of strawberry-colored hair tickled her bare skin.

The voice remained low and sensual in respect of the late hour, not wanting to wake anyone else in the house as she said, "I saw your candlelight."

"You should be asleep."

Emily kissed the side of her face, then pressed her lips softly to the empty space between Nox's neck and shoulder. Nox's tension ebbed as she allowed the intimacy, exhaling as the small pleasure pulled her mind away. Emily slid her hands slowly down Nox's arms.

Emily murmured against her throat, "I couldn't sleep."

"I can never sleep," Nox admitted.

Nox's heart would never belong to the freckled girl. Neither of them had explicitly said it, but they both knew. Still, the nights were long and cold, and the men who visited their chambers were sources of income, secrets, and power. Perhaps love could take many shapes and forms. Affection, companionship, and time didn't need to last forever to be meaningful.

"I can help," Emily whispered. "Let me help you sleep."

Nox's eyes drifted up to meet the bright, hopeful eyes that gazed at her. Emily was offering more than sex, and she knew it. Every time they connected, it was a bid to prove that she could fill the void in Nox's heart. She would make a wonderful partner. She was pretty and clever and compassionate. She'd had endless patience for Nox's guarded heart, her cagey answers, her wayward emotions. Nox didn't know much of what the male patrons thought of Emily's performance, but she was particularly skilled whenever they were together. And, Emily was right. She did know how precisely to help Nox unravel from the tight coils of the day.

Nox's brows pinched as she sighed.

Emily ignored the weak attempt at protest entirely.

"Come on." Emily pulled Nox back into her bed and she obliged, giving herself over to the tug as she abandoned her notes for the night. She dipped to blow out the candle at the bedside. Emily slid in first, lifting the covers. They tucked themselves between the silk of the sheets, Nox dropping the cashmere blanket from her shoulders before crawling in.

Emily's face wilted over the heaviness Nox carried, and Nox's heart squeezed with guilt over it. She didn't want the weight she carried to be a burden for her friend, her lover, her partner under the Selkie's roof. Life in the pleasure house didn't require new hardships. Perhaps Emily was too empathetic for her own good.

Emily kissed her deeply on the mouth, attempting to draw her mind away from the pain that plagued her. Her lips were an anchor keeping Nox in the present. It was working, as it always did. Emily used one hand to draw long, sensual lines up Nox's side. Whatever the quill was unable to siphon, their time in bed certainly could.

Nox sighed, feeling the effectiveness of the distraction. There was nothing more she could do for tonight by scouring notes and studying maps. Her mission would still await her in the morning. She allowed the door to her mind to shut, opening the one that belonged to her body alone. She let go of her troubles, choosing instead to use the hands that had clutched her worries and wrap an arm around Emily's full, curvaceous waist. She flipped the freckled beauty onto her back, appreciating the understanding face that looked up at her. Nox lowered her mouth slowly with her lips twitching upward in a smile, allowing herself a little fun, and a promised release, if only for the night.

✦

Infuriated heat rolled off Millicent as she paced in tight lines behind her desk.

Nox was decidedly bored by the woman's unimaginative brand of fruitless anger. She inspected her nails, pushing on her cuticles while she allowed the Madame her rather predictable outburst.

Millicent was going to wear the carpet bare if she continued marching in the small, lavish space. Nox stood, unimpressed, using her attention to pick phantom strings of fabric from the silken wrap around her shoulders. Agitation was an unbecoming emotion on the woman's face. It carved lines into her, betraying her age.

"I never meant for you to be the one to go to Yelagin," she said with clear exasperation. "Send his men and stay here, where we can continue gathering our forces."

"Our forces?" Nox asked. She narrowed her eyes slightly, looking up from her fingernails. She relaxed her back against the wall of the crimson fleur-de-lis of the Madame's office.

Millicent's anger did nothing for her.

"The forces you need! You'll need manpower if you intend to march north of the border. What do you have now, a duke and his men? A few merchants and their money? Why would you be so reckless! You can have it all! The manpower is at your fingertips! Stay here until we've convinced the Captain of the Guard to visit. I'm already sorting it out to send Emily to lure him to the Selkie. She was meant to go out later this week!"

Emily was an excellent lure, but Nox wasn't comfortable sending the girl into danger more often than necessary. This was not her fight, and it wasn't fair to continue using her. She knew that Emily would go whenever asked, particularly as Nox was involved, but the strawberry girl was fully human. She had nothing but her wits and prayers to protect her when she went out into the world to aid in their agenda.

With cool calm, Nox said, "I don't need the Captain of the Guard. What I need is information."

Millicent froze mid-stride. She trembled with her rage, looking like she might flip her desk. The Madame forced herself into stillness, an unusual practice for the mercurial woman. Her nostrils flared until she'd dragged in enough air to calm herself and find an authoritative tone. Nox watched all of this with the amusement of a single arched brow.

"You are being foolish. You're letting love blind you."

Nox was in no mood for Millicent's temper, nor could she be swayed by her scolding. The Madame was transparent and annoying. While Millicent had never been cruel to the girls at the Selkie, she wasn't exactly a joy as an employer either. Nox's mouth twisted dryly as she eyed the brothel's mighty Madame amidst her tantrum, knowing that she was privileged for her ability to disregard the rage altogether.

Nox had spent the last two years in a particularly advantageous position. After discovering her gift—or curse—Millicent had helped her to both cultivate and master it. For the first few months, the Madame had been a steadying force. Nox may have even considered the woman a mentor. Between Millicent's greed-laced avarice and Nox's power, they'd forged a tenuous alliance for their symbiotic destruction. As Nox learned more about the politics between the north and the south and the truth of Amaris's ensnarement, their plan had taken shape. Millicent helped her in her hunt to gather intel on her northern enemy. They learned the weak points in Queen Moirai's army and the best ways to access her troops. In turn, Millicent benefited directly from the array of puppets she gathered around the kingdom so that she might get closer to Farehold's courts.

Nox refused to feel guilt, even if her manipulation of Farehold's nobility and power structure was *technically* treason. Nox and Queen Moirai had a common enemy in Raascot. She saw her actions as in line with the royal highness's own wishes, even if the queen might not look kindly upon the unsanctioned vigilante efforts. Hopefully, if all went according to plan, the intercalation would remain undetected.

After all, what Moirai didn't know wouldn't hurt her. But Nox would be damned if the southern queen advanced on her plans to invade the north and left Amaris imprisoned by an oversight. Amaris was an orphan without a name, as Nox had been. Who would risk their forces for a nobody? If anyone was going to liberate the moonlit girl, it would have to be her.

"The Captain of the Guard isn't going anywhere," Nox said with detached calm. "Once I return from Yelagin, there will be nothing but time to accrue the needed men."

"You can't go to Yelagin!"

"Can't?"

Her gaze wandered away from the Madame, scanning the opulence around her instead. Millicent's office had felt so grand the first time she was in it. Now she saw it for what it was: expensive trinkets of a hoarder, and nothing but manifestations of Millicent's greed. She felt that avariciousness now in her insistence that Nox stay. It was no surprise that Millicent would want more. She always wanted more. More men, more forces, more titles, more power, it would never be enough no matter how long Nox remained in Priory.

She didn't have the energy to frown at the woman, though she could feel the way her brows remained quirked in between amusement and irritation.

Nox was no idiot. She had been aware from the beginning that the Madame was using her abilities as a succubus for her own, power-hungry objectives. Every duke, lordling, official, merchant, or noble she gained belonged to them equally, which was why Millicent was so willing to lay the traps, provide the lures, and facilitate the snares. Nox knew that Millicent's help was not altruistic and that the Madame would do nothing if it didn't serve her. Nox would have remained a no-named servant to the Selkie if she hadn't proven herself valuable. But her worth had rapidly transcended numbers or objects or things. She was more of a treasure than anything Millicent could deign to possess. Perhaps Millicent bought people, traded in secrets, and hoarded coin. But when Nox took someone up to her room, she didn't simply receive payment for the hour—she took everything.

And so, their begrudging alliance continued, even if it was particularly challenging for Nox to remain calm with her business partner in times like these. Nox permitted the tantrum, understanding precisely what upset the woman. If she was free to roam about the continent, Millicent risked losing her hope for the future. With the puppeteered support nobility throughout Farehold, Queen Moirai might consider the Madame for her court adviser. A position of prominence in the castle was the Madame's endgame, after all. The southern queen would never consider an audience with a Madame, as no monarch would ever openly associate with someone of disrepute like Millicent. If the weight of every male title-holder in the south put the woman's name up for adviser, Queen Moirai would have cause to look twice.

Nox had no need for titles, nor did she care what Millicent chose to do with the power that came her way. The Madame helped bring her the men she needed, and so their alliance continued. As long as they were bonded by the common goal of amassing their forces, the Madame's ulterior motives were not Nox's concern. After all, Nox had protected Amaris from infancy. She'd taken her place at the brothel. She'd be damned if she gave up on her now. Not when she had the power to make a difference.

"I can't allow it," Millicent said.

Nox's brows rose until she felt her forehead line with a testing disbelief.

"You may be the one with the abilities, but you can't move forward without my people, or without the home we share. If we're going to continue to work together, you need to stay here."

Nox's mind combed through the empty threat. The woman did have an essential band, to be sure. Millicent provided her protégé with a number of effective allies in their games of chess. The bartender, the lutist, the girls who worked the floor, the lures who would wander into the world to draw in the men, they were all cut in on the profits reaped.

Nox saw the faces of the others, certain they knew nothing of her dark power, though they weren't foolish enough to mistake her for something entirely human. Men would go up to her rooms excited for a tumble and descend the stairs ready to hand over their homes, lands, and lives. The Selkie had more money than it knew what to do with. The succubus kept up her life as a courtesan, allowing men to wander into her bed whole and departing once beholden to her power. Not only was it an endless supply of fresh prey as she absorbed soul after soul, but Millicent was tirelessly willing to clean up after her botched missions. Besides, remaining at the Selkie came with the added benefits of the luxurious lifestyles and afforded Nox the freedom she desired.

She considered all of it, and none of it.

Nox was wealthy, she was beautiful beyond reason, she was quite literally vibrating with power, and yet she was utterly empty without her starlight. She was a night with no moon.

Millicent pursed her mouth into a tight line, saying, "I'm sorry, but you're being too shortsighted, and I simply have to forbid it." Nox sucked in a lip. It was perhaps the least visible way she could bite back a retort. She knew Millicent well enough to understand how this argument would play out. What was this discussion but another game of chess? The best thing to do would be to let the Madame feel she had won the exchange, then leave in the morning. If she sent word for the Duke of Henares, he'd have a horse and armed escorts waiting for her by first light. She would ride out ahead of the troops before the infiltrating Raascot men in Yelagin were spooked by word of their arrival.

"Perhaps you're right," Nox said. She did her best to make a show of her reluctance to accept the truth.

The Madame's brows collected in the middle. "Yes, I...I'm not trying to prevent you from your goals. You know we want the same thing," she continued cautiously. "I'm just trying to help you get what you want in the most responsible way."

"I know you want what's best." Nox dipped her head.

Millicent was still poised for a verbal fight and seemed slightly surprised, if not quickly flooded with relief that Nox was able to see her wisdom. She hadn't realized how tightly she'd been clutching the back of her chair from where she stood until her white-knuckled grip eased, blood returning to her fingers.

"Good." The Madame nodded skeptically. "That's that, then."

Twenty–Seven

THAT WAS THAT.
Emily tried to breathe through her pain. Everything about her felt heavy, as if her heart struggled to pump paste through her body rather than blood. She would win no favors by revealing her shaking hands or her struggle to breathe. She'd always known this day was coming. Whether from their days at Farleigh or the way that Nox refused to meet her eyes even in their nights tangled in the sheets, she'd always known Nox would leave her.

It didn't make her ready for the day once it arrived.

Emily was up before the twilight hours, helping the Selkie's most prized possession as she packed. Her eyes raked over Nox's midnight hair, her berry-dark lips, the curves of her body, the straight posture she wore as she moved with intentionality about the room.

She said the young woman's name softly. "Nox?"

Nox paused, but it was clear that it brought her anxiety to do so. Her body jittered against the halt in movement. Nox's eyes weren't the lovely, bottomless trenches that Emily loved to tumble into. They were distracted, flat with their inability to focus.

Emily shook her head to withdraw her question. It was moot. Nox's willingness to let the moment slide from her like rain from the roof was just another drop in the lake of evidence that Nox belonged to no one. Especially not her.

Emily wanted to offer to ride with her to Yelagin, but she knew before even asking that Nox would never entertain the idea. She knew how useless it would be to beg Nox to stay, and how heartbroken she'd be to have the one she held so dearly look her in the eyes and tell her that. Though Nox had enjoyed Emily's intimacy and appreciated her companionship, she would go to the ends of the earth to save Amaris. Emily didn't need to hear what she already knew.

She continued to watch Nox move around the room and convinced herself not to cry. She was in the worst kind of love: the one that would never be returned. She knew it, and yet, she couldn't leave.

Her eyes squeezed shut as memories flooded in and out like water passing harmlessly through a net.

Emily had clung to her little sister, enviously watching Nox and Amaris together for nearly fifteen years within the walls of the mill. The pair had always been off in their little worlds, specks of black and white against the earth and its inhabitants. The other children at Farleigh may as well have not existed for all they were worth to those two. Everyone had their reasons for being spiteful toward Amaris and Nox. Their preferential treatment had made them unbearable for everyone within the manor's miserable walls. They were set apart, and the tallest flower is the first to be cut, after all.

Emily had felt just as much displeasure when she looked at them, but never for the reasons of her peers. Why should Nox give her love so intensely and chaotically to someone with whom no intimate barrier had been crossed? What a waste of time and attention it had been, watching Nox day after day as she had eyes for no one else.

Emily'd had her younger sister, Ana, to keep her company. The two of them kept their heads low and their hands busy. They did their chores, stayed quiet, shared their meals, and planned for an escape that would never come. They'd been little more than flies on the walls to the matrons and orphans alike for years, but nothing about her bond with Ana was the same. What Nox and Amaris had was infuriating. She hadn't thought it possible for her jealousy to grow with time, and yet here she was.

She chewed on her lip, hating herself for how desperately she wished the dark silhouette that cast its form through the hour before dawn would stop and give her the slightest bit of reassurance. She knew it wouldn't come. Nox wouldn't stay in Yelagin. She knew that much to be true. But she wasn't sure if she was ready to face life at the Selkie without her.

Nox's delivery to Priory had felt like a small blessing from the All Mother, but the goddess hadn't stopped there. Emily had Nox in her arms. She had the funny, brilliant, cunning, beautiful raven in her bed. She clung to her softness, her body, her moans and gasps and flavor. Nox had her whole heart. Emily crossed her arms in front of her chest, holding herself together against the ache that threatened to cause her to fall apart as she watched everything they'd built disintegrate.

Here Nox was, thousands of miles from the moonlit girl who had never kissed her the way Emily had, who had never touched her, never made love to her, never made her cry out or see the goddess or feel as Emily had, and Nox still chose Amaris over her time and time again. Emily hadn't pressed the issue, knowing that when the beauty had breathed her name in bed, her heart had been with another. She'd wanted to fool herself into believing that one day, with enough time and space, things might change. Hope was all it was.

"Are you sure you don't want company?" she asked, hating herself for voicing the question after all.

Nox shouldered the bag, finally ready to depart. Her face softened with kindness as she scanned Emily's wilted features.

"It'll be a hard road." Nox shook her head, squeezing Emily's hand.

"I could make it easier."

"Em…." Nox's brows were the most expressive part of her face.

Emily searched her eyes, allowing her pained expression to say everything she couldn't. She looked away, hiding the pink shame of rejection that doubtlessly colored her cheeks in the dark of the night. She couldn't bring herself to hear the rejecting words. She didn't deserve the heartbreak that would follow when Nox inevitably said everything they both knew to be true. Nox was a lot of things, but she never lied to the women with whom she shared her bed. And Emily wanted the lie.

"Emily, I don't know what I'll find there…"

Emily moved away and grabbed Nox's traveling cloak. She hated herself for helping her. Her heart still struggled to pump blood through her body. Every piece of her fought to stitch herself together as her tiny piece of the world fell apart.

"I know," Emily said quietly.

Nox wouldn't lie.

Emily wouldn't hear the truth.

There was nothing left to say. Her wishes floated from her heart to the ground like plucked feathers landing gently at her feet. It was clear from her posture that Nox's mind was already on the road. She brushed a peck against Emily's cheek and whispered some promise to be safe along with a quiet apology for the impending wrath that they both knew was coming from the Madame.

Nox disappeared into the darkened hall without looking over her shoulder.

Emily watched from the third-story window of the Selkie as Nox navigated out of the pleasure house and left the brothel behind her, walking swiftly down the lawn and mounting a night-black horse, matching the hair of its rider. She'd called for the Duke of Henares to send a horse and escorts, and he'd delivered without question. Two men on similarly dark horses flanked her as she urged her steed into a trot, putting as much distance between herself and the pleasure house before the citizens of Priory began to stir. The sky had scarcely begun to show hints of gray when their horses turned a corner down the cobbled streets, and Emily could see them no longer.

Twenty-Eight

AMARIS HAD FORGOTTEN HOW BADLY HORSES MADE her legs ache. How could sitting in one spot for hours engage every muscle she had plus thirty she hadn't remembered existed?

Despite her stiff muscles, she was thoroughly enjoying traveling the continent. Each day overflowed with new flora and fauna. The rocks ceased peeking through the soil as they ventured farther and farther from the mountains, cresting rolling hills and spectacular grasslands in between the dense clusters of trees. She even noticed shifts in architecture and garb as they went, from the thatching of roofs to the colors of tunics. They passed plenty of farmers with their wheelbarrows or carts laden with whatever might be intended to be brought back to their village for various markets in any number of towns. There had been at least a few carriages over the last several days, doubtlessly pulling a wealthy something-or-other to whatever destination the silver-spooned society members deemed worthy of their presence. At one point, a white-and-gold carriage had passed them while heading in the opposite direction. She'd only seen those colors on one other person. Amaris suppressed a shudder as she thought of the bishop who'd visited Farleigh each month. His arrival had been a recurrent signal that it was time to be weak, to make herself small, to hide.

She was not that person anymore.

The scenery wasn't the only thing worth watching. Each time a traveler passed them on the road, she kept an eye on the stranger's face, eager to gauge their reactions as they eyed the reevers.

Amaris supposed Ash would have drawn stares wherever he went. Between the dying-ember color of his hair and the point of his ears, there'd be no passing an ordinary citizen of Farehold. Ash had been raised in Farehold with his human mother, and as he never volunteered information on his fae father, Amaris kept herself from pushing him on the topic.

Malik, as amiable as ever, would most definitely have drawn smiles from the passersby if he'd been traveling alone. He had a face that could fit in anywhere. His easy aura was disarming to even the most suspicious of folk. Wariness melted into pleasantries as strangers' eyes slid from Ash and Amaris to Malik, which made her appreciate and envy her cheery, golden brother in equal proportions.

His likability was an asset that they weren't quick to dismiss. Ash and Amaris sent him into towns alone on more than one occasion to fetch dinner or supplies when they needed to be in and out without raising an eyebrow regarding their whereabouts. The journey from Uaimh Reev to Aubade was too long to subject themselves to unnecessary skepticism at every village.

The game of watching faces worked in both directions.

Maidens always seemed to favor Malik, which was just as fun for Ash and Amaris to observe as it was uncomfortable for Malik to experience. The way his cheeks flushed, humbly shying away from the attention, only made him more attractive to the village girls and their giggles. There was nothing quite like the strong, muscled shoulders of a man who didn't carry the weight of his own ego.

While she deeply enjoyed traveling with the boys, she wasn't sure if they could say the same. They loved her and trusted her, of course. It was her inability to go anywhere without drawing attention that made discretion nearly impossible.

After the first day of drawing gaping stares, she'd kept her hood up even in the heat of summer's midday sun. She grumbled with discomfort as sweat dripped down her sternum on the front of her shirt and slicked her hair. The shadow cast down over her brows and eyelashes hid her prominent features. Cobb, ever the mount, seemed unbothered no matter how many farmers skidded to a stop in front of him or horses were steered wide of the road to avoid them. Cobb's reliable calm always drew affectionate, appreciative strokes from his rider. The sweet, gray beast didn't have two thoughts in his head to rub together. She didn't care. She'd met Cobb on the day of her liberation and would always tie her love for him to her freedom. Weeks on the road would give them plenty of time for conversation, though it seemed she was the only one interested in discussing horses.

Malik and Ash didn't possess emotional ties to their mounts the way Amaris did. Their steeds had both been sired by the same highland pony that had fathered half of the horses in Stone, making their horses half-siblings.

When Amaris had asked the boys of their mounts' names, the young men had informed her they were on mares Nine and Fourteen, respectively.

"Your mare's name is Nine?"

Ash had shrugged. "Naming can be deeply meaning-ful, or it can be perfunctory. This one, of course, has the deeply meaningful title of being the ninth horse born to its mother."

Nine, Fourteen, and Cobb were pleasant road companions and trustworthy horses. She'd have to see if she could do something about the colt and filly naming process when she returned to Uaimh Reev.

Conversations ebbed each night as the sun dipped and their stomachs began to grumble. She wrinkled her nose at the thought of yet another meal of bread, hard-boiled eggs, and hard cheese that awaited them in the saddlebag. Amaris had considered her tiny sachet of salt as valuable as her waterskin. Her assertion had been met with eye rolls at the keep, but Ash and Malik were quick to eat their words as they dipped their bland traveling foods into her salt each meal to make them palatable.

"Shall we?" Malik asked, patting his stomach.

He'd either heard her stomach or read her mind.

They steered their horses from the road and away from prying eyes once more. The woods were filled with toppled trees, thickets, and thorny bushes. Amaris was halfway through a tight cloud of gnats before she began swatting at the air, choking on her tiny, disgust-ing nemeses. Between the scrapes, scratches, insects, and hunger, they were all feeling relatively soured by the time they made camp.

"I would love to not eat eggs again." Ash frowned, looking at their meager supplies.

This was something they could agree on. There was leftover bread from the previous village, and if they could catch a rabbit, the hot, gamey sandwiches would be a nice break from whatever hard, sharp white cheese and apples they'd acquired from the last village. While she normally loved cheese, this one was dry and crumbled in a way that made her think she'd rather skip a meal altogether than suffer through another block of the stuff.

Malik insisted he didn't mind the cheese, but she was sure he only said that because he'd been the one to purchase it. Instead, they split their hunt three ways in search of game, both for efficiency and for safety in case one was to fire an arrow. Enough reevers died at the hands of beasts and men. They didn't need another in their dwindling league falling to friendly fire over a hare.

She let the men keep themselves occupied as they hunted for supper. She had more important things to do.

Amaris had made a ritual over the last several nights of walking into the forest and quieting herself. She searched for the inexplicable intuition she had felt the night she'd been led to the pond. The instinct had been something silent but potent within her, and she clawed for it, begging it to reactivate. Many uneventful hours, camps, and slumbers had passed between the night she had met the demon general, but no matter how long into the night she lay awake or how hard she strained her ears for alertness, she felt nothing.

Ash had teased her over the last few days for being a lousy huntress when she had repeatedly returned to the camp empty-handed, but her attention remained elsewhere. She'd rather the boys believe she was terrible at collecting game than know the truth. She wasn't ready to hear their disapproval if she explained she was searching for the fae. What had happened that night at the pond? How could she learn to understand it?

The winged men certainly hadn't seemed like demons. Zaccai's wings had been feathered, not like the membranous, batlike wings of the twisted beasts in her tomes. He was not the monstrosity of the ag'imni. Even though Ash insisted an ag'imni was what they'd seen in the clearing, she couldn't understand how; where he had seen a twisted gargoyle, she had seen a winged man. Ash had asserted that her eyes had been playing tricks on her in the moonlight. He'd maintained that her weak eyes had no gift for sight in the dark. She'd been annoyed at his dismissal, but she knew arguing was useless. She ignored him, focusing instead on the desperate need for relief that plagued her following the incident. The unrelenting sensation akin to the kernel in her tooth gnawed at her whenever she thought of the exchange.

She gave up, frustration and disappointment filling her for the second, then third, now fourth night in a row. The evening passed as it did, cooking, eating, cleaning their weapons, and never bothering with the sentimentalities of good-nights. Amaris continued to lie awake long after the men at her sides had fallen asleep.

As she stared into the woods, she felt for the first time in days that something was staring back.

She swallowed, listening to the instinct that told her she was not alone.

Amaris sat up, straining her eyes against the darkness. She didn't make any move toward the woods but watched intently, waiting for a sign or the telltale absence of noise. She looked for the flicker of wings or the reflective flash of swords that the fae might have holstered. Without moving, she scoured the blackened shadows of the forest around her, searching for any hint of movement.

Then she saw it. It was the flick of a shadow. It was the slight, unnatural extension of darkness from one of the trees.

Amaris rose into a crouch. If she was about to encounter the pair she'd met several nights ago, she meant to show them she didn't intend to harm them. She wanted to have a conversation, not fight. Amaris flattened her palms to reveal that they held no weapons.

The shape moved closer. It was about the height of a man. The half-moon glow didn't show the face of a person, and she screwed her eyes as intensely as she could against the dark. An uncomfortable tingle in her belly perceived a threat long before her eyes. Something was wrong.

Despite the warm season, a cold breeze snaked through their campsite. Goose bumps chilled across her arms and the back of her neck. Inexplicable anxiety, like the tang of metal, filled the back of her mouth. Her senses switched from curiosity to fight-or-flight as the chill permeated the campsite. The sensation slithered down her spine, and she knew she was not about to face any mortal. The shadow hadn't moved closer, nor had she stood from her crouched position, but the reek of rotting flesh filled her nostrils.

She didn't have to know precisely what she faced to know what that scent meant.

She had to move.

Amaris lowered her hand with the slowness of molasses as she reached for her sword. If she could keep the creature from stirring before she was armed, she might stand a chance at defense. The moment she wrapped her fingers around the hilt, the monster drifted out from its space between the trees. It took her a moment to connect the monstrosity before her eyes with the horrible pictures, the lore, and bestiaries she'd studied. She had seen this face sketched in the tomes at the fortress and heard the war stories of reevers who had faced it and lived to tell the tale. She was looking into the face of a nightmare embodied.

She stared at the slackened, inhumane, corpselike

face, the sunken eyes, the reeking, smokelike tendrils of the beseul.

Her fingers flexed against the metal of the hilt as she readied for action. It was time to make her move.

Swift as a crack of thunder, Amaris cried out. Her sound was not fearful but instead intended to alert her companions while she sprang into action. She'd barely been spared a moment to react, and she knew they'd be slaughtered in their sleep if they were caught unaware. She was already moving as the men jerked from their slumber, their limbs a disoriented flailing for weapons without knowing how or why.

Amaris had to create time for them to mobilize while buying herself time to survive.

Giving the others the life-or-death chance to get on their feet, she took off into the forest, the smoke-like corpse tearing from the trees and covering the space of the campsite as the beseul glued itself to her heels in pursuit. She ran through the woods with the outright panicked sprint of someone who knew death was licking her heels.

Amaris tried to think of what she knew of the beseul, but she couldn't split her mind between her studies while avoiding fallen logs, dodging trees, and navigating shadows. She knew the creature sizzled in sunlight, forcing it to be a monster of the night. Unless she planned to keep her sprinting pace for the next six hours, the wafting, animated corpse would have its teeth upon her long before the break of dawn.

Think, think, *think*.

All she knew was that she wasn't fast enough. She wasn't running hard enough. She wasn't agile, or lithe, or strong enough to survive this attack. No matter how hard she pushed, she felt the stench in her nostrils flare, the smoke crawl up closer, the cold bite into the skin of her back. She could not outrun it.

Bob under the branch. Weave through the trees. The voice within her cried for her to move faster. She needed to watch her feet! Breathe, breathe, *breathe*! She cursed inwardly, obscenities cracking like hail against glass as her feet hit the branches, the leaves, the rocks underfoot. She pushed herself to run faster, *faster*! The obscenities continued to spill, one word over the other as if her feet did not belong to her. They were separate entities working of their own volition as they refused to trip. Her thoughts remained scattered demands, jumbled anxieties, and a desperate search for a plan.

Amaris didn't know where she was running, just that she was pulling the unholy entity away from camp, away from her friends. She couldn't confront the monster in the forest while it was on top of her. There was no room to swing a sword, no room to attack, no room at all. She knew from the whipping wind that she'd never run this fast before, her strong muscles forcing her into a full-out sprint. She called on years of hardened calves and thighs as she'd powered her way up and down the sheer trail at the reev for such a time as this. This is why they'd forced the reevers to run up and down the mountain. This is why they trained. They ran to survive. They ran to live. They ran for exactly this moment.

Her training did nothing to quell her terror.

The beseul's speed was not that of man or fae; it was the speed of shadow and time. She gagged on its scent as the creature closed on her. She could barely duck branches, allowing them to whip at her face, tear at her clothes, her skin, and grip her in sharp, painful stings as she barreled forward. Her face was being torn to ribbons, pain, sweat, and blood stinging her vision.

Amaris had intended to loop back to camp, counting on the three of them to take on the creature once her brothers had gotten to their feet. As its putrid, unholy wail sounded at her back, the foul stench of carrion overcame her. It was over. She knew she couldn't turn.

She choked on the horrible odor of death, knowing it would be the last thing she experienced. Amaris was buying not minutes but seconds between her and the beseul.

Pain. Pain from her muscles, her lungs, from the thin branches that whipped her, from the inexplicable cold of the icy death that pressed into the skin of her back. She knew only panic, fear, and pain.

Then she saw something.

The thinnest sliver of hope.

Amaris spotted what she hadn't realized she'd been looking for. She urged herself further, exerting the last of her reserves of stamina, pushing herself to her limit. She locked in on the open space in the forest where the dull, metallic glow of the half-moon illuminated grass rather than shrubs. She barreled for the opening. This was her only chance. Each leap over logs and brambles threatened to slow her, but maybe, *maybe*, if she could create enough space to maneuver without careening headlong into a tree, she stood a chance.

She was almost there. Almost.

The monster's chilled tendrils froze her as if ice itself had been pressed against the raw skin of her calves, her shoulders, the back of her neck, a liquid smoke on her heels.

Either she succeeded, or she was seconds from having her jugular shredded by a demon.

She had only heartbeats to make her move. In the few seconds it took her to burst from the trees, she dove—not fell, truly *dove*—plunging into the grass below and rolling to her back, her sword coming up in an arc as the beseul, too close to stop, practically flew on top of her. She cried out, the sound of an involuntary yelp tearing through her throat as her sword met its mark. The dead-winter chill of its half phantasmic form grazed the space above her.

It was the maneuver she had hoped for. Inertia carried the beast of nightmares over her, inches from her sliding body as her sword made contact with some serpentine spine beneath its death-scented shadows. She felt the crunch of bone, and the creature careened to the side, pummeled from its trajectory by her blow. The strike had not killed it. No, the beseul didn't even look wounded as it flew to the side. The creature hit the ground, then rose, howling with the force of a legion of demons as it loosed its bloodthirsty cry into the forest. Years of training had Amaris acting on instinct, back on her feet and ready with her defensive position.

That had been her only move.

She had no more tricks. No more advantages. Now, she would fight. If she was going to die, she would go down swinging. She blazoned her sword at her side, egging it on as she danced on the balls of her feet, urging the demon to make the next move. She raised her sword, tensing for impact as the creature lunged for her.

A sound cut the impact short.

Amaris flinched as the monster was knocked from its course by something. Rather, someone?

She stopped herself in the middle of a leap, unsure as to where her sword should land. Amaris forced her muscles to freeze in their descending arc.

Something new was in the forest. Her breath caught as she jerked her blade away at the last second. Someone had come for her. Panting a groan from the exertion, the man—Ash? No, it was neither of her companions—threw his own sword into play, and Amaris leapt to the side, flanking the creature without a second thought.

A flare of black, feathered wings blocked out her view of the moon. With the deafening beat of wings and rumble of thunder, a third party slammed into the earth. Enormous, crowlike wings blotted out the forest. It lifted a long, silver rapier overhead and slashed it toward the beseul. Together, they threw the power of three warriors at the ghoul. Now triangulated between the three of them, the gossamer terror was outnumbered.

She didn't have time to appreciate the magnificence of their entrance or the relief that crashed over her.

The black-haired man took the finishing blow in the brief second it had taken the beseul to assess its opponents, severing the creature's head from its body. The blow sent its loose, corpselike face spiraling for the earth with a final, wet scream. Its mouth continued gaping as its head disconnected from its neck, continuously animated despite its decapitation.

The fight was over nearly as soon as it had begun.

Amaris pulled in several ragged breaths as she struggled to adapt to the battle and its outcome.

The icy shock known only to those who survived combat pressed down on her. She'd studied the beasts. She knew of demons. She knew that she was supposed to separate their heads from their bodies, that pieces were to be cut, sliced, and buried. She knew that demons couldn't truly be killed. Now that Amaris faced it in the moment, she was paralyzed. She couldn't force herself to move or to speak. She knew neither whom to thank or how to proceed. Instead, she remained motionless as she trembled with sweat, adrenaline, and confusion.

The three heaved for air from their respective places within the clearing, eyeing one another in the wake of their victory. Amaris had outrun death itself and doubled over, pulling oxygen into her lungs from the flight. The blackened, stinking blood of the beseul stained the earth between them. The reever opened her mouth to speak when a cry erupted. For the briefest of moments she jumped in her own skin, terrified the noise had come from the beseul, but no—the noise had come from the trees.

They hadn't been given more than ten seconds of relief before a new threat descended upon them.

With the crash of breaking branches, pounded dirt, and the grunt of a hero's battle cry, Malik thundered from the forest with Ash fast on his heels. Malik body-checked the winged soldier, catching him off guard in his post-slaying pause, wrestling him to the ground. Of course it was the reevers. She had cried out to alert them to the beseul and then taken off into the forest with death on her heels, running for her very life. They'd sprinted into action and pursued the nightmare, destined to eliminate the threat.

Amaris couldn't understand why her men didn't stop when they saw that they weren't facing the beseul. Confusion, horror, and exhaustion tore through her in equal pulls, the fingers of each emotion clawing at her from the inside out. She'd already suffered and survived far too much in such a short stretch of time. She couldn't make sense of the chaos as it unfolded.

Ash crossed blades with the dark-haired general, who twisted his position just in time to throw up a defensive sword. The redheaded reever moved with the agility of the fae as he swung again and again, relentless. The motion of the clash had happened so fast, Amaris could barely see her friend wince as Malik took a dagger to the shoulder and rolled away as if it were a bee sting.

Amaris watched with something between dread and

disbelief. The beast had been slain and pandemonium had ensued with such immediacy that she could scarcely find her voice.

"No!" she shouted, recoiling from the anarchy unfolding. No one heard her. Nothing stopped. She didn't know what to do, how to help, how to intervene. The moon sang down on them, casting an incongruent pearly glow over the bloodlust on their faces.

The men brawled, poised to kill whatever had thundered through their campsite and torn them from their sleep. The light of the moon continued glinting in time with the clang of their weapons, washing their battle with its white glow. Amaris raised her hands helplessly, unable to do anything, to stop anything. She'd already expended too much energy, she'd fought, she'd run, she'd clawed for her life, and she no longer had the stamina to beat Ash or Malik in sparring. If she had to fling herself into the fight to slow them, she wasn't sure that she could hold her own.

"Please," she begged again, her voice weak.

The dark general seemed to have found his footing and began to advance on Ash, using his wings to thrust himself forward with one powerful beat.

She couldn't stay still.

Amaris threw herself between Ash and the man with her arms outstretched, landing in the pool of blackened blood leeching from the fallen beseul. In the time it took for her to raise her hands, she saw the one called Zaccai fall, the weight of Malik's foot pinning a single wing beneath him in an awkward bend. Zaccai's weapon clattering to his side as he twisted for his wing. The fae raised a hand to stop the imminent killing blow. This was it. The general made a lunge to protect his man just as Amaris screamed.

"Malik, stop!" she cried. Her voice was the loudest thing in the forest.

The world stilled as he did as he was told.

The reever froze in time. Malik's sword had been in the throes of full descent. Arms rigid above his head, he felt his emerald eyes widen as he found himself trapped mid-action, unable to complete the arc of his sword.

"Drop your weapon!"

Malik's hand opened in a horrible, forced obedience, blade clattering to the ground. His panicked expression was exactly that of a caged animal. The reever slowly lowered his open hands, fear and revulsion coursing through him. He had always been immensely kind. Now his seething expression oozed only vitriol.

She shook her head wordlessly as he burned with pure, unadulterated betrayal. Amaris looked between the men—her brothers and the winged strangers. She soaked them in, unable to understand the conflict that tore her in two.

Ash stared at the events unfolding with open-mouthed disgust. The winged general skidded back, ignoring the reevers as he moved for his fallen man. Ash and Malik remained motionless as the general offered his hand and helped Zaccai to his feet. The silence that resounded between them was so much louder than the sounds of battle, thicker than the tarlike blood of the beseul, and more painful than any cut of the sword.

Pain flashed between her companions, though it was from no physical wound. She didn't know what to say, how to help, what to do.

The first noise was the snarl of her copper friend, his voice scratched with raw emotion. Ash's words came out hoarse and feral.

"They're demons, Ayla!" he gasped.

She used her eyes to silently plead with him as she fought against his loathing.

"No, that's the demon," she insisted, pointing to the still-gaping head of the beseul. The viscosity of its black blood stuck in weblike tendrils as it dripped from its severed head. Her voice stuck with her emotion. She couldn't stand the way Ash was looking at her. She was desperate to make it go away, to make them understand, to heal what had broken between them. "The dark fae saved me from it. The beseul would have bested me."

She saw it in the reevers' faces: this was insanity. If their eyes were to be believed, Amaris's actions spat in the face of everything for which the reevers fought and believed. They had trained with her. They had accepted her. They had loved her. They had trained against magical imbalance, against evil, against the forces that thwarted the world and sent the continent into chaos. And the first moment they were dispatched onto the road, she had turned on them. They had been wrong to let a witch in their walls.

"*We* were here to save you!" Malik insisted, the injury in his voice more prominent than whatever wound he had taken to his shoulder. An invisible knife twisted in her heart as she searched Malik's face. What was he feeling at that moment? The panic she had caused with her single command was something she had never seen in a man.

"They're ag'imni, Ayla," Ash pleaded. He sounded like he might cry. She understood what he was asking: how could the girl he'd sparred with, the one he'd fought side by side with, the one he'd trusted, have chosen the demons over her brethren.

"She can see us." The man's voice was low, looking at his similarly winged friend. "She can see us," he said again.

"The demon is slain," Amaris said desperately, ignoring the winged fae as she focused on the reevers. "I need you to believe me."

"How can I?" Malik asked, his voice heavy with distrust. Nothing remained of the friendly, honey-sweet tone she'd grown to love from him. She'd never seen him hurt like this. She'd never seen him angry. She should have never been responsible for causing injury to such a pure human, and yet, she was the source of his pain.

How could he trust her, indeed.

She hated her power, but she'd needed it. Her gut twisted with the knowledge of what she'd done. She'd wielded a paralyzing, hypnotic evil when her friend was poised to strike, brainwashing him into little more than an unwilling servant bent to her will. Amaris knew how they must see her. They had to be wondering how such a poisonous serpent had been living in their roof, disguised amidst their family so long without anyone realizing the dangers that had slept mere feet from them.

Her heart clawed at her from within its ribbed cage. She could see into his eyes that Malik's kind, happy heart was utterly broken. She wished for a moonless night so she wouldn't have to witness their expression, but instead, the pearly light hid nothing. She couldn't even bring herself to look at Ash.

"They aren't here to hurt us," she emphasized. "Can't you see that? Have they made any move to attack? The only thing they've hurt is the beseul. They saved me."

"I have a dagger to the shoulder that says otherwise," Malik said, his voice low and bitter.

"It was a defensive wound." She motioned in a desperate attempt to placate. How could she make this right?

The fae stayed silent, watching Amaris as she pleaded

their case. They were not poised to strike, but they did seem prepared to flee if the situation between the reevers soured.

She needed to speak to the winged men responsible for her turmoil. She had questions and deserved answers. She blamed them for the wound in Malik's shoulder and the pain on his face. She blamed them for the thick anguish in Ash's voice. She blamed them for what had shattered between her and her men. She had a lot to ask and just as much to say, but none of it would happen while the reevers remained present.

"Go."

Her command was to Ash and Malik.

Their faces were masks of genuine repulsion. Her heart split, bleeding onto the ground around her as it emptied. They were her family. They were her brothers. She was angry, and confused, and desperate, and had no idea what to do. There was no clear path, no right answer, but there were wrong ones. The only wrong answer now would be to forsake the chance at understanding.

If she didn't get answers from the winged fae, this would have all been for nothing.

Ash went to Malik, grabbing his friend's fallen sword. The golden reever had already begun obediently limping away, bound to her curse of persuasion. Ash stared at Amaris over his shoulder as they disappeared into the forest. As long as she lived, she knew that look would haunt her. She would beg for their forgiveness soon. She would do whatever it took to prove that she did not stand against them. She was one of them. She loved them. For now, she needed answers.

She was finally alone with the dark fae.

Twenty–Nine

SOMETHING ABOUT THE FLAVOR OF HATE MADE HIS BEER taste like bile.

He scowled into the pint, unable to shake the near-tangible emotions from the night.

Ash had never punched another reever outside of the sparring ring, but now seemed like as good a time as any to start. Fury and shock felt an awful lot like loathing as he burned at the memory of Amaris commanding them to leave. He wanted to shout at her for her betrayal. He'd never been this angry with his sparring partner. He'd never been this angry with *anyone*. It was probably for the best that they'd left her in the woods with the beasts. Let them tear her to shreds on his behalf for all he cared. He wasn't entirely positive he wouldn't have killed her if he'd stayed.

He drained his beer and blanched, disgusted at the taste. It was probably a perfectly fine ale, but acrimony colored every memory as his thoughts drowned out the babble of the tavern and he recounted the evening.

Not only had Amaris chosen demons, but she'd yielded an unforgivable witchcraft against Malik—one she'd kept hidden all this time. The disgust burning within him had reduced his heart to little more than cinders. To think he'd trusted her. To think he'd fought with her. To think he'd...no. He stopped himself from wherever his mind had been tempted to wander.

They needed to create space between them and their white-haired witch before they said or did something they'd regret. He and Malik took off for the nearby city, ready to put a bitter distance between themselves and the one they'd left in the woods.

Yelagin was the halfway point between their far-off mountain home in the keep and the royal city of Aubade. As mad as they were and as eager as they felt to leave her in the woods to be eaten by ag'imni, they couldn't fully leave Amaris behind. She was their brother-in-arms, and even if she was a mutinous, hateful witch, her place in the stocks should be for the reevers to decide as a whole. Desiring a hot bath and a night on a mattress while Malik's shoulder healed, the men urged Nine and Fourteen into the city below, a rare treachery clouding their hearts.

Ash had caught the smooth scar on his palm as he'd gripped the horn of Nine's saddle, and he knew that her blood ran through him, just like every reever before him. They were joined, whether or not she was a witch, no matter how much he hated her.

Unlike the thatch-roofed villages and farm towns centered on churches or fields, Yelagin was a sprawling city on the shores of a long, deep lake hidden behind the hills that nestled it. If Ash had been in a less goddess-awful mood, he may have found it pretty. While the rolling landscape wasn't comparable to the gargantuan peaks and ranges that scraped the clouds in Stone and the reev, the terrain here rose and fell around the lakeside city, concealing it completely with the elevation changes of its bluffs until the men crested the hills and found themselves above its twinkling expanse. From their vantage point, they could take in the smokestacks and glowing windows from the metalsmiths, taverns, shops, and buildings. Docks lined with the fishing boats that trolled the lake stretched like black extensions of the city itself, carving paths into the reflective surface of the water.

The men hadn't spoken much on their ride, just as they'd remained silent upon returning to their camp, mounting their horses, and leaving Amaris behind. They left her pack, her things, and her gray steed for her to find whenever she returned. Ash had scribbled a note and left it on her blanket.

We'll see you in Yelagin, you traitorous bastard.

It got the point across. They were angry, and they did not forgive her, but they also would not disown her. Not yet, anyway.

The reevers had let themselves into a tavern near the edge of the city closest to the water. It had taken a moment to shake off their cloaks and settle at a table, but the other patrons seemed to give them and their foul dispositions a rather wide berth. They shared their pints in silence, drinking in the sour ale, allowing the tap house's commotion to drown out the turmoil of their thoughts. Jeering, heat, merriment, smells of fire, bodies, food, laughter, music, sex—it was all the senseless background noise of civilians who never left the safety of their city. How could the naive residents know what evils dwelled in their forests, or what witches lived amongst them, masquerading as their friends, their family, their lovers. None of them would sleep, toast, or gamble with the weight of unholy powers anchoring them to the bottom of the sea.

"Another beer?" Malik asked, raising his hand to order a second round.

Ash looked from the empty pint to the crimson wound blooming on his shoulder. He said, "I'm not one to judge, but maybe you should prioritize the tonic over alcohol."

Malik scowled at him but left the table to inquire about a room for the night. He took his pint with him, leaving Ash with a chilled, frothy glass to finish on his own. Ash was right, and he knew it. Malik needed somewhere to lie while the tonic worked its way through his bloodstream and his shoulder healed. The injury had been relatively shallow, but it was to his right side—his sword hand—and he couldn't risk any damage to the tissue.

While Malik found the innkeeper, Ash scanned the faces of the patrons. The faeling's character was normally amiable and open to townsfolk when he traveled. He'd done quite well with the ladies when he'd wandered into towns, more than happy to use his ears as a conversational opener and see where the night took them. This night was different. He felt sickened at the sight of their simple faces as they went about their merry, superficial lives. What must it be like to have your greatest worry be the springtime taxation or the anxious hope of an invitation to a mayoral dinner party. He admitted he might be feeling a little bit biased by his own bitterness as he drained his ale. Ash intended to shoot back as many as possible tonight. He was on a mission to get as shitfaced as the innkeeper would allow before he was cut off.

He set the pint down as the barmaid approached.

He glanced up to order another drink, but it wasn't the barmaid at all. Ash was looking into the twinkling eyes of the single most beautiful woman he'd ever seen. He straightened a bit, clearly surprised as he looked at the oddity standing at his table. She seemed to glow from some unseen inner flame. Her bottomless eyes were utterly mesmerizing as she looked directly into his. She leaned onto the table, pressing her palms onto its wooden surface. A cinnamon smell overpowered the honest auroras of stews and breads that had filled his nose only moments before.

"Hello." She smiled, teeth glinting. "May I sit?"

Ash was baffled, certain everything about his face betrayed his surprise. He had been radiating acidic energy from the moment he'd stepped into the alehouse that night. There was no reason anyone should have wanted to come within three table lengths of his bitter company.

"I'm sorry, m'lady. I don't think I'm particularly good company tonight," he offered as both an apology and an attempt at dismissal.

She made a somewhat amused face at that. "I'd rather a man be honest with his emotions than feign pleasure while concealing pain. Would you share your table with a lady? Maybe I can make your bad day better."

Making some unintelligible gesture in an attempt to recover, he motioned his hands toward the seat across from him. He'd meant to tell her to be his guest, but there was nothing charming or elegant about the way he'd reacted. Doing his best to compose himself, he asked, "May I buy you a drink?"

"You may." She grinned, delighted. She eased from where she'd been standing and leaned onto the table, seated directly across from Ash.

The young woman clasped her delicate, bronze hands in front of her. Apart from himself and Samael, he hadn't seen many people with her particular coloration. The lovely, tanned skin would have made her stand out in the tavern by itself, but the woman was a testament to the goddess's eye for beauty, as she was a masterpiece. Her glossy black hair shone like wet ink. Her white, pearly teeth flashed with unnatural allure in an effortless, winsome smile.

His eyes grazed from her hair, the rouge of her cheeks,

her berry-dark mouth, and her elegant throat to the curious cloak she still wore. It had been too warm of a day for the royal-blue cloak draped over her shoulders. The girl unclamped it at the neck, draping it on the chair behind her. When she removed it, it was clear why she'd been covering up. Her dress left astonishingly little to the imagination, plunging and hugging deliciously around her shape.

"Are you from Yelagin?" she asked.

Ash had forgotten the common tongue. All thoughts vacated his mind as he did his best not to gape at her. He wasn't convinced he'd ever known how to speak. He'd only had one pint, but he was feeling terribly drunk by the shock of her presence. He shook his head mutely, doing his best to keep his eyes on her face. Maybe the All Mother had seen what a terrible night he'd had and taken pity on him, sending him a silk-wrapped present. The thought, however foolish, warmed him. He managed to strike what he hoped was a casual tone.

Finally, he answered, "Just passing through, I'm afraid. Are you a local?"

She feigned offense, bringing one hand to brush her chest as she pointed to herself. The brush of her fingertips as they grazed the space below her collarbone served more than one purpose, truly testing his resolve to retain eye contact.

"Of this landlocked town?" she asked. The girl tossed her hair easily to one side with a charming grace. "Oh, I could never settle somewhere so far from the sea. Where's the sense of freedom in that?"

She was a coastal girl, then. He supposed there were probably people in the far southern isles with dark hair and tanned skin. That was more logical than believing the girl to be from Raascot, but though he tried to take matters of geography into account, he found his mind distracted from thoughts of her lineage. He could have sworn she leaned in to press her breasts together, which made discerning her origins rather challenging. How absurd that a woman so stunning would have to do more than glance at a man to have him at her beck and call. It was a bit *too* absurd.

Ash kept his voice casual, but a guarded caution had crept into his gut. The woman was art. Ash knew enough of the world to have learned that the prettiest flowers often had the moist, poisonous fruits. Vigilance aside, her presence remained immensely distracting.

He cleared his throat, offering, "How fortunate that two travelers' paths should cross, then."

He was thankful that their conversation was interrupted. The barmaid brought yet another ale for him, and a glass of red wine for the lady. He certainly didn't need another drink, but he couldn't have anticipated how the night would reveal itself. He slid the woman several pennies, and two extra as a tip.

The young woman lifted her wine glass in a toast.

The barmaid cut in, "It's only silver if you're wanting a room for the night as well."

The dark-haired girl raised a conspiratorial eyebrow, amused at whatever foregone conclusion was being implied.

"Your friend said you were the one with the coin purse," the woman clarified. The barmaid seemed a bit frazzled at the night's crowd but waved a hand to where Malik watched from the bar. Malik raised two fingers in a mock salute as Ash spotted him. He must have seen the lovely young woman take a seat at their table and taken his cue to make himself scarce, ever the valiant wingman, despite his injury.

Ash procured a silver and the barmaid went on her way, presumably handing a room key off to Malik.

"And staying at this inn as well?" she purred. The woman's lips twitched up slightly, eyelashes lowering as she looked into her wine, then back up at Ash. "Fortune smiles upon us. My room is just upstairs."

Was she inviting him into her bed? Ash hadn't bathed in nine days and had been scowling at the world for the hour leading up to their arrival. There was no way this stunning creature wanted his company tonight. Feeling a twinge of something that may have been an irritation for letting himself believe she could have been interested, he course-corrected by asking her, "Is there anything I can help you with, ma'am?"

Her smile was unchanging, ever the picture of grace, but something nearly reptilian had twitched in her eye at his question. This was not a woman used to men rebuffing her advances.

She kept her tone unbothered, bordering on flirtatious. "Tell me about yourself, traveler. Are you also from the coast?"

He shook his head, returning to his ale. "That's where I'm headed. I'm from up north, just into the mountains."

"The north, you say," she repeated. Once again, there was something imperceptibly ominous within her easy smile. It was a glint behind her dark eyes that he couldn't quite place, though he felt quite sure that whatever he saw was something untamed and predatory. "That must be why such a handsome young man is armed to the teeth. Who would think one gentleman would need this many bows and blades? Treacherous roads, I hear."

"It's just the one bow, miss. But you can never have too many blades."

"Mmm." She nodded amicably. She seemed to consider the swords and daggers as she drank deeply from her glass. The reddish-purple liquid nearly matched the ripened blackberry shade of her lips.

Every moment that passed, Ash became more and more certain of...something. She was beautiful—perhaps even the most radiant woman he'd ever seen. But there was a sinister edge to her beauty. Something he couldn't quite put his finger on, like a word on the tip of his tongue. The jovial sounds of the alehouse didn't match their exchange. The music was too bright and the laughter too loud for the rising suspicion he shouldered.

The men at the tables around him eyed him with thinly veiled envy. Surely they were asking themselves what a ruddy demi-fae would have to offer a woman of her caliber. Perhaps she was a thrill-seeker, he told himself, as occasionally women would see the arch of his ears and seek him out just to have lain with one of his kind. The stares from the neighboring barflies assured him once he left, the men would be swarming the table. Perhaps it was time to let them have their shot.

Ash was ready for a bath and a good night's sleep. He exhaled, looking for his exit. Maybe Malik would give him a few minutes to himself in the room while he thought of the beautiful body hidden just below the curtain of her generously revealing dress. He had no doubt that making love to her would be the most spectacular event of any man's life. She had the hungry look of a true man-eater, after all.

He spun from the table, swinging a leg over the bench as he readied the polite process of departing. Posturing oneself away from the chattier party was usually an effective method of letting them take the cue on their own. Taking another sip of his too full pint glass, he looked to Malik, who seemed just as bewildered as the men around him.

Malik had watched him go home with many a girl in

the village of Stone, usually as his golden friend had stayed behind to salute appreciatively and continue playing his card games with the villagers. Tonight's events did not track with their pattern of camaraderie.

Malik gestured to convey his confusion and moved his mouth, silently asking a single question from across the tavern.

What the hell?

Ash didn't know how to answer. There was no way to explain it to his friend. It was a feeling. A distant one, but one he couldn't ignore. Maybe it was because he was angry with Amaris. Maybe it was because a beseul had torn through their camp, and their white-haired friend had betrayed them, and the ale was too expensive and too sour. Maybe the reason didn't matter.

"I wish you a safe journey on your roads, miss," he said. Ash began to stand, but the woman clamped a hand down on his, perhaps too eagerly. He paused before rising.

"Are you going to make me finish my drink alone?" she asked, running her thumb softly over the top of his closed hand. "Don't leave a lady unaccompanied in a place like this."

The surge of emotions he felt was powerful. Her cinnamon scent seemed to pulse, growing stronger with each moment that passed. Her contact was electric, weakening his resolve. His blood flowed from his rational mind to somewhere else entirely.

Two wolves fought within him. One distinctly male wolf clawed at him to take her to bed, to rip her clothes off, to ravage every inch of her. He'd love nothing more than to pin this stunning creature to the wall of the inn or take her on the table right here while the patrons watched and cheered. The second wolf stood its ground. It was the cautious, lone wolf dressed for survival. It bit back the desire, nipping at the throb in his manhood, urging him to keep his wits about him.

The first wolf was loud, but the second wolf was powerful.

Out of politeness, he remained seated.

"Tell a girl about the north, would you?" she prodded. She had an incredible charm about her, as if it was a tangible aura shimmering around her. With every word that tumbled past her lips, his mouth filled with the sweet flavor of her presence.

She said, "I've never made it much farther into the continent than this lakeside town. It seems like a dreadfully long way to the mountains. I'd love to hear more."

She bit her lip as she waited for a response, undoubtedly knowing what an effect such a subtle action had on men. Ash did his best to comply as he watched the wolves fight, curious who would win. As the taste of cinnamons and plums overcame him, he began to silently cheer for the first hungry, male wolf.

He nodded. "It is quite the journey, and not one for anyone who fears heights, I'm afraid."

She looked impressed, saying, "You're on a mountain itself, then?"

"I am."

"And what is the name of your city?"

Hundreds of years ago, when the reevers were welcomed as guardians and respected for the peace they brought to the kingdoms, Uaimh Reev had been a household name. He would have told the girl of the reev, and she surely would have been delighted to have been sharing a drink with a guardian. Over the years, however, as their kind grew fewer and the continent more suspicious, it had proven pertinent to keep to the shadows. On the best days, people thought of them as assassins. On the worst days, they were equivocated to nothing more than hired swords. Samael had said the past fifty years had been the most challenging to live amongst the humans. This young woman wasn't old enough to know any reputation of the reevers that would serve him.

Ash opted for a deflection. He shook his head, saying, "I'm not sure the northern names would hold much meaning to anyone from outside of the area."

"Try me," she pushed. Was her brow arched with curiosity, or something more hostile? It was the second wolf again, clamping its jaws down into his flesh to draw him to awareness.

"I'd rather hear more about you, miss," he replied.

Her frustration was unmistakable this time, if only for a moment. It took the young woman a beat to steady herself, and Ash noticed. She took another drink of her ruby-red wine. She took her time eyeing the tap room and its patrons, its music, its tables and scents and sights, presumably regrouping her thoughts. She didn't lower the glass from her lips, still looking away. Clearly, he'd rattled her more than he'd intended.

Finally she'd summoned the casual air to say, "You're too kind. Men don't often ask much about me. What can I say? I'm a simple girl. The most exciting part of my day would be hearing about your adventures in the north."

"I doubt that very much."

She sucked on her teeth, and he finally recognized the look behind her eyes. He'd seen it on more than one occasion, whether crossing blades or beating back talons. It had taken a while to place, given the distraction of her night-black hair, her painted mouth, her tanned, glowing skin and otherworldly beauty. The dress was simply the cherry on top, an invitation meant to bait her prey. She had the distinct look of someone who was going to kill him.

Thirty

RAGE PRECLUDED HER CONFUSION AS AMARIS GLARED at the fae, blaming them wholly for this nightmare. Her world had fallen apart, and she was not to blame. She'd lived with her reevers for years and had never had to use her dark gift until these crows had flapped their stupid wings into her life.

"First you hold a knife to my throat, and now you—"

"Rescue you?" one finished, voice amused. The general, Amaris had learned, was a fae man called Gadriel. He raised a single, challenging brow. Though she hadn't yet gathered enough information to be certain, she was already quite sure she hated him.

As Amaris eyed them, her understanding of why the southern kingdom had taken to calling his breed of fae *dark fae* solidified. She'd assumed it had been to call attention to powers that were more familiar with nightlife. The black, fallen-angel wings belonging to Gadriel and his companion, and the nocturnal eyes that allowed them to see in the dark were just the most apparent features that set them apart as residents of Raascot. Everything she knew to be true about them gave them a more ominous edge.

Northern fae, Gadriel had said, were no friends of what Amaris had referred to as demons—despite what primitive superstitions and prejudices spread about the northern kingdom. Raascot, he'd said, had as many common enemies in the vageth, the ag'drurath, and the beseuls as any other human or fae on the continent.

It had been a long while since Ash and Malik had departed. Zaccai got to work shoveling the monster's disembodied head under the earth, as was tradition, while Amaris and Gadriel remained locked in a wordless stalemate. Eventually, the stench of the slain monster and black blood around them pushed them toward Cobb and where Amaris had initially made their camp for the night. Though she hated herself for it, Amaris was relieved her friends were gone upon her return. She didn't have the energy to verbally battle with Ash or Malik right now. These were the answers she needed.

"Have you been following me?" Amaris asked.

She'd spent long enough staring at them in the glen. She wasn't sure if she could continue scouring their features before her eyes dried out from staring. Amaris turned her back on them and busied herself with flint and kindling while she waited for an answer. She lit a fire, perhaps only because it gave her hands something familiar and comforting to do. While she was usually intentional about avoiding fires at night, it seemed as though the worst thing in the nearby woods had been slain and that the general and his winged companion were just as terrifying as anything else that might be attracted to their flame.

"We hadn't intended to," Zaccai answered for them both. "We're joining a few others over the hill in Yelagin. Then, after that night by the pond..."

"I could tell you saw us," Gadriel finished.

"Of course I can see you," she bit, her voice as sour as her mood.

Amaris hoped they could feel the ire in her words.

She knew she should be grateful that they had intervened with the beseul, but what had it cost her? They owed her answers, and though unable to articulate why, she couldn't bring herself to be afraid of the winged fae. Whether or not they were friend or foe, they didn't seem to pose immediate bodily harm.

"No," Zaccai corrected, running a hand through his hair as he looked for his words. "You see us for who we are. The others see…something else. How do I…" His words drifted off as he looked between Gadriel and Amaris. "I'm sorry—it's been so long since we've spoken to anyone south of the border. You saw the way your companions reacted, didn't you?"

"It's a spell?" she asked.

It took a while for their tentative nods to confirm.

Amaris narrowed her eyes as she evaluated them. She pushed, "You're enchanting people to see you as monsters? What sort of defense is that?"

Gadriel was quick to disagree, saying, "This is not our doing. Cai is pretty beastly and wins no favors with the ladies—"

"I do just fine, thank you very much."

The smoke rising from the fire was comforting, but the flame didn't warm her heart. She couldn't explain what she felt, but there seemed to be a glass shard jutting from her most important organ. She'd spent three years cultivating community and family, and in mere moments she'd lost them. Amaris took a half step closer to the flame, willing it to melt the frost that clung to the wound in her chest. Sitting around a fire felt distinctly human, even if no one sitting around its warmth could claim to truly be one. Ash and Malik may blame her for her treachery, but it was Gadriel and Zaccai who had destroyed her life with the swoop of their wings.

The arrival of the dark fae had been little more than tea spilled onto the map of her life, scattering the ink and dissolving her plans as her slate was wiped clean.

When Zaccai spoke again, it was with quiet resolution. He stared into the crackling flame as he said, "One day, it just happened. We were fine, and then suddenly, we weren't. For the last twenty-some years, there seems to be a curse on the border. It doesn't matter how we cross into the southern kingdom, how high we fly, how far around we deign to go—once we cross the border into Farehold, it happens."

Their words were illogical. Amaris's brows collected as her lower lip rose in disbelief. She asked, "When you cross the border, you look like monsters?"

Gadriel corrected, "No, when we cross the borders, we are *perceived* as monsters."

"Then why cross the border?"

Irritation flooded her. She didn't just want to know why they'd bother to cross the border if it held such a curse; she also wanted to know why they'd put her in this position, why they'd used their demon faces to turn her friends against her. Why had they followed her? Why hadn't they stayed behind their border and stayed far, far away from anyone who might spy them? Instead, she allowed her original question to spread thickly between them, its weight hanging in the air.

They exchanged looks. Zaccai offered, "This spell hasn't put a stop to things that have to get done on the continent. It's just made it substantially harder to accomplish them."

Gadriel scowled. "We've lost more men than I can count."

Amaris returned to the fire, if only to keep herself from making more enemies. She was tempted to make a comment about how they must not be great spies or warriors if they were picked off like flies, but she thought better of it. The moment she'd seen the beseul, she'd possessed the single need to end its wretched life, if only for her own survival. When Ash and Malik saw these winged fae—particularly given the rude awakening that had startled them from their sleep with the ice of carrion and death—they'd surely felt the same. She gritted her teeth, doing her best to reach for whatever emotion was closest to sympathy.

"How often does this happen?" she asked as she gestured between them across the orange of the campfire. "How often can people perceive you?"

Zaccai had been speaking for most of the night, but Gadriel looked at her very seriously for a moment, holding her eyes as he answered, "Never."

"Never?"

Gadriel crossed his arms and leaned back into his explanation. His deep, growling voice still sent the same chill of low, dark authority she'd felt in her ear when he'd held the blade to her neck, even if his words were amicable.

"Relations between the kingdoms have been strained for the last two hundred years," he began, "but there has always been an open route of communication and the cordial politicking expected from neighboring kingdoms. As was said, roughly two decades ago, this curse hit the border. At least, that's the most we know of it. No one has been able to see us, nor hear our words in the common tongue. Whatever this perception spell is, it has a death grip on its people."

Zaccai made a face but said no more.

Amaris allowed a small, appreciative sound as she considered his information. Finally, she responded with, "Well…that's pretty shit if you ask me."

Zaccai, who'd been swigging from his waterskin, almost choked.

Gadriel laughed, his teeth reflecting the light of the fire with his crooked grin. It was a genuinely amused smile. "Yes, I'd say it's pretty shit."

Wiping his mouth with the back of his hand, Zaccai looked to her and said, "This is where you come in. We've never had someone south of the border who could intercede on our behalf. Gad and I have been talking about it for the last several days, ever since you saw us in the woods. We can't get near anyone without having arrows or spears or torches and pitchforks—"

"Yes, I get it, the things for demons." Amaris raised her hands in conclusion. "You want me to be the demon whisperer."

"Well, that's rather rude." Gadriel arched a brow.

She shrugged. "Listen, I'm sure you're both perfectly lovely. Most women love having their missions disrupted and their friends abandon them in the middle of the night because demons were stalking them. Thanks for the beseul, by the way. But however noble your spying cause for infiltration of these lands may be, you saw how my companions reacted. I love those men. I've trained with them for years. They are my family. We would die in battle together if the occasion called for it. And now I am a—what was the word?" She held up the slip of paper Ash had scrawled. She looked at the note as she read, "That's right, a *traitorous bastard*."

Gadriel began to move around one end of the campfire, unable to stay fully still. She didn't seem to understand the weight of this exchange. "I sympathize with your position," he said.

"Do you?" she asked, making no attempt to conceal her contempt. "Because I did not ask to be hunted for days by two winged assailants. I certainly didn't request the company of anyone who would further alienate me. Look at me. I don't exactly fit in. The reevers were the only family—"

"You're a reever?" he asked. Zaccai's face lit at the word.

She paused, feeling a protective flare for her family. She slowly answered in a cautious affirmative.

"That's great!" Zaccai grinned. He looked like he might hug her, which was not the sort of reaction anyone had given her to such a word. "We've lived with a reever in Gwydir for nearly ten years! The reevers have helped out Raascot for hundreds of years. He's quite instrumental in our monster control."

Gadriel remained unimpressed. He paid his friend's enthusiasm no mind as he said, "I expect a citizen of Farehold to use words like 'dark fae,' but Uaimh Reev should know better than to speak without knowing the weight of your words."

"Well, I'm a little late to Uaimh Reev, and forgive me if I don't live up to your expectations." She glared. Amaris turned to Zaccai, who'd maintained a smile over her title. She asked, "Cai, right?"

He nodded, as cheerful as ever.

"Is your reever red of hair?"

"That's the one!" he said, unbothered by Gadriel's mood.

She was almost sorry for them as she responded, "Yes, it's his son who tried to kill you tonight."

Gadriel's mouth curved in amusement as he said, "Ah, well, that's unfortunate. I'm sure Elil would be disappointed that we didn't make a better first impression, though I can't say I'm surprised. The man is rather singularly focused on his mission. The apple must not fall far from the tree."

Amaris realized she'd never asked Ash of his father's name. She wondered if that made her a bad friend, though she knew Ash didn't particularly care for his father. Perhaps she could excuse her poor manners as an orphan, surrounded by other discarded children of dead or unwanted heritages, for failing to instruct herself on the polite ways of inquiring of lineages.

"Perhaps I can help you," she began. The men perked, glittering at her words, but she mitigated their excitement before they got ahead of themselves. "But I don't want to."

Zaccai looked to his general while the warm, orange fire popped between them. The reddish firelight caught the black feathering of their wings in a way that made them seem more like the fabled phoenix than the crows they were. Gadriel's face made it clear that, as a general, he was far more familiar with obedience. Amaris was somewhat certain that a defiant, silvery girl was beyond his realm of comfort.

The general leveled his gaze once more, unsure as to her sense of where her humor and impropriety intermingled. He asked, "Are you serious?"

"I find you disrespectful, invasive, and suspicious," she said. Amaris crossed her arms firmly. "Why would I help northern spies? But even if I did want to help—and believe me, I do not—I'm on dispatch at the moment. My companions and I need to seek an audience with Queen Moirai."

"Regarding?"

Her initial reaction was to tell him it was none of his business. Then, she considered the coincidence. On the one hand, no one was entitled to the assignment from Uaimh Reev aside from her, Ash, and Malik. On the other hand, she was open to believing in a world where accidental happenings might be mutually beneficial. It didn't seem useful to withhold this particular bit of knowledge, nor could she see a disadvantage in sharing it. Amaris chewed on it and made the decision to tell them.

"Well, *you*, I suppose. Two other reevers who left Uaimh Reev were sent into Raascot to investigate why your king is sending his men south of the border. They need to learn why spies have been reported throughout Farehold and to confirm or disband rumors of infiltration of the southern borders. Meanwhile, I'm meant to find out why the queen is ordering the slaughter of all northerners in her territory, and perhaps ask her to stop. Now that I know northerners share a striking resemblance to ag'imni, I can't say I blame her, though."

Gadriel's sharpened canines glinted in the firelight as his dry amusement twinkled.

"And they're sending a bear-mauled reever because of the witch power you exercised in the glen? This sounds like a flawless plan. Who's the seat of power in Uaimh Reev—is it still Samael? I may have to have a word with him."

"First of all," she said, sinking her weight into her hip as she tightened the grip of her crossed arms, "This bear mauling is of my own infliction, though that's a story for another day.… I realize upon saying it that it doesn't sound like it helps my cause. But, second of all, I'm no witch."

"You're right." Gadriel eyed her dryly. "You're absolutely delightful."

She narrowed her eyes, conceding, "Yes, I suppose your conclusion is about right all the same. Still, who the hell are you? Why are you here? I've learned what I needed to know: you're Raascot fae. I don't see a particular benefit in prolonging this exchange."

When she'd commanded Malik to stop his death blow, everyone had seen her power for what it was, friend and fae alike. She wondered if she'd be welcomed back in at the keep once Samael learned she'd used it on another reever. Perhaps once she pleaded her case, the others would understand.

Gadriel clapped his hands together suddenly. He grinned. "That's it!"

"What's it?" she asked.

The other two looked at him expectantly, the dancing flames filling the campsite with the warmth of its crackle.

"You need me."

"I'm quite certain I do not."

Gadriel's eyes were wicked with delight. He drew a few steps nearer to her, causing her heart rate to spike inexplicably as the distance between them closed. Reaching for her arm, he pressed, "Believe me, you do. You need to get to the queen to tell her to stop killing northerners with your persuasive sorcery? Excellent. I couldn't love a plan more. Coincidentally I, too, would like her to stop killing us. What do you say, Cai? Want to be conscripted swords-for-hire to a surly, white-haired witch girl?"

Zaccai grinned. "I haven't heard a better plan in quite a while."

Amaris attempted to yank her arm away, but Gadriel tightened his grip. His calloused fingers didn't hurt, but they also didn't allow for her retreat. She scowled. "I told you. I'm not a witch. I don't think I see much of an advantage in accepting your demonic help."

"Fine, you're not a witch," he conceded, loosening his hold. "What are you going by these days? Enchanter? Conjurer? Magician?" He did his best to goad her into further reaction. She refused to take the bait.

"Your abilities are..." Zaccai searched for a word.

"I'm not a witch!"

"That's not what I was going to say," he corrected.

"They're just very powerful. You saved my life when your friend would have killed me. I've never seen a power like it."

She understood Zaccai was attempting both to thank and compliment her, but she didn't have the space in her heart for his words. He seemed friendly enough. But then again, so did any snake before it bit you.

It was too much. She couldn't think of what she'd done to Malik. The general was too close, the wound of the reevers' abandonment too painful, and the fae were too bothersome. Amaris had already endured enough of the conversation. She began to gather her things.

"Between the two of you, you can work out what to call me while I make my way to the city," she muttered, sheathing her weapons and draping her bow over her shoulder. "Two ag'imni couldn't possibly follow me into its streets anyway. Think of the children."

Gadriel was not amused.

"See? Not so nice, is it?"

Zaccai raised his hands reassuringly. He was undoubtedly a pleasant person, but Amaris was not interested in his olive branch. Still, he kept his voice calm as he said, "This will give us time to talk to the others at the outpost in Yelagin. Once they know what a resource we have in this wi—um, this girl, this reever, I mean—they'll want to help as well. I'm sure of it. They're going to be thrilled to learn about you."

"I don't think I want demons talking about me."

"We're not—" Gadriel bit back annoyance, overcoming whatever agitation he felt with her by breathing through his nose. She felt a spike of pleasure at his agitation; her lone moment of joy this evening would be in not giving this man whatever it was he felt entitled to.

"Gad, she's—"

"I know." Gadriel cut off his friend with a sharp, silencing look. He finally cooled enough to say, "You're going to need our help, whether or not you understand as much at the moment."

Amaris untethered Cobb and made a few steps to lead him out of the forest, the brambles and thickets crunching beneath his weight. He'd been marvelously unbothered by the tumultuous events of the evening. She waved a few fingers over her shoulder as she said, "Great, I'm sure an army of the damned is exactly what I need to have Queen Moirai opening me with welcome arms."

While she began to lead Cobb away, Gadriel chided her. "Go—see if you can salvage what's left of your friendship. Let me know when you manage to relieve yourself from that attitude and see my offer to help for the asset that it is."

Zaccai wasn't nearly as sour as his general. He kept his tone level as he said, "For what it's worth, I'm pretty sure I'd find it in my heart to forgive you if it were me. We'll meet you on the other side of the city within the next few days. If you're anywhere near the road, we'll be able to find you."

"Don't bother," she called.

"Wait, witchling—"

Cobb nickered in annoyance as the fae invaded their space.

"Stop it, demon!"

Gadriel ignored her, his rough hand chafing her forearm with his hold for the second time that night. She looked down at where his hand encircled her arm, then back up at him, feeling a spike of heat at the closeness of his body and the intensity of his gaze.

"You've saved us, and I don't even know your name."

She motioned to shake off the manacles of his grip, but he denied her the liberty, holding her to him.

He took a step closer until there was almost no space between them. Amaris's throat bobbed to counter her flooded senses, from anger and adrenaline to the vague spice of pepper, leather, and something dark and sweet. She barely kept the scowl from her face as she answered.

"Amaris."

He seemed to chew on the name with a bit of a smirk, as if appreciating a dark, private joke. When he finally spoke, it was a whisper.

"Of course it is."

✦

Amaris made it into Yelagin just after the two o'clock bell. Compared to the events of the glen, the burning stars, the smell of the lake, and the cool night air should have been a relief. She appreciated none of it. After the silver spikes of adrenaline had worn off from her fight with the beseul, she was left with nothing but heaviness. It was the burden of remorse, of the way Malik had looked at her, of the disgust that Ash had shown her, and the weight of the sleep she desperately needed on her eyelids. Of course her fellow reevers hadn't known the layout of Yelagin or its establishments well enough to tell her where they'd be going. She'd hoped that their oath could carry the weight between them in moments like these when their faith in her had faltered.

She hadn't been sure she'd be able to experience relief, but its soothing waters washed over her the moment she caught a glimpse of Nine and Fourteen. The hearty mares were tied to a post with a few other road-weary horses on the first tavern at the edge of the water just as she began to enter the town. She edged Cobb toward the familiar beasts and began to dismount when the tavern door swung open.

Relief had been short-lived as her veins filled with shock once more.

She jolted in her saddle at the sudden rush of bodies and noises, pulling the reins tightly as she stopped Cobb short of the chaos. She blinked back the mayhem as two recognizable shapes sprinted from the threshold, running through the yellow rectangle of light cast by the open door. Ash and Malik spilled out into the street, clutching their belongings, the cries of angry men and screams of a barmaid following close behind them. Ash saw her the moment he hit the pavement.

"Go, go!"

Amaris gaped at the sight, then urged Cobb forward, cantering over the hill and away from the furious mob. The boys were on their horses behind her within moments, their steeds urged into gallops as threats to never return and vulgar curses from the mouths of the men chased them past the city. They slowed their horses farther down the road when Amaris widened her eyes and whirled to them from where she sat in her saddle.

She could barely choke down her surprise as she demanded, "What the hell was *that*?"

Malik, who had been smiling from their harebrained escape, seemed to remember that he was angry at her. "I should be asking you the same." He scowled.

Ash said decidedly, "Let's talk about it in the morning after we've had some sleep." The glower in his voice made Amaris's gut twist. She wasn't sure she wanted to hear what conclusion they might reach in the morning.

"You still want to sleep after that?" Malik was aghast.

Amaris chastised, "It's a big city. Surely word won't have traveled as to what sorry bastards you are if we make it to the other side of the lake. Besides, you're hurt."

"Takes a sorry bastard to know one," Ash spat at

Amaris, and she was glad for it. Anger was something she could handle. Antagonistic exchanges were so much better than the icy indifference she had feared. Instead, the banter told her that no matter how long his temper might last—and surely, it would burn for a day, a week, a year—when it passed, he would forgive her.

As they took the wide road around the outskirts of the town, avoiding as much of Yelagin as possible, Amaris asked, "Are you going to tell me what you did to the poor citizens of Yelagin?"

"I'm pretty sure I was almost eaten by a witch. Speaking of witches, are you going to explain to us what sort of black fucking magic you've been hiding?"

"I wish people would stop calling me that."

The cloudless night was no longer refreshing. Shadows leached into her from every pore as she slumped into her saddle.

"It's what you are," Ash said darkly.

She looked at his silhouette in the moonlight and felt the dagger that had been used to connect their palms, their blood, as it was driven into her heart. It twisted within her as she felt herself losing them. She suspected it was the very same dagger he envisioned plunged into his back. They were going to leave her, and she would deserve it.

It was a long, three-mile semi-loop on horseback around the edge of the city before they were comfortable reentering the outskirts of Yelagin. While they were unable to exchange more than a few words on the topic, they decided that if they rented a room in another tavern now and left first thing in the morning, they'd be long gone before word spread of their blacklisting.

Perhaps it would give her enough time to begin to right the many wrongs.

Her hope dwindled as the minutes stretched on and their demeanors did not soften.

As they rode, Amaris told them what she could about her persuasion. She kept her voice quiet as she explained she hadn't known about it until her meeting at the reev, nor had she used it since. She informed them that Samael was not only aware but had saved her power for just such an occasion as this. This was why she needed to speak to the queen. She assured Ash and Malik that the road to Aubade would be long enough to give them all the time they needed to tell stories of demons and whatever enchantress had nearly eaten Ash—that, or whatever nonsense he claimed had occurred within the tavern's walls.

Yelagin's permeating odors of fish, seaweed, and algae disappeared the moment the door closed behind them. The tavern they'd chosen was half the size of the one she'd initially approached, but it came with the added benefit of not having patrons who wanted to kill Ash and Malik. Unfortunately, its size meant there were only two rooms available. Given his pierced shoulder, Malik had earned his own room, to take up as much space on the bed as he needed to heal, undisturbed.

Typically, their nighttime routine was filled with companionable chatter. Instead, they wordlessly untethered themselves from their numerous weapons, fingers working nimbly around straps and buckles as they went through the painstaking process of settling in for the night. Amaris let herself into Malik's room and offered to help him while he sat shirtless and bloodied, but he kicked her out with no room for argument.

"Give Malik a moment, then you can go," Amaris said to Ash.

He didn't respond as he left the room to check on their friend.

Amaris was the last to visit the bathing room, using a pressed bar of homemade soap smelling like milk, almonds, and honey in her hair and all over her body. It was cleansing to wash the road away in more ways than one. Under the water, amidst the comforting scents of nuts and sugar, she could forget about her mission to see the queen, forget about Ash and Malik considering her a traitor, forget about the dark fae begging for an intercessor and, most importantly, forget about her evil witch's power.

She was fae. It was a truth she repeated again and again as she tried desperately to justify her gift. Samael had told her himself that she wasn't fully human. As she dipped beneath the warm waters of the bath, she clung to the wisdom he had instilled in her on their first meeting as a source of comfort: a power is no more good or evil than the one wielding it.

Maybe soap, a hot bath, and the comfort of Samael's sound judgment would be enough to scrub away all her hurt, pain, and shame. Maybe the water could wash away the weeping wound in her heart. Maybe Ash and Malik would forgive her, and they could go back to the way things had always been.

Maybe.

✦

It was terribly late by the time she finished in the bath. Her eyelids were weighted by the stones of the world as she forced herself up from the grayish, lukewarm tub. From the silence that met the swish of her body against the bathwater, she was confident not even the innkeeper was awake. No one in the building could judge her for her pain.

Amaris didn't bother to redress. Instead, she walked down the communal hallway wearing nothing but a towel. Her white hair dripped honey-scented puddles in her wake. The emotional exhaustion was a burden far heavier than the hour's fatigue. She wanted the load of her misery lifted more than she wanted sleep. She was desperate to be free of its shackles more than she wanted food, or water, or air. In its place was the soaking need to feel the love she'd lost.

Each barefoot step down the hall echoed two syllables with rhythmic consistency. Over and over again, one foot after the other, it repeated *alone*.

Rejection's sharp sting showed her a fear worse than death. The dagger within her twisted again as she remembered the hurt, the betrayal, the disgust in their eyes. More than anything, she needed to feel whole again.

Amaris opened the door to a wet-haired Ash, who looked poised to continue their argument. He halted when he saw her, mouth open for the fight. He was clean, dressed only in clothes for sleep. The anger had evaporated from his face at her wanton state of undress. She let the door close behind her with a loud, purposeful click and leaned against it, refusing to break the amber gaze of the man staring back at her.

"What are you doing?"

She said nothing as she looked at him, wondering if he could see the dagger that pierced her, and whether or not he would be the one to fix it.

"Ayla," he cautioned. His throat bobbed as he eyed her.

Ash took a careful step toward her, almost as if he were warning her to stop.

She didn't. Amaris had suffered too greatly. She'd had too much taken from her in her eighteen years on earth. She wouldn't let herself lose anyone else.

She wasn't afraid—not of this. She didn't look away

as she felt the gentle drip of milk, almonds, and honey continue to pool on the floor around her from where the bath had washed the remnants of the night. She could replace the dagger with something good, something fun, something he'd wanted. Where once a gaping wound had been, they could fill the chasm with something they'd teased and flirted with and danced around for years.

Amaris brought her hand to where the towel wrapped around the space beneath her arms. She watched him, needing him to know that every second, every stroke of her fingers, every twist of her wrist was intentional. She dropped the towel completely, bare before him as she leaned against the door.

It was an invitation he'd wanted for a long, long time.

Ash didn't need further encouragement. Whatever arguments he'd been ready to have were gone. He closed the space between them in a flash, pressing his body into hers, his mouth on hers. It wasn't the gentle kiss of a lover but the hard, anger-tinted kiss of a man who had thought she might die tonight. He gripped her to him, the contrast of his rough, tan hands against her soft, milky skin heightening her arousal. She kissed him back with equal ferocity, desperate for the healing closeness. She gasped as endorphins and dopamine swirled into the wound, moaning lightly at the alchemy of pain's transformation into pleasure.

He put a hand beneath each of her thighs, hoisting her naked body up against the wall. Her back hit the wall with a thud as she pressed into him. She wrapped her legs around him and reveled in how it spurred him on. Every touch, every movement, every brush of lips or flex of each muscle heightened as he pinned her against the door.

They weren't close enough. She needed more. Amaris wanted to pull the reever into the pain, into the fear of rejection, into the sense of abandonment and use his body, his love, his hands, his mouth as a promise, a bandage, a sense of forgiveness. She dug her nails into his back, arching her spine as she pulled him in. His body pressed into hers, air rushing out of her lungs. Her movement left her throat exposed, and she inhaled sharply at the sensation.

"Take me to bed," she breathed against his cheek.

He growled in response, a positively animal sound at the opportunity.

Ash carried her across the room, tossing her thin, white body onto the bed. He tugged his shirt over his head in one swift movement. She propped herself up on her elbows, watching. He moved on top of her with an intensity she only saw in him when they were sparring in the ring. Amaris wrapped her legs around him once more from where she'd remained prone, attempting to flip him as she would if they were in hand-to-hand combat, but he resisted the flip, asserting his place on top. She leaned into the pressure, wanting him to crush her. The more she felt Ash, the less she could feel anything else. He throbbed against her skin until she was ready to let him in. She craved the fullness of it, the forgiveness, the love and understanding and absolution she'd feel if he was inside of her. Her heat, her thirst was pounding down her veins. She wanted—no, *needed* the intimacy—to feel enveloped by acceptance.

She arched her hips to meet his, and the motion seemed to bring him back into his body.

Something changed in him, as if waking himself from a spell. The impulsivity fell from Ash like raindrops off a roof. Frozen in his stance, his features transitioned from fierce to contemplative to soft. A muscle in his jaw throbbed as he eyed her. The copper reever looked down at her, the fury of his passion turning into a different emotion as he drank her in.

He closed his eyes as he exhaled slowly, unmoving. It was clear it had taken him a great force of will to stop himself. "Why are you doing this?"

She swallowed, feeling the nerves of rejection even more profoundly now that she was vulnerable. "No, don't stop." She reached for him again, hoping to recapture the magic of the moment. It had been working. They'd been connecting. They'd been healing. "Please, I want...I don't want to lose you. I—"

He opened his honey-colored eyes again, and his brows knit with a deep sadness.

The moment rushed between them, snipping the taut cord of tension that had drawn them into this intimate, vulnerable embrace. The strand of the moment fell on either side of them. As the energy shifted, she relaxed the grip she'd had around him with her thighs, sinking down into the bed once more. Her eyes looked up to touch his, but he looked away. He remained poised above her while she waited for him to speak the thought that had hung itself on his shoulders.

He was quiet as he said, "You're not going to lose me. You're not going to lose the reevers. It's I who thought I was going to lose *you* tonight."

"Ash, I–"

He lowered himself slowly to the space next to her. Despite the fact Amaris remained fully naked, he draped an arm around her midsection, turning her to face him. She tried to bring her knees up to her chest, wanting to curl into a ball. When he brought his hand to touch her face, she felt the tears that she didn't know she had been holding back. The weight of everything crashed through her. She wouldn't be forgetting. No, not tonight.

"We're angry because we care. Don't you know that by now?"

She turned her chin away, shame burning through her. She understood why she'd thought this was what she needed and wanted in order to restore their intimacy, but her miscalculation made her sick. She wished she could turn back time. She wouldn't drop her towel. She wouldn't betray Malik in the forest. She never would have met the demons responsible for this turmoil.

"Stop that," he chided softly, pulling her into a hug. "You're a witch and a bastard. Just let me be angry. But you don't have to do or be anything other than what you are. Except for the witchcraft. Maybe don't do that one anymore."

She couldn't look at him. It took her a while to whisper, "I…I'm sorry."

"Oh, please don't be. I've wanted to see you naked for years."

She laughed through the discomfort, feeling the rush as the tension cracked between them. She smiled into his chest, chuckling. "Fuck you."

"You sure did try."

"*You're* the bastard."

"Always will be."

Instead of pushing it away, she would face it. The sorrow, the humiliation, the pressure, the fear of abandonment poured out of her in hot, salty tears. He tucked her close to him and held her while she cried. After the single tear shed on her first day at Uaimh Reev, she had never let herself show weakness around any of the men. Years of tears spilled out, shaking her shoulders. The orphanage, the Madame, Nox, all of it crashed over her like the ocean's waves until she had no more water left in her sea. The desperation she'd felt in the moments she'd thought the reevers had left her had been paralyzing. She had gone mad with the need to be loved by the only family she'd truly known.

But they were family. Not by birth but by rite, oath, and choice. What they had was stronger and deeper and more important than heritage. It couldn't be broken by a mistake, or a perceived treachery, or a foolhardy attempt to use sex as a bandage. Ash didn't release her, holding her as her tears broke. She wasn't sure if that made things better or worse. A few ragged inhalations and exhalations punctured the noise of his calming shushes. And eventually, between his soothing, her tears, and the warmth of their skin, they fell asleep.

✦

Morning light filtered in through the window, catching the dust in the air like ten thousand specks of gold.

She was the first one awake, stirring from a much-needed, dreamless rest. As she stared at the still-naked faeling in her bed, guilt itched her behind the ear. She fully understood what had possessed her to desire intimacy the night before, but this hadn't been a union she'd truly wanted. Even in the heat of their embrace, he'd known it. Their flirtation and friendship had been an affable source of joy, of inspiration, and of kinship. She did love him, though not in the way a woman might love a man when standing naked before him and wrapping her legs around his waist.

Usually when she was this close to Ash, the scent of autumn was tinged with sweat, dirt, and the midday sunlight from the ring. Occasionally the red and orange smells of maples and oaks in the fall would mix with the oil from their blades, the leather of his armor, or the hide of his horse. She inhaled the perfume of fallen leaves and chestnuts, knowing it wasn't one she wanted to smell again. Not like this. Not in the morning, against his skin. Not in the wake of her shame.

Amaris vowed to put the embarrassment of this misstep into the airtight box within her. It would have to suffocate deep inside her chest if she was to stand a chance of forgetting her botched attempt at seduction. She tested the invisible container to ensure that it had room to hold yet another traumatic experience, and then she slipped the night inside, securing the chains around it, never to be thought of again.

With the lid tightly closed on her emotions, she dragged her gaze down the sleeping man a final time, eyeing him for exactly who he was.

He looked peaceful. The reever was one year her senior. Though he'd been lean and sinewy when they'd met, his chest, arms, and back had filled out beautifully, matching the firm, strong legs that had carried him up and down the mountain. They were not the muscles of an overgrown brute but those of a body prone to action. His hair had dried in the night in wavy, coppery locks around his face. His grit, his might, his will had relaxed into perfect silence as he slept. She might have thought him dead if she hadn't been slumbering beside them night after night in the forest, knowing he never snored.

There was a friendly love in her heart that wanted her to press a kiss to his coppery hair while he slept, but no. Their chapter had closed. They were brothers in arms. That was the only love she wished to foster.

Amaris slipped out from beneath the covers. Redressing silently, she allowed him his sleep. He didn't stir as she let herself tiptoe down the hall and into the tavern below where bread and eggs were being served. Malik was already awake, sitting at a table by the window.

Warm, morning sunlight lit his features, creating a halo against his golden hair. There were no other patrons in the dining room at this early hour, only a friendly-looking innkeeper picking his way quietly around the room as he set up for the day with a broom and a dustpan. Malik's eyes were on the road beyond the windowpane, scanning. He saw her walk in and smiled. Perhaps a bath, a night on a proper bed, and a healing tonic had been all he'd needed to forgive her. His heart had always been a bit too pure for this world.

"So, about last night. Should I go first, or do you want to?" she asked as she slid into the seat across from him. Tea and a plate piled high with breakfast meats were set before her moments later, the innkeeper appearing happy to be working in the quiet hours of the morning before most patrons awoke. The man tittered off with a rag and his chores, leaving them be.

Malik shrugged. "I'll go first, though I'm not sure that I have much to tell. We were at the tavern—room already paid for. I was watching some night-haired girl with these gorgeous coal-black eyes try to get Ash into bed. The woman was a goddess. Honestly, I don't know what happened. I would have sold my soul to have taken her for a tumble."

She bit back her amusement. Apparently, two women had tried unsuccessfully to get Ash into bed that night. She was in good company.

"Well, I guess I'm glad you made it out with your soul." She rolled her eyes.

He shoveled a few forkfuls of egg into his mouth and took a long sip of his tea to wash it down. The breakfast had been over-salted, but it was hot and better than the cold dried goods they ate on the road.

"Like I said," Malik continued, "I really don't know

what happened. It was after the second time he'd tried to get up from the table. I can't quite explain it, but the girl lost her damn mind. It was bizarre. First, they were flirting. The next thing you know, she was screaming at Ash, and by the way he stumbled backward, the other patrons thought he'd done something truly terrible to her. Isn't insanity the curse of all beautiful women?"

"I don't know. I'll have to ask the next one I see." Amaris smiled, picking at the warm center of her bread. "Did you find out what the girl was looking for? Or why on earth she thought Ash had anything to do with it?"

Malik shrugged. "Your guess is as good as mine. Maybe it was a case of mistaken identity."

"Does he look a lot like his father? Maybe she knew him."

"She did seem to single him out because he looks like he's from the north." Malik chewed on the information, pondering. "I suppose that could be it. Or maybe she had a thing for would-be assassins. Maybe I should make an effort to display my blades a little more prominently next time I'm drinking. One of life's great mysteries, I guess. Honestly, sometimes the crazy ones are better lays."

Amaris tossed her half-eaten bread at him. "You're disgusting."

He laughed, his emerald eyes twinkling their delight. She beamed back at him, feeling the healing wound of whatever had been broken between them. She also knew Malik well enough to know he was a perfect gentleman with the women, no matter how foul his mouth was this morning.

"Your turn."

Her smile faded slightly. "Malik, I just wanted to say how sorry I am."

She had already explained persuasion in broad strokes

while on the ride around Yelagin as they'd found a new inn. As it had been well past the two o'clock bell, and given the chaos of their escape from the first establishment, she hadn't gone into detail. She'd just wanted to get off the road.

She gave him every detail she possessed, explaining precisely why she'd been tasked with speaking to the human queen of Farehold.

He offered a dismissive half shrug. "That's what I get for being human, I suppose."

She didn't know what to say to that. Was it better to be fae in this world? Long life was their most coveted trait. Youth, beauty, gifts that manifested themselves in various ways throughout the bloodlines were a source of envy, even of hatred from the humans. But was it a gift worthy of such contempt? What gift is it to be forced to relive heartbreak on an endless cycle until you become so cruel, cold, and desensitized that you cannot love, cannot be vulnerable? Perhaps the humans should pity the fae instead.

She thought that if she could choose her fate, she would have elected to be human, born with a small magic. If she could be human with the ability to heal, to summon wind, to manipulate water, then she could experience the favors of fate without the cruelties of time. Her mind wandered to Brel and thoughts of his human parents, terrified of his gift. Perhaps there was no one born under the All Mother's preferential treatment. Everyone suffered in their own ways once they entered this earth.

Movement in the room's corner drew her eyes to the red hair, now neatly pulled into a knot once more, of her friend. Ash eyed her cautiously as he crossed the room toward them, checking her face for signs of regret or shame from the night before, but she held none. Nothing had changed between them, and by the time he slid into his chair, she felt sure he knew it. While he took his turn on the bread and eggs, she began to explain her encounter with the ag'imni.

"They're fae," she whispered.

Ash looked up from his forkful of eggs but continued chewing.

"There's some sort of enchantment at the border—that's what they said, anyway. For nearly two decades, when northern fae pass from Raascot into Farehold, they're perceived as the demonic things you saw last night. They were just men, two fae men, only as evil and grotesque as myself or Ash or Samael."

Malik chuckled. "I guess that's her way of telling you she thinks you're ugly."

The men exchanged elbows as she continued.

"I don't know why, but I didn't see ag'imni when they were speaking to me. I saw them for who they are."

Ash considered this. His eyebrows slowly lifted as he processed the information in real time. Finally, he offered, "Here we've been wondering why your night vision was so terrible for a faeling. Maybe this is your gift of sight. Amaris, perhaps you can see through enchantments."

She could feel the weight of their gaze as they studied her purple irises. Amaris tucked a strand of hair behind her ear and continued, "I made a judgment call last night, and I need both of you to support my decision."

Malik gave her a dry raise of his eyebrows. "Yes," he said, "we were there. You made the call to brainwash your favorite friend and spare the demons."

"I'm pretty sure I'm her favorite friend."

"You definitely aren't. Amaris, which one of us do you like better?"

She winced, ignoring them and their ill-timed humor. She tried again. "Okay, I made a few judgment calls last night. I told them of our mission."

The boys stiffened briefly at that piece of information, breakfast meats freezing halfway between their plates and their mouths as they waited for her to explain.

Amaris went on, "Samael instructed us to find out why the queen has a vendetta against the north and to see if we can't persuade her to stop the killings of men or fae from Raascot. It seemed pertinent to tell the dark fae that my mission, in so many words, is to save their lives while on this side of the border. Also, I like Malik better."

"Told you."

She knew they weren't thrilled that she'd made the decision without them, but they saw the wisdom in her choice. Her companions nodded, ready to accept her rationale—Malik was particularly agreeable since he'd been established as the favorite. Their dispatch wasn't exactly of utmost secrecy, and it would only grant them more allies if the northern fae knew the mission was to find amnesty for them. Besides, what was the harm of one or two fewer demons in the woods who needed to be slain?

Ash finished his final swallow and drained his teacup. "The question, then, is how are we supposed to know if we come across a real ag'imni? Swinging first and asking questions later seems like a bad policy for prospective allies."

"I guess you'll have to keep me around." Amaris smiled.

"Oh," Malik amended, "and what is your punishment if you ever use that on me again? Can I hang you from a tree by your thumbs?"

The boys took their time discussing various methods

of suitable torture while she finished her breakfast. While most of their ideas revolved around particularly cruel and unusual ways for her to apologize, they landed on using a hot iron brand to burn "I'm sorry, Malik" across her forehead.

"For what it's worth, I *am* sorry."

"Tell it to the iron brand."

While their night at the inn hadn't been an eight-hour slumber of down pillows and crackling fires that one might have hoped, it was certainly refreshing for them to have taken a break, however brief, from cold nights on the ground with insects and wild hares as their only company. The baths and hot meals had done them a world of wonder. Even the horses seemed to have enjoyed their night in the stables with fresh straw and the bag of oats mounted on the walls of their stalls. It didn't take long for the threesome to saddle their steeds. Soon Cobb, Nine, and Fourteen were carrying them up the hill out of Yelagin, the road to Aubade stretching out before them.

Thirty-One

EMILY HAD COME TO DESPISE THE SMELL OF VANILLA. She choked on it now as it coated the back of her throat. The perfume mingled with the burn of anxiety. She didn't know why she'd been called to the office, but after Nox's clandestine departure, she suspected it wasn't over anything good.

"Do you know what the most dangerous force in this world is?" Millicent purred. She clasped her hands in front of her, resting her elbows on her desk. The ornate walls of her office populated the space behind her. Today she wore all black, including a small, black hat atop her pinned hair, and her ever-present inky gloves.

Over the years, Emily had been summoned to Millicent's office for numerous reasons. In the past, she had sat in this chair to discuss clients, techniques, and procedurals. In more recent visits, she and the Madame had gone over Emily's instructions for how to target and lure the Duke of Henares to the Selkie or her upcoming plan to ensnare the Captain of the Guard. The duke hadn't been her first act as bait, but it had unquestioningly been her most successful. The power of suggestion was more effective, she learned, when the target believed the idea to be one of his own creation.

This was not a meeting of the minds. There were no conspiratorial whispers or maps of men and their whereabouts. Emily shifted uncomfortably as she tried to adapt to the sticky, unpleasant energy.

Too much time had passed since Millicent had asked the question. She was taking too long to answer, and the failure stuck in her throat like a dry pill. Millicent raked her eyes over Emily as she waited for the response, taking her time as if counting every one of her infinite freckles.

"Death?" Emily offered, heart skipping a beat as its pace increased to match her nerves.

"Oh, not a bad guess at all. Yes, death can be an effective motivator. But, no, death motivates only from fear. The brave and the foolish alike do not fear death, at least not as they should." Millicent leaned forward onto her elbows, bending in closer to the girl. "Money is also quite powerful, of course. A man with no title can still buy the lands, the forces, the wine and women and the obedience of others. But money, like death, is motivated by selfishness. Selfishness can be predictable. It has its limits."

Millicent stood from her chair, leaning on the edge of her desk. Emily remained seated, her unease growing as the woman in black continued to speak. "Knowledge," she said, "has kept universities running, it has kept politics flowing, it has aided in the ebbs and flows of kingdoms. Yes, knowledge is certainly important." She took a few steps around the desk and was now on the same side as Emily. The choking vanilla cloud intensified. They were within an arm's reach of each other. Millicent shifted her hip, perching on the edge of the desk, looking down at the young woman as she leaned against the piece of furniture.

Moments like these, she was reminded of how truly powerless she was. Her discomfort meant nothing to Millicent. She couldn't get up and leave. She wanted space. Emily wished the wooden desk had stayed between them. The closer Millicent drew, the thicker the constricting fog of vanilla became.

The woman continued talking, but she was only speaking to herself. She purred, "Power for power's sake is preferential, as it requires little effort aside from being born a crowned prince, but who amongst us outside of the royal family can claim true power in and of itself? Even the royals probably have limits, as they're not the goddess herself."

Emily looked up helplessly.

"No? No guesses?"

Emily shook her head, desperately wishing this lesson would end so she could leave.

Millicent began to slowly tug at the sleeve of her left glove as she answered her question with an air of resolution. "Love," she said, "is the most dangerous power we know. Men will lay down their lives for the love of their country. Mothers will throw themselves into the teeth of wolves to save their babes. Kings will ride into battle to fight for love. It's why I knew the Selkie would be such a success. No little girl dreams of owning a pleasure house for its own account, you see, but to sell synthetic love? To market an opportunity to taste love, even in its most bastardized form, if just for a minute? Well, it has made this the most established line of business in all the lands since the beginning of history. You, my dear, are a proud member of the oldest profession in the world for a reason."

Emily's jaw fell open in astonished revulsion as Millicent removed the glove.

She struggled to comprehend what she was seeing at first as the fabric was tugged from the elbow to the wrist, exposing the Madame's hand entirely. She was left staring at the gray, amphibious hand that slithered down Millicent's arm, ending in blackened, razor-sharp talons.

"Unrequited love will keep Nox collecting the men I need in her desperation to ride north for the object of her affection, and love will drive those very men to her doorstep—*my* doorstep—in droves. But do you know the one thing I will not allow love to do?"

Emily was instantly petrified. Her eyes peeled in shock as she gaped, speechless. She shrank like a mouse attempting to disappear into the corner of her chair.

Millicent placed the reptilian claw on Emily's bare throat.

Within an instant, Emily fell sick. The limp muscles of a terrible fever, the shakes of illness, the weakness of death consumed her. Her mouth opened, desiring to scream, but only dust escaped her lips. She tried to writhe, to fight. She had no energy, no power.

"I own love. I trade and barter and profit in love. Love works for *me*. Love will *not* defy me. It will *not* aid in my most prized tool's disobedience and escape from Priory when I need her here. It will not offer her comfort or confidence or strength when I need her angry. I need her to be hungry. I need Nox, and Emily—you stupid, foolish cow—you and your love will *not* stand between me and my victory."

Emily felt the withering void as it sucked her dry. She looked at her hands as she tried to get them to rise, to beat against the Madame, but what she saw was alien. Her hands were dehydrated, paper-thin features belonging to an elderly grandmother. She lifted them to fight, but she no longer possessed the strength to move.

Millicent towered down on her, eyes flashing with her power and burning with anger. She tightened the grip of that shriveled, monstrous arm on Emily's throat and leaned in close as she said, "Your love has no place here, and it is your love that has killed you."

Thirty-Two

NOX'S RAGE FILLED HER WITH THE RUBY-RED HEAT OF her failure. The curtains were pulled against the late hour, and the tavern had died down as the patrons had gone to sleep. Not her. It would take a long time for the fury that coiled within her every muscle to unravel.

Nox was incensed. She had never lost control like that. How had that man—that idiotic, red-haired, dagger-covered mercenary—resisted her charms? This was her power! This was what she possessed! This was what she did!

She walked all the way into the far room of the wall and pushed off, using the leverage to dramatically spin on her heels as she paced. She needed something to do with her energy, something to throw, something to break. She scanned the inn for something inconsequential, something glass, something fragile that she could shatter against the floor. A lovely blue vase with three wilted peonies tempted her, but no. It wouldn't serve her to further prove that she had no restraint.

Nox admitted she'd been rattled the moment she'd spotted the faeling, but she had still seen the path forward in their game of chess. Perhaps her opening hadn't been the simple forward pawn she'd intended. He'd sensed her eagerness.

She had felt utterly stonewalled as turn after turn she had sensed him pulling away, the young man making it clear time after time that he wanted to leave their exchange. She paced the suite at the inn on the outskirts of Yelagin, nearly overturning the table with her rage. That fool, that *imbecile* had publicly displayed his weapons, ones nearly identical to those she had seen on the assassin years ago in Farleigh. After learning that the northern assassin had abducted Amaris, she had reached into her memory and written down everything she knew about the man. She'd made a thorough record of his height, his hair color, his clothes. She had drawn the swords and daggers and crossbow in sketches on the papers of her desk over and over. She had sketched his face, burning it into her mind. She'd flitted in and out of seven taverns in Yelagin that evening, and there it had been: a nearly identical sword, slung onto the back of the telltale bronzed skin of a northerner.

She'd stopped breathing.

It had taken her a full minute to compose herself before she slipped into character. She would need to use everything she possessed to get the answers she needed from the northerner.

She'd slid out her pawn as an opening move, and he'd responded with one of his own, cautiously guarding the conversation. Her interactions with men had always been a game of chess, and she'd never lost a match. Now, when she finally did, she had failed spectacularly. Her round with the coppery mercenary had been a two-move checkmate, and she had not come out the victor. Their exchange had been a textbook execution of the Fool's Mate. It was the single, worst opening in the game.

That's what she was. A fool.

So what if the boy's complexion matched her own? She would not go north of the border for camaraderie but for vengeance. What had the north done for her but breed her mother with its demons, abandon her at a child mill, and spirit away the only person in this world she had ever loved? What would a band of assassins have done with such a fragile girl?

She felt like she was going to be sick. How had she let the man get away, and how could she find him again? Her reaction had revealed her hand, and he had fled. Why hadn't she taken a horse and followed? Why hadn't she screamed that the young man had stolen from her, or sent someone else after him? Why hadn't she kept her wits about her? She'd been too hysteric to think rationally. She'd run this race since childhood, yet here she was, tripping at the finish line. Nox had simply let her knees go weak, sinking to the floor of the tavern as she'd wormed away from the grip she'd had on his tunic. The surrounding men, eager to defend her honor, had taken off after him, hurling their curses and threats while she'd remained slumped on the ground.

She hadn't just lost; she'd failed.

Surely, he had returned to whatever Raascot men of his had been in Yelagin and alerted them to her hunt. She had been careful not to use any specifics, like her name, or even Amaris's, lest she risk spooking them into discarding the problem. If she had been able to get the young man back to her room, she would already know everything. He should have been hers. He had been within her grasp. She had sat across from the answers she'd needed. She had touched his hand. She had been so close to everything she'd ached to know.

She hadn't just failed herself; she'd failed Amaris.

He should have been a husk of a man at this very moment. He should be slack-jawed, consumed with love, willing to take her north and give her anything she might need. Had she been able to pin the assassin beneath her in her chambers, she would know where in Raascot Amaris was being held. She would know how to get there, the conditions of the girl's life in the north, and what it would take to infiltrate and conduct a rescue mission with a northern escort to guide her way. Whether Amaris was tortured in a prison cell or happily married to a damned northern farmer, the point remained that she had been taken. Nox rarely let herself consider the latter option.

If they'd hurt her? There would be no hell prepared for the mangled bodies Nox would send into its fiery, sulfur pits. She had but one talent at her disposal. Her succubus power was meant to work in the night; it was a skill for behind closed doors, for the influence of time with a victim who was in her clutches one-on-one. And if she used it well, it was all she needed.

She eyed the blue vase once more, craving the satisfaction of hoisting it above her head and shattering it into ten thousand fragments at her feet. It symbolized her failure. It symbolized exactly what she would do to Amaris's captors. And perhaps most importantly, it would feel really goddess-damned satisfying to break something.

She couldn't bring herself to return to Priory just yet. It had been more than a week of travel by horseback to get to these lakeside knolls, and to have faced a swift and total defeat was demoralizing. Tonight, she would rest. Tomorrow, she would flex her seduction and work the men of Yelagin until she found at least one morsel of information to make her travels worthwhile.

She didn't remember falling asleep.

She didn't even remember lying down, and yet, clearly her rage-fueled pacing had come to an end.

She blinked awake, stiff from falling asleep in her clothes.

Nox had never been one to rise with the sun. As the years went on, she preferred to stir later and later. Especially now that she was both a lady and creature of the night, she would sleep until noon if circumstances allowed. She had paid for three nights at the inn upon arrival and had tipped handsomely for her privacy. No one disturbed her as she rested well into the late morning. The sun was bright and in her face through the suite's window when she blinked her eyes open through a curtain of thick, black lashes.

Today she opted for a more subdued approach to finessing the fine people of Yelagin. While nothing she owned could be considered particularly modest, the emerald dress she selected scooped to display her collarbones and hint at her cleavage without exposing her entire upper body quite as dramatically as she had the night before. Her attire wasn't the layers of fabrics worn by most proper ladies, but a long skirt with a rather daring slit up to her thigh was the best she could do. Her blue cloak would help conceal her body from the additional attention, as it had the night before, until she locked in a potential source of information. The cloak was a rather flowy scrap of fabric appropriate for the summer temperatures, and though it was unusual to wear a cloak in the middle of the day, doing so shouldn't draw too many strange looks.

The innkeeper had desperately wished he could have been more helpful to her when she explained that the redheaded gentleman had lifted a very precious heirloom of hers while trying to sweet-talk her over drinks last night. The man apologized profusely for not knowing more about the boy or the blond mercenary with whom he traveled. He swore he'd ask the barmaid as soon as she came in to work if she had any more information on the miscreants and that he'd send word to Nox right away if any news filtered through the chain of innkeepers regarding the thief. When she'd inquired about Raascot's presence in the town, she had been reassured on no uncertain terms that no one from the neighboring kingdom had set foot in his tavern for decades.

Nox not only made stops at the taprooms but also chatted with any shopkeeper, vendor, or young boy who ran through the square. Most of what she heard was superstitious nonsense. The news consisted mostly of the gossip of peasants who bemoaned how their once safe woods were now home to demons and monsters of all varieties. She didn't doubt that a pig or two had been killed by something like a vageth, and their education had only offered them what little vocabulary they had access to describe the incident.

One elderly cobbler informed her in a hushed voice that a customer not two weeks back had a daughter go missing, and when they found her, the blood had been drained from her body. Nox wasn't familiar with too many blood-drinking creatures in the bestiary aside from sustrons. Many a thief who sought to kill the creature for the cloaking power of its scent would wind up in its clutches instead. She'd even heard a story from a regular at the Selkie of a peasant boy who had kept a sustron chained in a stone root cellar, stealing its blood to spy on the naked maidens of the village. She had discerned it for the hopeful folktale told by the aspiring voyeurism of men who wanted to see tits for free. What a fateful irony that a creature with blood so useful to humans would find the humans' blood equally delectable. She thanked the cobbler for sharing his story, though the tales of the bloodless maiden were not helpful to Nox or her search.

Frustrated, she took a seat near the water fountain.

She was beginning to hate Yelagin more with every second that passed. The lake's soaking odor was inescapable. Whether she was smelling seaweed, fish, or algae, she didn't know, but it didn't have the same exciting salt and brine of the sea. She'd learned nothing. She'd embarrassed herself. She was exhausted and irritated.

She extended her palm to let her fingers dangle into the water and shuddered, stopping just short of breaking the surface. She wondered what sort of bacteria and illness lurked in the inconspicuous waters of the fountain and withdrew her hand. The only water she trusted was that of a hot, soapy bath she'd drawn for herself.

Nox continued sitting on the edge of the town square's fountain. Her feet were tired, her spirits just as damp. Enough townspeople milled by that she was able to stop someone now and again to interrogate them. She was just asking some awestruck teenage boy about any sight of tanned-skin peoples like those of the north when a young girl approached from the side and tapped her on the shoulder. Nox turned curiously to address the child, who appeared to be no more than five years of age. Her hands were clasped behind her as she rocked back and forth on her feet.

"There are demons, you know. My mama says they come from the north."

Nox smiled kindly. She felt her heart soften, despite the wave after wave of frustration that had been drowning her ever since her failure the night before. It was a nice break from the parade of male faces to speak to the little girl.

"Where are your parents?" Nox asked, frowning at the sparsely filled square.

The girl clasped her hands behind her back and wiggled proudly as she said, "I'm not to get into any trouble! But I can play in the square while Papa sells at the market. Mama stays with the farm."

"What's your name?"

"I'm Tess," she said. The child's grin was proud despite missing its two front teeth. She was small for her age, with gorgeous dark hair nearly as long as she was tall. It had been set in a braid, but the exuberance of child-hood had scattered much of the loose ends from what had surely once been neatly plaited hair into a muss of tendrils around her face. While Tess's hair was as black as soot, her face was as fair and milky as that of the common folk of Farehold.

Nox felt a tinge of something like sadness as she regarded the girl. She felt the inexplicable urge to pull the little one into her lap and cuddle her deeply, but out of common decency, she resisted. She knew it wouldn't be appropriate and would most definitely frighten the child.

"I'm sure your mother is a very smart woman. I know she'll keep you safe from any demons." She didn't feel the need to hurry the little girl away. Her life had sorely lacked human conversations with women and girls who weren't her colleagues or employers, or ones who lacked ulterior motives. It had been far too long since she'd had an exchange with anyone that was simply two normal people just talking.

"The demons don't hurt us," Tess said with confidence.

"Oh?" Nox asked, amused. "Do you have charms at your house? Wards etched into the doorway?" She had seen several runes scratched into the tops and sides of the frames of homes as she'd wandered about Yelagin earlier that day. She wasn't sure what sort of iron grip the demonic lore had over this city, but she supposed it had something to do with how isolated it was. Yelagin was very far from the castle and from the buzz of civilization.

It was even farther from the university, where one would probably learn just how useless those runes were for the creatures in the forest. She didn't know much about the art of magical manufacturing, but she greatly doubted that the doorways had been crafted by someone trained and gifted to actually create something effective.

"No, but when they meet in our barn, they never bother us. Mama has said they're not bad and to leave them alone."

Nox's lips parted. She was struck with genuine surprise. No one in the town square was listening, but she still found herself lowering her voice, counting on the burble of the water fountain to cover her words. "The demons meet in your barn?"

The little girl smiled, delighted to have shared her confidential information. She whispered, "Mama says we're not supposed to tell people about it. It's a special secret."

"That does sound special indeed," she said quietly. Nox stared at the child for a long moment, soaking in her wide-eyed innocence, heart pinching at the utter lack of goodness in her own life. She longed to snatch the child into her lap and squeeze her until she disappeared. "Tess, would it be all right if I gave you a hug?"

It was the best hug she'd had in years.

Tess waved happily at Nox as she trotted off to meet her parents. Nox wiggled her fingers in return, knowing that as soon as they turned their backs, she'd be following them home.

✦

It hadn't taken long for the family to repack their cart and leave the city for the evening. Nox trailed at a reasonable distance, urging her horse toward the trees once they

380

neared a small farmyard. Her beast protested slightly with a whinny, acting the part of a temperamental prima donna. It jerked to show its disapproval as it was forced from its comfortable path to the brambles of the underbrush.

"Oh, hush. As if your life is hard." She rolled her eyes at the horse.

The night-dark horse objected rather adamantly, nickering as she dismounted. She leashed its reins to a tree and began to slowly pick her way through the forest toward the farmhouse.

Nox was at home in the lateness of the hour. She had been a lady of the night for years now, and sleep was the furthest thing from her mind. If Millicent and her damned tome of monsters were to be believed, Nox might very well be a creature of the night by blood. Should they truly be meeting in the barn, perhaps they'd welcome their long-lost succubus kin with welcome talons. She nearly snorted at the mental image it conjured.

Nox had never struggled with the way her vision had adjusted to the dark. Perhaps it was the goddess's humorous gift to her namesake, or maybe it was a blessed curse from whoever—or whatever—had sired her. Her eyes didn't strain as she watched the candlelight in Tess's house blink out for the night. The absence of their orange glow made it easier for her to monitor the silhouettes of the home, the henhouse, the hills in the distance, and of course, the silvered outline of the barn as the light of the half-moon lit its frame.

It was a beautiful, if modest, home. The idyllic country coupled with the rolling hills and view of the lake made it the kind of place Nox would have loved to live in. In another life, she could envision herself in such a home, waking up to a glass of tea by the window, looking out as the sun came up over the water. She could picture herself waiting for Amaris to finish her book just there on the stuffed settee or see the life they'd lead tending chickens and selling eggs in Yelagin's square. She imagined their shared conspiratorial smiles as the towns-folk made comments about what very good friends the two maidens must have been to share a home and to have never taken husbands. She was sure she'd learn to love the ever-present freshwater smell if she shared this home with Amaris. It was ridiculous to let the daydream cross her mind, no matter how fleeting.

As she waited, she uncovered a very tiresome truth.

One thing no one had told her about espionage was that it was dreadfully dull. There was no excitement that the spying heroes of folk tales and ballads had led her to believe. There was no thrill from the deception as she watched the barn. Her mind wandered elsewhere—not to Amaris this time, but to the girls in the salon. She thought of troops she needed to gather. She thought of the toffee-haired Duke of Henares and of oxytocin and power and of the bluish-white glow that every soul had as it left the body. Her mind wandered to her childhood days at Farleigh, to the teachings of the church, to the bullies she'd met and the peers she'd hated. She thought of Emily—of her lips, her smile, her compassion—and regret tugged at her.

The memory of her speckled face was just starting to fade when Nox saw the distinct flash of blackened, batlike wings.

Thirty–Three

OVER THE PAST FEW YEARS, NOX HAD COME TO THINK of herself as brave. She rarely, if ever, met an opponent she couldn't tackle. The matrons and the Madame had favored her. The townsfolk had opened doors for her wherever she went. Men had swooned at her feet, handing over their mortal lives for a chance to be with her. As she sidled along the edge of the barn, painted in its shadow, she couldn't hear anything inside over the furious thundering of her own heart. She willed her knees to bend, her feet to move.

Bravery, like cunning, was a skill that required regular practice. She was strong, resilient, and clever, but her courageousness had atrophied from years of disuse.

The barn was traditional in its structure. The lower level was meant to house animals, with an upper loft intended to store their hay. The two enormous doors on the front opened and closed for cattle and horses, both of which had been shut in for the night. A human-sized door on the side that divided into two parts, top and bottom, was the entrance she angled for. She knew it to be common for barns to have such a division on their doors in case farmers might need to toss in food or check on the animals without risking a lamb too small and nimble to grab, or a flock of chickens rushing out. Nox reached the handle of the door, and each movement took her every drop of strength. If the rusted handle let out even the smallest sound, she was relatively sure she'd faint. How heroic.

She rallied her heroism and turned the door's handle with painful slowness. Unfortunately, only the top division opened.

"Fucking goddess-damned piece of—"

She felt quite confident that opening this door was the most frightening thing that anyone had ever done in the history of the continent, and it was outright offensive that she had to do it not once but twice. Her string of obscenities was contained to the quietest of furious whispers. She steeled herself to try again.

"Come on, you spineless jellyfish," she said, cursing herself as she summoned her grit.

She didn't mind the strong wave of hay and animal smells that hit her as she slipped into the barn. There was an honest, bucolic reassurance carried on the scent of farm life. The homeyness was comforting, which was a feeling she needed if she was to make forward progress tonight. Choosing her steps carefully, she closed the top half of the door but left the bottom half ajar should she need to make a quick escape. She didn't need the light of the moon seeping in and alerting them to the intrusion any more than necessary.

Nox crept closer to a ladder that she was just barely able to make out in the center of the barn. A horse in one of the stalls, obscured by the dark of the night, made a shuddering noise, perhaps shaking a fly from its skin. The sound caused her to pause, but the voices above contin-ued, unbothered. There was something unsettling about the way they were talking. She wasn't close enough to understand what it was, but the voices were something distinctly unlike the common tongue.

Nox's mind flicked like a candle illuminating the dark of her memories.

An omnilinguist had once visited the Selkie. While some humans were born with the small magics of palm reading, of fire, of scrying, or of stone, this young man had been invited to hold an audience with the queen for his gift of gab. He'd been eighteen—nearly a man in his own right—before he knew he'd even been born with such a magic, as he hadn't done much traveling before taking work on a ship. Everywhere they docked, whether the remote southern isles, the hot sand shores of the Tarkhany Desert, or even across the Long Sea, he'd understood and spoken with anyone he'd met without ever having encountered their people or studied their words. It didn't take long for word of his gift to spread. It was a delightful power, to be sure. While some magics terrified simple folk and villagers, there were few ways the power of language could frighten the citizens of the continent. The proud man had just concluded his meeting with the monarch when he'd marched directly to the best brothel on the coast to celebrate his honorific title as the court's translator.

It had been comparatively exciting to hear from someone directly who dealt with the queen rather than rumors or cityfolk's opinions of the lordlings. The omnilinguist claimed Moirai was a sharp and suspicious woman, wary of all who entered her throne room. After her daughter, Princess Daphne, had passed, she had sequestered herself to rule as Queen Regent while the young crowned prince grew to maturity. Once probed with enough drink to loosen his omnilingual lips, he'd described Moirai as a paranoid old witch and declared himself ready to serve the young king whenever he ascended the throne. Nox had smiled at that, always finding new ways to be amused at the pliability of men. What wouldn't they say in the company of women?

No matter how much coin he'd offered, Nox had refused to go up the stairs with him the night of his visit. At the time, she had not yet managed to sleep with a man without killing him, and this man of many tongues would have been a shame to murder. She hadn't particularly liked him, but she had seen the potential for usefulness in keeping him alive. She made some laughing, vague reference to her moon time of the month as an excuse, promising that if he were to return to the Selkie, she'd give him the ride of his life. Now that she'd mastered her curse, she'd love the chance to add the queen's omnilinguist to her harem of puppets.

She knew, however, that she did not possess such a gift for speech. Two of the men she'd killed in her journey of mastery over her feeding frenzy had been from foreign lands. The sea-fresh faces of the foreign sailors had been safe practice marks, Millicent had said, as they were too far from home for their families to come looking for them. The Madame had always applauded Nox for her effort, reassuring her of her progress whenever she had to clean up a body. Hers and the Madame's companionship was not a virtuous one, but she had been grateful for Millicent's assistance and encouragement in those early days.

She thought of this now as she listened to the voices above. While she knew in the pits of her stomach that the sounds were not the vowels and consonants of the common tongue, somehow she found herself comprehending their words. Their male voices carried well enough as they floated down through the barn.

"I'm telling you, she saw us. Gadriel can confirm."

Nox positioned herself behind the ladder. She had

gone as close as she dared before the demons in the loft might spy her. The dullest murk of moonlight filtered from the upper windows of the barn's loft down into the lower levels. She kept herself hidden from sight of whoever, or whatever, sat atop in the hay.

"He's telling the truth," the one they'd referred to as Gadriel responded. "I don't know how it's possible, but she saw us. Truly saw us, and wasn't afraid. If it weren't for her gift of sight, her companions would have killed us."

"And? How do we proceed with this information?" asked another.

Nox absorbed their words but felt as if the sounds were coming out in monstrous shrieks. There was something inhuman and beastly about what her ears heard, yet deeply sentient regarding what her mind understood. Perhaps if Millicent was correct and Nox was part demon, it was her demon half now that found itself able to comprehend the shrieks and gnashing teeth of the damned, no matter how her human ears attempted to block it out. The contradictory noises horrified her, but she pressed herself into the ladder and continued listening.

The two voices above pushed each other for plans and seemed determined to head southwest toward Aubade. If they were going southwest, she could leave and intercept them closer to home where she had the safety of reinforcements. She could have the troops of Henares rallied the moment she arrived. What good would she be now, caught in a legion of demons alone on a lakeside?

"I'll leave another letter for Theresa telling her we're headed south but to leave our outpost in Yelagin available for retreat," the first voice responded.

That explained how they were communicating with the farm family, but not why anyone would accept the unholy scribbles of demons as any form of command.

Perhaps they had threatened Tess's mother or her precious child. Nox didn't know much about demons, though nothing she'd read on the ag'imni had led her to believe them to be very intelligent. The bloodthirsty humanoids were rumored to have some gifts of speech, but only for the purpose of spreading lies and instilling fear. These voices seemed like the astute plans of men, not the serpentine whispers of the damned. Her head swam with questions of Tess's mother and the woman's affiliation with demons, but she pushed them aside to listen.

"How does she expect us to help?"

It was the third voice again. From the sounds of shuffled weight, there seemed to be more than three. How many additional diabolical presences were loitering overhead in the hay? Nox had wasted all her fear outside. Fortitude settled over her as she became determined to absorb every scrap of information disseminated from the loft above.

"She didn't ask for our help. We offered it" came the insistence from the only name she'd learned—Gadriel. "This is the chance we've been looking for. I'm telling you—this is the one. She's southwest bound on the regency's road as we speak."

The first voice chimed in with cautious optimism. "She travels with companions, but I don't believe they'll pose a threat to us. At least, I have high hopes."

A new voice now, a fourth guttural and bitter one, responded.

"I have too many dead men to trust your beliefs, Cai. How many years will it take for you to see the bodies of your friends and countrymen before you stop hoping for the best in these people."

Cai was the first voice, then. She had two names to work with now. She'd remember them for her ledger when she made it back to the Selkie. Nox was sure she'd think of nothing else for the entirety of the nine days she was to spend on the road back to Priory, pushing her horse within an inch of its life on the hard ride home.

"I need you to trust me," the one called Gadriel said. "I don't know if we'll survive. I've never guaranteed our safety. But we all know why we're here. The king has not stopped searching in over twenty years, nor has he shown any sign that he intends to stop. How many men will be sent across the border to die at Farehold's hands? How many of your brothers will you see filled with arrows? For the king, that number has no limit until he finds what he's looking for. This girl is the first time in twenty years I've held even the smallest of hope that we might end the carnage. I'm telling you, she's the one."

"Damn the mad king, and damn his useless fucking plot to lead us all to our graves," said the fourth voice with vitriol.

No one responded to this, but the silence that followed was not a comfortable one. The sounds of night loomed about them. The soft noises of horses shifting filled the quiet. The summer sounds of nighttime insects and nocturnal birds made a dull, comforting chorus beyond the barn's wooden doors. The loft creaked as demons above moved, seemingly troubled by the treasonous tone of the fourth man, before Gadriel offered his final words.

"He is our king. That's the last word on his charge. This is the order, from here on out. We know how to stay alive, how to cling to the shadows. Travel by night and avoid the villages, but follow the girl to Aubade. Keep her safe. Our only hope rests on her meeting with the queen."

"How will we recognize this *savior*?" asked a fourth voice bitterly.

"She fits the description," Gadriel said quietly.

"She's hard to miss," Cai added. His voice was the

cheeriest of the bunch as he went on, "She's traveling with two men, one half-fae. The girl herself is as white as the moon."

Weightlessness swept her from her feet as Nox's soul left her body.

No human or fae on the continent fit that description—no one, save for one. A sound like the ringing vibrations of her own blood clouded her ears as she clung to consciousness, desperate to hear the men's next words. She reached for the ladder, feeling splinters bite into her fingertips as her vision swam. They were still talking, but she could scarcely hear their words.

"Look for her silver hair," Cai continued, his voice a controlled excitement, "and if you're close enough, her eyes are as purple as lilacs in the spring. Come to think of it, though, she might be traveling with her hood up to hide her features for exactly that reason. If she's concealed, keep an eye for her companions. We met her human and her fire-haired faeling in the woods. Between the three of them, they shouldn't be too difficult to spot."

Though Nox knew she needed to remain concealed, both hands were gripping the ladder for dear life. If she fell to her back, they'd be alerted by the thump of her lifeless body. The ringing in her ears grew louder, drowning out the voices that had suddenly stilled. A horse whinnied, but something about the sound felt far away. Where blackness had been, suddenly stars began to swim in her vision, coloring her sight with their light. This was not the detachment that called to her as a friend. This was darkness at her door, threatening to take her against her will. She felt drunk, as if wine swam through her head. Nox began to sway and knew with certainty that no matter how tightly she gripped the ladder, she would faint.

She fought against the black that swam before her eyes, but void would win this battle. She took a ragged breath in as she began to fall. The last image as she drew in a final moment of consciousness was the monstrous face of an ag'imni staring down at her.

✦

Straw and manure were the first things to enter her consciousness. The smell of animals and barnwood were in her nostrils before her eyes dared to flutter. She raised herself to her elbows, straw clinging to her hair and her cloak. The quiet was pressing. When no sounds of voices or stirrings of demons moved above her, she knew the barn had been abandoned. She brushed away a piece of straw sticking to her face and forced herself into a sitting position. The creatures were gone and she was alone. All things considered, she was lucky to be leaving with her life. She should have been torn to ribbons after they'd discovered her. She should be a gory shell of entrails, left for Tess and her parents to discover in the morning. Instead, she was about to walk out of the barn, unscathed and armed with knowledge—even if she had failed rather spectacularly at making it in and out of Yelagin's demonic barn unnoticed.

It took a moment to find her feet, but soon blood returned to her limbs. Nox slipped out of the half door and latched it behind her on shaky legs. She hadn't been unconscious for long, as the moon had made markedly little progress across the sky. She continued picking pieces of straw from her hair and her cloak as she made her way amidst the shadows across the farmyard into the trees. The horse was extraordinarily impatient as she mounted it and urged it onto the road. It was a decidedly unfriendly beast, and perhaps if her wits ever returned to her, she'd ask the duke for a new steed.

They had been talking about Amaris.

The demons had been talking about Amaris.

How many ways could she turn the revelation over in her head? She was in a barn filled with ag'imni discussing Amaris.

She rolled the long-lost name around from the front of her brain to the back. She said it out loud a time or three. It would make more sense to convince herself that she had hallucinated the entire encounter than to believe that four damned creatures of hell had been discussing the white hair and lavender eyes of her Amaris.

That hadn't been the only information they'd shared. She made herself focus, desperately wishing she'd had a pen and paper. Amaris was heading to Aubade. Amaris was not alone. Amaris could see them. What did that mean, that Amaris could see them? They were not invisible; Nox had seen the membranous, stretched skin of their batlike wings as a demonic entity had entered the barn's upper window. She had seen the gargoyle's face as it had peered down at her. What else had she heard? There had been more; she knew there had been more.

There had been four voices, yes; of that much she was certain. She'd learned two of their names. They were talking about Amaris. She was traveling south with… what had they said? She was traveling southwest toward Aubade to meet with the queen. She had two male companions. One was fae. One was fae? Had there been another word used to describe him?

Yes, she realized. One was a fire-haired fae. That's how the beast had described him. Nox had been sharing drinks only one night ago with Amaris's ruddy, faeling friend. Not her captor. Not her enemy. Her riding companion. She had been across the table from Amaris's friend. She had grabbed the hand of Amaris's friend.

What else had they said? Nox felt strongly that there had been one more piece to the puzzle, but the voice inside herself continued to shout, *"Amaris is alive! Amaris is here, in Farehold! Amaris is heading south! She's alive, she's alive, she's alive!"* Whatever the demons had said, they had clearly wanted to ally with her. Nox knew she'd fight on the side of the ag'imni if they were truly Amaris's allies. But that couldn't be true. The ag'imni were creatures of nightmares. They were damnation personified, clawing their way up from the earth, escaped abominations who had wriggled free from the goddess's hell. In what conceivable plot could Amaris be the champion of hell?

The sooty horse was happy to keep to the road, moving forward of its own volition while she was left to her thoughts. It carried her far from the farmhouse and the forest and its trees, keeping the freshwater lake on her right side all the while. The road led straight into town, right to the first inn on Yelagin's outskirts, nestled on the edge of the lake. Nox dismounted numbly, leading the horse to the orange glow of the inn where the blessed release of sleep and perhaps several tankards of ale awaited her. If her head weren't so foggy, she'd press herself to ride out now in the dead of night, with or without the duke's armed escorts. But no, a few hours of rest would do her a world of good while she sorted through all that had been said.

She was nearing the inn's stables, swinging her horse wide to avoid the annoying blockade of another patron's glossy, black carriage, when a sharp voice preened to her from the shadow looming against the carriage's side.

"Isn't it the oldest lesson in the book? You tell a strong-willed woman not to do something, and it's the first thing they do. I do take full blame for that one, my dear."

Nox skidded to a halt in front of Millicent.

Thirty-Four

How—"

"Yes, yes, I travel rather fast. This is something you know of me, darling. Don't be dull."

Nox gaped at the Madame in her black dress, the color of shadow. She was a mere arm's length from the light and safety of the inn. Nox gripped the reins of her horse, in a true state of shock for the second time in one night. She'd thought she'd gone numb, but she could still feel the leather of her horse's reins, still smell the animal's sweat and the leather of its saddle, still feel the chill down her spine from the Madame's voice. She was present, and once more, she was not. This was how she'd learned to survive. She'd found a common retreat in the ability to stay present while wandering far, far away. Seeing Millicent had been her final straw as she felt the tether that kept her in her own body snap, whipping in the wind like a rope on the docks amidst a storm. She was taxed, physically and emotionally. Her head and heart whirred with too much force for her to process the woman before her.

"Climb in, please. I haven't got all night."

Millicent opened the door to the carriage and beckoned her forward.

Nox shook her head mutely. She was positive she did not want to go anywhere with the Madame. She pulled her horse closer, but it was not a loving animal. It resented the movement and tugged its long snout away from her, making her feel even more vulnerable than she had before.

"Traitor," she whispered to the horse.

The Madame arched a curious brow as Nox fidgeted with her inky black mount. "Would you like to return the horse to its master? I can certainly leash it with the others. We don't have to leave your beast behind, if that's the issue."

"Millicent…" she exhaled the Madame's name, too deadened from the night's turmoil to form the words she needed. She was a shell.

"You act like you haven't ridden with me before. It's childish, dear, really. We'll be back before the morning. You can sleep in your own bed tonight."

"My bed?" Nox repeated, uncomprehending.

What were her options? She was powerless against Millicent as far as succubae were concerned. Her charms held nothing except the sweet song of likable favoritism with most of the world's feminine parties. If she dashed into the inn, then what? Perhaps the innkeeper would shelter her from the Madame for a moment, so she could…start a new life in Yelagin? That wasn't in the cards for her, particularly as she knew that Amaris was already more than a day's ride southwest toward Aubade. Priory was just another stop along the way to the castle. What was the point in resisting if it was indeed the most effective means of getting her where she needed to go?

Nox found her words long enough to ask, "You can fast-travel?"

"Me? No, dear. This carriage, however, was the most marvelous trinket I picked up when I studied at the

395

university. I'll tell you all about it sometime—marvelous chapter of my life, it was. My manufacturing professor was something of an inventor, always fabricating this from that. Very compelling man. He was reluctant to part with it. You and I both know that women have our ways of being persuasive, through one method or another."

Millicent leered at the memory, flashing her teeth at some distant man from her past.

Nox moved forward in a daze, knowing only that she did indeed wish to go southwest. Amaris was headed southwest. Her room was there at the Selkie, her notes were on her desk, and Emily would be waiting for her there. She felt a pain somewhere below her ribs at that. How would she find the words to break Emily's heart again once she told her Amaris was close? Nox handed the horse's reins to Millicent, though the awful midnight animal put up quite the protest. She didn't care whether or not it came with them to Priory or if it was set free to roam the hills of Yelagin, but the action seemed like the only way she could consciously force her body to move. The chestnut horses bound to the Madame's carriage were equally unpleasant creatures and did not care one bit for the additional companionship.

Nox crawled into the carriage, feeling utterly disembodied as she did so. Her legs moved her forward, mind numbly replaying the events from the night. She was focused on envisioning Amaris and her riding partners, on remembering the words of the ag'imni, on combing through her thoughts to remember what else it was they had said.

"Let's get you home."

Nox must have fallen asleep, though she didn't know how. She hadn't remembered resting her head or closing her eyes, yet when she opened them again, the glows of

Priory were scarcely one mile away. She was choking on the sickly, familiar scent of the Madame's vanilla perfume.

Millicent's carriage was perhaps the most interesting piece of magic she'd ever thought possible. Nox had never heard of such devices that allowed the map before you to fold just as if it were no more than a piece of paper, with one destination meeting its opposite through the crease as they poked through locations. It wasn't the only magic item she'd seen. The Madame had shown her a spelled quill once, claiming it was able to write its letters and have them appear on papers anywhere on the goddess's earth, so long as the recipient had its matching feathered counterpart. Nox had heard stories from men at the Selkie about spelled objects, but it had been hard to tell fact from fiction when they spoke of such things while intoxicated and in the presence of beautiful women. The Madame had also told tales of coming close to owning an enchanted mirror once, claiming it reflected one's possibilities rather than their present, and she seemed a bit more reliable a source on such things than the bragging of drunken patrons.

Nox recalled a day more than three years ago when she'd opened her eyes and been in nearly the same spot, watching as the carriage approached Priory. Could it go anywhere in the world? Or was it tethered to exits predetermined by its enchantment? If she stole such a device, could it take her to Amaris?

"Did you learn much on your travels?" came Millicent's cold cadence.

Anger would have been easier to understand, but something about this restrained attempt at friendliness was inexplicably chilling. Nox considered what to tell the Madame. She knew precisely what she wanted to say. She could inform Millicent that yes, she'd learned that Amaris was alive and that she would no longer be acting as a pawn in the Madame's game to amass forces. She wanted to say that she wouldn't be helping her in her quest for puppet titleholders any longer. She wanted to wish the woman and her elaborate curls luck on their mission for domination and damnation before bidding her adieu, but she said none of this. Millicent was not a reasonable person. They had been accomplices over the last few years, thinly bound by common needs for their mutual ulterior motives. They were not friends.

Come with me instead, the darkness within her beckoned.

She shook her head, answering the void while ignoring the Madame.

Millicent considered her expectantly while awaiting a response, and Nox thought of the enchanted mirror and its possibilities. The happiest possible future would show her a vision where she immediately reunited with Amaris, aiding her in her apparent quest to speak to the queen. This future probably included more demons than one might hope, but if the ag'imni were to be believed, it was a possibility. One future would perhaps display the possibility of her liberating the other girls at the Selkie and rallying them to her cause, or taking the reins to the carriage and urging the trotting horses into a gallop toward her friend. She'd love to see a possible future where she opened the door and kicked the Madame out in a swift motion, watching her extravagant, jewel-toned attire roll on the ground as she sped away. In the most probable future, the one she felt quite certain the carriage was taking her to now, Millicent would surely keep her under lock and key at the Selkie, ensuring nothing allowed the precious succubus to slip away again. Millicent needed her puppeteering ability far more desperately than Nox needed the Madame. The possibilities were contingent on what happened next. What would a mirror that reflected the present reveal?

The shadows inside herself told her to just let go. They urged her to release her grip, to release her fear. They promised she would be safe if she sank into herself and allowed herself to float away.

"No," she said quietly to the shadows.

"What was that, dear?"

"I said no."

"No you didn't learn anything interesting?"

She could not allow them to get to the Selkie. She couldn't yield to the seductive temptation to let herself drift free from the world. No. She would not go. Not to the brothel, and not into the dark.

"Let me out," Nox said, reaching for the latched handle to the carriage door as its horses plodded forward outside the enclosed cab's walls. The numbness began to ebb as she found the words she needed.

Millicent's surprise was tangible. She intercepted the girl, her painted mouth opened in a startled gasp. The Madame attempted to subdue Nox's movements, treating her like one might a drunken companion who insisted on swimming in the river after a night at the alehouse.

"Are you mad, girl?" Millicent gaped, blinking in horror.

"Let me out!" She wriggled, freeing one arm from Millicent's restraint.

Millicent made more attempts to contain her, using her body to block the exit to the carriage as she grappled to restrict Nox's flailing arms. As the scene unfolded, Millicent's eyes bulged, not dissimilar to those of a dying fish. Nox had never snapped like this. It was as if the Madame were wrangling a crazed animal rather than a human woman.

Nox grew more rabid with every moment that passed, each heartbeat an increase in her ferocity, consumed with the singular need for exit.

"Let me out!" she screamed, grabbing a handful of the Madame's hair as she yanked her to the side, battling for her life, her survival, her freedom. "Let me out, let me *out!*"

She went feral with her singular need. She tore at Millicent, willing to rip the woman to shreds if it would release her. She'd found every drop of her warrior's heart, and she would not allow herself to be locked up in the Selkie again.

The Madame had her teeth set in a grit and was releasing a snarl in protest as she fought back, not caring how crazed Nox had become.

If she could just open the door enough, Nox would roll onto the road and begin running. Even if they both tumbled out onto the ground together, carriage in motion, she would twist herself free and run until she made it to the woods. She would hide, she would intercept Amaris, but she would not go back to the pleasure house. She would not enter the gilded, silk-tufted jail cell that awaited her.

"Stop!" Millicent shrieked, her voice like that of a banshee in the midst of the disaster.

There would be no stopping. Nox would sooner have them both die here having scratched one another's throats to ribbons than be locked away. She was so close to Amaris, there was no coercion or command that would confine her to the tawdry cave and be Millicent's puppeteer for one moment longer.

With barbarian effort, Millicent managed to rip a glove free from her hand and grab for Nox's bare wrist with the steeled cinching of a manacle. The inertia from

Nox's movements, propelling her forward only moments prior, crashed into her like the ocean's waves breaking against a cliff. The thrust that was meant to send her flying past Millicent and out of the carriage exploded instead within her. Her motion landed her in a crumpled pile on the coach's floor. Millicent had released Nox's wrist nearly as soon as she'd grabbed it, but the effect had been immediate.

The fight was over.

Nox was instantly still. She was limp, silent and neither willing nor able to move her arms, her legs, her voice, her dark hair in tendrils covering her face and neck.

Gloves now covering her fingers and forearms once more, the Madame, badly scratched and hair torn from its updo, knelt nervously over the slumped girl. She quickly put Nox's head on her lap in the tight space of the carriage's floor where only feet had been meant to rest, brushing the night-black hair from her face with indelicate motions. Millicent felt for a pulse, slapping Nox several times in quick, successive taps. The Madame's voice was panicked.

"No, no. Nox. No," Millicent repeated. "Come on, you're okay. Wake up. You're okay."

Millicent's distant assertions sounded as if they were filtering through dark and terrifying water, as if shouting to her from beneath the waves as she sank into the ocean's trench.

"Wake up," Millicent urged, voice hitching with desperation. Each word grew quieter, farther away than the one before. "It was just a touch. It was the quickest touch. You're okay, Nox. I need you to wake up. You're going to be okay. Please wake up."

But Nox, drifting into the black abyss, did not open her eyes.

Thirty–Five

"THIS SEEMS AS GOOD A PLACE TO CAMP AS ANY," MALIK said as he led their horses toward the sounds of running water.

As far as Amaris was concerned, the last two days had been blissfully uneventful given their chaos in Yelagin. Encountering demons, being betrayed by her hidden power, and then being chased from a tavern had been enough excitement for one journey. The boys hadn't attempted to hide their gratitude that they had not seen the ag'imni in several nights. Now it was time to stop for the night and relax against the peaceful serenity of fresh water.

The river they discovered was fast but not treacherous. Its chilled, crystal-clear waters were shallow enough to wade into without fear of being swept off one's footing. The horses enjoyed it nearly as much as the reevers. Both man and beast splashed into its waters, dunking themselves against the heat of the road and washing the dirt from their faces. Cobb's snout dripped from the exuberant way he continued to dip his whole nose into the river to drink.

The line of trees stopped a few arm's lengths away from the banks of the river, allowing grass and stones to stretch between the bending trunks and the rippling water. They took idle turns kneeling on the gentle slope of the bank and filled their waterskins, each disappearing from the group for stretches at a time to rinse the grime of travel from their bodies. While Malik warned them that the babbling of the river's current might drown out sounds they needed to hear from the forest, his caution was overruled by the other two. The lure of clean, fresh water took precedence over better judgment. They decided to sleep along its banks for the night.

The three had laid out their blankets and were gnawing off bites of salted meats with the watery light of the moon illuminating the river's surface before them. A dark shape shot above them, blotting out the stars. The reevers noticed immediately, eyes trained on the sky. The shadow like that of a large bird passed overhead once, then twice. The dark figure felt terribly foreboding against the indigo of the late hour. Ash set his sorry dinner down and reached for his bow, gripping its limb.

"Do you see that?" he asked cautiously.

Amaris spoke quietly. "I think that's the northern fae."

"And they're ominously circling as a greeting?" Malik asked, voice ripe with distrust. The man was not a coward, nor would anyone believe the title if it were ascribed to him. His worry came from his education, training, and instincts when it led to battle. He knew fear for what it was: an intuition that kept champions alive when an enemy approached.

"If I had to guess, I'd think they're doing it *so* we see them. That way they won't startle us when they land."

Amaris continued mechanically chewing her meat, not entirely convinced at her own argument. She was not particularly pleased with the fae's arrival either, but if she could stay relaxed, perhaps it would convince the others to stay calm as well. Ash did not release his grip on his bow, and Malik left his fingers on the hilt of his sword in solidarity. They eyed the large, dark bird as it swooped lower below the tree line on the same side of the river. All was quiet for several minutes as the three listened, but little could be heard over the gentle burble of the stream. When the first sounds of movement through the under-brush hit their ears, everyone was on their feet.

"Amaris?" a voice called out.

She breathed a sigh of relief. She glanced to Ash and Malik and found their hackles up. Palpable dread stretched between the men. Their eyes remained screwed onto the shaded space between the trees, disregarding how her posture had relaxed. She grazed over the tensed reevers and realized they'd need a bit more reassurance than she'd thought.

"Don't worry," Amaris whispered. She turned and shouted into the woods at the Raascot men, "They aren't monsters, just the very persistent, obnoxious bird-fae who don't know where they aren't wanted."

Ash whipped toward her with incredulity, body still angled for the trees.

"That is no screech of fae," Malik agreed.

Amaris scrunched her face apologetically. She lifted and lowered one shoulder in a shrug as she said, "From what I understand, you can't hear them for how they sound. The curse affects all facets of perception. I can't imagine what noises you're hearing, and I'm sorry for that, but he just called my name."

Malik gawked, turning his head while his sword remained raised in front guard.

"That's how your name sounds in *demon*? It's good to know we'll be able to properly address you in hell."

Amaris ignored him and called into the forest, "I hear

you. My friends won't hurt you—probably. Just walk in slowly so you don't spook their gentle sensibilities. And if you're particularly annoying, I'll be sure to tell them that you're going to drink our blood and let them attack."

Malik's jaw clenched in irritation. The tendons in Ash's forearm were taut from how tightly he held his bow, refusing to lower his weapon. They wanted to trust Amaris, but they would not do well to fully lower their guard and be caught unprepared against a true enemy. Several moments dripped with tangible anxiety as they waited, eyes trained on the dark spaces between the trees. Finally, Malik released a long, low breath as four ag'imni stepped out from the shadows of the forest.

✦

What ensued was the most delightfully uncomfortable campfire shared in the whole of recorded history. Amaris knew it was wrong to chuckle. She knew that empathy was demanded of her and that both parties of men must be going through their own personal brands of torment. That being said, the absurdity was perhaps the single funniest thing she'd ever been privy to, and she savored every delicious moment of it. If this moment had a flavor, it would have been orange slices covered in chocolate— delectable for those with a very specific palate. Amaris, however, adored chocolate oranges and was positively delighted at the comedic discomfort of their campfire.

Their seven bodies had formed a horseshoe around the crackling fire. They were without a doubt the seven strongest and most terrifying things in the forest, a fact that allowed them to forgo the general wisdom of avoiding fires at night. As the only one who could successfully translate between the reevers and the Raascot fae, Amaris took on the role of deeply reluctant host. She assigned the men tasks just to give them something to do; otherwise they'd be forced to sit and stare at one another. Amaris ordered the Raascot fae to gather wood and kindling and had the reevers use their flint to light and foster a warm fire. She then told the men of Raascot to take a seat on one side, the river to their left, and the men of Uaimh Reev to take a seat to the opposite, the river to their right.

"She's really bossy." Malik frowned apologetically at the demons.

"Oh, it's good to know it's not just toward us," Gadriel responded.

Ash and Malik cringed but tried to remain polite.

"What did he say?"

"He said that I'm delightful and that you should be grateful to have me."

Gadriel gave her a withering look as she continued coordinating their evening.

At one point, Amaris was the one who left to collect more firewood. She was quite sure that no one had moved a muscle in her absence, everyone too rigid with discomfort to risk speaking or shifting.

She sat precisely in the middle at the top of the horse-shoe as the intercession for the two groups of men and folded her hands over her legs.

"You're a chatty bunch tonight, aren't you?" she mumbled to herself. She would be the first to admit that she was taking entirely too much pleasure in their distress. They deserved their bitter medicine—both the reevers and the winged fae alike. Their intersection in her life had nearly cost her everything.

The northerners tried to keep their conversation to a minimum for the first while, since every time they opened their mouths, Malik and Ash seemed to be performing a two-man act in displays of winces, disgust, and the stoic bravery to conceal their obvious discomfort. Amaris knew that, in theory, her friends were being very courageous. She understood that they must be seeing and hearing something from which nightmares were made. Even knowing that to be the truth, the boys had to be witnessing four demons just…sitting there. Surely, Ash and Malik saw ag'imni relaxing around a campfire, hissing and snarling in the language of the damned with the charming ease of scary monsters at a tea party. The ridiculousness of picturing an ag'imni warming itself by firelight while it chatted politely with its companions was enough to fill her belly with smiles.

On the other side, it was clear the fae had not been this close to southerners in decades. While Ash and Malik flexed and tensed, the men of Raascot shifted uncomfortably, self-conscious at their effect on the others. Amaris, on the other hand, wished she could bottle the night and take sips of it for years to come.

"Stop laughing," Malik scolded with muttering disapproval.

"You'd laugh too if you could see what I see!"

While she knew Gadriel and Zaccai, the other two were introduced as Silvanus and Uriah. She did her best to serve as interpreter and aquatint the two parties. Ash and Malik were easy enough for the dark fae to recognize, but Ash mumbled something about the four creatures' needing to stay in their assigned seats or their names wouldn't matter, as all ag'imni looked exactly alike. He did seem to be making an attempt at acceptance. When enough time had passed with no one being maimed, eaten, or hunted, the reevers appeared genuinely convinced that everything Amaris had said was the truth. They knew enough from their bestiaries to know that monsters did not sit for civil conversation. The beasts before them were simply enchanted fae, little more than men under a perception curse. While that didn't make it any easier on the eyes or ears, they would find a way to deal with the reality.

Malik, in a triumph of bravery, stretched his arm over the fire barrier between them and offered some of his salted meat to the slick, gray creature nearest him. Zaccai looked startled by the gesture but stood to receive the cured, meaty olive branch. The transaction was the catalyst they needed, as the men breathed out a collective sigh of relief, relaxing their tension slightly.

"Do you have a plan to get in to see the queen?" Gadriel asked of the group. It was the first time anyone from either side attempted to speak to the opposite party.

Amaris took it upon herself to translate to the reevers, answering, "I planned to wing it. No pun intended."

Several of them seemed to flex and flare their wings in response.

"I don't think we can help you get into the city—at least, not during the daytime."

"Then it's a good thing I didn't ask for your help in entering the city, is it?"

"Could you at least try to be pleasant?" Gadriel asked dryly.

She chewed her meat for a moment, considering it. "No."

Ash frowned. "What are they saying?"

"They want to be even more problematically involved in our lives than they already are."

Gadriel ignored her response. He had spent hundreds of years serving as a respected general in Raascot, and the goddess's humor had forced him to collaborate with a headstrong, disrespectful witch. He pretended she hadn't said anything as he answered.

"If you can travel by night and try to call an audience

with her majesty after the sun is down, we'll have your back to the best of our abilities."

Amaris frowned. "I do think there's something we haven't considered. While we know the queen was ordering the killing of northern men, often the simple folk are just as responsible as Moirai's armed troops for hunting you, correct? The citizens of Farehold are not slaughtering fae; they're killing what they believe to be demonic abominations. How would my persuasion change that? I mean, if I saw what Ash and Malik saw, I'd kill you too. Come to think of it, I still might."

It was Zaccai's turn to speak. "I think you need to give us a little more credit. A pitchfork flung by a spooked farmer isn't what's taking us down." His lips twitched in a half smile. "I don't doubt any reever's ability to face us in battle—you'd make a formidable opponent. But you've had plenty of opportunities to kill us. Admit it—you're our friend."

"I most certainly am not."

Gadriel arched an eyebrow. "Are you sure you want her as a friend?"

Amaris's eyes narrowed.

One of the new companions, Silvanus, a brutish, unpleasant man, spoke. "Queen Moirai—goddess curse her to hell—knows what she's doing. She's sending orders knowing where we are and what her troops are to be on the lookout for."

Gadriel answered this time. "It could never be an open battle with a fight like this unless she marched north and came to us. We exist in small pockets throughout the south. We travel by night, and our unifying gift is flight. Moirai can't send any true war band to take us out in her kingdom. What she has done for the last twenty years is ensure that wherever she has a duke or lord who

409

serves her anywhere in Farehold, his men are conscripted to hunt us. Her troops are readied with weapons meant for us and us alone. They're given intel on our outposts. While townsfolk might take a swing or loose an arrow, her men have been equipped with metallic shredding arrows specifically fabricated for our wings."

It took Amaris a moment to relay the information to the reevers, who had been straining the muscles in their necks and faces as if they might, through some miracle of the All Mother, be able to comprehend what was being said. The perception curse allowed nothing through its cracks to be heard except for the grating of monsters.

"I'm sorry," Malik said apologetically, "but your dark fae demons sound like they're cutting knives on plates with their vocal cords. You don't hear it at all?"

She frowned. "True ag'imni are said to be able to speak—even if it's only for mischief or fearmongering. All the texts say so. The fact that these crows can't be understood at all is a testament to the thoroughness of this curse, don't you think? Whoever created it had no intention of allowing anyone from Raascot to be seen or heard south of the border, ever again."

"We're not crows."

"Hush. I'm not talking to you."

Gadriel's face made it clear he'd never been so openly disrespected in his life. If she wasn't mistaken, his men seemed to enjoy the exchange. Zaccai was making no attempt to conceal his delight. That being said, none of the men from Raascot appeared to appreciate Amaris's comparison to crows, though she did have a point.

Malik's frown deepened as he said, "So they weren't even made into real ag'imni. Just…demons."

Ash spoke, looking first to Amaris, then to the creatures. "If we are to work together, I need to know

410

what Grem and Odrin were sent to find out. Our reevers are in Raascot seeking an audience with your king, because if the reevers are to have any hope of keeping the peace, we need to understand his motives. Why are you here? Why risk your lives to infiltrate Farehold at all of these outposts? What does Ceres want?"

There was a tension that needed no translation, as the pause that stretched between them transcended linguistic barriers.

The happy burbles of the stream filled the responding quiet. The dark fae seemed to fight an uncomfortable internal battle. The men looked to Gadriel, their general, as their spokesperson. Amaris had offered the purpose of her dispatch many nights ago, but they had yet to reveal theirs.

It was clear that their honesty rested solely on the shoulders of the general. After far too much time had passed, Gadriel exhaled slowly and looked at Amaris.

"King Ceres believes he has a son."

Ash and Malik looked expectantly at Amaris for the translation, but her brows were knit together in a study of Gadriel's face. Her interpretation came out as a reiterated question, asking them for an explanation.

She repeated, "The king has a son?"

The reevers discussed this information while she continued to search the general's expression.

Maybe it wasn't that they had expected him to reveal this information, but his men continued to trade looks. Zaccai's eyes briefly touched hers but quickly looked away, allowing the general to continue to speak for them. She felt a strange pinch of discomfort for the first time that night, but she didn't know why.

"We've been searching for the child since it was born. Something about its birth seemed to set off the curse."

She tested the words carefully, rolling them back and

forth in her mouth, repeating herself as she worked out the material.

"The king has a son, and his child is the reason for your curse in Farehold. The king has an heir in Farehold. The curse is a result of his heir?"

Zaccai shrugged, still not meeting her eyes.

"It would seem that way. The curse is about twenty years old, so we expect the heir should be in his twenties, if he lives at all."

Uriah, who hadn't spoken all night, was quiet as he said, "If the son had died, the curse would have broken."

"We don't know that the curse and the heir are related," grumbled Silvanus.

"If they aren't, then that's one hell of an unfortunate coincidence," Amaris mused.

"What else do we know?" Malik asked. He looked at the creatures but kept his question on Amaris. "Why would his son be in Farehold and not in Raascot? Was it a stolen baby? Is this a witch's dealings?"

Gadriel was the only one who maintained unwavering eye contact while the other fae looked into the fire. "The king believes it to be hidden somewhere in the southern kingdom. It would seem that this curse is a way to prevent him from ever being reunited with the heir to his throne."

Amaris conveyed the message.

Malik's mouth tugged down. Gadriel had sidestepped several parts of his question.

"What of the mother?" asked Malik.

"We don't think she lives. The king made it sound like she passed long ago. He's…" Gadriel searched for the correct word. "King Ceres has been a bit difficult for some time. We haven't uncovered much, but we do have a lead as to how we might find out."

"Difficult how?" Amaris prodded.

"Being reunited with his child is the only thing he cares about. Occasionally, his obsession seems to cause Ceres to stand in his own way."

"I'm listening," Malik prompted, hoping Amaris would continue.

"By this time tomorrow, we could be at the Temple of the All Mother."

Amaris made a face, asking, "And what? Pray for answers? I didn't take ag'imni to be so religious."

It was a taunt, and even though the faes' expressions ranged from flashed teeth to scowls, their anger was playful enough. Perhaps after all these years, it was validating to hear the words from the voice of a southern girl. They'd undoubtedly come to understand how they were perceived, and yet she was not afraid. She did her best to empathize with whatever relief they must be experiencing to finally feel seen.

Zaccai smiled hopefully. "We haven't been able to ask the priestesses our questions. We've tried writing letters that have been left at the temple's door, but for some unknowable reason, she doesn't seem to want to put the great secrets of the universe down on paper, so we've never gotten a response. We have reason to believe they have an item of great power that could help us find the Raascot's heir."

Ash turned to her. "Ask your dark fae—"

From his flinches, Amaris could tell he was cut short by what he perceived as screeching.

"Even Uaimh Reev is using such terms?" Silvanus said, his voice thick with disgust.

Gadriel sighed. "We all live on the same continent, but Farehold seems to be the only kingdom that gets to believe it's alone in the world, with the rest of us existing in their peripherals. If the reevers are full of citizens of Farehold—"

"It's not Uaimh Reev's fault," Zaccai said softly.

Everyone spoke as if she weren't there. Amaris melted amidst her brothers while the fae spoke around her. Zaccai continued, "If no one from Raascot has joined the neutral territory and taken up with their cause in a century, how are they to know better?"

Gadriel glared. "The same way they know about sustrons and vageth and the whole of civilized history. Education."

"What are they saying?" Ash whispered for what felt like the hundredth time that night.

Amaris blinked at the exchange, shaking her head. "I truly have no idea."

The hour was getting late, and Amaris was tired. The northern fae may have been nocturnal, but the reevers had not had the necessary time to adapt to such a sleep schedule. They planned to transition into night life so that the winged men could better aid them in their mission. For now, they needed to rest. They decided to reconvene the following night at the Temple of the All Mother. Zaccai informed them that if they followed the river, they would find the temple over the edge of its waterfall.

Uriah, who hadn't spoken much that night, made himself quietly useful and smothered the fire as they stood. The Raascot fae would be patrolling the forests while the reevers slept. As they were saying their parting words, Amaris inhaled sharply, face pinched in a question. The fae paused to hear her.

"One more thing, before you go," she began. She tilted her head to the side as she looked to Gadriel. "How does the king know it's a boy?"

◆

Despite her years of cultivating tenacity, Amaris was the first to admit that she was easy to frustrate. Recognizing what was arguably one of her more unflattering qualities did nothing to expand her patience. The day wore on her with the agitation of one dozen mosquito bites.

It took them nearly a full day to find the temple. It was for the safety and sanctity of the priestesses and their sanctuary that the temple was far from the main road, discouraging travel for all but the devout. This would have made it difficult to find even if they'd been traveling through conventional methods, but the reevers were following the river. Unlike the easily traveled road that bisected the continent, the river wound in tight, snake-like coils. The woods on either side of its banks made it difficult to cut a more direct path with their horses. They hugged the twists and turns, almost definitely doubling their travel time. Hours had passed without the hope of any progress until their ears picked up the distant, telltale thunder of a waterfall. Ash was the first to hear it, motioning the others forward. The faeling rushed ahead and made it to an overlook, skidding to a halt at what he saw.

They had most definitely located the Temple of the All Mother. Reaching it would be a separate feat entirely.

The Raascot men had failed to mention that the waterfall's pool at which the temple sat was no gentle slope; rather, it was the bottom of a rock face far too sheer to climb. Their initial assessment told them there was no straightforward route to descend. Though they'd met the river's edge and found the waterfall near what the evening sun told them would have been the six o'clock bell, it took the reevers several hours to navigate the trees, pick their steps along climbable slopes, and create paths wide and safe enough for them to lead their horses down to the temple's glen. By the time they had tied their horses, they were in the twilight hours of dusk.

What they saw took their breath away.

The Temple of the All Mother was no church, nor was it any common temple. The sacred space belonging to the goddess and her high priestess practically hummed with the intrinsic magic of the goddess's power. The forest of their day's trek through the summer sun had been a mix of rough boxelders and oaks along with maples and buckthorns. Their shins had been scratched and torn by weeds and brambles and snagged by the underbrush. As they approached the temple, the woods surrounding this holy place had changed slowly but completely, as if each step they'd taken had brought them closer to a better, lovelier world.

The trees lining the temple's glen were made of papery, silver-white bark, gently quivering in the breeze. The vegetation underfoot dwindled until they walked only on soft, cool grass. The twisted brown trunks had grown lesser and lesser as they'd drawn nearer to the temple, slowly replaced with the consistency of aspens, birches, and willows. Amaris knew their leaves to be green, but it was a blue-green bordering on silver as they rippled from the wind and flashed their underbellies, rubbing together with the whispers of a haunting forest song. Their wooded scent was both mellow and fragrant, refreshing and filling. The waterfall tumbled from the cliff, but it was not the jagged, looming cliffs like those found near Stone. This river had ended in a seemingly obsidian lip, scooping inward to hollow out the hill below it in a dark, shallow cave. The water fell, free of the interruption of rock, plunging its bridal-white mist into the pool below—a basin that seemed unnaturally clear and still for a body that was receiving tumbling water from above. All of these elements of beauty and wonder were before one even considered the temple itself.

"Oh my goddess," Malik whispered, his voice hushed in reverence.

"I didn't know such a place existed," Amaris agreed, lips parted in wonder.

Ash said nothing, his posture honorifically stiff as he stared at the building before them.

Amaris looked to one brother, then the other. She'd never seen their cheery faces this slack-jawed. There would be no witty quips, no banter, no commentary about the Temple of the All Mother. For once, they were both gloriously silent. They'd stayed at the tree line, standing amidst the shadows of the aspens. Something about the space seemed nearly ominous in its glory, as if their grubby, world-weary presence would be an insult to the art of the goddess's temple.

The Temple of the All Mother was hewn from the cream-smooth of white marble. Enormous, unbroken pillars connected the floor to the lofted ceiling. Its height, width, and length were that of a glorious cathedral. The roof of the temple towered nearly to the lip of the cliff, though far enough back that neither crowded the other. The marble glimmered with shimmering gold flecks that appeared to be embedded within the milky rock itself. Steps led up into a wide-open entrance, one with no doors or hinges or locks, allowing them to see directly into the temple's innermost places. The size of the temple, the beauty of the waterfall, and the stillness of the forest were nothing compared to the reason the enormous temple required such a space, for even from where the three reevers gaped hundreds of yards from the entrance, they saw what rose from the center of the temple.

Growing in the middle was what appeared to be the ancient, twisted expanse of a living tree. The tree had few leaves, but its knotted arms wove throughout the temple, lit by some ethereal light that seemed to glow from both above and below. It wove its way upward and outward, filling much of the temple.

"What do we do?" Ash asked, breaking his silence.

Amaris shook her head. She had no answers. She knew they were meant to wait for the fae, as it had been Gadriel and Zaccai who had suggested that the temple would be where they found information of great importance. She felt like no amount of time would be long enough. She would never feel ready to cross the glen and mount the steps. She would never feel worthy of setting foot anywhere near the tree, older and more beautiful than time itself.

There were few times in life that Amaris had been truly unaware of the passage of time, but their feet felt glued to the bluish mossy grass underfoot, soft enough to be plush carpeting. She and her companions may have stared for ten minutes or one thousand years. She would have stayed in that spot, soaking in the temple and its glen, its aspens, its moonlit pool, the lavender sky overhead, and the incredible tree in awe and wonder for the rest of her life. Only the sound of a demon could have torn them from their reverie.

Though the sun had not quite set, the sky was purple enough to have emboldened the northern fae to travel. She heard the general before she saw him. His voice was hushed, not wanting to startle the others. Gadriel approached her and stood at her side. Perhaps they'd used whatever dampening wards had enabled them to stay hidden on their first encounter, because he had been utterly silent until he was upon them. Ash and Malik stiffened at the horrid contrast of the amphibious, humanoid monster in such a hallowed place but said nothing.

"We couldn't have prepared you. No words do it justice," Gadriel said quietly.

It felt wrong—*sinful*, even—to enter this temple with any motive other than that of prostrating oneself before the All Mother. Last night she had mocked them by asking if they had gone to the temple to worship. While she had never been a religious girl, she could imagine no other purpose to enter this temple.

"What do you need me to do?" she asked. Her voice was so quiet she felt as if the quaking aspens might have whisked her breath away. For once, she felt no irritation as she looked at Gadriel. The surroundings seemed to have a similarly calming effect on the general. For the briefest moment, she thought he looked at her under the silver light the same way she looked at the temple.

From across the glen, a woman's voice called to them.

"Step out of the forest," it said.

The musical sound of the call was so beautiful, so serene. Her sudden presence did not alarm them but tugged at the recurrent sense of true, unadulterated awe. Amaris had not seen the woman before, though now that she looked, she could not imagine how anyone could have missed her. The woman was as onyx as Amaris was white. Her skin glistened with its depth, something richer than night. While the Raascot fae tended to be bronze, this woman was the true, dark, resonant browns of the whispered beauty of the Tarkhany Desert. They were known for their gorgeous depth of skin, but Amaris knew that even in the desert, this woman would have towered as a goddess of beauty amongst the rest. Perhaps this woman *was* the goddess. Her long black hair, in thick, elegant braids independently fused together, was clasped up in a golden band. Her dress was marbled like the temple around her.

The woman beckoned them to approach.

Gadriel did not linger behind the way she'd expected. As far as Amaris had understood, the Raascot men had tried for decades to stay concealed. She stifled her surprise when the ag'imni matched her stride toward the temple. Zaccai was close at Gadriel's opposite shoulder while the reevers flanked her opposite side. What a motley group of five they were—dirty and travel-weary, human, fae, and ag'imni, approaching the most magnificent place on the continent. They stopped when they arrived at the base of the steps, looking up at the priestess where she stood.

The priestess regarded the winged Raascot fae, but she did not seem afraid. Her face was nearly impassive, containing perhaps a touch of curiosity. She moved with the slightest tilt of her head as she looked at them.

The woman's voice was not loud, unkind, or excited. It, like her expression, was almost entirely blank. The serene priestess simply *was*.

"Why do you seek the Temple of the All Mother?" she asked.

The reevers took a nearly imperceptible step backward, urging Amaris to speak. Uncertainty spiked through Amaris as she looked first at the northern fae, then to the priestess. She wished she had something grand or eloquent to say. She didn't feel like this was a place where any words could do justice to its splendor. She struggled and came up short, but Amaris did her best to summon reverence and make her words important.

"We…" She twisted her mouth, looking over her shoulder. Amaris lifted her eyes to the priestess and tried again. She finally decided upon "We seek knowledge and believe the answers we need may live here at the temple."

The ghost of amusement flickered behind the priestess's eyes. "Live," she mused quietly.

Amaris had chosen her words either very well or very poorly. She couldn't discern which.

The woman extended an elegant hand. Moonlight reflected off her arm, silhouetting her as she held her palm still in a beckon.

"You are welcome here, child," she said. Then with serene finality, she added, "Men may not enter the temple."

Amaris didn't need to look at the others to know that they would not press the issue. She would enter alone.

When Amaris and Nox were children, the matriarchal religion had always won small favors with both of them for this reason alone. The bishop who had visited Farleigh was the lackey sent ever on the road in service to the All Mother. The only role in their faith that suited males who opted to worship the goddess were those outside the sacred temples. Bishops were permitted to lead in lessons in their town churches, but they had no place in the presence of the All Mother herself.

Men of the cloth existed throughout the kingdom. They could worship through upholding the Virtues and ensuring that the All Mother's graces were valued in her outposts of charity across Farehold through the hardships of travel, rather than the honorific positions of power within the temples granted to the priestesses. Perhaps this is how the All Mother was worshipped in other kingdoms as well, but Amaris had no way of knowing. She knew that the love for the goddess was felt in other lands, but she could not speak to their practices. She hoped men were kept from the sacred temples in Raascot, Sulgrave, Tarkhany, and the Etal Isles alike.

Amaris took slow, solemn steps toward the priestess, following the woman as she led her into the temple. She was vaguely aware that there were other rooms, other pillars, other shadows and alcoves and perhaps things to be seen, but she saw only the tree that served as the temple's heart.

"Wow," she'd murmured, not aware she'd made the sound out loud.

"The goddess is beautiful," the priestess said knowingly, not shaming Amaris for the childlike way in which she had absorbed the tree. It was not brown like an oak or white like the birch. There was a grayishness to the way its large trunk rose at an angle, twisting back with its arms intertwined and outstretched to the heavens.

Amaris caught moments just as they passed, like grabbing for a piece of dust in the sunlight only to have the air send it from one's fingers. Had she heard that correctly?

"The tree is the goddess?"

The unreadable priestess sounded lightly pleased and somewhat amused, her mouth the ghost of a smile.

"Yes," she continued with her melancholy smile, adding, "And no. What have the worlds called our All Mother? She is the Tree of Life. She is Bodhi, Genesis, and Yggdrasil. She is here with us now, and in the worlds between. She is our All Mother. From her, all living things come."

Amaris had never considered herself slow of wit, but these words, though intelligible on their own, made no sense to her when combined by the priestess's lips. The names held no meaning, no knowledge.

"There is more than one tree?" she attempted.

"The All Mother will not limit herself to one body. A single body can be cut down, destroyed. A single name can be forgotten in the wind. But what of a forest? What of the earth? Can all tongues forget 'tree' even in its absence? Ideas surpass the bounds of worlds. Her concept is everlasting. It is transcendent. That is the All Mother."

Perhaps Farleigh had not offered the most rigorous

theological education. She knew the All Mother to have no face. She knew of the goddess's graces, her virtues, her joys and charities. She had learned the prayers and recited them in her lessons. There had been no mention in her studies of a tree.

The symbol of the All Mother that she'd seen emblazoned in iron in churches of Farehold or even the one that had been welded to her orphanage filled her mind with a sudden, sharp comprehension.

The symbol was simple and recognizable. Once again, she saw its two parallel lines and the upturned horseshoe that intersected them. It could be made with three strokes of the quill and was easy to embroider into cloth or hang in the homes of believers. As she reflected on it now, she had been looking at a tree. The two lines were its trunk, the horseshoe its branches.

Amaris extended a hand as if to press her palm to the source of life itself, though she was several scores of arm's lengths from the trunk of the great, twisted life that expanded before her. She held her hand aloft, no intention of truly pressing her fingers to its wood.

"I was never taught that we worshipped a tree."

For the second time, the priestess displayed emotion. This was the downward turn of her lips, the puckering of her brow. It was a combined displeasure; maybe it was sadness, maybe frustration.

"She is, and she isn't," the woman said, looking first to Amaris, then to the tree. "She is here, and she is all. Why should she not manifest in a place where those who wish to revere her may worship."

Though the woman's riddles were beautiful, Amaris did not find them particularly helpful. Perhaps she'd make a note to live a more virtuous life and actually read the theological tomes. In the meantime, she had questions.

"I need to ask you for answers."

"I expect so."

"What can you tell me about the curse on the land?"

The priestess offered the ghost of a smile yet again. "Me? I can tell you nothing."

There was an impropriety with which the priestess answered. Amaris felt as though she was being intentionally difficult, holy woman or no.

"What can you tell me?"

"I can tell you many things."

She pursed her lips. "Will you share them with me?"

"What would you like shared?"

Amaris's fingers flexed and relaxed once more at her side as she fought frustration. Answers were only as valuable as their questions. She sighed. "How can I learn about the curse on this land?"

This phrasing appeared satisfactory. The woman looked to the tree, then to Amaris once more. Her face had been a nearly unreadable mask through the duration of their visit, yet there was some emotion in the distance behind her eyes that the reever almost recognized. She scrutinized the priestess while the woman spoke.

"Magic is energy," she said. "It is neither created nor destroyed. It exists before it takes shape and maintains its presence after it is uttered. If you find the orb of its physical shape, there too you will find your answers."

"Do you have the orb?"

"I do not."

She stopped herself from asking the priestess if there was *anything* helpful about the woman. Amaris prevented herself from the insult, knowing it for the disrespect that it was. Even in her agitation, the woman's presence was calming, returning her to her senses.

If the priestess frustrated her, perhaps she should

focus instead on the tree. What had the woman called it? Bodhi? Genesis? Yggdrasil? The tree absorbed her attention. As she asked her next question, she realized the tree had seemed to pulse every time she spoke.

"Where can I find the orb?"

Again, her question earned little reaction. Perhaps the priestess, lost to the reverie of her worship, had detached from this mortal world that she had little connection to. She did almost look too magical to be human. Her dress looked like the pillars and marbles had offered some of their milk and gold to be sewn into an elegant, flowing fabric. Her arms were bare, save for an elaborately engraved cuff on her upper arm. She was as much art as she was human.

"It is held where all magic's secrets are held. You will find it there."

Amaris's fingers flexed for the second time. Why couldn't she contain her irritation? Maybe it had something to do with that curious, unidentifiable emotion that the priestess had displayed. Perhaps this woman didn't realize the importance of the mission, and that's why she felt no requirement for helpfulness. The woman was communicating to her that she was concealing something, while simultaneously telling her that whatever she hid was to remain that way.

That was it, she realized. The distant flickers in the priestess's eyes were the shrouded defenses of secrecy. The look in the back of her gaze was like a wall covered in beautiful, flowering vines, guarding all that she would not share. She knew more than she was saying.

Amaris took a stilling breath, begging her temper to ebb.

"And where is all magic held?"

Amaris drank in the woman's appearance one last

time. No pointed ears. No enlarged irises. No extended canines. Her ethereal beauty notwithstanding, she was not fae. Hoping her next action would not damn her to hell, Amaris gave a command.

"Tell me where to find the orb."

The priestess considered her with taciturn amusement.

She did not answer Amaris, nor did the holy woman scold her. Instead, she laughed. Her voice was the music of tinkling bells, the sound of the quaking aspens whose leaves had trembled and descanted in the glen. The unrecognizable secrecy was there, but there was also something a bit like pride. Yes, the woman looked distinctly proud. Not of herself but of Amaris.

Her face mellowed into a soft, distinctly human smile. The gentleness was almost maternal as she eyed Amaris kindly for the first time that night. She took her time soaking in the reever's appearance. Amaris remained still, allowing herself to be studied. Nothing about their interaction had been similar to any conversation she'd had with man, fae, reever, matron, demon, or the like. Why should this careful examination be any more usual than the rest of their exchange?

The priestess began to raise a hand as if to touch her, and Amaris flinched in surprise. The woman seemed to return to her senses, allowing the near-happy expression to fade as her composure engulfed her once more.

Rather than give her any sort of answer, the priestess offered a question.

"Why is it that those who walk this earth need such finite limits to understand the world around them? The binary ways of fae and men are trivial to the All Mother. I hear your words for what they are: a gift from the goddess's tongue. Humans are meant to bow before your will. That is your blessing."

Amaris blinked in surprise, lips parting as she wordlessly attempted to make sense of what had happened. She couldn't. The woman showed no traits of the fae, yet Amaris's command had glided off her like water on a glass.

"I'm sorry," Amaris said finally.

And she truly was, but only because her attempt at persuasion had failed. Perhaps the command would have been justifiable if it had led to something useful. With the priestess laughing at her attempted flex of power, she felt only shame. She was a small, dirty, pitiful thing in an enormous, pristine, sacred space. She did not deserve to be here.

"You use what you have in the only ways you know. The goddess will wield it for you at the fullness of time," she said. The priestess waved it away as if it hadn't offended her in the slightest.

The woman began walking in long, elegant strides. Her footsteps were quiet, not the authoritative clatter of heels that one might expect from a woman at court but the muted movements of the pressing silence in the temple. It was a silence that was, and wasn't. For though there was no sound, it was not stifling. The air glowed with life.

"Can you tell me anything I need to know?" She watched again as each time she spoke, the tree pulsed almost imperceptibly. She nearly tripped on her own feet as she followed the priestess around the tree, her attention focused on the effect her words had on the tree. "My friends seek King Ceres's son. It's why they're here from Raascot."

The priestess continued her slow, stately circling of the tree. She did not look at Amaris, only at the twisting limbs of her goddess.

"I know why your men come from Raascot."

Amaris followed. Her brows knit as she asked, "Can you see them? The dark fae?"

"Ag'imni do not wait politely at the feet of my temple. True demons have not bothered entering these holy woods for one thousand years, since their unholy birth in the wilds. I know men and fae when I see them, and I know an enchantment even if I cannot perceive what it conceals."

What a beautiful, political way of always responding while never answering. Perhaps in Amaris's second life, she would sit upon a throne in the courts and remember the lessons learned here, authoritatively speaking to the questions of the people while revealing nothing. It was effective for the priestess, and mind-numbing for Amaris.

"Can you—or will you—tell me where the king's son is?"

The woman paused. She tilted her chin to look over her shoulder, not facing Amaris as she spoke her solemn response. "The king has no son."

"He has spent twenty years believing something to the contrary," Amaris countered carefully.

"Yes, he has."

Was this priestess a friend or an intentional obstacle? With each obtuse question and indiscernible answer, the woman felt more and more like a foe.

Amaris reached into her heart and stilled herself, prepared for the riddles. Perhaps the visit to the temple would not be succinct, but she would not let it be cut short by the immaturity of her own disquietude.

"Does the king have an heir?"

"He does," she responded, continuing to circle the tree.

"Why is the king certain it's a son?"

"His beloved gave unto him a son."

"He sired a son?"

"He did not." The woman did not look back as she continued their volleys.

"A son was born from the one he loved?"

"A son was the result of their union."

"But King Ceres has no son."

"The king does not."

What a fruitless game. Together they were the ouroboros, a snake eating its own tail in infinite futility. Each step, a question deflected. Each movement around the tree, a frustrating nonanswer. The king had a son. The king didn't have a son. Both seemed equally true and equally false. The line of questioning was getting her nowhere. She shifted her questions to a matter of geography, following the priestess one step at a time as they circled the tree.

"Do you know where the heir is?"

"I do not."

"How can I find out?"

The priestess came to a full stop. They had finished their resolution, ending with the trunk of the tree exactly where they had begun. She brought her hands together, pressing her fingertips lightly in front of her as if in a relaxed, gentle prayer.

"May I ask you a question instead?"

Amaris blinked. Perhaps this would be a refreshing change of pace from their spinning evasion. "Yes," she said.

The woman stared at the tree for so long that when her eyes found Amaris, she shrank under the weight of the priestess's gaze. The woman asked, "Why do you seek to aid the kingdoms?"

"I'm a reever," she responded. "We've taken an oath for magical balance, and this curse is an obvious imbalance in magic. I was trained at Uaimh Reev—"

The priestess moved her head once, a cut to the side.

It was the most elegant way to slash a sentence where it landed. She repeated, "Why do *you* seek to aid the kingdoms?"

Amaris's lashes fluttered her confusion. She found herself shrugging—like a child—at the holiest woman on the continent. She had no satisfying answer. Could she say it was because of her dispatch? Was it because a knife had been held to her throat and she'd been forced into a hasty alliance with the tenacious crow-fae of Raascot? Was she helping the kingdoms because she had been an orphan with no purpose who latched on to the first meaning her life had been given?

It was all of these, and it was none of them. Her final response was a weak one, her voice tilting upward at the end as if she were asking rather than telling. "Because it's the right thing to do?"

Following the priestess's steps, they began to walk away from the tree toward the entrance where four male silhouettes had not moved from their mark in an unknown length of time. Two reevers and two winged fae waited for her just beyond the palatial walls of the temple. Gesturing a long, elegant arm, the priestess bid Amaris adieu. "When you know the answer to my question, you will have the answer to yours."

"Is that…" Amaris paused at the top of the stairs, looking out onto the glen. She looked back at the woman. "Is that everything?"

The priestess allowed herself the same softened emotion once more. "If I may… What were you named?"

"Amaris."

Her face softened for the final time that night, eyes rimming appreciatively with another in a long string of strange, conflicting, distant, unreadable emotions. The priestess turned her head before any feeling might betray her, discovering her quiet once more. The flowering garden of secrets within her would remain impenetrable. She glided away from Amaris with slow reverence, returning to where she kept watch beside her tree.

Amaris walked away from the temple, her feet carrying her of their own accord. Her legs felt numb as she descended the steps, rejoining the men. She couldn't explain why, but she felt like she wanted to cry. It was as if she were waking from a dream. It was surreal enough that Amaris could convince herself it had never happened at all. She felt this with greater intensity as she left the smooth, holy walls and stepped amidst the shapes of men. Their exchange had come to an abrupt, dissatisfying end before she'd learned anything. Her companions flashed glances between their friend and the holy woman expectantly.

"So?" Malik was the first to speak, his voice ripe with anxious tension. His tone was hushed despite his eagerness in honor of their sacrosanct location. "Did the priestess tell you what we needed to know?"

"Yes," Amaris answered as she led them away from the temple.

Gadriel spoke up next, forcing his voice to control his eagerness at the debriefing. They'd barely passed the line of trees before he pushed, "And? What did you learn?"

"Nothing."

✦

The men were not patient with her as she recounted her experience. Amaris thought she'd been agitated in the temple, but she had underestimated the men's capacity for irritation. Their frustration over having not been present compounded with testosterone resulted in a rather unfortunate explosion of helplessness. The cross-examination that ensued was not particularly pleasant. Reever and Raascot alike found themselves pacing before her, throwing up agitated gestures with questions like "Why didn't you ask this?" or "Why didn't you say that?"

Amaris let them rant, idly wondering if outbursts like this were amongst the reasons men were not permitted in the temple. Sure, the paths forward seemed obvious to the boys as they stomped through the forest, retrospectively analyzing the events that had taken place at the foot of the Tree of Life. If they had been there, maybe they would have made more demands, and perhaps they would have learned even less, been discarded even sooner. Amaris had played the priestess's game to whatever dissatisfying end it yielded. While Gadriel was furious and Ash was beside himself, Amaris felt relatively confident that she had learned something, even if she didn't know what it was. She sat between Malik and Zaccai, who seemed content to watch their prospective counterparts storm about.

"She was beautiful," Malik offered. It was a comment of admiration.

"She was."

"And that tree," Malik mused, more to himself than to the others.

"Have either of you heard anything about the Tree of Life?" She looked to Malik, then to Zaccai. Perhaps the men couldn't communicate effectively with each other directly, but that wasn't going to stop her from conversation. "Yggdrasil? She said several other names for the tree, but I've never heard anything about this. If we worshipped a tree, shouldn't we know?"

Both shrugged against Amaris's question, admitting to not having been raised particularly religious on either side of their border. Malik's parents had taken him to their village's church on the solstices of the year, always with donations and offerings to the All Mother. He had supposed it was a practice born out of community solidarity as much as it was any sense of spiritual obligation. His mother had never made a pilgrimage to a proper temple, he'd said.

In the north, Zaccai said, many worshipped the goddess, but his mother had raised him outside of the views of the church. His mother had believed in more tangible magics than the abstract offerings of an unseen goddess. Malik looked at Amaris as if waiting for her to translate, but she did not. Instead, she sat in a long, pensive silence while considering the continent's faithful.

"It's a tree," she finally said.

"What's a tree?" Zaccai asked.

"The symbol of the All Mother. It's a tree."

They considered the iron they'd seen, and it clicked into place just as it had with her. Three minimalistic strokes had been the goddess's sign, but they'd seemed meaningless in and of themselves. They had been lines and a curve, nothing more. Now they saw the symbol for what it was.

"It seems obvious now," Malik said quietly, looking into the distance. His eyes peered through the shadows of the distant woods, presumably off to where the enormous plant had grown in the temple's heart. Of course the iron symbol would be born to represent something sacred and beautiful.

"Forgive me if I'm wrong," Zaccai said politely, "but aren't the reevers a religious organization?"

Amaris had only been a reever for a few years, but this was something she knew the answer to. She didn't translate, but it was clear from Malik's expression as he listened that he agreed, nodding along slowly.

"They call us 'the sword arm of the goddess,' but not because we're an extension of faith. We're just agents of balance. The church shares our goal and supports us. We can't very well have bishops and priestesses running around with swords."

Her answer appeared to satisfy Zaccai and Malik alike.

Amaris considered the tangible magics and thought only of Brel. She wondered how many humans she had met with the small magics and never known them for what they were. She then found herself wondering if those with tangible magics were considered human at all. Was sweet, young Brel, with his ability to speak to fire, what the superstitious folk would have called "witch"? What was it that caused magic to bubble up in a human lineage?

Hoping her question wouldn't be taken with offense, Amaris pressed Zaccai further. "Cai, when you say your mother was more interested in tangible magics... Was she a witch?"

He shook his head, unprovoked by her question.

"Both of my parents are fae," he said. "'Witch' is usually a term ascribed to humans with the small magics—though I've heard plenty of people use 'witch' on the fae as well if the fae has a power feared by others."

"You mean, you use 'witch' for other fae? Wouldn't they just be 'dark fae'?"

From across the campfire, she saw how the term drew the briefest of eyes from the other men of Raascot. In the same unwavering nonchalance she'd come to appreciate, Zaccai answered her question.

"No, it has nothing to do with geography. It's not unusual to hear humans and fae alike refer to those who possess feared traits as witches. My mother herself had discovered no skills beyond that of a typical northern fae—flight, health, long life, ease of nocturnal sight—though she saw those with power for their value, not their fear. A healer, a water-speaker, a medium, and a grower all held far more practical value than the goddess, at least on a day-to-day basis. Unless, of course, you ever meet a manifester."

"What is a manifester?"

Zaccai paused a bit too long before answering. He considered the question as if it held more weight than Amaris understood.

"From what I understand of it," he began, "manifesting is something like dreaming, and making your dreams into a reality. You just"—he snapped his fingers—"create. From what I've heard about manifesting, it's only been seen a few times over the course of history. It cannot be used freely, quickly, or lightly. It may not exist at all, save for the All Mother. Some think it's how she got her name. Most think the power is little more than a fairy tale."

Amaris was just intelligent enough to spend every passing day feeling less and less educated on the realities of her world. The more the world opened up for her, the smaller she felt. How could she have spent fifteen years studying at Farleigh and have learned little beyond her letters, maths, and recited prayers? Uaimh Reev had trained her body, developed her muscle memory, and created a formidable warrior. In the keep, she'd learned of beasts, of tonics, of poisons and health. She was frustrated that she'd spent so little time learning about gifts, abilities, fae, witches, and power. She'd wasted years with the matrons on reading, writing, and drawing, but she knew nothing of the magic that flowed through the world.

She took a different approach, and still speaking to Zaccai, she asked, "Do you not believe in the goddess?"

"I believe that the world is full of magic, both good and bad. Who's to say whether it is or isn't from a superior power? It seems a bit pointless, don't you think? We just have to take our days one day at a time, no matter who is or isn't watching."

The conversation should have concluded, but she had one more question. His answer may have been irrelevant, but she pondered it nonetheless.

"What is a witch, do you think?"

He had an easy wisdom about him. Zaccai always seemed thoughtful without being arrogant. He looked off as he considered her question, then answered, "Perhaps 'gift' is just the favorable term for when we see a talent we can appreciate. For the others, perhaps people needed a word like 'witch' for the magics they neither liked nor understood."

She was exhausted. The only truth Amaris had learned was that the more she studied, the more lands she visited, the more people she met, the more faiths she uncovered and things she read, the more she realized how profoundly little she actually knew.

PART FOUR

What Must
Be Done

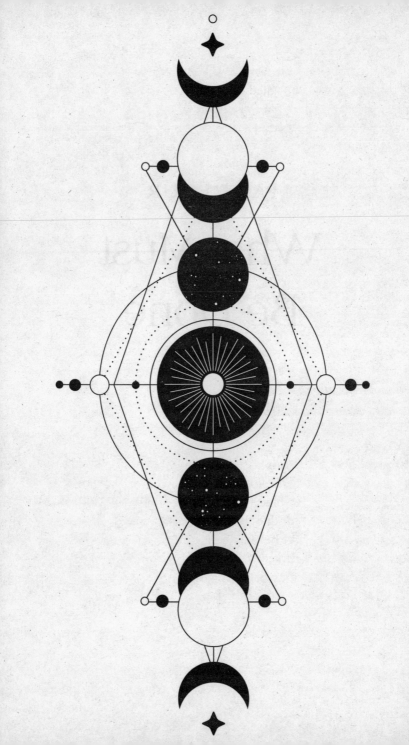

Thirty–Six

NOX WAS DYING.

She'd felt mortality's talons grip her for days now. Here she was on silk sheets she'd sworn she'd never feel again, surrounded by the gauzy curtains she'd never intended to see. She had refused to return to the Selkie, yet now it would be her tomb. She remained immobilized on the bed of her room in the brothel as girls had been filtered in and out, their faces plastered with worry.

The Madame had done this, and Nox had nothing but time to put the pieces together.

Once the wake of fretting girls became overwhelming, Millicent forbade anyone from visiting her. Not only were the other young women afraid for Nox, but they also feared that whatever mysterious illness she'd contracted might be contagious. Millicent leaned into this fear as an excuse to lock them out. The only people allowed into Nox's chamber was the healer whom the Millicent had summoned, and the Madame herself. Much to everyone's dismay, the healer had no answers for them. The unhelpful healer stayed under the roof of the Selkie at the coin of the Madame, if only to clean up after the soporose young woman.

Nox was too weak to speak.

Trapped as she was inside the comatose illness of her own body, her eyes could only flutter open to blink yes or no to answer the simplest of questions. They didn't seem to understand her rapid "no" blinks anytime the vanilla cloud of the Madame drew near. The healer would dab a damp cloth to her forehead and her chapped lips, urging small dribbles of water or broth into her throat and holding her head and neck aloft, allowing her to swallow without choking. Nox had scanned for the telltale freckles of Emily in the faces that had come and gone, but she was a shell of a woman. She'd become little more than sentient eyes caged behind a withering body.

She had no eyes through which to see herself, but from the way Millicent and the healer spoke, she knew her supple cheeks had become gaunt and sallow. They'd commented in hushed, harried tones over how her tanned skin was chalky and clammy. Even her hair, they said, had become dull and limp.

Nox had nothing to do but think and sleep and think and sleep and think and sleep. Her mind dwelled on how it hadn't been until after her succubus powers had manifested that suddenly she'd "learned" everything about the day Amaris had ridden off with an armed northern assassin. Millicent had told her Amaris had been abducted and led her to believe the girl was being held in the north. The lie was so elegant. So simple.

No one had ever told her how much loathing tasted like molded fruit and rotten meat. The putrid flavors swirled in the back of her throat as Millicent's tales festered within her. The world's best lies, after all, are composed from truths. She'd been groomed to hear such a lie, and she hated herself for it. She'd been too thirsty for knowledge. Her need for answers and tangible solutions had opened her up to a beautiful deception.

The anger of her manipulation burned hotter than her fever. She despised how blinded she'd been. Of course, given the craftiness of Millicent's motives, Nox had been willing to gather forces. How else could the Madame have possibly convinced Nox to create her small army? Nox had known that Millicent wanted the power all along, but it had been presented as a shared need for conquest. It was a brilliant lie in its effective subtlety. Nox would amass the troops for a sham, and Millicent would swoop in to use what she had collected.

Nox had become a murderer. She'd justified every still-warm body, every botched mission, every corpse carried from her rooms. Everything she'd done had been for justice, for liberation, for love.

Millicent had been the marionette all along.

If she'd never been purchased by the Madame, taken in the stead of the deposit paid for Amaris, she never would have been touched by a man. She would have lived her life without knowing the dark curse that lurked within her womanhood for any male who dare come near her.

Her anger grew as her mind would meditate on nothing else, trapped in a cycle composed only of sleep, wake, think, hate, plan, repeat.

Nox relived the moment in the carriage over and over again, grateful she hadn't said what had been on her mind. She had wanted to call the Madame out for her lies, to scream that she knew Amaris was alive and beholden to no captor. She knew Amaris was free and in Farehold. She knew everything. Instead, she'd tried to leave, and the evil bitch had all but killed her. How lucky she was that the woman could not hear her thoughts.

I'm going to kill you. I'm going to get better, and I'm going to watch you die.

Nox's only satisfaction came from watching precisely how her grim condition affected the Madame. Though she couldn't possibly burrow into Millicent's marble skull, she knew the woman was losing her mind.

Good.

Thirty–Seven

T HIS COULDN'T BE HAPPENING.

Millicent refused to believe it. She nearly tore the pins from her curls as her gloved fingers continued to work their way against her scalp, balling in her hair as she panicked.

She'd been so close, so *close* to everything she needed. Nox was her missing piece! Nox had basically been gift wrapped and sent to her doorstep by the All Mother herself.

Millicent was crazed. She had nearly run a threadbare line into the carpet of Nox's room from all her fretting and pacing, watching the coal-dark eyes of the incapacitated young woman follow her back and forth in the room. She had muttered everything from excuses and apologies to pleas as Nox lay on the bed, motionless. Millicent was a harbinger of death, but her innate ability only seemed to pull her further from the things she craved, not bring her any closer to the power she desired. The powers of death that coursed through Millicent's gray, otherworldly hand rarely brought her a single step closer to anything resembling victory. Millicent had said it herself once to Emily: death was powerful, but its influence rested only in fear. The hand of death she possessed would have her hung by the noose sooner than it would bring her nearer to any sense of fulfillment this empty life had offered.

She needed Nox to get better. She needed the girl to see reason, to forgive her, to rejoin her team. If she could heal her, perhaps the young woman would feel indebted to her. If she could explain herself and make things right, they could work together again. All she needed to do was to keep her alive. She would not let her die.

Millicent had been a child when she'd learned of the powers of love and death and the line that severed them. Her arm had been deformed and discolored from the moment she came from the womb, but her parents had loved her all the same. The left arm did not stretch or reach or grasp as did the fat, happy hand on her right. It was not the hand itself but the claws that tipped her nails in shiny, black talons that had her parents hide her mutation away.

She had inherited her golden hair from her mother and the tight ringlets from her father. They were a simple family of kind, beautiful people. Her mother had sewn her a sling in her infancy, as her mother had sewn all things in their home, from her dresses and skirts to the curtains and pillows. It kept prying eyes from ogling their other-wise healthy, happy baby, wanting her to live a normal, judgment-free life. No one needed to see the bizarre coloration, nor the dark, hooked barbs that protruded from where healthy fingernails should have been.

Millie, they'd called her. Merry little Millie, with her tenacity, her willingness of spirit, her dauntlessness in the face of adversity, was the apple of her parents' eye.

Her father had played and laughed and taught her all the things a girl must know. He brought her to his bakery on many days to learn about flours and breads and pastries. She knew how long they needed to rest and rise and how thin to make the laminated, buttery layers of delicate desserts. She was exceedingly capable with her right hand, managing everything any other child of her age could do with two. All of her clothes were lovingly tailored to keep her left arm snuggly inside of her shirt, resting against her.

If Millie wasn't following her father to the bakery before the four o'clock morning bell, she was staying home to learn stitchwork from her mother. Their home had been happy and their life had been full.

It had been her mother who had decided that she should begin to exercise her left arm. The woman was wary of the talons her daughter possessed, avoiding them completely as she taught Millie to stretch and grab and hold.

Millie was given small, light objects to grasp, nothing more than quills or spools of yarn. Then she was given tasks, like to pick up the knitting needles or embroidery hoops from where they rested and carry them to where her mother sat. Her parents allowed the growing girl extraordinary independence as she began to master her arm and its movements, watching it heal and come into its shape much faster than anyone could have expected. If she left the house, she was to do so with the use of her sling. Inside the protective walls of their cottage, she could continue to practice her exercises.

She didn't recall how old she was, only the look on her mother's face when the woman lifted her eyes from a particularly intricate threading design to see the family cat dead in Millicent's lap. Millicent was looking up at the woman with the silent, screaming eyes of a confused child.

Her mother had buried that cat quickly, but her

parents' suspicions had begun to grow. They'd hushed her, returning her arm to its sling. Their loving eyes had been etched with fear. Their open hearts had been instilled with guarded spirits.

Now that Millie had learned how to use her left arm, she struggled to obey their simple instruction. She did not want to keep it in its sling any longer.

Her father saw it for what it was the day his beautiful, perfect, joyful child threw both of her arms around her mother's neck in a hug, clasping the grip of hands firmly against the back of the woman's neck, talons grazing his wife's fair, exposed skin. He had ripped Millie from his wife, throwing his daughter to the ground. She had unleashed an unholy wail, a tantrum erupting through her pain and confusion while the man cradled his beloved wife in his arms. The woman was sick for nearly three weeks before her soul left her body to be with the All Mother.

Death was the parasitic spirit leeching on the household, and everyone felt it. Millie, though a child, had understood what she was and what she possessed as she watched her mother lowered into the earth. Death gripped her and her father with a hand just as twisted and gray as the one that belonged to her.

Love had shown its face every day as the three of them lived their contented, simple lives. Love had taught her how to bake, and love had urged them to encourage their daughter to stretch herself and grow, not limited by what others perceived. Love had caused her father to throw his daughter to the ground and cradle his wife on the floor of their cottage. Love made a child kill its mother with its embrace. Love forced the man to sneak off into the night to have tailor-made gloves for the child that would run to the length of her elbow. Love protected her as the baker ardently defended her against the bishops of the church when they came for her, insisting that he had it under control. Love kept her sequestered in her home as the months stretched into years, as the seed of fear planted in her father grew into a weed, its roots deep and tangled. Love put her on a three-week carriage ride at the age of fourteen with a strange crew of westbound men with a letter begging the university to accept her and train her to master her gift. Love wrote her a farewell letter before she was able to graduate, telling her she'd always be in his heart as his spirit went to join her mother. Love broke her heart time and time again until there was nothing left but death.

It brought her to the present, where the bridge between her past and her future withered before her.

Millicent knew of love and of death. Over the decades, her heart may have grown to be as grotesque as the talons at the end of her left hand, but when she saw Nox glowing with the light of her gift in her office those years ago, Millicent's own light had ignited. Love may not be something that would grace her doorsteps, but perhaps it could be something she could control and possess. Its embodiment had crossed her threshold. Nox was the perfect complement to complete her puzzle, the missing link between love, death, and power. If Nox died, the bridge would die with it.

Millicent knelt at her side, her words hurried and manic. "I will heal you. You just have to feed."

She'd twiddled her thumbs for days. She'd fidgeted. She'd contemplated. And ultimately, she found herself at a crossroads of evil.

There were many horrible things in this world.

She knew of the malicious horrors of hate, of enslavement, of torture. She knew the horrors of nature, from the plagues that swept through the villages, and winters so cold that they froze whole families in their beds as they huddled for warmth, to the curses of magic decided well within or before the womb. She knew the common horrors of the ravages of time, and the unspeakable horrors of the cruelties of mad kings and their violent delights.

Then there were the horrors that went on within the Selkie. Nox was too sick to move, and Millicent knew of only one way to heal the young woman. She turned away from the horror as she sent the intoxicated patron to Nox's room, closing her eyes as the man shut the door behind him.

Thirty-Eight

RECOVERY AND HEALING WERE NOT ONE AND THE SAME. Though Nox's strength returned, she remained fractured with anger, betrayal, and revulsion. Her legs worked once more. She could sit, and speak, and eat. Though feeling better, she was anything but fine.

For years, a cocktail of emotions had wrapped themselves around her abilities—whether gift or curse, who was to say. Nox had struggled to separate the disgust of self-loathing from the rage born of justice as she brought the judge's gavel down on any man who deigned to enter her bed. Perhaps her soul was cursed, but if she was to go to hell, she'd drag every wretched, indulgent male soul who took from women with her.

The quiet, white-hot anger smoldered within her as she considered that the Madame was something else entirely. No longer could she expend emotional energy on herself, on men, or on the Selkie. She had no room for anything save for her hatred of the Madame.

Millicent had fussed over Nox for three solid days after she had risen from her nearly paralytic state, fetching her any wild thing the woman suspected she might want. Nox, who had made a remarkable recovery from death's door, did not leave her rooms. Chocolates and a ginger-colored puppy with curled fur and paintings of the landscapes near Farleigh and friends from the salon were all sent up to her, all turned away—all except for a single, dusted truffle, though one piece of candy would hardly be missed. Millicent sent jewels and dresses and the doting compliments of would-be suitors, should Nox have wanted either their companionship or their life force.

Emily had not come to see her, nor had anyone at the Selkie heard from the freckled girl since the day Nox had ridden for Yelagin. Emily's face had been the only one she'd hoped to see. Perhaps now that she knew Amaris was riding for the south, it had been divine intervention that the young woman who'd warmed her bed would choose such a time to run. Maybe it would save her from a deeply unpleasant conversation.

For nearly a week, Nox treated Millicent like a phantom, refusing to acknowledge her presence. Instead, she focused her attention on her notes and her books, furiously scribbling everything she knew about Amaris, about the demons, about Millicent and her powers, about herself and her own curse. She listed all the enchanted objects she'd ever heard of or encountered. She wrote and re-created through her command of language every gift and magic known to men and fae and witches alike. She recorded everything she knew of the kingdoms, including every trait or possession or inclination mentioned of Queen Moirai and the crowned prince. She wrote names, drew places, kingdoms, and objects. She drew the barn with the silhouette of a bat overhead. She drew the leering face of the ag'imni on page after page. She even drew Millicent's ungloved hand.

Why she did these things, she did not know. Her mind was a busy, violent place. Writing and drawing the thoughts drained them from the cage of her head, leeching the terrors from her body onto the papers.

Knowing that she was always one touch away from death, she decided to do whatever was necessary to survive. She stayed in the safety of her rooms, never venturing down to the lounge. She would entertain no clients; she would work at the Selkie no longer. When she left, she would not return.

By the end of the sixth day, Millicent let herself in with a quiet knock.

"I was hoping we could talk."

For nearly a week, the Madame's voice had been unrecognizable. It was not the cold preen of a bird or the authoritative demand of a madame. It was a soft, uncertain, pleading thing. From the onset of Nox's "mysterious illness" to her seemingly miraculous recovery, Millicent had not once spoken to her with the force or prudence that the Madame had worn like a suit of armor for years. Instead, her voice was always colored with a tinge of desperation. Nox knew three things. The first was that Millicent needed her more than she would ever need the Madame. The second was that the woman was terribly dangerous. And the third was that no matter what penance was paid or amends were attempted, Nox would see personally to the witch's death.

It had been six days since she'd blossomed aglow with health once more, and still the young woman had remained in utter silence. When Nox spoke, she was almost surprised at herself that any voice remained at all.

"What do you want, Millicent?"

The Madame was in magenta today, a color not unlike many of the silks around her room. A similar color flooded her face as she nearly slumped in relief. She sounded like she might cry as she said, "I'm just here to check on you, dear. How are you feeling?"

"Physically? I feel fine."

Millicent considered the specification, wringing her gloved hands.

"Nox, about what happened in the carriage—"

"You did what needed to be done." She kept her response matter-of-fact before turning her body away, her attention once more on her drawings.

"What?" The Madame paled.

Nox did not look up from her desk. Her words carried over her shoulder with little emotion. She said flatly, "I was in the middle of an episode, and I would have flung us both from a moving carriage. You stopped us the only way you knew how."

Millicent nodded, her movements jerky with extreme hesitation. It was, of course, the excuse she would have wanted to hear, no matter how hollow or false it sounded. Surely it was the very words the Madame would have used to plead her case in defense of her actions.

"If it's all right with you, I'm quite tired today," Nox said, still not bothering to look up.

"Of course, dear."

"But…" Nox stopped her before she could exit the room, twisting in her seat to look at the Madame. "I'll send word when I'm ready to see the Captain of the Guard."

Nox used the excuse of the closing door to hide her expression from the Madame, though the woman's confusion had been unmistakable. Let Millicent think whatever she wanted. She didn't need to be convinced of Nox's allegiance in order to desire the advancement of her plans. If Amaris was going to seek an audience with the queen, Nox would too. If she happened to have the kingdom's chief executioner and head of all of Moirai's troops at her beck and call through its commander, maybe that wouldn't be such a terrible thing.

Thirty–Nine

Cities were fine for nobility, Amaris thought. They were probably considered both wonderful and necessary by monarchs and lordlings alike. A city's civilized sensibilities surely made lovely content for tomes and ballads.

The nobility could keep their cities. The sights, sounds, smells, and overcrowding garnered no favor with Amaris.

The road to Queen Moirai's castle ran through the heart of Priory, a sprawling cluster of buildings, markets, homes, and shacks belonging to the people outside of the walled city of Aubade. Priory served as a port town and began along the coast, but it had grown in a way that hugged the sea as it wrapped around the shores all the way to the castle.

The boys wanted to stop for food, but Amaris urged them forward. She had no pleasant affiliations when she thought of this city. All she knew of Priory was that she had marred her face and run to the mercies of a would-be assassin rather than allow herself to be taken here. Now she was on Cobb's back, Nine and Fourteen at her sides with their reevers atop them, surrounded by the very city that had plagued her nightmares.

Everything on the coast looked and smelled different. The stones were an unfamiliar color, from the cobbled streets to the buildings themselves. The roofs were of reddish clay tiles, the bricks, mortar, and rocks all shades of beiges and custard. Some homes that clung to the cliffs seemed to be entirely white, as if the foam from the sea had splashed upward and frozen in time, creating houses and structures for the coastal residents. The fishy scent of salt and brine followed them wherever they went, accompanied by the pungency unique to large, packed cities. She had never smelled the overcrowding of people before she'd entered Yelagin, but compounded with the ocean and its odors, her senses were overwhelmed.

Cityfolk shuttered their windows like common, superstitious villagers as the three rode by. Perhaps it had less to do with their appearance and more to do with the weapons that were strapped to every space on their bodies. Each reever was equipped with sheathed swords, daggers, and wrapped with a bow across their chest. Amaris, accompanied by her ever-visible scarring, knew she looked like a living testament to their willingness to put those blades to use.

Nothing about Priory was particularly welcoming.

The roads were narrower within the city than she liked. Most of the villages she'd entered had large, grassy areas between homes, or the cobbled streets meant for wagons and markets. Unlike the farmyards and set-apart homes of country villages, these town houses melted into one another with alleys that allowed an intersecting pedestrian to get entirely too near before they were spotted. Everyone seemed to be on foot as they scuttled about Priory, few carriages, horses, or carts gracing the roads. Fishermen and salesmen would push past the three with things like flat-bed crates of dead fish yet act as if the reevers were the unpleasant sight rather than their stinky, scaled corpses of dead things. The feeling of discomfort pressed down on her.

"What exactly is our plan?" Ash hissed. He kept his voice low, knowing that even if the citizens had closed their windows and slammed their doors, they'd remained pressed to the frames as any good gossip might.

Amaris was unmoved. "I've told you several times."

"We've had weeks to come up with a better plan than 'wing it.'"

"Why am I the only one responsible for planning! Though I am flattered that you assume I'm the only one of us with a working mind."

Malik didn't appear overly bothered, nor did he attempt to speak in hushed tones like the other two. He even deigned to wave at a woman as she scurried past them. She began to lift a hand to return the friendly gesture to the handsome young man but thought better of it. "Not that you've asked, but my plan is to get through the walls into Aubade and then find us something to eat."

Amaris raised a hand from where it had rested on the saddle's horn. "See?" She waved appreciatively. "A man with a plan. Thank you, Malik."

"At your service, m'lady."

Differentiating itself from the casual strides of towns-folk, a clattering of hooves was rounding a corner up ahead. The sources of the oncoming commotion hadn't yet turned into their line of vision, but the horses were moving with purpose. The three had barely begun to pull on their reins and exchange looks when the constabulary cantered into view. Six men on horseback dressed in the queen's seal urged their uniformly black mounts, cutting them off. The reevers weren't given the opportunity to breathe a question before the Head Marshal took charge.

Clearly, they would no longer be needing a plan. Their fates had been decided without them.

A throaty, armored man boomed, "State your name and your business in Priory."

The trio's armed presence must have caused more concern amongst the citizens than they'd realized. Three travelers should have been able to filter in and out of the city without detection, but typical travelers wouldn't need the kind of weaponry they boasted.

Okay. This was it. This was why she'd been sent.

Amaris steadied herself, focusing on the comforting truth that she'd been sent by Samael to be the mouthpiece for the reevers specifically because of her abilities. Perhaps she could use education and kindness before flexing persuasion. Before launching into demands, she attempted diplomacy.

For the barest of moments, her mind flitted to long-forgotten lessons under Farleigh's roof. The matrons had forced her to read, to trace and retrace her letters, to sing, to practice her command of the room, and to perform in all the ways that might make her a marketable society lady. It had been an exercise in torture, but at the very least, it had readied her for impromptu speeches to those in authority.

"We're reevers—peacekeepers from Uaimh Reev. We seek an audience with Queen Moirai."

Despite having been told with the repetitive defensiveness of someone trying to convince themselves that reevers were an important and respectable stronghold for justice, the title was not received with any such reverence by this particular subsect of guards. The lawmen chuckled to themselves, and Amaris felt profoundly tired. She was exhausted from travel, emotionally drained from the trials, and taxed from the weight of the responsibilities that had revealed themselves with each new passing day. She didn't have the energy to put up with their ignorant, stilted laughter.

Amaris had been reassured her gift was useful. She'd been promised it was morally neutral. That said, she still struggled to justify its use as she eyed the hostile men before her.

Even within the recent week, her ability had been a source of both contention and shame. However, the constabulary had caught her on a bad day. The priestess at the Temple of the All Mother had said with every bit of authority that persuasion had been a gift from the goddess for humans to bow to Amaris's will. She wasn't sure if it had been the priestess's words or her own fatigue, but with the nonplussed expression of a woman who was weary from the world, she exchanged a look with the men before her. With an unimpressed calm, she said, "You will now escort us to see the queen."

The effect was instantaneous.

Amaris found herself looking to Malik to see if using the ability on the other humans triggered an emotion in him, but his face was unreadable. She sensed nerves and relief muddled into whatever amalgamation of emotion her friends were feeling as they nudged their horses onward. In immediate obedience, the marshal had simply nodded, and he, with his men, had turned their horses and led the way from the long road of Priory into the city of Aubade. As they walked their horses forward, she heard Malik say under his breath, "I guess this means we aren't getting food."

✦

It had taken no small stretch of time to get through both Priory and past the walls of Aubade to the castle at its center. Priory and the royal city beyond were far larger than any of them had anticipated. The constable and his men cleared an easy path for them. "We're escorting them to see the queen" was a perfectly reasonable answer no matter who of importance might ask and was met with no resistance.

The guards at the walled city of Aubade would have certainly stopped the reevers, though Amaris could have probably handled them just as effortlessly. Instead, they were waved forward as the Head Marshal escorted them beyond the opened, iron gates into Aubade.

Amaris had spent years in Uaimh Reev and referred to the keep many times as a castle throughout her stay. It had been hewn from the mountain's granite—made, not built—into the side of the sheer rock. When she was little, the children of Farleigh had often thought of their stone manor as a castle, for it had been large and stately in many ways, with enough rooms and corridors and alcoves and turns that their imagination was able to conjure importance and intrigue into its walls. It wasn't until they were within Aubade's walls that it became clear she had truly never seen a castle.

If the walls surrounding the city itself hadn't been protective enough, this cream-colored citadel was a solid stronghold, built to the teeth with fortifications. The beige stones had been rounded for uniformity, lending a bricklike appearance to the vast, thick walls and towers that covered Aubade's center. While the reev had been cold and gray, the coastal city offered warm, earthy tones to the megalith, forged from the earth, clay, and rocks of its climate. As Priory was on a lip of the coast, the three travelers had been able to see the castle from a far-off angle, appreciating its size and shape from miles away. It had taken on a familiar, animal frame from a distance.

Amaris found herself able to discern precisely what shape it was as they drew nearer.

Now that she was nearly upon it, four primary towers, countless windows in height, jutted from the angles of a rectangular backside, but a long, secondary rectangle with a curved front angled its way forward, as if the castle had been created to resemble the head of a horse. The snout-like portion of the castle seemed composed of at least five levels. From Priory's coast, she'd gathered that there was another structure at the back of the castle looming over its cliffs. While she couldn't be sure, something circular seemed to frame the back of the castle, as if the beast was wearing a halo atop its head. She smiled to herself at the idea of the bird's-eye view of the ruddy-cream, horse-faced, halo-wearing angelic fortress of Queen Moirai and its crowned prince. The southern kingdom sat within a horse's head. It was strange what idle thoughts brought one comfort in uncertain times.

There was something oddly comforting about the expanse before her, as if she found some small relief in knowing how easy it would be to slip away in a fortress this large, hiding in the castle for days or weeks or twenty years without ever being found. She and Nox had found ways to hide in Farleigh, and it had been a thimble compared to this megalith. Surely, she'd find safety in the expanse of its custard walls.

The constabulary, having completed their primary task, were held up not by security upon arrival at the castle, but rather the castle's servants halted them. The reevers may as well have been grimy street urchins at their door. The guests would certainly need to bathe, they insisted, before they could be ushered in to see Queen Moirai.

They were right. Suddenly self-conscious, Amaris

became acutely aware of the grime and filth that clung to her and her friends.

Other than their dips in the stream, they hadn't had proper baths with soap since their night in Yelagin. Feeling rather embarrassed at the implication, the reevers dismounted and allowed their horses to be led away by flustered servants. She realized the attendants were dressed to reflect the neutrals of the stone, as if they were merely living elements of the castle, scarcely discernible from the rocks on which it was built. Even in their simple linens, they were impeccably clean.

She hadn't thought a bath would stand between her and her dispatch, but she understood the need. Perhaps a good cleaning would give her time to calm her nerves. Amaris's heart pounded at having come so close to completing her task. Adrenaline flooded her veins as she racked her brain for speeches and words important enough for the queen, a simple comment grounded and comforted her. Despite the severity of their situation, she could have sworn she heard Malik asking about when they might be fed.

✦

Amaris knew she was being ungrateful, but she didn't care.

She would rather burn down the castle than be forced into a frilly dress. She argued with the personal attendant about the attire provided for her, and it was clear that her obstinance had driven the woman to the verge of tears. Amaris had not worn a dress in years, and she absolutely wouldn't be forced into one now. She'd barely been old enough to transition from pants to dresses in Farleigh before she'd escaped and returned permanently to the male garb of the reevers.

"Miss, please, see reason…"

"You will find pants and a suitable shirt," Amaris said coolly, flexing her persuasion yet again. Perhaps she was abusing her gift, but she would rather brainwash every servant in the kingdom than be forced into a girdle.

The woman dipped her chin obediently and turned to find something appropriate.

Amaris comforted herself that she was in the right. She couldn't possibly wear a proper lady's dress. What if things went poorly? What if she needed to run or fight? How was she supposed to dive or roll or crouch while wearing skirts and lace and petticoats? The personal attendant's nose had reddened in the moments before crying, clearly taking crimes against fashion very seriously. She left Amaris with two other young servants to help her bathe and wash her hair—despite her protestations that she was capable of bathing herself—and ran off.

When Amaris asked why she couldn't wear her tunic, the stewardess informed her that her filthy road things were to be burned. The servants revised their plan with immediate obedience after a flex of Amaris's power. She had grown a little more generous with her guidelines for acceptable usage regarding her gift over the last few hours, it seemed.

She examined the newly proffered outfit before her, then slipped into its components. It looked like something worn by a court entertainer that—though hideous—did include a pair of pants that fit her small stature. At least, she wanted to call them pants. The bottoms provided resembled black jester's tights far more than the riding leathers she'd preferred.

The outfit was composed of four pieces. The first was a lovely, clean, off-the-shoulder sari made of a gauzy, white fabric. She examined herself in the mirror, appreciating the way the blouse gathered around the smallest part of her waist, giving her thin, boyish shape the illusion of a womanly figure. She would have preferred to wear the white sari on its own, but unfortunately, the ensemble included both a black bustier and something that may have been a gaudy attempt at a silver, puff-sleeved jacket.

Amaris slipped into the black tights and white blouse but required the attendant's help in lacing up the bustier.

"Who in the court has worn this?" Amaris asked. She gasped as they cinched her waist tighter and tighter.

The attendant finished lacing the bodice as she answered, "The court juggler, I believe."

"Wonderful."

Of course, she would be assigned the juggler's clothes. It was a fitting punishment for a woman who refused a dress. Why be taken seriously when seeking an audience with the queen? The outfit made it clear: she would be allowed no dignity in the eyes of the court.

Amaris sighed, resigned to the fact that it didn't matter. Whether she'd worn the formal, royal dresses or her grimy travel clothes, or had rolled in red paint and entered the throne room naked, none of it had any bearing on her dispatch. At least her attire would give Ash and Malik something to laugh about on the ride home. Soon they'd be finished with their mission and the whole keep would share its ale-drunk commentary about the humor of a reever in juggler's clothes before Farehold's queen.

"It will have to do," said the displeased attendant. "I did think the silver jacket was a lovely complement to your hair, given your objections. Though if you change your mind about the dress, I have the most stunning lavender to match your eyes—"

"The juggler's attire will do just fine."

Amaris considered the extra space in the room. She remembered how isolated she'd felt in her early days in

Uaimh Reev. It had been cramped but well loved. It was old but clean. This bedroom space in Aubade was revolting in its opulence. Between the abundance of furniture, the lavishness of the decorations, and the excess of the golds and jeweled features in the space, Amaris had missed a key detail. She'd been so distracted with the finery of the beds, the chaises, the tables, the windows, and the bathing room that she hadn't taken stock of anything that mattered.

She stiffened as she looked around.

With wide eyes she turned to the attendant, asking, "Where are my weapons?"

The steward who'd stood in statuesque attendance throughout Amaris's series of ridiculous requests looked horrified. She began fixing Amaris's hair as she answered, "You can't carry your weapons around the castle! Honestly, child, what sort of question is that?"

"But where—"

The steward did not seem like a particularly strong woman, in the emotional sense of the word. Everything seemed to rim her eyes with the silver threat of tears. If it wasn't Amaris's protestations about the dress, it was her queries about the weapons.

Through choked frustration, the attendant informed her, "They'll be returned to you when you fetch your horses—though truly, the idea that any untested, mysterious outsider would be allowed to meet Her Majesty with daggers and swords and arrows is preposterous. It's downright offensive!" she said, nearly spitting her disbelief. She had been combing Amaris's hair into some elaborate updo of braids and seemed to pull a little harder than necessary as she punctuated her words.

Amaris reeled at the information. She didn't even have her daggers.

Was this why they had bathed her? In seeing her nakedness and combing through her hair, there was truly nothing she could hide. There was a cleverness to the seemingly perfunctory acts of the servants that she both admired and feared. She wondered if Ash and Malik had been set to the same shameful stripping and scrubbing, rendering them weaponless.

A distant memory recalled a time when Odrin had been forced to remove his weapons before he could shelter for the night in the kitchens of Farleigh. While the servant tugged brutally at Amaris's hair, she felt a surge of sympathy for Odrin at the memory. Removing a reever's sword was like removing a limb. Still, the knowledge that this was somewhat common practice comforted her. If the man she called her father could be gutted of his weaponry for a night in Farleigh, so could she.

The door to her room opened, which annoyed her. Would there be no end to the disturbances before she met Queen Moirai? Would she have no time to process her thoughts or plan?

A new servant popped in her head through a crack in the door. They informed her that the queen was in the middle of a previous engagement and Amaris was to take dinner in her rooms until Moirai called upon her later that night. She fidgeted uncomfortably at the knowledge that she was not to be reunited with her brothers.

"My companions?"

"—are also being served in their rooms."

At least Malik would be fed, she thought. She inquired as to the whereabouts of her friends and debated whether or not to slip from her rooms and go to them. Though she knew they'd be in the same room soon when reunited before the queen, she hadn't been separated from the reevers more than a handful of times over the past three years. It felt unnatural to be unable to access her brothers. Perhaps it was more than just the unfamiliarity that was disquieting.

An anomalous instinct filled her stomach with stones. She ignored it, certain it was just anxiety over the unknown. She was afraid of doing something new, and if she was to succeed, she would need to learn to adapt. Of course, the castle was unfamiliar. Of course, being bathed by servants and dressed by attendants was new. How would she survive in this world if she felt a surge of fear every time she faced a unique situation?

"Will you be needing anything else, miss?" the attendant asked. She pulled her fingers from Amaris's hair, finally finished with the ornate braids.

Amaris stared at herself in the perfect, glassy mirror. She soaked in the snow-white hair that disappeared against the milk of her skin. She regarded the charcoal they'd smudged around her lids and gazed into the lilac eyes staring back at her. Even when she'd been up for auction at Farleigh, she hadn't felt as dressed and stuffed like a pig off to market as she did now in Moirai's castle.

"No, I'm fine. I'll just stay and eat until I'm called upon. Thank you."

Eventually, the attendants left her to her thoughts. She remained in the chair, tapping her fingers against the desk as she stared into the mirror and watched the stranger who stared back at her with impeccably clean hair and goddess-awful clothes. Amaris's nose scrunched against the sickening smell of florals, as though she'd been bathed in perfume rather than soapy water. If she didn't get some fresh air, her stomach would be too unsettled to appreciate dinner. She moved from the bed to the desk to the window, trying to find a comfortable spot to relax while she eyed the unfamiliar coastal food.

Amaris opened the doors to her balcony, enjoying the sea breeze that rushed in as it stole the choking scents of flowers and spiced, coastal foods from her room. Satisfied that the breeze would do its job, she abandoned the balcony in favor of the tiny buffet that had been left for her.

Amaris tried to take at least a few bites of the meal, but her gut was already stuffed with apprehension. It was truly a pity, as she hadn't seen a meal this fine in her entire life. Not only had fishes and cheeses and vegetables been beautifully plated and seasoned, but chilled fruits and hot pies and caramelized tarts and exotic wines dotted the table in a veritable cornucopia of options. She should have been gorging herself. Instead, she was wasting a once-in-a-lifetime dining opportunity on fretfulness.

Amaris reassured herself that the fear was perfectly natural. Everything was fine, she said. Even if the queen was a nightmare and the meeting went awry, she had nothing to fear. Her power had emboldened her for such a time as this. This was her divine purpose. Amaris would simply command Moirai and her men to stop their bloodshed and hunting of northmen. She would command the queen to release her. She told herself her plan over and over again, using it as a meditation. Everything was fine.

Her words were lies, and she knew it. She couldn't explain her certainty, but every repetition of her false mantra clanged hollowly through her mind.

Amaris gnawed unenthusiastically on her bread but couldn't stay still to enjoy her meal. She returned to the grand glass doors of her balcony, wandering outside to view the setting sun while she picked at her loaf. It truly was a marvelous view. The sky colored magnificently on the western coast in a way she'd never seen before. The smell of salt and the ocean spray reached her even from where she stood on the balcony. The birds who dove and cawed near the cliffs were large and wild and unfamiliar in their songs, providing a welcome distraction. The sea was the sort of thing children scribbled with blues in their etchings without ever fully comprehending its vastness. She had been like any other peasant, uncomprehending of true infinity before she'd seen how the horizon met the blue line of the ocean. Her fingers continued to absently move her bread to her mouth, nibbling at the simplest of foods provided to her. Watching the sun change the water from gold to pink as it descended while warm sea air drifted up to her perch was a magical experience.

Her jaw unclenched. Her muscles relaxed. Maybe it was the sound of the waves breaking, the homeyness of the bread, or the fresh air, but tension dripped out of her as she appreciated the sun descending over the western sea. She still itched to leave her room to find her brothers and could picture them pacing their rooms, feeling the same about her. Perhaps if they had to be apart for a few short hours, a sunset over the ocean was an acceptable conciliation.

This is where she'd sit until Moirai's attendant came to get her.

The enchanting, silvery glimmer of distant waves reminded her of sparks of magic. She frowned at the bewitching sparkles as she remembered the tasks before her. Her mind wandered to the priestess's cryptic instructions as she mulled over the woman's inscrutable message on the orb.

It is held where all magic's secrets are held.

She puzzled over what it could mean but remained baffled. For now, there was nothing she could do about mysterious orbs or holy riddles. Instead, she'd eat her bread and relax into the knowledge that they'd made it safely to Aubade. She'd melt into the sunset, becoming one with the distant, blue line on the horizon. The fingers of relief had just begun to massage her stress when her eyes fixed on a particularly large seabird against the dusk of the disappearing sun. It vanished entirely, leaving the last indigos of its dying light in the sky before the stars began to sparkle into existence.

She saw it again and knew it was not a bird.

"Goddess damn it," she cursed to herself, all semblance of peace leaving her. "Can I not get one moment of peace?"

Anger raked her as she knew her only chance at relaxation had been snatched from her. She ran back into her chamber, blowing out the room's candles to further obscure herself and the unwanted visitor in the shadows. She then slid a chair against the door, lodging the handle in place. She'd barely crammed the back of the chair against the handle before she heard a flutter of air and the gentle footsteps of a man. Somewhere on her balcony, Gadriel had landed as quietly as he could. His great wings folded behind him as he muted his footsteps.

"What are you doing here?" she hissed. Her room was dark, but not dark enough. If someone really wanted to spy, they'd be able to see the Raascot fae and his angelic, feathered wings—that, or the batlike wings of a demon.

He didn't bother greeting her. He did a quick, careful pan of the room, presumably assessing it for weak points. Gadriel took several steps into the room before using the rushed, militant voice of a general.

"Silvanus hasn't reported in since our night at the river. We thought we'd meet up with him after the temple, but I have a bad feeling."

Amaris responded in a harried whisper as she said, "Your presence is going to give us away! What were you thinking?"

"Do you think I want to be here? Ask yourself—does

a man who looks like an ag'imni feel particularly safe inside Moirai's castle?"

Gadriel closed the space between them. He did not look kind as he grabbed her arm. She tried to jerk away, but his grasp was firm. Agitation flashed through her at his strength. She looked up at him with anger. He fixed his gaze on hers as he spoke.

"Listen closely, ungrateful witchling: I need you to succeed. I'll have your back if it kills me. Oh my goddess—"

"What?" Amaris looked around, head jerking nervously at his sudden shift in tone.

"What's that smell?"

"Go fuck yourself." She rolled her eyes. As if she weren't already suffering enough.

His anger and support were incongruous. His words clashed defiantly against his tone and posture. His fingers began to hurt her arm as his dark eyes burned into hers. Yes, she definitely hated him. She was fairly certain that she didn't want the others to die, though.

"Get off me, demon," she said as she attempted—and failed—to shake him loose.

"You're stuck with me."

"And Cai? Uriah?"

The general relaxed his grip slightly but continued to hold her forearm loosely.

"Both instructed to hang back. You might need help in the castle or outside of its walls," he said. He made a face, his touch grazing against her forearm as his grip slowly fell away. "I guess I'm your man on the inside."

She was both baffled and appalled. How could a man who claimed to lead militaries have been this foolish?

"I am telling you with absolute confidence that your presence is going to do more harm than good. I already have backup."

"You have your reevers," he agreed, "I know. But the queen and her men know Ash and Malik are here. They don't know I'm in their walls. You can never be too careful."

Amaris seethed with his recklessness. How could Raascot trust him to lead troops if this was the sort of thing their general found acceptable? She took a few steps away, moving with her back to him as she paced toward the wall.

"How could you even risk coming here?" she asked angrily. "If the queen is hunting for dark fae across her lands—"

Gadriel didn't let her get too far. With one swift movement, he turned and spun her until she faced him. With a steadying grip, he used both hands to hold her at the elbows. He squeezed gently until she looked at him. The moment she met his burning gaze, she regretted it. Heat filled her, and she jerked her head to the side.

"What?"

He cupped her face with gentle intensity, forcing her to look at him. This arrogant, insufferable crow had never touched her like this. It was too familiar, too intimate. She raised her hands to grasp his forearms, intent on dislodging his hold. As she tugged at his grip, Gadriel tightened his hold.

She squirmed. "Gad—"

"We have never had a hope like this."

Her anger and fighting spirit stilled wholly. Something deep within her understood. Her anxiety remained high over the risk of her mission, and her stomach churned knowing that Gadriel was putting himself in such danger, and yet, she understood. If this was truly the first glitter of hope in decades—if it had been her in their shoes—she would have stopped at nothing to see the mission through.

Hope was dangerous. Hope was reckless. Hope was essential.

Her eyes lit as she realized suddenly that his presence may come with more than a few perks. She shook her arm free once more, and this time he obliged. Amaris caught him off guard with her topical change. "Can I have one of your daggers?"

Gadriel's face tightened in disapproval. "You let them disarm you?"

"They made a very persuasive argument as to why I can't meet the royal family dressed with the ability to chop off their heads. That, and I was stripped and scrubbed naked. I didn't have much choice in the matter."

Gadriel was wearing no fewer than six blades, he informed her, though none of them were the heavy weight of a sword that might impede his flight. He winked like the perverse show-off he was as he showed her the glint of a knife strapped to his forearm, hidden up his sleeve. He fished a lightweight throwing knife from his boot. Amaris thanked him and tucked it securely against the small curvature of her breasts just beneath the front of her tightened bodice. Even if she was searched before meeting Moirai, no one would think to check her sternum.

The general touched her forearm lightly as he dragged a thumb over her exposed skin. It was so gentle.

"Stop touching me," she said, but her command lacked conviction. He was fae. Her persuasion would have done nothing for him, even if she'd been trying to wield it.

She looked at him fully, ceaselessly amazed at how beautiful he was, irritating though he was. It would be much easier to glare at him if he hadn't possessed such sharp, perfect features. Gadriel had the strongest jaw she'd ever seen, such bottomless eyes, such night-black hair. His eyes were gorgeously dark, as deep as the ocean's trenches, identical to ones she'd known from her childhood. His dark eyes reminded her too much of Nox—everything reminded her too much of Nox. Maybe that was what kept her from stabbing him whenever he was particularly rude or difficult. This demon should count himself lucky to share any commonalities with an angel.

"Amaris?" he asked. Her name on his lips was a whisper.

She wanted to snap at him, but her tone came out gentler than she intended as she looked back at him. "Yes?"

He looked at her intently and she waited for his words, an unfamiliar want leaning against her ears. He finally said, "You look ridiculous."

Her mental to-do list now read *Persuade the queen to stop killing northerners, escape the castle, and kick Gadriel in his manhood*, in that order.

She heard footsteps in the hall and turned to him to tell him to get lost, but the northern fae was already on the balcony, slipping into the shadows around the corner of its opened door. Amaris ran to remove the chair from the door just in time for it to swing open.

"Her Majesty will see you now."

Forty

H ER GREATEST ACTING ROLE TO DATE WAS EXPRESSING patience with Millicent, as Nox wanted nothing more than to step on the woman's throat in pointed, high-heeled shoes. It reeked of vanilla perfume and the stench of overexplained failure as Millicent tried to rationalize the situation. She hid the vitriol that dripped from her every pore over Millicent's lie. She painted a neutral expression over the atrocities that had been committed in the name of healing. Considering the loathing that consumed her, Nox's ability to plaster on a mask of boredom was nothing short of an award-worthy display of thespianism.

Nox wanted to raise an unimpressed brow as the Madame's arguments grew less and less convincing, but she resisted the urge. Instead, she allowed Millicent to explain why nothing was working. The Madame informed Nox that she had sent two of the Selkie's girls over the past few days to plant lures and whispers about the marvels of the Selkie, but no one had the gift of suggestion quite like Emily. Millicent repeated to Nox over and over that the girls would be fine but that they could also use it as an audition of sorts to see who might serve as valuable lures for the future.

So far, the answer was no one.

Despite Millicent's attempts, no one could lure the Captain of the Guard to Priory. They hadn't even been able to get close enough to the armed man to try. Surely Emily would have succeeded, but she had not returned. They were left with no plan and no captain.

While none of the working girls Millicent had sent into Aubade had been able to speak to the captain directly, they'd learned all about his inglorious reputation. They'd returned with information regarding the captain's inner circle, his regular schedule, and his reputation. The man was named Erasmus. He was said to be a nightmare of a leader for his men and was often caught leaving the tavern with a new woman more nights than not. Even if the girls hadn't been particularly effective in setting snares, they'd gained more than enough for Nox in newfound knowledge alone. She found the information of the guard's reputation lovely—she vastly preferred a man of low moral fiber. It was unspeakably comforting to have a target in her sights with no guilt attached, let alone one for whom she could exercise unbridled contempt.

Nox pulled on her black silk dress and grabbed her cloak. The other escorts hadn't failed her; they'd simply set the stage for the final act. A dark twinkle coursed through her as she set her plan of action. She hadn't selected jewelry for her endeavor; she was ornament enough.

Why would she send amateurs to do a champion's job? This was her game, after all.

Nox's years at the Selkie had taught her to read minute expressions as if they were printed text on a scroll. From her face alone, it was clear Millicent was torn in three directions. In the most potent way, she wanted Nox under her roof where Nox—whom she considered her most prized possession—was safe. On the other hand, she wanted the Captain of the Guard with unspeakable greed. This many-armed beast provided yet a third hand, and it was on this final branch that Nox had pushed all of her hopes. After their altercation, Millicent needed to believe that she'd reforged the badly damaged trust between them. Nox knew this was the only bargaining chip she'd need in order to come and go as she pleased.

Nox focused her thoughts on her target.

If the castle and its resources were a locked door, then Eramus was the key.

The man was said to live within the castle's walls. This was perfectly logical, as the queen would need to be able to call upon her most trusted man regardless of the hour of the day or night. Though Nox had never been inside Castle Aubade, she didn't think she'd have much trouble buttering palms into an invitation. She'd grown rather confident in her charms. With the unification of their target, Millicent had a few more intelligent tricks than flirtation. The Madame had called upon a calligraphist to forge a letter of invitation.

Nox made a face as she lifted the letter to the light in the Madame's office. She questioned, "Are you sure this looks convincing?"

"Used it myself," the calligraphist swore, solemn as a saint. "Got myself invited to a banquet. Ate the finest pies of my life and nearly bedded a courtier—well, she was married and her husband was also in attendance, so perhaps 'flirted with' a courtier is more accurate."

Time was running short, and Nox had made it clear that she would wait no longer. Millicent ignored the forger, not taking her eyes from Nox.

"Do you know where to find him?"

Nox nodded. "The girls have seen him each evening at a tavern called the Bird and the Pony just outside of the castle."

Millicent's hands were on her hips, her eyes averted to some distant corner as her wheels turned. She asked, "If he isn't there? Your plan then?"

Nox wiggled her forged document in mock triumph. She smiled. "I don't need a plan. I have an invitation."

"There is no banquet to crash tonight, Nox. There's no crowd to get lost in," she said.

Usually, the Madame referred to her as the more pejorative "dear." The usage of her name belied the jeweled woman's nerves about the night to come. Nox had just returned from the brink of death days after an escape to Yelagin, and now she was to infiltrate the castle. Their relationship had undergone an undeniable shift that neither of them would address outright.

Millicent went on, "Perhaps we're rushing our plan. Surely there will be a masque—"

"He will be at the Bird and the Pony. There's no need to wait for an excuse."

"But if he isn't—"

Nox had no time for discussion. "If he isn't, then he isn't. Do you believe me to be clever?"

The Madame nodded somewhat reluctantly, and Nox knew why. Millicent would have been far happier if she'd found herself a simpler, more naive girl of such great, formidable, terrible power under her care. Yet it was the very same cleverness that might win them their captain and eventually their rank in the castle.

"Then trust me when I tell you, I will not fail tonight."

Nox would not fail, nor would she return. After her feet crossed the pleasure house's threshold into the city beyond, she swore she'd never look back. These would be her parting moments in the Selkie. If she came back, it would be to sit atop a mount outside while a fleet of men beholden to her rushed in to behead the Madame, not emerging unless they clutched her by her golden ringlets. That particular detail would have to stay concealed for now.

"Here," Millicent said as she pushed three bejeweled hairpins into Nox's hand. All three were meant to go above the same ear, slicking the hair back on one side. The underside of each pin had been sharpened into a thin, strong blade's point. Nox felt a twinge of emotion. She hated Millicent with every fiber of her being, but the begrudging, distasteful alliance was unavoidable.

She was grateful for the covert weapons, slipping all three into her hair. They had been an excellent addition to her outfit, as she was to appear alluring and unarmed in every conceivable way. They were perfectly delicate, harmless adornments with a deadly purpose.

The time for arguments had come and gone. If Emily had reappeared, she would have used this time to say her final goodbyes. Instead, Nox walked rather unceremoniously from the front doors of the Selkie. Millicent, of course, had assumed return the next morning. Nox had no such intention.

The Madame sent her in her personal glossy, black carriage, though it did not fast travel to the castle. A woman and a carriage manifesting from thin air would draw more than a little suspicion, Nox supposed. She had wanted to take a horse but saw the wisdom of avoiding the elements of wind, salt, and air, staying in her most pristine condition. Tonight, she was both bait and huntress.

✦

Though Nox had insisted with an air of confidence to the Madame that the captain would be at his regular tavern, she was sick with unease throughout the carriage ride. In three years, she had failed only once to lure a man.

Learning that her charm was less effective on those with fae blood filled her with trepidation. What if Eramus had fae heritage?

Nox absentmindedly wondered if this also meant someone of full fae lineage would survive a night with her, though she wasn't morbid enough to try it just for the sake of experimentation.

She stepped out of the carriage and paused, gripping the edge of the doorframe.

"Are you okay, miss?" asked the driver.

She'd never learned the man's name, nor did it matter. She had no interest in the men Millicent kept in her employ. Nox would never see the driver again after tonight, after all. No matter what happened, she wouldn't be returning to the brothel.

"I'm fine," she responded unconvincingly. But she wasn't fine, not truly. The task at hand was a drop in the venom-filled bucket of reasons why she hadn't been fine for days.

"Shall I wait here for you then?"

She wanted to smile kindly, but didn't have it in her to feign the emotion. She reserved her masks for her target. So she just said, "No, that won't be necessary," and waved him away.

Nox wasn't sure what was more terrifying—spying silently on the demons in the barn or opening the door to the Bird and the Pony. Tonight would be her first kill as a succubus outside of the walls of the Selkie. She corrected that thought: tonight would be her first near kill, as she did intend to keep the captain alive. It would have been preferential to hunt, feed, and capture on familiar soil, but she had to work within the conditions provided. No stretch of time would have any impact on her bravery. If she went, it would be now or never.

The relief she felt when she pushed open the pub door and immediately saw Eramus sitting like a prize-winning pig in the center of the pub, surrounded by his cronies and adoring maidens, was like a cool, refreshing bucket of cold water in the suffocating summer heat. The forged note she'd taken from the calligrapher had been a gamble at best, and a death sentence at the behest of the royal family for conspiring to infiltrate the castle at worst. She was exceedingly grateful she would not have to use the document.

The pub had been like any other. It was full of patrons and wenches and the smell of spilled beer, hot with the crackles of fire and the warmth of bodies. The roar of men seemed to ebb as she entered and faces turned to regard her. Her opening move in this match had been little more than walking through the door. Nox was aware of the effect she had on men, especially since she'd recently fed on a drunken bastard who'd deserved a fate worse than the death that swallowed him in her bed. The recent feeding had set her skin aglow with an unearthly beauty, making her all the more alluring. She was glad he was dead. Any person who would touch an immobi-lized woman shouldn't have just been killed, he should have been hung from the city square by the bloodied stump of his ripped-apart manhood. Once Nox had the captain under her guise, perhaps she would see to it that he implement precisely that as the new punishment as the law of the land for any man who forced himself on another. The hatred fueled her, manifesting itself as the glimmer of beauty. She was glowing and she knew it. She was the perfect bait.

Nox removed her royal-blue cloak, feeling greedy eyes on her as her dress worked its delectable magic. Her black, silk dress was the ultimate temptation. It had been her favorite weapon on more than one occasion. Her stunning, curve-hugging gown was a pawn in the game in its own right. The piece revealed enough to let others know that she was confident and sensual, while covering enough to make them want to see what secrets it kept beneath the contours of its fabric.

She relaxed into its effectiveness. It had never failed her.

That being said, hunting in the open air like this was nothing like the task of bringing men upstairs from the salon. When patrons entered the Selkie, they knew not only precisely why they'd come but also what rules governed their permission to stay. Her only challenge at the pleasure house had been to get the men to forget that they were at a brothel at all, convincing them to pursue her and want to win her despite where they'd met and the role in which she lived. It was a mistake many girls made in the Selkie. She knew enough from the pleasure house that no one who hoped to win a big spender could act like a sure thing. She'd learned the rules of life in a brothel enough to excel within them.

Vulnerability wrapped itself like ropes around her belly as she navigated the unfamiliar tavern. She'd assumed the pub would also be an inn and kicked herself for jumping to conclusions. Nox had realized her mistake the moment she'd crossed the threshold, but it had been too late to change course. There would be no simple slip upstairs when she was ready to seal the deal.

The Bird and the Pony was a crowded joint, lively with its own popularity. An enthusiastic fiddle player and his songstress entertained the crowd with drinking song after song, leading the men in familiar choruses. The crowd was jolly with the opportunity to join, sloshing their pints and spilling their ale as they slurred their rough, off-kilter contributions to the music. The musical pair was skilled at commanding a crowd, keeping their attentions jovial and the spirits high. The bar itself was crowded to the gills with a particular brand of rough, militant men and the maidens who were either supplied by the establishment or the young women of Aubade drawn to the masculine exterior of such brutish energy. Everyone had their motives, and as long as everyone in the bar was mutually benefiting, it seemed like a perfectly lovely place. This was only Nox's second time hunting on unfamiliar soil, and her first experience in Yelagin had gone disastrously. Hunting was an art, and beyond the walls of the Selkie, she was a painter without a brush.

There was no reason to be nervous, she told herself. This was her game.

Nox eyed an open spot along the main bar, far from the tables of men and their swooning women. She draped her cloak over her arm, allowing her bare back to be seen by the patrons as she maneuvered through the pub. Nox arched her spine slightly, ensuring that she was the picture of feminine beauty.

Nox avoided the men's eyes entirely, choosing to play coy. She knew precisely who had seen her when she walked in and whose eyes were on her as she took her seat across the room. Men liked to think something was their idea, after all. This reliable method was the very technique that had gotten the Duke of Henares and countless others to the Selkie. Nox lifted a finger and ordered herself a glass of red wine, though the lifted finger had been unnecessary. The bartender had noticed the unfamiliar face the moment she'd entered.

She made a show of scanning the bar, pointedly ignoring the soldiers bearing the queen's crest. The men, their armor, their weapons, their sigils were meaningless to her. She was no clout chaser, interested in titles or the authority that might entice one to seduce those within the court. Instead, she looked past the guardsmen, feigning mild interest in a tawny young man of barely eighteen far across the tavern. He'd noticed her immediately and practically spat up his beer. She did feel a bit sorry for the heart attack it appeared to have given the boy as he choked, sputtering ale onto the table. Hopefully, this boy and the collateral damage of his emotional confusion would be the final pawn she played before stronger moves were required of her.

Nox knew more than enough of timing and the role it played in seduction.

If the fiddle player and his songstress were beginning a new song now, she estimated it would take until the second chorus for the captain to approach her. All she had to do was graze her eyes over his, touching them briefly to extend an invitation, and he'd be on his feet in a moment.

She was ready. It was time to put her next piece into play.

The song lifted, rising in the notes of its first tawdry chorus. Nox began her scan, knowing very well that Eramus, along with more than one of his men, was looking in her direction. With an idle disinterest, she allowed their eyes to meet. Nox held the captain's gaze for the briefest of moments, and then she continued her scan with indifference. The bartender caught her eye with something of a knowing chuckle. He recognized her ploy. Good bartenders made their living off reading people, she supposed. If the other girls at the Selkie were to be believed, Eramus was a known hunter. Perhaps it was refreshing for the bartender to see the captain be the prey.

The first step in her job was nearly done. Her eyes

abandoned the tap house altogether, ignoring the amused barkeep, the gaze of the men, the eyes on her bare skin, and the envious looks of the women, who wore far more appropriate clothing than she had. Nox lifted her cup, studying the wine in her glass as the first chorus ended. The second verse began, and like clockwork, the captain was standing. If she knew anything of timing, she knew he wouldn't rush to her. There was an order to this dance, as predictable and important as any waltz. His men were cheering on some good-hearted mixtures between encouragement and envy, mostly unintelligible hybrids between grunts and cheers as the captain worked his way around them. It would take him the length of the verse to acknowledge his men, pat their shoulders, accept their envy and move. Slowly, he approached—bypassing the subtlety of opening pawns, he went right to his knight on his own. By the beginning of the second chorus, he was leaning against the bar, ever the picture of suave relaxation.

Eramus was just as the girls described, save for a curious, innocent quality. His golden hair was cut a little shorter than that of most men of the age. His locks were a bit curly, hanging to his cheekbones. His eyes were a bright, sky-blue color that stood out against his hair in a nearly virginal halo. Eramus didn't possess the rakish, bawdry handsomeness of her duke. Instead, he had a disarming angelic aura about him that the women had not explained when describing him to her. He asked if he could buy her a drink, and she tipped her nearly full glass to him.

Nox smiled, pressing her lips to her glass, allowing it to tug her mouth open ever so slightly. She waited until his gaze snagged on the shape of her mouth.

"I have a drink, but perhaps instead you could tell me your name?"

He twinkled wickedly. "I'm Eramus, but you can call me 'sir,' depending upon how the night pans out."

It was the second time in one night she should have been handed an award. If a trouper had spotted her performance, they would have shaken her hand and whisked her away to a life in the theater. Years at the Selkie had been an education in acting. It was a battle not to cringe or laugh at the man who fancied himself terribly dominant and charming. She recognized the angelic face for what it was: the beautiful coloration of a venomous snake. Disarming, attractive loveliness was how the goddess's most dangerous creations hid in plain sight under the guise of beauty. After all, it was how she operated, wasn't it?

Clearly, his combination of innocent loveliness and assertive domination worked on women who favored the company of men. Nox didn't always hate men. She had found some friendly, and others tolerable, if not occasionally charming in their own way. Eramus, however, was borderline insufferable.

Fortunately, she felt confident she could throw out the chessboard altogether. He was making this too easy. He'd won her the match with his arrogance.

He arched a brow, smiling at her over his pint. "And what should I call you?"

"Call me yours."

✦

One of the centurions clapped the captain on the back as he left the Bird and Pony, arm slung loosely around Nox's hourglass waist. The rough calluses on his hands grazed her bare lower back as he guided her through the crowd before he returned his hand to its resting place on her hip.

The pub had been intended for the castle's traffic,

as it truly was mere steps from the royal gates, but she was surprised to find them entering the enormous regal structure. She'd known the captain resided within its walls, but it was another thing entirely to be led into the castle. Did he genuinely bed women on castle grounds? Was she to lie down in a royal bed?

Every step brought her deeper into the cream stones of Aubade, carrying her further into the depths of uncertainty. She continued to chastise herself, saying her nerves were only a product of unfamiliarity. If she was to thrive in this world, she couldn't allow alarm bells any time she was in new territory. Nox justified his actions, supposing his quarters made right and proper sense. Queen Moirai couldn't very well be the one to ring the bell for men to awaken from their various townhomes interspersed amongst the coastal city if the castle found itself under siege. Still, it seemed unwise to be leading a strange girl into such a private space, especially if rumor was to be believed that the man took women home with regularity.

After all, what if she was a spy for Raascot? Or a member of the working class's resistance party? Or, say, a succubus?

It wouldn't serve her to dwell on the wisdom of Eramus's actions, so she focused on her surroundings. The castle was colder than she thought it would be. There were lanterns all around. The castle was insulated, and his arm was around her. Why was she cold?

Something was wrong.

No. No, she was allowing her nerves to better her. Nothing was wrong. Something being unusual didn't make it wrong. A man being atypical didn't make him bad. A situation being unfamiliar didn't make it dangerous. She was okay. She convinced herself that she was looking at everything through the lens of hostility. Her freshly stoked spite couldn't burn the bridge between her and the work to be done. She needed to quiet herself if she was to remain the cool, collected picture of confidence.

She did her best to keep up the alluring flow of idle chatter, and he answered in polite, bright tones. There was something stilted about their conversation that she couldn't place. Nox had facilitated many a night of chatter with drunken and sober patrons alike. Between everyone else, their conversation flowed as easily as the meads, ales, and wines that had refilled their cups. She knew how to ask questions and how to prompt responses. With Eramus, she found herself bumping against an odd disconnect. They both seemed to be the one facilitating the flow, relying on the other to fill the void. She'd been on unfamiliar ground in the bar and then taken to a new second location. The unexpected change happened as their stilted conversation continued to ring the warning bells from deep within her belly.

Once again, she told herself that it was her anger at Millicent, her revulsion toward men, her enmity for the world setting off undo alarms. She steeled herself against the quiet tug. Paranoia was unbecoming.

The castle was ominous after sundown, though she assumed that half of her impression stemmed from knowing she was on a mission of devilry. All castles were sinister by design. What use was a fortress if it felt jubilant and inviting? She used this rationale as she scanned the corridors, noting that the inner halls held no windows, only closed doors to chambers beyond and the staggered placements of haunting torchlight. The passages wound in a way that made the wanderer feel quite lost. The plush running carpet, the monotonous layout, the sameness of the cream-colored stones in the corridor all led to a consistent feeling of déjà vu. It was unnerving, knowing she was far from an exit and too disoriented to know how to properly escape.

She was deep within the belly of the castle with no sense for east or west, before they stopped.

The captain gave her a white-toothed grin as he paused in front of a large, wooden door and riffled in his pouch for a key. She continued to hold his arm as if she were an excited, lovelorn maiden of the city while he fiddled with the lock. Eramus flashed her a reassuring smile that didn't feel at all reassuring. He opened a door and ushered her in.

Nox stepped inside first.

For a moment she didn't understand what she was seeing.

There was no bed, nor were there windows. There were large chests, racks and shelves of…weapons. He had brought her into an armory. There was an oversized wooden table in the middle with something that appeared to be manacles embedded into each of its four corners. No, this wasn't an armory. Why were they here? Like a deer hearing a tree snap in the forest, she felt all her senses go wild, straining against the predatory sensation that loomed down on her.

Then she heard the clink of a metallic lock sliding into place behind her.

Yes, she saw it now. She saw everything.

She'd fallen for a move that had been meant to placate her into assumed victory. She'd let her guard down in premature celebration. She'd concluded their game of chess without realizing he was still playing. Not only were his pieces still in play, but Eramus was countless moves ahead.

This was his check.

Her heart quickened as she absorbed the weapons on

every wall. She heeded the chains meant to strap and constrain. She saw the brownish smears of blood. The objects meant for entrapment, for entanglement, for torture. At long last, she beheld the man who was not a man at all but a monster. He did not crave the bodies of women for any human lust.

Their stilted interactions suddenly made sense. It had been the conversation of two predators not knowing how to interact. The warning signals had originated from her having spotted a fellow hunter who'd found her as his intended prey. She had cursed herself for her counting on her senses, and now she hated herself for ignoring her intuition. She'd made only one mistake all night, and it had been her refusal to heed the wisdom of her gut.

She was in grave danger.

Eramus hadn't moved from the door. His smile had remained unchanged. It was a cruel, bizarre mask against his virginal features as it mixed with the scent of dried blood and metal.

It was suddenly obvious how important the captain's innocent face had been as camouflage, allowing his angelic features to hide in plain sight. She understood the frequency with which he needed new women, never bringing the same one home twice. Nox doubted that anyone brought into this room was left alive, and she fully comprehended why she was in a windowless room with the door locked behind them. How cruel an irony that the huntress had been the one to let herself fall victim to the teeth of a beast.

In that moment, Nox knew a few things with certainty. The first was that no charm or seduction would help her now. The next was that one of them was about to die, and she certainly didn't plan on it being her.

This is not how I go.

The steel cage of her mind clamped down around the sentence, and Nox was prepared to fight for her life. This would not be a battle of fists. He may have spent his life in preparation for steel, flesh, and his role in the guard, but she had something that he didn't. Nox had only one advantage at her disposal, and it was that of a player who had not revealed all her cards.

He wanted fear.

She was nowhere near triumph, but she could see the chess pieces move. These were not the guaranteed clutches of defeat. Not yet. She would win; her life depended on it. There were moves to be made. She could strategize her way out of this.

"Oh, sir," she purred, referencing the submission he had mentioned at the bar. "I do love a good sadist."

Nox bit her lip and slid her hands onto the table behind her, ignoring the smudges of uncleared blood. With the perverse delight of someone sharing in blood-lust, she did a backward hop onto the table, hoisting herself up by her hands and spreading her legs open for him. She allowed her dark eyes to fix on the bright blue sapphires of his angelic face. She was the picture of lust, spurred on with excitement. This was the performance of a lifetime, and she would not fail.

Perplexity flashed across his face. Good.

He was shaken from his regular pattern. Nox watched a piece on the chessboard shuffle as she understood how he'd strategically put himself at every advantage. She wasn't sure that she was out of his check, as her would-be king remained carefully pinned in their match. Surely, he had expected a panicked woman, the look of terror, perhaps even a gratifying scream.

Maybe he dined on fear the same way she fed on love.

Surprise, curiosity, and even a bit of disappointment

danced behind his blue eyes. She maintained her mask of confidence as she watched him regroup.

No matter, said the calm that settled over his features. The room had not rattled her? He was sure to have a few more tricks up his sleeve. The Captain of the Guard took a few steps to a cabinet, eyeing the options after opening its doors. He ignored her fully, fingering the barbarous selections it held. Perhaps this was his next step meant to unnerve and terrify. Through the power of sheer, desperate will, Nox forced her exterior to remain the picture of calm amusement, channeling pleasure. The metallic, spiked glint of a flail was the first thing she saw. There were blades, whips, and arrows. Next to the flail hung a crossbow. She had no hope if the man picked up the crossbow. Her eyes attempted to glaze over so she wouldn't see the terrible things inside, but she chased off the temptation with a harried, violent urgency. She would not live through the night if she didn't remain her sharpest.

Nox made the slightest, most sensual hitch of her breath, drawing his attention.

Another bold move.

She lifted one palm, using the index finger of her right hand to beckon him forward while her left hand began to slide up the side of her dress, slowly tugging on its slit to reveal her thigh. She kept her voice low and feral, leaning in to whatever animal nature she hoped possessed him.

"I like it rough," she practically moaned, her low voice a sensual whisper. Everything in her fought to keep her tone easy and aroused. She clamored for a balance, wondering what words would strike the subservience of someone who enjoyed sexual torture while still expecting to make it out alive.

Did Eramus carnally consummate his unholy

sacrifices before maiming the women he brought here? The blood pounded in her ears, drowning out any hope of using her senses. The battles she fought were raging in her mind: Who were the other women? Did their families know that their daughters were dead? Were any left alive when he finished with them? There was the faintest remnant of blood in the air, no doubt from the ruddy brown smears on the table and mortar between the stones from nameless others. She couldn't let herself be afraid. She couldn't let herself picture the women. She had to focus. She was the predator. He was the prey. There was no other alternative.

Eramus made his decision. His fingers wrapped around a nine-tailed flogger and turned toward her. A stab in her heart, the burble of terror as she remembered the crack of the whip, the sting of her blood as it pooled around her in the courtyard of Farleigh a lifetime ago. The pain of the whip would be nothing compared to the flogger in his fingers. He took a step toward her.

"Bend over."

Her mind echoed the unspoken word. *Check.*

The board was not moving in her favor. All his pieces were advantageously positioned to keep her cornered. There had to be a way out. She couldn't let him move one more piece, or he'd be the first to reach checkmate.

The room was too cold. It was too small. Her heart was beating too fast. She needed to keep up the ploy. She needed to win his favor, to sweet-talk him, to urge him into letting down his guard if she was to gain the upper hand. She needed to keep her face relaxed, her lips parted, her eyes filled with lust and excitement, no matter what she felt. The next move had to be hers.

No. She would not turn her back on him. If he were simply a man asking for a sexual favor, bent would do the trick as well as any other. But if she was in a vulnerable position, she'd have no way of knowing if he was bending her to enter or to break her skin with the weapon he held. Floggings ripped at the flesh and broke the ribs and backs and spines of their victims if the wielder refused to stop.

The only way to get out of check was by interposing a piece between the threat and the king. Death awaited one of them at this match's conclusion. She moved her queen.

Nox spread her legs farther. She bit her lip as she ran her hand up her thigh, purring her words. "Warm me up first, and I'll let you do whatever you want to me."

He glimmered as he said, "You'll eat those words."

"I can't wait."

He flashed his teeth in a snarl, agitated by her seductive taunt as he advanced on her.

Yes.

She'd done it. She'd made the most aggressive countermove, and it had paid off.

Nox had only a moment to seal her victory. She licked her palm, wetting herself as she enticed him forward. He stepped toward her, taking himself out of his pants. It was not with lust that he advanced but with the cruel monstrous need to dominate, to silence, to exert power and control and force. The moment he moved for her, she locked her legs around him, unwilling to let him leave. These were the moments that separated life from death for both of them, for terribly different reasons. This was not the passionate embrace of lovers. He had no intention of kissing her, but as he jammed himself inside of her, she smashed her mouth onto his and sucked.

Nox had known she'd won well before the captain realized he'd lost.

He'd continued with the full force of presumed domination for a breath before his eyes widened in panic.

It took less than a beat for Eramus to begin to fight as she drank him in. She felt his fear within a single heartbeat as he appeared to understand on a primal level that he was being devoured. She clamped down harder, engorging herself with the life force of the animal in her grasp. He attempted to claw at her, pulling at her hair, pushing back, fighting with his dying heartbeats to wriggle away, but no strength remained.

"Checkmate," she panted aloud, anger, triumph, hatred, and relief surging through her as her lips broke free.

The battle was over. His life was forfeit. Nox had won.

With one kernel of life remaining in him, she shoved him off her.

She needed a moment to heave in disgust just as she'd done years ago after her first kill. She'd seen death. She'd met wicked, cruel, and repulsive men. She'd encountered soldiers and warriors and power-hungry military officers. This was the first time she'd met a true demon.

Eramus was a monster. She bent herself over the table while he remained trapped in whatever remained of his shell of a person-suit. Nox held her head in her hands and wasn't sure if she would scream, laugh, vomit, or cry. After a time, she felt herself begin to grin, though not with joy. The smile was not one of happiness but of vitriol. She was a force of nature; she was lightning and thunder and the pewter gales of the stormy sea personified. She was the night. She was the creature in the shadows.

"How are you doing down there?" she asked. Nox feigned a pout as she looked at the crumpled man, her conviction returning.

Her calm was replaced with something else entirely as delicious justice tingled on her swollen lips. She pulsed with triumph.

She straightened from the table as she examined her

conquest. She wiped her mouth clean of him, teeth glinting from her victory. Nox ran her hands down the black silk of her sensual gown, straightened her dress, smoothing it like a lady. A hand went to her hair, fixing it as she raked her fingers tenderly through her inky locks, appreciating the soothing familiarity of grooming.

Perfectly presentable to claim her prize, she crossed over to him and spat on him. Nox lowered until she was at eye level, the water of her spit glistening upon his unmoving features. She stared into his baby blue eyes for a long time, allowing herself to see into the depths of the blackened soul she'd stolen.

"You still in there, Eramus?"

He let out the barest whisper of a terrified moan.

"Good."

She took the tailed flogger from where it had fallen on the floor and brought it to one of the blades on the wall. Nox snipped the long strand from its flog and returned to Erasmus. Nox sighed as she began the laborious effort of shimmying the captain's pants farther down his hips, revealing his testicles. She made a noise to express her displeasure before she set to work. She wrapped the leather strand tightly around his scrotum, watching the testicles grow purple instantly as they filled with blood. She knew enough from the gelded horses in Farleigh's stables that it would take two weeks for his manhood to fall off in its entirety, and she wasn't sure she'd let him live that long. Two weeks was too long for a man who did not deserve to draw breath. Still, castration—even a slow one—was a relatively satisfying victory. He would never, ever be removing this leather band.

"How does it feel? Nice and snug?" She feigned something like friendliness, a pout on her lips as she scanned the rapidly fading terror in his eyes. Soon, he wouldn't feel anything. She needed him to stay awake for a bit longer. She needed his consciousness for a few more minutes.

Another defiant, ghostly groan scratched over his lips.

"Oh, I hear you, Captain. It's scary to feel trapped and helpless, isn't it? Nowhere to go, no help in sight, right? That must be terrible."

She rose from where she'd knelt and eyed the tools on the shelf. She smiled at her dress, her arms, her legs, the curve of her breasts, and the silky strands of hair she could see brushing around her shoulder. She knew beyond the shadow of a doubt that she was the picture of perfection and found it deeply satisfying. There was something particularly malevolent about her curated loveliness cast against a backdrop so evil.

Nox turned to him from where she stood, smiling as if they were children on the yard at playtime. "How about I point to one, and you tell me if you've used it on a woman. Does that sound like a fun game?"

He grunted again. The sound was nearly human, presumably meant to be a cry for help.

"Ah, I see. Not so fun because you've used most of these, right? Or has it been all of them? Busy, busy boy," she tsked. She decided to keep it poetic and, after considering her options, landed on the same nine-tailed flogger—now with eight remaining tails—that he'd intended for her.

Nox knelt again, grabbing his chin and feigning another pout. She painted her face with mock sympathy as she spoke, saying, "I'm not a cruel person, Eramus. I've never tortured—not physically, anyway. Though I do suppose you and I have a thing or two in common. In a way, I use men as you use women. We both take. We're takers, you and I. The primary difference is that the men I use…well…for them it's a disembodied heaven on earth. Of course it took a few tries to get it right. Now not only can I control it, but I can stop just shy of that euphoria, should I please—which is where I'd love to leave you, if you didn't serve a greater purpose. I do feel bad for the men who fell to my trial and error before I learned to wield my puppets. Really, I do. I'm not a killer by choice. Maybe that's our primary difference."

Nox rose and looked down her nose at where he remained slumped against the floor, his purpling bulge still visible. She nudged him with her foot.

"Don't fall asleep now, Captain. Stay with me. I have something to tell you. You see, sometimes I feel bad about who I am and what I do. It's true! Can you believe it? Occasionally, I get all tangled up in things like morality…but then I meet men like you and I remember exactly why I don't need to feel *anything* about what I do. Justice can be a cruel mistress, can't it, Captain?"

He breathed again, and she knew with a wicked delight that he'd given up all hope. His sounds weren't those of a plea. They weren't even noises of pain. Had he already resigned? How disappointing. She continued to allow him the twinkle of consciousness he needed to stay himself for a moment longer. Somehow, she felt quite sure this was not cruelty. She was no more evil for this than she had been for discovering her heritage in the first place. In fact, if she had to ask the ghosts of the women who'd been lost to this room or their families, she'd be considered an avenging angel.

She kicked him again. "Stay awake, soldier. In a bit, I'll put you in a daze. Trust me, you'll love it. But the thing is, I don't quite feel like you deserve to love anything just yet. I just want to make sure you're still *you* for the next few minutes. You'll get to live for a few more days while I see how you might atone for your sins—and trust me, you will atone. For that reason, I think I'll leave your limbs on for now." She ran her fingers along the eight-tailed whip, enjoying the luxury of its sadistic leather against her skin. She smiled as she asked, "We shouldn't waste any time. We have a long night ahead of us before your daze begins. Is that all right with you?"

Nox would never doubt herself again. Instincts were meant to keep her alive. Telling herself she had been wrong for feeling nervous, convincing herself that she had been crazy for her worry had almost gotten her killed. She'd protect and honor those intuitions until the end of her days, never again allowing the past and its horrors to guide the instincts of her present. For now, she'd enjoy the end of his days.

Forty–One

THE IMAGE OF A HORSE WAS STILL IN HER MIND AS AMARIS pictured Castle Aubade's architecture. From the outside of the castle, Amaris had assumed its snout to be roughly five stories high, and now she understood the reason for its height. The horse's nose belonged to the throne room.

Moirai's throne room was a long, grandiose cathedral. Three levels of balconies had onlookers curiously watching the three reevers as they approached the thrones, with two additional pseudo-floors left solely for the light and expanse of palatial luxury. At least, there would have been light pouring in from the upper levels of skylights if it hadn't been nightfall before the queen summoned them. Amaris, Malik, and Ash had scarcely had a chance to exchange two words in reunion before they were ushered into the room. She absently hoped Malik had been fed before they were shoved from the landing through the double doors of the monarch's room. The entrance closed behind them as the reevers were led into the magnificent, imposing space to meet with Queen Moirai. Guards stepped from their place on either side of the doors, stoically safeguarding the only exit.

"Are you ready?" Ash asked her under his breath

before they took the final steps down the long, carpeted aisle to see the queen on her throne.

Amaris nodded once. She was as ready as she'd ever be, yet acknowledging it and feeling it were two very different things. At least she had more than enough to look at to distract her from her inner turmoil.

Enormous columns connected the floor to the vaulted ceiling. Equally large stained-glass windows lined both sides of the throne room, and Amaris was sure that during the daylight hours, the rainbow they cast was spectacular. The only thing they could do was put one foot in front of the other.

She continued scanning the cathedral-like space, wondering if Ash and Malik were better at concealing their gapes than she was. The three reevers made their way down an ostentatiously long, plush rug of deep burgundy, trimmed in golden thread, that created a perfect runway from where they'd entered to the two imposing thrones, seats far too gaudy to feel noble, awaiting them at the end of the runner. The thrones, presumably one for the queen and one for the crowned prince, sat upon an elevated platform so the royals could look down their noses at anyone who approached.

Amaris vastly preferred the clean, honorable grays, furs, and leathers of Uaimh Reev to the gaudy reds and golds of Farehold, but then again, no one had ever consulted her opinion on decorating.

It appeared that only Queen Moirai would be taking an audience with them, as the throne beside her sat empty. Amaris did her best not to move her head away from the queen, understanding enough of courtly propriety to know it to be improper. From their brief meeting in the hall, her friends also appeared to have been dressed as fashionably as she had and walked with as much stately reverence as they could muster. Ash and Malik flanked her, a man on each side keeping an arm's length behind. Their flanking was meant to ensure that Amaris was showcased as their speaker, as she would likely be the only one with the opportunity to exchange words with the queen. When she spoke, she needed to make every word count.

The reevers reached the end of the rug, and all three knelt in an appropriate bow. Their lessons on poisons, monsters, and ways to be one's own battle medic hadn't exactly prepared them for decorum, but Amaris had had the fortune of being educated in such ways at Farleigh. Ash and Malik followed her lead, bowing their heads with their knees bent.

Moirai struck an intimidating figure at the end of the aisle. Dressed in a bloodred gown trimmed with gold along the collar and large, she looked like Farehold's banner come to life. An ornate gold belt studded with rubies hugged her waist; it may have been lovely when she was younger, but given her advanced age, it seemed misplaced. Her crown was just another accessory in her collections of crimsons and golds. The gilded circlet rested atop the loose curls of her unpinned hair as she frowned at the reevers.

"Your majesty—" was meant to be said in unison, but Amaris distinctly heard both of her companions pluralize the word. It was an odd, jarring moment that Amaris almost tried to convince herself hadn't happened. She kept her eyes lowered until the queen motioned for them to rise. Amaris scanned again to ensure she had not missed the crown prince. It was more likely that she had misheard her friends. She stilled her inner voice, focusing on the task at hand while Queen Moirai spoke.

"Why have you crossed the continent to call for an audience with us?" she asked. Moirai's voice was not kind, nor was her cadence particularly beautiful. It was the robust, irked voice of a monarch who had better things to do than to entertain the league of guardians who were best left ignored.

This was Amaris's moment. This was precisely what she had waited for throughout the weeks of travel. This was why Samael had looked at her that day in the reev and had known her persuasion was more gift than curse. Diplomacy came first, she told herself. First she would ask the queen, then she would tell.

"Your majesty." Her voice came out quieter than she had intended. Amaris rose to her feet, watching the reevers on either side mimic her actions as they straightened their postures. She lightly cleared her throat and summoned her courage. She locked eyes with the queen of Farehold as she said, "Your highness, I am Amaris of Uaimh Reev, and these are my reever companions, Ash and Malik. As you know, the reev has only served to keep peace. That is why we seek an audience with you today."

The queen made an unimpressed face. She was the perfect picture of inconvenienced boredom. She clearly had dinners to eat, nobles to meet, baths to take, books to read, peasants to spit on, and all manner of things she'd prefer to accomplish rather than be in the company of whatever assassins operated outside Farehold's law.

The courtiers in the balconies were not especially numerous, but the ones who did observe appeared to be listening intently. A few could be seen whispering behind laced gloves or outstretched fans. The reevers had been around for centuries, but Samael had said himself that their numbers had dwindled. He had not left the keep in practically five decades. No one in this room appeared to surpass that length of time in years. Amaris wondered how much may have changed in the dozens of years Samael had remained sequestered.

She noted the courtiers only with the studiousness of the warrior she was trained to be, then blocked them out for the distractions they were. It was not useful to dwell on her audience. The only other bodies in the throne room that mattered belonged to the fully armored soldiers, still as sentinels, holding lavishly feathered spears on either side of the twin thrones. When she spoke, it was with authority and finality. She may be a girl with no family and no title, but she was a reever. She had a right to speak on behalf of balance regardless of the monarch before her.

"We are on dispatch to inquire as to the killings of Raascot men throughout Farehold."

The queen's transition from disinterest to amusement was abrupt. She nearly snorted at this, casting an entertained look to the empty seat beside her, then gesturing as if to the audience of courtiers. Her defensiveness was immediate.

"Killing! Please. Have any bodies been produced? Show me evidence that I have killed a single northman on my lands."

A few humorless chuckles bounced off the stones from the overhanging balconies.

Amaris refused to look at the nobility lining the lofted floors. She kept her eyes on Moirai and remained uncharacteristically neutral as she restated her purpose.

"We are here on behalf of the reevers to request that Your Majesty stand down on her orders to kill northerners found south of the border," she said.

Moirai let out another laugh before raising her eyebrows further. It was surprising that there had been any skin on her forehead remaining to experience the ever-arching eyebrows, but somehow they'd climbed. If she managed to be any more surprised, her brows would disappear beneath her curls and join her crown.

"What do you think?" Moirai asked the chair.

Amaris flinched at the oddity. She shot a quick look over her shoulder to catch Malik's attention, as the mop of his golden hair seemed a bit closer to the tilt of her chin. He did not meet her eyes.

Moirai raised a hand to her ear as if to better hear. Amaris blinked several times in an attempt to maintain her poise. Had the queen gone mad? Surely, there would have been word if a mad queen sat upon the throne. Even in Farehold, gossip had spread about the instability of the man who sat on Raascot's throne. How had nothing been dispersed about the woman who spoke to furniture?

Raising her voice to its loudest, most regal bellow, the queen announced: "The crowned prince is quite right. He and I find it offensive that Uaimh Reev—a keep that has claimed neutrality for hundreds of years—comes into our kingdom and makes such accusations about our people and our intentions. What kind of peacekeeping is it, then, when you march into our throne room and defend the north from some offense invented by your reev? What sort of northern agenda have you truly come to press upon the good people of Farehold?"

The onlookers murmured their agreement.

Amaris knew she was supposed to keep her eyes on the queen, but they darted to Ash beside her. "What prince?" she breathed, barely a whisper.

His amber eyes widened with horror at her idiocy. Ash angled his head forward, using the barest of motions to gesture toward the throne. She was fumbling her dispatch, and they both knew it. Amaris was botching the mission. With the intensity of his urgency, Ash mouthed, *"The crowned prince!"*

Her eyes tore from her copper friend. She stared at the empty seat for a moment longer. The queen and all her courtiers watched Amaris expectantly. The inelegance of finding herself mute at the foot of Queen Moirai when an answer had been demanded of her was its own catastrophic failure of adherence to courtly standards. The expectant sounds of fidgeting silence of the courtiers around her pressed down on her. But she couldn't speak. Not yet.

This wasn't right.

Amaris dipped her chin again, doing her best to conceal the movement of her lips as she continued to angle her head toward Ash.

"Do you see a prince?" Her question was low and hurried. She widened her eyes at him, signaling her seriousness. He blinked several times at her, perhaps thinking she'd lost her mind. He was disappointed. He was horrified. He was pleading. Ash flared his nostrils, using all of his nonverbal signals to urge her to pull herself together.

Amaris couldn't pull herself together. She looked over to the remaining reever.

"Malik!" she said in a hushed cry for help.

"Talk to them!" he urged as quietly as he could.

She looked back at the queen, realization slackening her jaw. Samael's musings as he'd looked upon her purple eyes ran through her, just as Gadriel's had on their second encounter. The first meeting she'd had with the leader of the reevers rang through her memory with a single sentence: "…*with those eyes, I'd love to see what gifts of sight you possess.*" Her mouth dried as if stuffed with cotton.

Her next statement came out, barely the ghost of a murmur. Her heart fell into her stomach. Her blood went cold. She felt as though she tasted pennies on her tongue.

Amaris swallowed. "There is no prince."

Her voice was too quiet. The queen made a motion of annoyance, looking to the chair again and nodding.

Moirai was conversing with a phantom. No one was there. Amaris blinked a second time, then a third.

It was an act. Amaris had the gift of sight. She had the gift to rightly see. She heard a ringing in her ears as she stared at the empty space beside the queen. Slightly louder, she repeated, "There is no prince."

Her voice found purchase this time. She knew from the expression on Moirai's face that she had been heard. The queen's eyes instantly tightened. The woman gripped the arms of her throne, knuckles flexing white. Perhaps Amaris's exclamation had been a mistake, but she was possessed with her realization.

"What are you doing?" Malik asked. His voice was a hoarse, desperate rasp beside her. They were losing the favor of the crown with every passing second.

"There is no prince" was all she could say, repeating herself stupidly. The pieces of the puzzle clicked together. Her heart was in her ears; her breaths, shallow. There was no prince. Everyone saw a man who was not there. They perceived something that did not exist. Everyone saw it…but her.

Why? *Why?*

"It's an illusion."

Then louder, the accusation bubbled up, her hand nearly raising to point an index finger, though her fingers crumpled inward. She was too horrified to find the strength, and she didn't have the time to do what was right and proper. She wasn't afforded the luxury of discussing things with the reevers. She locked eyes with the queen and fully lifted her finger. "You have the gift of illusion," Amaris said. "You—Your Majesty…the perception at the border…it's *your* curse."

The reevers at her side had gone rigid. They felt the court's tide turn against them.

Her heart thundered in her ears with the high, drowning sound of the ocean's tide.

Moirai blinked rapidly, gripping the handles of her throne before she barked out a single word: "Guards!"

Amaris had found her voice fully now. She was not timid. She was not anxious. She sounded demented to all looking on, but she knew. She knew the truth and demanded that all hear her as she screamed at Moirai. "It's *your* curse! The border is your curse! You have the gift of illusion!"

She tried to gulp air by the bucketful. It suddenly seemed impossible to breathe.

The guards advanced as Amaris seemed to remember her only task, one she had failed. She'd been sent to persuade, not to reveal. She stared at Queen Moirai, the world around her melting into a tunnel, but she saw only one woman's face and summoned her power. "You *will* let us go!" Amaris shouted past the bodies that closed in around her, ignoring the world and rallying her persuasion for the Queen of Farehold alone.

"Guards, seize them!"

She leapt to her feet as she pointed at her accusers. Moirai's intensity and hysteria should have betrayed her guilt before her court. She had been discovered. She had been foiled. The woman's voice was too loud, too frenzied.

Bewildered anger coursed through Amaris as she gaped at Moirai. Her heart thundered in her ears as the centurions closed in within seconds.

Her companions were helpless, knowing they could not fight. They were unarmed and outnumbered. They were in couriers' clothes, weaponless and powerless. Even if they initiated hand-to-hand combat, how many trained centurions could Ash and Malik truly fight before they were overpowered? They'd counted on Amaris to persuade the queen, and in a single moment, their hopes had been dashed. The struggle beside her was little more than the sounds of grunted protest.

Her voice was shriller than they'd surely ever heard. She was little more than a girl being plunged underwater, sputtering her desperate screams against the lapping surface of the waves, but she tore her gift of persuasion from its resting place in her belly and flung it at the monarch.

"Queen Moirai, you will let us go! You will set us free from this castle!"

But the queen was unyielding, trembling with rage as she held her hand firm, pointing with all the venom in the world.

The throne room had descended into colorful chaos. Courtiers were burbling their shock. Flashes of color and jewels swam from the balconies. Metallic breastplates and the tinkling of armor filled the air around them.

"Silence her!"

Amaris fought to ignore the guards as they grabbed her arms. Her words were little more to the sentries than the mad ravings of a lunatic bouncing off the enormity of the throne room and all its finery. Courtiers continued gasping and shouting at the eruption of excitement. The reevers beside her were omitting gasps and grunts as they wormed to keep their feet on the ground. She saw none of it, heard none of it, willing herself to see only the queen.

"You will let us go! You will stop killing the northerners! You will—"

A thud deadened everything, and stars swallowed her vision. She fell to the ground as the pommel of a sword hit her over the head, and the world around her winked into black.

Forty–Two

C APTAIN ERAMUS!" A VOICE SHOUTED FROM SOMEWHERE down the hall while the sounds of doors opening and clattering shut filled the air. The voice's owner continued their hurried searching as they made their way toward the succubus and her prey.

Nox, still in her black, silk gown, remained perched on the torture table picking at her nails, the picture of boredom. Whatever chill she'd felt in the night had long since dissipated. It had been hours of exertion, and her muscles had warmed her body. Now she enjoyed the relaxing hours of morning as she eyed her accomplishment. Nox was careful to avoid the red-brown stains of the table before sitting down, not wanting to dirty her dress. She looked to her glazed-over captain with just her eyes, lifting her brows slightly.

"You ready, pet?"

Eramus had been redressed for some time, though the bulge in his pants as his purpling manhood throbbed beneath from its leather-tied death grip looked a bit improper. To the untrained eye, it looked merely as though he was having filthy thoughts unable to keep to himself. No one would expect the swelling castration to be anything more than a distinctly male blunder.

Her exercise in vigilante justice had taken all night. Once she had finished cracking down her punishments, ensuring he'd heard and felt every moment of his lessons, she had used what remained of her power to breathe into him the droplet of life she'd need for him to be under her charm. Hours had passed, and she had no doubt that had this room possessed any windows, cheery morning light would be filtering through. She smiled at the thought of the sun shining down on her and her painful brand of divine, feminine vengeance.

Nox hadn't worried about her enchantments when she'd sent the Duke of Henares from the Selkie. The toffee-haired lordling had quite the reputation for being a lazy, debaucherous noble. Diddling about his estate in Henares babbling like a drug-addled, love-sick puppy wouldn't draw too much suspicion, as it was within his line of character to do so, relatively speaking. Nox had no doubt he'd do just fine handling himself while out of her sight. This captain, however, would require a bit more of a hands-on approach. His responsibilities were far greater, and due to the inflexibility of his title, his margin for error was practically nonexistent. Nox would have to stay close to Eramus, firmly steering him until she'd used him for everything he was worth.

She inspected her nails once more for the telltale signs of dried blood as the panicked sounds of searching echoed down the hall. She'd been using a slender knife to remove traces of her punishment but set it to the side as the noises drew nearer. Her nails were rather short given her romantic proclivities, but the speckles of blood and struggle had found their way beneath them nonetheless. She was unbothered as the noises grew nearer. She had nothing to fear. The mighty Captain of the Guard was at her side, after all.

This morning Nox had assumed that she would have the bewitched captain to escort her out of the castle, but if the commotion in the hall was any indication, it appeared now that they would be taking a detour. This was fine, of course. If Yelagin's demons were to be believed and Amaris had need for the queen, then Nox had no problem staying close to a royal resource. There was nowhere Eramus could go that she couldn't with him posing as her chaperone— even if it might raise more than a few eyebrows. Eramus was roughly as high-ranking and authoritative as one might get without possessing a noble title. She very much doubted anyone, save for the regents themselves, would be able to deny him his sultry, black-haired companion.

Someone—presumably a servant, from the deference used in the title—continued calling the captain's name. The individual used the clanging of keys to lock and unlock every door in the corridor until finally the entrance to the sadistic armory flung open.

The servant's eyes darted with surprise as his gaze flitted between the captain standing loosely in the middle of the room to the woman resting against the table. Nox continued to look both relaxed and unimpressed, allowing her puppet to lead the way.

"Sorry, sir" came the uncomfortable explanation. The servant fidgeted, unsure about what, exactly, he'd walked in on. "Captain Eramus, you're urgently needed at the arena."

"Regarding?" the captain asked.

Nox puckered her lip and cocked a brow in appreciation. She was impressed with her own handiwork, as he did not sound quite like the opium-drugged lovers who often left her chambers once entranced. His tone held almost enough authority to pass as competent. She had told him, under no uncertain terms, that she wanted to know everything he knew from this moment forward. This was more than likely why he was obediently asking follow-up questions of the agitated servant.

The servant squirmed slightly from where he stood in the doorway before approaching Captain Eramus and whispering in his ear, presumably to discuss matters of utmost secrecy out of the earshot of whatever lady friend the captain had been entertaining. It was clear from the discomfort of the servant's flickering eyes that he had noticed the captain's bulge. It took a few moments for the message to be relayed before he backed away, offered a quick bow, and took off down the hall.

"So," Nox asked calmly, "what takes us to your arena?"

✦

Amaris opened her eyes. At least, she tried. One of her lids seemed impossibly heavy, perhaps swollen from the blow she'd taken to the face as a thick memory of a sword's pommel had connected to her skull. Discomfort pulsed through her entire being. She remained disoriented while her eyes slowly widened to take in her surroundings. Her head throbbed. Her shoulders ached. She absorbed every sickening sensation of lying facedown on a cold, filthy floor. Still unmoving, she took a moment to orient herself before she realized that her face was pressed into the dirt and stone of the ground. As she breathed in through her nose, the odors of unwashed bodies, mold, animal musk, and waste assaulted her.

She had failed.

She had barely awoken, yet she already knew with definitive certainty that when her abilities had been required of her, she had been useless. Amaris made a motion to push herself up into a seated position but found herself unable. Hands restrained behind her back, she knew there'd be no escaping her tight bindings. She swallowed, but her tongue connected with an obstacle. A thick band of fabric was gagging her, disabling her ability for speech. Her mouth filled with saliva around the foreign object as if her body willed her to swallow the obstruction away. Despite the desperation of her situation, some part of her accepted the act. She supposed if someone tried to use powers of persuasion on her, she'd also have them gagged and rendered speechless. If she'd truly been suspected of persuasion, perhaps she was fortunate that her tongue had not been cut from her mouth.

Amaris let out a muffled choke as she rolled onto one side. She bent her right knee, bringing it up to her chest to create space between her torso and the stone floor with her left leg outstretched behind her, toes rolling her onto the ball of her foot. Using her knee as leverage, she pushed herself up and was able to get her feet underfoot.

Her eyes struggled to adjust to the dismal, drab space. Her vision had never served her well in the dark. Her gaze filtered through the gloom, one shape at a time. The light from windows around corners illuminated just enough, yet nothing at all. She was in a cream-bricked room—no, a cell—not with the straight four walls of a jail but in a hall that seemed to curve ever so slightly. While three walls of her cell were made of the iron bars one might expect of a horrid dungeon, the wall that should have been the barrier to the outside was made from wood, containing a single slit down its middle.

Despite her pounding headache, she forced herself to study the wall. Her best guess was that she was on the wall closest to the outside world. She'd barely absorbed the layout before something far more important leapt to the forefront of her mind.

Ash and Malik.

Her heart stuttered painfully as she searched for the others.

Her eyes now fully adjusted, she spotted her companions in the cell opposite hers, still unconscious. Their cell, like hers, had its iron bars, but their far wall was the same cream stone of the Castle of Aubade. Why did hers have a slitted, wooden wall? She shoved the thought to the back of her mind, deciding architectural design was the least of her worries.

Amaris tried to call out through the muffle of her gag.

Ash's red hair was easy to spy. He faced away from her and made no movements at her sounds. Beside his motionless form, Malik stirred. He had been left in a sitting position, head slumped to his chest with his hands behind him. Amaris cried out again against her gag, then nearly cried in relief as her friend's emerald eyes fluttered open.

Malik was quick to consciousness.

He attempted to stand the moment he realized she was trapped behind bars but quickly discovered his hands were similarly bound like hers. She continued to stare with frenzied intensity as he fumbled against his bindings, and she noticed that neither Ash nor Malik appeared to have any fabric muzzling him as she did. Perhaps gags were unnecessary for anyone who didn't contain a witch's malevolent power. After what felt like a grim eternity, Malik created enough leverage with his bound hands to get his feet underneath him.

He made it to his feet and pushed his chest against the bars as he gaped at Amaris.

"Are you all right?"

Despite her situation, she felt a lurch of sadness at his question. His empathy was a bottomless well. As miserable as she felt, she knew he felt it in equal proportion at his inability to help her. He'd go to the ends of the earth to save the ones he loved, yet he was rendered powerless while he watched her, bound and gagged behind iron, separated from them. This seemed a somewhat more tragic fate. She carried the powerlessness of her own scenario, while he shouldered the burden of everyone's destitution.

Amaris nodded, though she had no idea if it was true. Was she all right? She was bound, gagged, and in what was most definitely a prison separated from her brothers.

She channeled her senses, focusing on what she had to do to get out. For now, she'd ignore Malik and pour her attention into her bindings.

Amaris pressed her face into the cold iron bar, searching for something jagged or rough to rub on her gag. She ran her cheek along the bar, but there was nothing. Though it chafed her skin, the cloth of her gag stayed securely in her mouth, choking her lips in an open position as it remained tied tightly at the back of her head. While she searched for something—*anything*—to snag against the fabric, she saw Malik gently kicking Ash to a waking state. It took the groggy faeling a few moments to take in his surroundings, but he rolled to his side in a fashion similar to Amaris and was able to get on his feet.

"What happened?" Malik asked, knowing Amaris could not answer.

Drool was the only answer she could offer beyond her grunts. She waited as they tried to untie one another but realized that, though rope bit into her wrists, her companions had the irons of chains around theirs. Their bindings were different, and she didn't know why. At least the men had been spared the cruelty of gags.

They left her to her fruitless wriggles as they worked their way through their own bindings.

Malik lowered himself to the ground, rolling into a

sitting position as he squirmed his bound hands over his backside, down the length of his legs, and managed to maneuver the shackles to his front. He helped Ash do the same until their still-shackled hands were in front of them.

Ash gripped the bar, staring helplessly at her.

She could feel the grime smudged across her face and knew she looked exceptionally pathetic. Not only was she filthy, but she still wore flat shoes, black tights, and the puffy, silver-sleeved jacket of the court juggler. If she hadn't felt humiliated before, the furious burn in Ash's eyes told her everything she needed to know.

Ash's flare of anger called to the final insult to their situation. Not only were they bound and jailed, but they'd been stripped of their dignity. They were imprisoned not as proud reevers but as clowns—mere laughing stock for the queen.

Amaris could not maneuver her hands to the front of her body as her friends had. While Ash's and Malik's chains were loose, standard cuffs, her ropes did not end at her wrists. They coiled up to her elbow, fusing her forearms together in a viselike grip. She'd been kept separate, bound differently, and gagged. If their situation hadn't already been horrid, there was something unknowably ominous about these slight variations. They made no sense to her, but her gut told her that it couldn't be anything good.

The others spent a moment talking hurriedly to themselves in gruff, muddled tones.

Ash locked on to her gaze as he spoke aloud.

"Ayla, just shake your head yes or no. Are you telling us that the crowned prince we saw was an illusion?"

The relief was like the cold water on her dry, gagged tongue. They understood her. They knew what she had been trying to communicate. Alleviation smothered her, taking whatever small solace she could. Amaris blinked rapidly, nodding with urgency in confirmation.

He tried again. "You were able to see the illusion for the same reason you can see the Raascot fae?"

Again, she nodded with enough ferocity that the very tendons of her neck might spasm. She let out a choked sob, relieved at being understood.

Ash swallowed, leaning his forehead against the iron bars as he eyed the space between them. He continued, "And the last thing you had said was that if Queen Moirai has the power of illusion, it must be her gift that has cursed the border with this perception spell?"

Amaris groaned, able only to nod in encouragement. She pressed into the bars, desperate to be as close to her friends as possible. The reevers were at least three arms' lengths away from one another. Even if they had each been unbound and outstretched, they still would have found themselves unable to find the touch of comfort in reaching for one another. They were separated in a way that had been intended to leave them emotionally destitute.

"The queen couldn't be persuaded," Ash stated.

"But the queen is not fae." Malik's sentence was not a question. Moirai's traits didn't display a drop of fae blood. She had no ears, no large irises, no sharpened canines, not even a hint of beauty in her horrid traits. His voice was contemplative, lost to his own thoughts as he said, more to himself than anyone else, "Moirai is a witch."

Angrily, Ash snapped, "Why didn't you address the guards instead? Why didn't you command them? When your power did nothing to the witch, why didn't you turn your attention away from her!"

Malik kicked the redhead, eyes flashing. His voice came out in a snarl. It was only the second time in her life that she'd heard anger from Malik, and she knew it was for her benefit.

"What's done is done, you ruddy fool. She'd spent weeks prepared to give her speech to the queen and the queen alone. Do you want your last moments with her to be scolding her for not being all-knowing?"

Last moments, he had said. Malik was right. The queen would never let her live. In seeing through the monarch's illusion, Amaris knew more than perhaps anyone else in Farehold, and knowledge was a dangerous thing. There was no way she'd be permitted to make it out alive. It was through grime, tears, and a soaked, filthy gag that she eyed her friends. This might be the final time she looked at them. Ash, with his flaws, his joys, his angers, his arrogant flirtation. Malik, with his goodness, his generosity, his selflessness and strength. Wet tears joined the moisture of the saliva against her gag as they tumbled from her eyes, absorbed by the cloth that bound her mouth. She leaned her forehead against the chilled bars and closed her eyes.

This was it. The how and when remained an unimportant question, given that a death sentence loomed over her as inevitably as the sun rose in the east and set in the west. If this was how she went, she'd pass amidst the stench of mold and filth. She'd leave the earth and join the All Mother with her arms aching against their binds, her heart throbbing against her failure. She'd die unable to say goodbye to her brothers.

She understood Ash wasn't truly angry with her, even if his words had said as much. He was just angry—angry at his helplessness, angry that he couldn't have saved them or have done more. She wished she'd had the where-withal to engage the guards directly. She hadn't known enough of her power or its limits to think to address the ones surrounding them, focused solely on the queen. Of course, Ash burned against the injustice. His rage had nowhere to go, no place to fall but on the fruitlessness of *what-ifs*. What if, indeed. What if she had known, somehow, that commanding the queen was in vain and that her attention had needed to pivot to the captors around her? What if Amaris had been born a brown-haired girl to a happy family and a safe village, never having heard of child mills or places called Farleigh? What if Raascot and Farehold had excellent relations between benevolent rulers and there was no curse? *What if.* They were the two most useless words in the common tongue.

She didn't possess the vocabulary for everything she felt. Being trapped in this dungeon was like being kept away from market day, but with violence and bindings. Being thrust into Farehold's cells was like being torn from Nox all over again, but with the cruelty of seeing the ones she loved just out of reach. It was rejection, confusion, and fury tangled into Moirai's incomprehensible spiderweb.

Nothing made sense. Why would Moirai need a prince? What reason would compel her to spell for herself a perceived heir where none existed? How much power did it take for her to cast and maintain such a curse? And furthermore, what did Raascot have to do with any of it? Ash and Malik seemed to be having a conversation similar to the one brewing in her mind, but they didn't have any yes-or-no questions they could ask of her. Her guess was as good as theirs, and no theory could be uttered through the fabric that gagged her. She wasn't sure that she wanted their last moments to be spent arguing. She didn't know what fruitless guesses and speculations would benefit her.

Amaris shifted from leaning her forehead against the cool bars to her cheeks, her neck. She let the questions slide away, savoring what remained of her mortal life; whether in one week or one hour, these might very well be her final sensations. What did knowledge matter if she was about to die? How would the queen do it? Was Moirai famous for any particular brands of cruelty?

Amaris looked within herself for a happy memory. She didn't want to die thinking of pain, of destitution, of failure. Amaris didn't want to die at all, but it seemed like she might not get much say in the matter. If she was to be killed, she wanted to die thinking of how Odrin had beamed with such pride at her swearing-in ceremony. She wanted to die remembering the first time she'd kicked Ash's ass in the ring. She wanted to die in a cloud of plums and spice as Nox held her, allowing her to feel safe and loved in her arms.

Her search for joy was cut short.

A clang came from somewhere around the curvature of the beige-stone hall.

No time in the world would have been long enough to prepare her for whatever was to come next. She didn't want to spend her life rotting in a cell, but she wasn't ready to be torn from the reevers. Ash leaned against the bars of his cell and met her eyes while they listened to the boots. Wet, helpless tears matched her own. She saw it on his face. He was saying a silent, heartbroken goodbye.

The heavy scrapes against stones belonging to footsteps came bouncing off the jail's curved walls as armed guards made their way to the reevers.

Three men—none of whom seemed particularly interested in the reevers—strode into view. The faces before her were pocked, scraggly, and entirely forgettable. The unremarkable guards with their unremarkable faces and ordinary armor paused in front of the cell that held Ash and Malik.

Clinking metal was the only sound in the cell as the man in front retrieved the circlet of keys from where they tangled at his waist. He wouldn't be so foolish as to unleash the reevers. Instead, he located a smaller key and slipped it into a hatch on the cell's floor scarcely big enough for a cat. The jailer slid a metallic tray to the boys through a slot on their cell floor.

At least the reevers were being fed, even if it was a single loaf to be shared between them and a tin cup for water. The presence of bread and water in their cell sent a message perhaps as chilling to them as starvation was to Amaris. Ash and Malik were meant to be kept alive for whatever awaited them, perhaps making them wish that they, too, had died with her. Whether through their action or inaction by refraining from offering anything to Amaris, the guards had more or less said it themselves: Ash and Malik had been set apart to see her die. The guard turned to Amaris and smiled. His teeth were yellow, with a terribly greenish hue to the edges.

"I'm afraid you won't be needing a meal where you're going, girl. You seem to have made a powerful enemy."

The men walked away with a dark laugh shared between them, continuing down the hall rather than returning from where they'd come. Their footsteps echoed for a long, long while. From the sounds they made, the hall seemed to have no end. What sort of circular jail…

It was the halo.

Amaris remembered the animal in her mind's eye. The vivid imagery of the castle from a bird's-eye view filled her mind. She recalled the structure behind the castle she'd seen as it had betrayed its outlines from the shores in Priory. It looked like a horse. The throne room and surrounding space for courtiers had been its long snout. Castle Aubade had four towers. The two bottom towers would have composed the horses eyes, while a rectangular band attached two parallel towers for its ears;

those were presumably reserved for the regency. There had been a circular shape on the back of the castle, visible only in snatches between the buildings as they'd ridden up because of how the castle sat on a hill. It had stirred in Amaris a memory of the sparring ring in Uaimh Reev. Their cells were a part of the enormous ringlet of the circle, which would make the center...a coliseum.

They were in the dungeon of a coliseum.

She wasn't sure when she'd stopped breathing, nor was she sure she'd ever breathe again. No good could come from this realization. Amaris looked at the reevers, but she could say nothing. In the cell across from her, the boys hadn't touched their food.

Perhaps Moirai meant only to allow Amaris to starve to death, her secrets dying with her. What would become of Malik and Ash? Would they be tortured to see what they knew, to see if the reevers had a plan to bring down Moirai and her deception, using their oath to stand against unholy powers?

A new sound sliced through her dread.

Would there be no reprieve from interruptions? Could they not be left alone to mourn and grieve together before Moirai had her final word? Once again it was the sound of footsteps, boots scraping on stone. As she strained her ears, she heard two voices. One was a man's; the other, a woman's. Was it the queen? No, the voice was too young, too gentle to belong to Moirai. What were they saying?

The man stepped into view first, a soldier dressed in a golden breastplate adorned by the sigil of the queen. Behind him followed a young, bronze woman with supple curves draped in black silk.

Forty-Three

THIS WAS WHAT IT MEANT TO FEEL WEIGHTLESS.
Nox's soul left her body the moment she saw the filthy, gagged young woman in the jail cell before her. She couldn't breathe. Couldn't think. Couldn't move. The world evaporated away into a dizziness that may have been a dream, melting her feet into the cream-cobbled floor. She wanted to sink into the ground, though she needed to stand. Every motion flashed through her in the span of the second it took for a muffled shout to come from the moonlit prisoner.

It was her.

It was her snowflake.

Nox broke free from whatever had glued her to the ground, pushing past the armored shoulders of the captain. A primal cry—the cry of years of anguish, of longing, of love—tore from her as she fell to the floor in front of the iron bars and Amaris's name ripped its way from her throat. Amaris was pressed into the bars, the guttural screams of recognition and surprise and desperation and terror and helplessness scraping past her gag. Nox's fingers clawed through the bars and their slits, pulling her close, stroking too quickly at her hair, holding her too tightly through the bars.

"Amaris," she sobbed.

Nox didn't recognize the sound of her own voice.

Tears flowed in hot, salty rivers down Amaris's face, carving wet paths through the dirt that had smudged her milky features and running over the fabric that gagged her. As soon as she managed to look up from her embrace, Nox tore at the gag. The fabric that held the girl's tongue still was too tight. Nox fumbled through her hair, forgetting how to put her fingers into motion.

Her hands froze as she found what she was looking for. She produced a razor-sharp hair pin, slipping it between the bars and working at the fabric that wrapped itself tightly around Amaris's face. Nox sliced the gag free, and Amaris joined in the sobbing, their sounds rattling the very earth around them.

"Nox!" Amaris cried, throwing her shoulder against the bars. Her forehead clanged softly into the iron as she cried. "How are you here? Why? What—"

"Shh, shh." Nox pulled her into the tightest embrace she could manage through the bars that separated them. She continued stroking the girl's hair too fast, with too much built-up intensity as love and the need to comfort overwhelmed her, even if Nox was the one who needed shushing, given the shudders of her tears. These were the throttled, hysterical, gagged sobs of years of separation. Any emotion that had jarred and stunned her upon initially seeing Amaris had broken into countless painful shards, now the powder of a million fragments of broken glass that tinkled around them like the falling snow. She had spent fifteen years at Farleigh protecting and comforting Amaris—dedicating her life to shielding, loving, and looking out for her snowflake. What could she do now that she played the role of the wicked whore on the wrong side of the bars? It should be her locked up, not gentle Amaris.

Nox's shushes were useless. They were more for herself than for the reever, as Nox's shoulders shook and her sobs were louder than any other noise in the room. Her snowflake had never seen her tremble or shake as she did now.

"Can you—"

Amaris didn't have to finish her sentence before Nox's eyes widened in understanding.

"Goddess, oh goddess yes, turn around, turn around," she said, each word punctuated with a sob.

Amaris offered Nox her rope-bound hands. Nox immediately began to cut and slice at them using the tiny blade. She broke through one coil, then another. The rope's tendrils fell away, and with the tangled ropes fell their last tethers to sanity. They clutched each other as if they were about to lose hold on gravity and float from the other. Their arms wrapped through the bars, each gripping at the back of the other. Hair and clothes and skin and bodies gripped and pushed and held with unrelenting intensity. They couldn't be close enough, couldn't clutch hard enough.

"Nox, I'm so sorry" was all Amaris said.

"What?" Nox wiped her tears with the back of her hand, her smile a ragged, half-wild thing. "What could you possibly be sorry for? Oh goddess, Amaris…"

In ten thousand nightmares and daydreams, she'd never imagined this to be their reunion. She'd dreamed of the moment they were finally together once more. She'd pictured it, she'd wished for it, she'd wanted it. Now, her love was an uncontrollable wave breaking against a cliff. In one moment they were hugging, and in the next, Nox's mouth was on Amaris's. It was not the mouth she had offered to patrons at the Selkie, as those had been born of survival and manipulation. They were not the lips she had given to Emily, for those kisses had been stolen, as Nox's heart had always belonged to another. This salted, tear-soaked kiss was meant only for Amaris. Despite the anger and pain, despite the tension and tragedy, it was somehow tender, full of all the adoration she'd held in her heart for all of these years. Passion and hurt, separation and desperation met in the gentle, tragic connection of their lips.

Nox pulled away only long enough to truly absorb the dungeon. Rows of empty cells lined the curved halls, save for the two men who'd averted their eyes, presumably to allow Amaris her moment to mourn. She looked at the men only long enough to see the bread in their cells and how differently they'd been bound. Horrible truths clicked together. Nox pulled Amaris in closer, holding her, begging for an answer, kissing her with desperation. Their lips locked in anguish, mouths tasting of salt and plum and winter and dirt. This was not the moment they deserved.

"No." Nox choked against the kiss, unable to reel in her pain. "No, this can't be it."

Nox knotted her fingers against the white braids of Amaris's hair, tugging them into disarray as their kiss swelled with the love, sorrow, intensity, and agony of their seasons apart. She held her with a passion born from the fifteen wasted years before their fateful separation. The movement was shattered only by the ragged breaths of broken sobs as heartache and waves of emotion continued to crash over them.

Nox tore from the connection, touching her forehead to Amaris's.

"I'm going to get you out of here." Her voice was low and hurried, broken only by ragged sobs as she struggled to steady herself. Nox found her voice, whipping to the quiet centurion. Her dark eyes narrowed at the captain. "Eramus, where are the keys?"

Amaris's lips parted in a wordless question as she noticed the captain as if for the first time.

Answering the darting question in Amaris's eyes, Nox mumbled from the side of her mouth, "He's with me."

"The others—" Amaris had once been so articulate, but Nox could hardly blame her for the anguish that twisted her tongue.

Nox looked over her shoulder for the first time, gaze snagging on the stunned men averting their gaze— whether out of politeness or discomfort, who was to say. She caught the darting glance of the flame-haired faeling, who looked entirely too familiar. Her recognition wouldn't serve her. She'd have to save her regret for later.

"Yes, I've got them," she promised, urging Eramus to hurry.

Eramus wobbled an uncaring arm off in some distance, offering the name of a man they didn't know in a location they didn't understand. Irrespective of his words, the message was clear: there would be no key.

Metallic adrenaline spiked through Nox like a stake to the heart. Solutions. There had to be solutions. She grabbed for the very pin that had sliced through Amaris's ropes and thrust it into the lock, desperate to hear the freeing click of its opening. She'd barely begun to twist it before the pin snapped in her fervor. Three seconds of relief at her ingenuity were answered with thirty petrified seconds.

She froze. Nox stared at the cracked hairpin, horrified. She'd stopped breathing altogether as her gaze lifted slowly from the lock to Amaris's wide, lavender eyes. Bright, trusting eyes she'd looked into as her friend, her person, her only lifeline in the world for so many years. There was no hope in them now.

Nox's mind went wooden, unable to think, or feel, or profess. She couldn't believe it. It couldn't be possible. Amaris couldn't be trapped. She couldn't have failed.

Even if Amaris had known how to pick locks—which seemed irrelevant now—Nox knew she'd ruined any chance at freedom in her haste. Not only had Nox's attempt not worked, but the iron lock was jammed. The tiny, broken pin mocked her. Her other pins would be useless unless she had the tools to dislodge the evidence of her failure.

A numbness descended upon her as she surveyed Amaris in the wake of the lock she'd hopelessly wedged. She wasn't frightened, sad, or angry. She'd presumably emptied herself of whatever emotions one was supposed to feel. Instead, she offered Nox a small, comforting smile. Nox watched as the pale hand slipped from between the bars, this time serving as the source of comfort as Amaris ran soothing fingers through Nox's hair.

"Shh," she said, her voice quiet and calm.

Amaris had never been the bedrock before. Nox didn't understand any of it, almost as if she were seeing a dream.

"If I die—"

"You're not going to die," Nox said quickly.

"*If* I die," Amaris pressed on, "I get to go knowing the goddess was real."

Nox's brows puckered. She shook her head, not comprehending.

"I got to spend my last moments with you," Amaris said softly.

No. Amaris's calm was too much. It stirred a renewed sense of panic and urgency within her. She began to search for solutions, eyes scanning her surroundings. She tried to understand the bizarre makeup of Amaris's cell juxtaposed against the surrounding cages, but she couldn't figure out why Amaris had been put in such an unusual holding room. Her eyes kept snagging on the silvery slice of moonlight, too bright, too pure, too lovely for the hopeless grime of her fate.

"I'm going to get you out," Nox said again. Amaris may have been feeling peace in her resolution, but for every passing moment of calm and acceptance the reever felt, Nox's hysteria only grew. After all this time, they were mere inches from one another. The iron bars sent a clear message: they may as well have been a continent apart.

A sword composed of sound and light cut through their efforts. Its lurching noise jolted them from their moment, causing everyone in the room to flinch in surprise.

A golden, piercing beam cut into the prison, blinding everyone. Over her shoulders, the two jailed men who'd been watching with unhinged jaws raised their arms to shield their eyes. Eramus did the same, holding his hands up in front of his face like a child playing a hiding game. Nox and Amaris squinted against the bar of light as it grew wider, stretching from where the wooden wall of Amaris's cell was beginning to split open.

It was an effort not to keep from scrambling backward in horror as Nox realized precisely what she was seeing.

Amaris's cell was not three bars and a fourth wooden barrier. Amaris had been jailed against a great and terrible door into the coliseum. She wished she'd understood it sooner. She should have made the connection the moment Eramus was summoned to the coliseum.

Nox had no doubt that she looked every bit as unhinged as she felt. She saw the intruders before their hands were on Amaris. Nox reached through the bars and balled fists tightly in Amaris's clothes, hands tearing to maintain a hold on Amaris as they tugged her into the arena. Amaris twisted against the hands that held her, not to release herself from Nox but to free herself from their grip. Angered shouts and the metallic banging of fists on iron carried from the opposite cell, but Nox only watched as Amaris drove an elbow into one guard and flung a fist toward the other. The scuffle was tough but brief. The moment they caught her arms in their grasp, it was over. She continued thrashing, but their hold had separated her arms so fully that she had no room for an advantageous position. The men grunted as they began to move.

Nox had never felt more powerless than she did as the men dragged Amaris backward out of her cell. She screamed, clawing fruitlessly through the bars for Amaris as she struggled.

Nox's heart pounded through her throat. Her stomach turned as she looked over Amaris's shoulders into the open doors of the coliseum beyond, knowing both she and Amaris were seeing its horrors for the first time. Amaris whipped her head around wildly, taking in the enormity of the coliseum with its teeming crowds of onlookers and the heat of the high-noon sun, all absorbed in mere heartbeats. Her eyes swam painfully as they struggled to adjust to the change in light.

Amaris was still looking at Nox and screamed a command, eyes darting wildly between Nox and the jailed men behind her.

"Save them!"

"I love you," Nox sobbed, gripping the bars with both hands as she became smaller and smaller in the distance. Her cries were otherworldly, ripping from a depth of suffering known to the pits of hell. She didn't even know what she was saying. Her heart ached; her tears lubricated the iron of the bars. Her fingers gripped uselessly against the metal that had separated them. "I love you," she said again as the doors began to shut.

The lights, the sounds, the enormity of it all crushed down on them. Amaris's gaze stayed fixed on Nox for her final moments. This couldn't be it. Amaris couldn't be whisked off by assassins. Nox couldn't have taken her place in a brothel. She couldn't have spent years amassing forces, formulating plans, doing everything she could to reunite them only for the All Mother to grant them five pitiful minutes separated by iron.

Nox hurled her final words, her last plea before the doors drowned out the shouts.

"Just buy time!"

She begged Amaris to hear her, screaming the words once, twice, then as one final plea. Her command cut through the tiny slit in the wood in the moments before they snapped shut, a wooden barricade slammed down to lock it in place. She repeated it like a prayer. Three final words rang into the coliseum before Amaris was shut out from Nox's vision altogether.

"Just buy time!"

Forty-Four

AMARIS BOLTED TOWARD AN EXIT THE MOMENT THE men released her. The shock of seeing Nox had been just enough distraction to catch her off her footing. One of the centurions hit her with such rattling force that her jaw nearly dislocated. She collapsed to the sand, a cloud of dust surrounding her on impact. Her ears popped and the stars dripped from her eyes, but by the time she got to her feet, it was too late. Her only escape route was shut.

She turned in a slow, painstaking circle as she soaked in the horrors on all sides.

The coliseum at the Castle of Aubade was ten times the size of the ring at Uaimh Reev in the most modest of estimations. The ring at the reev had been a friendly place, with granite stairs leading all the way from its top to its bottom. Anyone training could easily run from the center of the ring to the crest of its stairs and back again. Here, flattened walls nearly forty—no, fifty—feet high surrounded every inch of the coliseum, save for another large door on the opposite end and a few other latched and bolted wooden openings, presumably to cells elsewhere in the dungeon. What mastery of masonry and crazed architect had decided on this smooth, cream fishbowl for its fights? The grandeur was absurdist at best, a display of the royal family's madness at worst.

She continued her slow, careful rotation, assessing the stadium while her swimming equilibrium settled from the centurion's impact. She couldn't let her guard down again.

Those in attendance weren't merely the courtiers from the throne room but the entire city, which seemed to buzz with excitement as they watched Amaris, child of snow and silver, stumble from her edge of the enclosure. Tens of thousands of voices and bodies screamed and roiled like insects in the stadium above. The heat of the blue, clear day felt suffocating as it reflected brightly off the sand. It was utterly disrespectful that the sun would bake down on them during a moment like this. This was not a day for cloudlessness but an occasion that called for the goddess's rain, thunder, and wrath.

Amaris shook off her insultingly hideous juggler's jacket and dropped it to the ground, leaving herself only in the bare shoulders of her linen shirt, bustier, and black tights. She would not die in the puffy sleeves of a court entertainer. The sun was directly overhead, which was something of a blessing as it did not shine into her eyes, allowing her to scan the stadium. She rotated, soaking in every detail of the enormous circular structure.

Only one small object accompanied her in the entirety of the great oval sands. The item was too far for Amaris to see what was with her on the arena's floor. If it wasn't moving, then it didn't matter. She ignored the dark blotch on the sand as she continued to look for a way out.

There had to be a way to escape. She thought briefly of the winged fae. Could they save her? If she looked to the skies, might they fly in and grab her? She squinted into the bright sky overhead, hopes dashed before they even had a chance to take root. No, there were no shadows to offer them cover. This was the high-noon heat of a blistering summer day. There would be nothing to shelter them here.

As she tore her gaze from the retina-burning sun, her eyes snagged on a new threat.

Even if it weren't the broad light of day, a row of what must have been twenty marksmen lined the bottom tier of the stadium fifty feet overhead, planting their protective weapons directly in front of Queen Moirai. They stood with the stillness of statues, all wearing metallic breastplates with the queen's insignia. The archers held their bows, strings drawn loosely in a ready but resting position. The glint of the sun on every one of the arrows they'd nocked told her that they were made of wing-shredding, Raascot-murdering metal. The queen was sending her a message.

Amaris stumbled farther to the center as she absorbed the sounds of cheers and jeers alike. There was no stockade, no noose. There was no executioner. Why hadn't the queen left her to rot? If her secret was so precious, why would she risk allowing Amaris to see the light of day? Was she just to stand in here and perish from thirst?

The chatter of the babbling audience swelled in excitement as her eyes refocused on the object that had joined her on the sands. Whatever it was, the onlookers were eager for her to reach it. In the center of the coliseum, she saw a single blade displayed upon two rough-hewn wooden stands of twin sawhorses on the sand. She'd been given a sword. Perhaps this was why she'd been tied with rope. She was meant to free herself before the public using this blade.

Amaris closed the distance between herself and the weapon. The garbled words of what may have been hundreds, thousands, or millions of onlookers created the white noise of a stream, completely unintelligible and of utter disinterest to her. She approached the blade cautiously, examining the single, simple sword before her. She and the blade were alone on the enormous sand floor of the stadium. The crowd hummed with excitement in a way that told her she would not be alone for long.

Somehow, she didn't feel afraid. She wasn't excited or nervous or even the sort of calm that came from preparedness. No, this peace came from knowing she was not alone. Nox was here. Nox had told her to buy time. The only people she'd ever loved or trusted were here.

If she had to die, it was okay to do it knowing that she was with the ones she loved.

A voice bellowed as if from everywhere and nowhere. Amaris spun, scanning the tightly packed crowd until she found the shaded alcove of the queen behind her archers, accompanied by a similar performatively empty chair to the one she'd seen in the throne room. She would have recognized the owner of that horrid voice anywhere.

The display of wealth before her was abhorrent but not the least bit surprising.

Queen Moirai wore a rich crimson gown. A matching ruby necklace gleamed upon her pale chest, and she donned a golden crown with red gems to complete the look. The red of her regalia was in such stark contrast to the homespun garb of peasants and commonfolk filling the stadium and its many seats. The wealthy courtiers sat near the queen, surrounding her on various sides of the shaded box. At least a few had joined her within the carved alcove, cooling themselves with elaborate fans. Several members of the nobility flanked her box seat, sitting primly beneath what appeared to be the shade of an umbrella. The nobility were dressed in their finery for the festive occasion. Amaris watched the queen, wondering what spelled object could amplify a voice like this. The way Queen Moirai's voice resonated throughout the stadium, she was surprised more people didn't cower or wince in fear.

"My people!" Moirai began, her crimson arms raised to greet the masses.

Amaris scarcely heard the first two words of the speech before her stomach churned in disgust. The crowd, apparently, did not feel the same. Their returning cry was none other than the barbaric excitement of men and women awaiting bloodsport.

Moirai addressed the crowd with ear-splitting volume as her words coated every inch of the stadium, drowning the people in her voice. "For centuries, the keep of Uaimh Reev has rested on the border between Raascot and Farehold."

The mention of the northern kingdom drew a swell of jeers from the people. Moirai offered appropriate pause for them to sneer and yell their anger at their enemies to the north.

"For hundreds of years," she boomed, "the reevers have pretended to be our friends, our allies against dark forces. We have offered them sanctuary throughout the churches and temples of our lands, believing their lies when they spoke of peace." Queen Moirai paused dramatically.

Enraptured, the audience clung to her every word.

The same ear-popping dizziness crept into Amaris once more as she understood why Moirai had brought her into the stadium to face her people. She froze, little more than a pillar of stone while she listened to the wicked deceptions of the illusionist queen. This was why Amaris hadn't been left to rot in her cell. The queen meant to make an enemy of Uaimh Reev.

"The crown prince and I offered our magnanimity just yesterday, inviting this reever before you into our palace. And what did she do?"

The pregnant pause hushed the crowd, pressing the question down on the people.

"She revealed herself for what she is: a demon sympathizer!"

The citizens of Aubade went rabid. They screamed at the blasphemy and outrage of the information. Men, women, and children alike hurled a cacophony of insults, their voices an unreadable outpouring of incensed sounds. Amaris's breathing came in short, shallow pants as she watched the tide turn against Uaimh Reev. Vitriol rolled in from the stands, crashing against her from all sides of the coliseum like nauseating waves.

She couldn't listen to them if she had any hope of survival. She scrambled to grab the emotions within her and bundle them tightly, refusing to let panic overwhelm her. Amaris tuned them out, stilling her heart against their anger. She screwed her gaze onto Moirai alone.

The queen spoke over them. "Not only do the reevers *not* seek peace against the dark evils that plague our land, but they would have us allow demons to roam freely, eating our children, raping our women, and murdering our citizens! Is this the peacekeeper of legend, or do we see her for the witch she is?"

The sun scorched Amaris, burning her white shoulders. Her hair felt hot from the light of the sun. Sweat beaded on her forehead, dripping down from what was left of the elaborate braids atop her head. Despite the heat, a bone-chilling cold leeched through her body. Her pulse was weak and distant. She tried to wet her lips but found her mouth was dry. The audience may as well have been a brick wall for all the attention she gave it, her eyes focused solely on the crimson speck of the despicable queen.

"Good people, I give you your demon–loving reever of Uaimh Reev, enemy to the crown. Show the citizens if I am lying, reever! And strike your demon down!"

The sounds of hinges and planks broke her fixed gaze. Pulse quickening, she shot her attention to the noise. A door opened then within the stadium. It wasn't the giant door opposite her but a wooden cell slightly off to one side.

She grabbed for the sword, holding the metal of its sunbaked hilt tightly as she looked to what was stumbling out of the dark space in the wall before the doors slammed and bolted behind him. She knew what the crowd saw the moment the shape lurched forward, its massive wings slashed to ribbons. While every citizen of Aubade shrieked at the ghastly, monstrous presence of an ag'imni, Amaris gaped in horror at the battered face of Gadriel.

Forty–Five

IRRESPECTIVE OF THE DISTANCE BETWEEN THE STADIUM floor and the lofted alcove, Amaris saw the unmistakable gleam of Moirai's purely evil smile. She locked eyes with the only other person in Farehold who could see that what stood before her was a dark-haired fae. When she tore her eyes from the queen, she was determined never to look at the crimson witch again.

"Gad," her voice called across the coliseum floor, mouth dry with sand, dehydration, and fear.

He moved toward her, hands still bound.

"I told you not to come," she said, her voice thick.

"It's a little late for that, don't you think?" he responded. He didn't look at her. His humor was empty. Nearly at the coliseum's center, he stopped and knelt on the sand.

What had they done to him? While the two primary ligaments of his dark, angelic wings remained on either side, grisly slashes had torn through their connective tissues and membranes. The blood that plastered his feathers together had dried, informing her that this had been an atrocity committed during the night. His hands were tied with rope like that of Amaris's former constraints, and his left upper cheek was purpling with bruises. This was the man who had held a knife to her throat in the forest to defend his soldier. This was the general who had fought for his king, knowing the risk every day. This fae warrior knew no fear. He had fallen to his knees before her now.

Amaris ran to him, cutting his bound hands free with the sword. The action won her no favors from the jeering crowd, but nothing she could do on the goddess's lighted earth would have pleased the queen or Aubade's deceived people.

He didn't look up as he said, "You have to kill me."

He wasn't regretful, accusatory, or frightened. The resolution in his voice was both calm and absolute.

"Gad—" She recoiled from his words as the ropes fell onto the sand below him.

Still, he did not look at her, and now she understood why. The task expected of her would be nearly impossible if she had to look into his eyes. The general offered her an olive branch to dehumanize himself, to spare her own soul. He had knelt before no one. He feared nothing. Yet here he was, on his knees.

"They see a demon, and you know it. If you spare me as an ag'imni, they will kill you. You're worth so much more to this continent alive, Amaris. Do it now."

Gadriel kept his head lowered, not to show his fear but to give her a clean blow to the back of his neck. It was an act of kindness.

"Gadriel—"

"Do it, Amaris," he commanded. He gritted his teeth between his words. "I die, or we both die. However you slice it, I'm not making it out of here alive," he said. His great, shredded wings folded tightly behind him as he spoke.

Anger surged through her. She grabbed him roughly by the arm, hoisting him inelegantly to his feet.

"Shut up unless you're going to say something useful."

"Amaris—" His eyes lifted to hers, their gaze touching as he resisted.

"I said shut it. And you never call me by my right name. Don't bother starting now."

He had seen his death as the only way forward, but her rejection of his solution was final. He'd offered, and she'd slapped it away. There would be no clean end to whatever befell them. Gadriel had spent too many years training in battle to act the part of a coward. Even in his sacrificial death, he'd meant to go with pride and honor. The general had been ready to give his life for Raascot's cause, but if the child of the moon would refuse to swing her blade, then he had no choice. If they were going to fight, then they were going to fight.

He found a smile. "A witchling even in death."

She returned the smirk. "Would you have it any other way?"

Whatever end they met, they would do it together.

Amaris bent her knees slightly in the readied stance of a warrior on a battlefield. The crowd around continued shouting, crying, repeating something. A word had started to form on their thousands of lips, taking on the consistency of a chant. The pockets of the chant were broken up enough that she couldn't quite hear what three syllables the people were bleating in unison.

She looked to Gadriel through the sweat dripping off her brow to see if he could understand the people any better than she could, but the general seemed to be scanning for something else entirely. An exit strategy? Another weapon? A plan?

"Do you see?" roared the queen.

Farehold's monarch had known precisely how this would play out. Of course Amaris—who had seen that there was no crowned prince, who knew of the curse at the border, who had exposed Moirai as a witch in front of her court—would never execute the northerner on whose behalf she'd come to Aubade to intercede. Letting Amaris die in her cell would have let the curse's secrets die with her. Showing Amaris's ag'imni sympathies to the people would rally the queen's loyalists against the reevers, deepening their hatred for the north and uniting them against any hope of peace that might have come from the intercession of Uaimh Reev.

"And what should we do to our enemies? What do we do with those who consort with demons?"

The chant from the audience grew louder as more and more mouths joined in its feral chorus. Hundreds of people repeated the word over and over again—the same three sounds like a howling, wretched prayer to the old gods, or the All Mother herself. Sadistic screams garbled out the consistency of their chants as bloodlust unified the citizens of Aubade.

She and the general might as well have been alone in the stadium, for she looked at no one else. The sun burned her shoulders and their sounds hurt her ears, but there was only her, her sword, and Gadriel. Moirai wouldn't get the satisfaction of her attention.

The queen continued her impassioned address to the bestial crowd, announcing, "We throw them to the monsters they worship, and we let hell reclaim them!"

Her sentence was punctuated by the cranking, metallic sound of gears. Wood groaned and chains strained. The audience lost its mind as the noise washed over the sand. Amaris turned her body to face its source, a blackened, rectangular shadow slowly spreading before her. The enormous door on the far side of the stadium began to open. The aching screeches of the mechanisms used to pry the door apart echoed throughout the coliseum. The ripping, ear-shredding roar of a monster tore from the inky darkness as the door continued its slow, mechanical opening. Amaris took a backward step, fighting off the dread that threatened her.

Her jaw dropped and, with it, her heart.

As she stared into the foreboding shadows and the monstrous screams that emerged from its darkened cage, she felt true fear.

Gadriel and Amaris moved their feet deftly, positioning themselves side by side, as they backed from the center of the stadium. They moved on instinct, putting as much space between themselves and the shadow as possible. Their eyes remained glued on the darkness of the enormous door's open mouth. Another thundering, unholy shriek pierced the eardrums of everyone in the stadium, causing the two to flinch. They remained on guard as they moved, Amaris with her blade held before her. Gadriel had no weapons, nor did he have his wings.

She comprehended the three syllables the people had been chanting the moment the black, four-legged obsidian snake tore from the dungeons. Its jaw unhinged, revealing layer upon layer of needlelike teeth, jagged and wildly strewn about its horrible maw. Its serpentine neck, unnaturally long and horribly flexible, wriggled skyward as it cried its terrible, hungry call to every unholy beast of the continent. The scarred wings, nearly large enough to fill the coliseum, beat in such a forceful, singular blast that it blew Gadriel and Amaris backward, almost knocking them from their feet. They remained firm though the sharp bites of sand and dirt assaulted their skin as they winced against its force. They stared as the beast adjusted its front feet, planting itself onto the sand and eyeing them with hunger in its demonic, soulless eyes. The crowd invoked the three sadistic syllables of its name over and over as they begged to see the justice of its wrath.

Ag'drurath.

Forty-Six

A NY IDEAS?" GADRIEL EXHALED SLOWLY BESIDE HER. His empty hands were raised to fight.

"Yeah," Amaris hissed. "Don't die."

In the tumultuous events following her confrontation with Moirai and her reunion with Nox in the jail cell, she'd forgotten an important detail. She remembered the hard point of metal between her breasts. Amaris fished the thin dagger Gadriel had given to her after he'd landed on her balcony from where she had stashed it in her bustier.

She passed it off to him, and even in their moments of peril, he managed sarcasm. "Perfect. I was just thinking if only I had a throwing knife—"

Another demonic shriek cut off any chance at a smart-ass rebuttal.

This was why the walls were so high. How long had this demon been enslaved by the royal family? The snake was covered in the scars, lashings and wounds speaking of abuses that spanned decades, if not centuries. The horrid monster had been carved and mutilated from its eyes and legs to its wings and tail. Odrin had once told her that if she ever came across this beast, she should say her final prayers to the All Mother. Amaris knew one and only one thing of the ag'drurath: they could not be killed.

Staying still would not serve them. Amaris may not have had the luxury of training with Gadriel before this moment, but they had the shorthand of warriors. The two sprinted for the far end of the arena as the quadrupedal serpent galloped for the center of the stadium, lurching backward against the night-dark well of its dungeon as its right hind leg caught on an iron manacle, the clamp and chains thicker and heavier than any work of rock or metalsmithing Amaris could have fathomed. Remaining pressed against the far wall offered them no safety, for the remaining distance could be closed by the black snake's neck. Its neck alone was the equivalent length of its body, and that was before one even considered the monstrous tail it possessed. The creature beat its wings again, nearly sending the pair off their feet with its hurricane force. The enormous dragon was a worm, serpent, demon, and monster all at once. Its shrieks were the legions of the undead, its teeth the thing of nightmares. Amaris couldn't look at it for too long or she'd lose her resolve. It may as well have been a large horse. A horse with millions of needlelike teeth. And wings. And one that knew no death.

"What do we do?" Gadriel asked, bracing himself against the gust. He was a general. He gave commands, not asked them—yet reevers were known for their studies of beasts and magic. If anyone would have an inkling of hope against one of the continent's demons, it would be a reever. So few of the draconic beasts existed that Amaris's only instructions had been, should she come upon one, to say her parting prayers to the goddess.

Yes, she was the reever. Still, incredulity surged through her. Gadriel was a leader. She should be asking *him* for battle plans. Yet whatever had led him to trust that it would be for the good of the continent if she killed him emboldened him to ask her now.

"We buy time," she grunted before abandoning him.

Amaris took off with foxlike agility. She hugged the stadium's edge as she moved. The dragon's serpentine eyes followed her as she sprinted, and she sensed the beast coiling up to strike. The moment she felt the tension snap and the needle-toothed maw propel toward her, she used a move she'd perfected at the reev: she dove toward the enemy, tucking the drive into a roll and continuing her sprint toward its legs while the face of the beast careened into the wall of the coliseum. Its face hit the wall with the loud crack of thunder. The ag'drurath winced from the great force of its impact, unleashing another scream meant to melt the bones and minds of its prey with terror. There was one thing Amaris knew about being small when facing a large enemy: weight and size were as much a disadvantage as they were an asset.

Amaris saw the recognition behind his eyes as Gadriel took no time at all to understand the task at hand. Whether they wore it down, knocked it out, or simply lived to battle the beast until they could stand no longer, they would fight with every clawing breath to buy themselves precious time. The ag'drurath was still shaking off the pain of its impact with the wall as Amaris caught the general's assessing glances of the creature.

While she was darting for the space near its legs, she could feel Gadriel's eyes on her. She trusted that he saw how the beast tracked her movements. The ag'drurath readjusted its snakelike head, bobbing to the music of an unheard song while it eyed her hungrily. The screaming sounds of the crowd were the music of war, composing a terrible symphony for their battle. Gadriel looked to the snake again, then to Amaris.

Its attention was fixed on her.

The dragon could snatch her in its needlelike teeth in a second. It focused solely on Amaris, its forked tongue darting past the horrible rows of jagged teeth as it tasted the air for her scent. She needed Gadriel's help, even if she had no idea what he could possibly do to keep them from a gory, horrid death.

With his slashed wings, the general could not fly, nor could he roll as Amaris had done due to the girth of his wingspan. She counted on him to do the only thing he could: distract. Gadriel rushed in the opposite direction, flaring his broken, bloodied wings to draw the attention of the monster as it poised to strike Amaris. She caught the pained look on his face as he bypassed her, spreading his shredded wings to draw the dragon's eyes.

The beast turned for Gadriel, its attacking maw fixed on his outstretched wings just as Amaris swung for its leg. As she'd hoped, the blow caught the ag'drurath utterly unprepared. The creature screamed, its eyes drawn to the pain at its front left leg. Her wound had been shallow, meant to divert rather than to maim. The black oil of its blood, stinking like the carrion from the beseul, oozed from the wound. Thin, smokelike lines wove their way through its blackened blood, stitching the skin of the creature slowly back together where she had sliced. The action seemed only to irritate the monster, as Hell itself sewed it together before her eyes. The monstrous dragon flapped its great wings, succeeding in knocking Gadriel to the ground with the attack's rush of wind as the fae's own wingspan remained outstretched. The dragon's wings worked against the fae, wielding wind as its weapon.

Amaris's breath caught in her throat as she saw the dragon's effects.

For just the barest of moments, Gadriel was on his back.

The creature made another lunge as if to close the distance, but its concentration was snagged by the painful jerk of the chain on its back right leg. The noise it loosed from its reptilian throat in anger was a chilling, unnatural thing. The length of its enraged scream was all the time Gadriel needed to be on his feet. When he drew its eyes, Amaris moved. They switched parts in a dance to the death.

She sprinted for the space beneath the dragon's belly again, slashing at its tender part. She cried out with exertion as she swung her sword, her sound joining the screams of the crowd and wails from the beast. Her shoulders ached. Tarlike blood splashed from its stomach and soaked her clothes with a dark, acidic burn.

There was no room for pain. They had no time for self-pity.

While one distracted, the other would wound. It was their only plan. They would buy minutes—seconds, perhaps. They gave everything they had as the citizens of Aubade screamed for their blood, watching a reever, an ag'imni, and a dragon battle to the death under the hot summer sun as their wicked queen grinned down at them.

The people, the queen, the season didn't matter.

Buy time. They were trading mere seconds for a chance at hope.

Time was not an easy ask when facing the ag'drurath. They didn't have the luxury that one might find while battling any normal beast, for the serpent's neck could swivel with the unnatural grace of something born only from the depths the goddess had cursed to her hell. Still, their plan was working. It was not a good plan, and it had no end game, but every second they bought on this earth was one more moment that they defied the queen. They would not go down as willing meals to be cursed in the infinite, pin-like fangs of the ag'drurath. The dragon swiveled its neck and looked to its stomach where Amaris still slashed.

She slid against the sand, kicking up a cloud of dust as she plunged her blade once more, grunting against the effort as she thrust upward into its belly a second time. The general was near the coliseum's wall. As long as she drew the dragon to the space beneath its stomach, he'd be safe for a few more moments.

Gadriel beat his wings against the clear hurt it caused him as she watched him find the barest of lifts from the ground. It wasn't the flight he should have been capable of, but the general took full advantage of his opportunity. He plunged into the monster's neck, stabbing the ag'drurath's elongated throat with the throwing knife. The pair would have had no hope of a killing blow even *if* the beast could have been slain. Nevertheless, the knife made purchase. Gadriel plunged the small steel into its neck while it flailed, once again drawn from Amaris to a new and more horrible attention as Gadriel's knife bit into its long, reptilian throat. The creature thrashed savagely in its desperation to shake him off.

Whether this was a good thing or bad, Amaris couldn't tell.

But they were still alive. Though Gadriel grunted through the pain of his shredded wings as he gripped the demon's neck, Amaris knew he would give everything he had until the moment the ag'drurath clamped its jaws around the general. They would fight until the very end.

Blood pounded in her fingers, her toes—even her throat swelled with her exertion. Her muscles ached. Her head rang from the screaming audience and the eardrum-piercing wails of the monster. Her senses were not her friend as she forced herself forward, deadening herself so she relied solely on muscle memory and instinct.

This game had no end. There was no victory here. Gadriel clung to the ag'drurath with unshakable fortitude, blade embedded in its gray-black amphibious skin while it writhed. She could continue to hack and slash, trading places with him for as long as they could muster their stamina.

They couldn't keep this up forever.

Amaris's lungs burned. Her legs ached. Sweat and heat and dust coated her face, her hands, her throat. She knew she couldn't quit, but while she had been told to buy time, she had no idea how to expend or preserve her stamina. Gadriel was badly wounded. The audience continued to scream their thrill at witnessing a slaughter. The ag'drurath was agitated, but the beast would ultimately outlast them both.

A buzzing cold swept through her as her faith leeched from her pores.

Helplessness coursed through her as she eyed the unkillable demon.

Each second required only one more move. Any hope for survival was contingent on focusing on the next right move.

Amaris looked for her next best action to draw the monster's attention when, from the door through which the guards who had dragged her had left, out stumbled a disoriented, gold-breasted Captain of the Guard.

The sight was so jarring that Amaris almost lost her wherewithal.

While Gadriel kept the beast panicked in its need to shake him from its neck, the gold-breasted captain rushed for the creature's leg. He lofted his ornate sword with the intent to attack. Confusion flashed to comprehension immediately.

The guard was their gilded sacrifice.

Amaris snapped to attention. She couldn't let the ag'drurath see the captain. Not yet.

She slashed again at the belly over and over again until the beast twisted its serpentine neck for her in agitation, keeping its eyes from the soldier.

"*Nox.*" Amaris whispered the name like a prayer on her lips, knowing what Nox had done. The name glowed through her as she slashed, repeating the blow as many times as she could until she knew she was within striking distance.

The captain closed the gap and began hacking at the great trunk of the dragon's back right leg, just above where the chain had cuffed it to the dungeon for goddess knew how many years. The dragon shrieked unnaturally, flinging the winged fae successfully from its neck with a *thwack* as he careened into the coliseum wall. Gadriel slumped on impact. The Captain of the Guard, gilded breastplate reflecting the sunlight, continued his barbaric attempts at amputation, feeling and seeing nothing around him, as he was possessed with the single-minded need to cut and slice exactly here, exactly this place, exactly now.

The dragon coiled, then struck.

The ag'drurath dove with its mighty, unholy maw and had the captain in his jaws in a second. The man's face and shoulders had been swallowed, disappearing into the void of its throat. The black creature raised its neck skyward, allowing gravity to aid it as its needle teeth crunched down on the captain's breastplate. The sounds of metal and bone against teeth echoed above the cries from the people as they screamed in shock, their world turned upside down by his appearance.

The captain continued swinging his sword hand from where it remained outstretched as if, even as he died in the monster's mouth, he was still consumed with the singular need to cut. The ag'drurath focused its efforts on swallowing, several disgusting, wet crunches of steel and bone and gore echoing through the coliseum as it focused on its bloody, metallic meal. The serpent struggled to swallow him, leaving the man lodged in its mouth. As the armored soldier went lifeless, his sword clattered to the ground, kicking up a cloud of sand around it with its earthbound thud.

Immediately, the demonic beast already began to show signs of whitish tendrils knitting together. Unwilling to let this wound heal as had the others, Amaris ran for the back leg to continue what the captain had started. The simple sword left by the queen had been a ploy. The blade had been intended to either behead the northern fae or reveal the reevers as traitors to the crown. Moirai's sword would be the very weapon she would use to mutilate the dragon's leg and free it from its shackle.

Exhaustion throbbed through her with every strike, but Amaris rallied her adrenaline and pushed past the fatigue. She called on her years of fortitude, ignoring the tremble in her arms as she battled tendon, muscle, bone, fiber, and the constantly reknitting, wicked tendrils that crept up through her hacks. She swung the sword in a butchering arc while Gadriel found his feet and sprinted for the captain's fallen weapon.

"Help me!" she cried out to him, but Gadriel didn't need the encouragement. He knew exactly what they were doing.

The audience in the coliseum felt the shift as the tide turned against their draconic champion. Ripples of the audience's confusion and fear splashed through the coliseum, joining the sound of Amaris and her fae counterpart as they hacked and battered the beast, using every second that its attention was on its meal as an opportunity to land their blows.

Through the All Mother's blessed distraction, the ag'drurath continued to choke in its attempt to swallow the captain. It was too busy asphyxiating on the captain to turn toward the pain shooting through its leg.

The ag'drurath gagged, then spat, discarding the armored body without consuming it.

The serpentine dragon relinquished its metallic meal, spewing the captain's lifeless body onto the sand with a loud, wet smack. An ocean of blood poured from the man's chewed, crumpled corpse. With the ag'drurath's focus no longer fixed on the captain, Amaris saw her window for amputation close. She escaped from where she had been mangling its hacked, bloodied leg and shot away from the snake. She counted on the silver gleam of her hair to pull its eyes to her movement while Gadriel slid under its belly. It was his turn to take a swing at the leg with the anger he held by the power and might of twenty years of his fallen men. The rage of Raascot rained down on the monster's leg as Gadriel unleashed his strength to the sound of crunching and shattering bone, relying on Amaris as she sprinted away to hold the giant, beady eyes of the serpent.

The crowd wasn't alone in feeling the change that crept through the coliseum. As the people panicked, hope filled the two lone warriors on the sandy battle-field. Renewed adrenaline surged through Amaris. The people's screams were a beautiful music, a shrieking wail of optimism that flooded the coliseum with their magnificent, horrible song. From across the sand, her eyes touched Gadriel's in the briefest of moments as his powerful arms descended on the beast and its leg. His teeth glinted in an angry, terrible smile.

There it was. They saw their escape.

The queen, amplified by whatever enchanted magic object allowed her to be heard throughout the coliseum, screamed to her archers. The men responded in a flurry. The archers loosed metallic arrows aimed at Amaris and Gadriel, their weapons intent on execution. Though charged to slay Gadriel and Amaris, these centurions had been chosen for their numbers, not their skill. Their action succeeded only in drawing the pain and fury of the ag'drurath, luring its beady eyes away from the dueling warriors to the men and their agonizing, glistening arrows fifty feet high.

The ag'drurath reared onto what remained of its hind legs, slamming its front feet into the stadium wall and arching its black neck up to its maximum height, striking for the archers. The dragon shifted its weight onto its back left leg, focusing its vengeance, its pain, its wounds and mistreatment on the men and their weapons. The centurions screamed their cowardice, scrambling from their posts. The crimson queen fell backward as she crawled on her elbows and knees to push herself as far away from the beast as her shaded alcove would allow before her back was against its stone. The ag'drurath struck successfully at one of the armed men, then a second. The first archer had been a strike to wound; the other was to consume. The archer was gobbled while his men in arms ran, terrified by the black serpent. Its attention remained fixed on the fleeing soldiers, leaving just enough time for Gadriel to land the final, mutilating chop at the demon's leg.

It was enough.

Amaris gasped against their success as the dragon appeared to feel its liberation. The screams of the people amplified as the craven wails of the wicked queen intermingled with the legion of the serpent's demonic shrieks. It released itself from its prone position against the wall and flapped its wings once, then twice. It began to move away from the chain before its smoky tendons knit together.

"Let's go!" Gadriel shouted.

She obeyed, following the general as he pulled himself onto the spikes that ran along the ag'drurath's spine. Gadriel hooked himself around a sharp, bony protrusion that jutted from its back in time with its movements, hoisting himself from the monster's tail onto its body. He reached an arm for Amaris, and she jumped from the sand, grabbing his forearm while he swung her onto the creature. She scrambled briefly against the slick surface of its body before Gadriel pinned her to the demon, allowing her to find the handhold she needed. The serpent continued to flap its wings, searching for a lift she imagined it hadn't felt in a long, long time.

She held her breath as she begged the dragon to take its chance.

The dragon sensed its once-chained legs lift from the sand below it and shrieked again, pumping its thunderous black wings while the audience erupted into chaos, screaming and sprinting, pushing from their seats to escape. The panicked fleeing sent several clambering audience members over the coliseum's edge, caught in the selfishness of the thrown elbows and arms around them as they plummeted fifty feet into the stadium below. The sounds of cracked skulls splattered against the unforgiving, packed sand. The cries of the fallen and the terrors of the onlookers continued to attract the serpent. Wholly distracted by the chaotic bloodbath, it paid no mind to the warriors who clung to its spine.

Gadriel used his body to secure Amaris against the beast, clutching her tightly with one arm, shielding her with his bloodied, tattered wings. He let out a low growl from the effort as he gripped the blackened spike with what she could only imagine was every drop of strength he possessed. Amaris craned to see that Gadriel's foot was lodged firmly on the spine behind him, pressing them into the space for a semblance of security as the winged serpent broke free. He had her. She was safe.

She may have been securely pinned to the demon, but the danger had not yet passed.

The dragon used its front feet to tear up the stadium wall, talons ripping apart the coliseum's stone and sending even more citizens careening to their deaths by either the force of its wings or under its claws as it climbed. Amaris peered between the gaps in Gadriel's torn wings to see Moirai as the ag'drurath hoisted them through the stadium. The queen continued screaming, her shrill, terrified cries amplified by her enchantment object, the gutless sounds of Farehold's spineless monarch filling the arena. The ag'drurath ripped its way to the coliseum's edge, throwing its great, black body off the back of the structure and over the cliff into the sea where the free fall could allow the monster to find the wind it needed to become truly airborne.

The instant buzz of freedom filled her like a gallon of wine. She nearly laughed as she pushed her face into Gadriel's shoulder, burying her face into the chest of the warrior who held her. They'd done it.

The great serpent shot like a blackened arrow over the city of Aubade, twisting its body away from the civilians' shores and toward the blue horizon of the ocean. It shrieked what may have been a horrible, blood-curdling scream of delight while it twisted in the sky, a tightly rotating spiral darting through the air. Gadriel flexed his wings, allowing them to act like an extra pair of hands at her back, cradling her in close to him while the gravitational pull of the dragon's whirl threatened to rip them from their grip of the monster. The ag'drurath shrieked again, its cry the sounds of tin and metal and demons while simultaneously the music of freedom, joy, and escape as it shot for the north, keeping the shore to its left and putting the coliseum with its captors and swords and chains as far behind it as it could.

They were free.

Forty-Seven

NOX NEARLY CHOKED ON THE SIGHT AS THE DARK, horrid silhouette pierced the sky. Her heart abandoned its place into her chest, lodging itself firmly in her throat as the shape shot into the distance.

She looked at the two men she'd rescued. They'd paused against the seaside cliffs, joining her reverie as the sight of the mighty ag'drurath dotted with a fae and a girl as white as the moon clung to it. They watched until it was little more than a speck against the horizon. The silence was interrupted only by the seagulls and waves breaking against the rocks as they resumed climbing down the cliff that led to the sea.

This had been all they'd hoped for and more.

The moment they'd witnessed the amputating blow to the dragon's leg, they'd run for their lives. Seeing the demon spread its wings against the sky, Nox knew she'd done it.

She'd saved her.

Wails shrieked across Farehold and over the sea as the ag'drurath's wings carried it into the distance. The sun was already lowering, but the summer heat on the cliffs had not provided any relief from the scorching temperatures.

Sea spray dotted them while they watched the dragon, immobilized as they witnessed the escape of their friend.

"Where do you think it's going?" Nox looked after it, her voice hollow. Her eyes followed what she knew would be the white speck of a snowflake somewhere on its back.

"As far from Farehold as possible," Malik said quietly, his gaze following hers as he watched the black dot disappear where land met sky. "If I were the ag'drurath, I'd head for the Sulgrave Mountains."

✦

After five hours in near silence, Nox, along with the men she'd acquired, had picked her way into the forest outside of Aubade. The reevers stayed with her as the sun began its plunge somewhere over the western sea. They'd abandoned the coast altogether in favor of the safety of the woods, leaving the crabs, seagulls, and castle at their backs. Fortunately, the frenzy that gripped the city had provided more than enough cover for three escaping criminals. No one looked twice at them amidst the shouts, looting, and the fleeing civilians.

The reevers had a lot more stamina for running than Nox, and despite her best effort, her adrenaline wore off. She'd scarcely escaped the city's perimeter before her legs were too wobbly to continue her retreat. With her hands at her elbows, the men kept her on her feet long enough to make it beyond the tree line. They'd made it. She was supposed to feel relief, but she was too disconnected from the world around her to absorb the events of the day and its consequences.

No one had the energy to hunt or to start a fire, but when they found a space that felt sheltered enough from the outside world, they stopped on the grass and began to remove their stolen weapons, allowing the heavy objects to clatter to the ground. Nox's delicate silken dress had been torn, shredded by the scratching fingers of the forest. She was too tired to stand. Angry red welts lined her skin from the branches and brambles. She clutched at her shoulders where the gooseflesh rippled down her arm, pulling her knees to her chest. The reevers, still dressed in the court's ridiculous garb, had no cloaks to offer her.

It shouldn't have been this cold in the summer, but as night descended and numbing darkness settled over her, Nox felt as though ice pumped through her veins. She shivered, teeth chattering.

Beyond learning their names, she didn't know these men, and they didn't know her.

Though their tentative alliance was new, it was abundantly clear each party knew and cared for Amaris. Whatever emotional turmoil the reevers had faced upon seeing Amaris bound and gagged, Nox had suffered ten times over. She hugged her knees to her chest as her eyes darted between the men. They were in truly uncharted waters.

She stiffened a bit as one of them approached her.

Without waiting for an invitation, Malik sat beside her and put a warming arm around her. It took her all of ten seconds to transition from feeling hesitation and anger to dissolving entirely like paper in water. Though she hadn't meant to, Nox let herself cry. She hadn't realized she'd been holding back a dam of tears from the moment they'd dragged Amaris away. She buried her face in her knees, and her shoulders shook with her sobs.

Malik's arm had undoubtedly been intended for warmth, but it stayed like a bandage, holding the pieces of her together as they threatened to spill into the world.

"I'll gather the things for a fire," Ash offered somewhat helplessly.

Nox sniffed, her face red and puffy from her sobs. She looked up, wiping her tears with the heel of her palm. Malik's arm was still wrapped around her, protecting her from the chill of the evening, the welts of the forest, the pain of the world. Awareness gripped her moments before the young man disappeared from her sight.

"Wait," she said quietly.

Ash paused as he turned to face her. His amber eyes met hers, face tense with a cautious question.

"I wanted to say I'm sorry."

Ash's red brows knit. "For what?"

She offered the ghost of a smile. "For trying to kill you in Yelagin."

His startled look erupted in a short, terse laugh. It was the moment they'd all needed for a break in the tension. It hadn't been nearly as funny as his smile made it out to be, but the pain of the day had allowed any small relief to paint his features with a grin.

"I'd say you've done more than enough to make amends."

He turned toward the forest with his intent to gather wood but stiffened, back tight.

Sensing his motion, the other two turned from where they'd huddled, following his stare. A snap from the trees drew their eyes to whatever Ash had spotted.

The shy face of a monstrous ag'imni waved at them from the underbrush. It made no attempts to advance, waiting for the reevers and the dark-haired girl to acknowledge it.

Though truly terrifying in its appearance, the sight was…silly. A demon…waving.

Nox tensed so much that the man beside her

tightened his grip in response, holding her steady as her heart thundered. Her eyes darted to the fallen swords, but the men did not reach for their weapons.

The ag'imni held up a single twisted talon as if to beckon them to wait a moment before he ducked behind a tree. He reappeared with a bundle of blankets between his spindly, amphibious arms. The absurdity felt like a dream. Perhaps they'd perished in the castle and this was the afterlife. Maybe they'd been knocked unconscious and their nightmares and daydreams of escape and of monsters had bled into one another.

Ash extended his hands to accept the bundled offer from the ag'imni. Nox's first instinct was to be baffled at the obscene partnership, or appalled on behalf of the goddess's decency, but there was something else that nudged at her from within her ribs while she watched the exchange. She'd watched Amaris spare a demon from execution. She'd watched an ag'imni hoist her snowflake onto the dragon's back.

"For the lady," the demon said, its voice little more than nails and rust and glass. The reevers winced at the shrill, grating sound.

Nox cocked her head, turning from where she sat and shaking herself out from underneath Malik's arm to face the creature fully.

"For me?"

The ag'imni tilted its grotesque head to the side. It peered at her with the soulless, molten eyes of a demon. It looked at her with both calm and uncertainty.

"You were in Yelagin," it said.

The reevers couldn't contain the way they shrank away from the noise, like silver forks squealing in high-pitched, painful tones while they grated across ceramic plates. Nox did not wince. She'd experienced too much

562

pain today. Her heart had undergone enough trauma. She'd learned something of herself: once she'd reached a threshold for horrors, she could transcend into a particular numbness. In moments like these, it was almost helpful.

"I was," she answered honestly. "I saw a demon there, at a farm."

Ash and Malik exchanged looks.

"You can understand us," the demon said.

"I can."

Malik asked carefully, "Can you see them? As dark fae?"

She shook her head, answering, "They are ag'imni. But I...I can hear them."

The ag'imni took a few steps forward, the talons on its gray-black, animal feet flexing into the ground as it moved.

"I'm Zaccai," it offered.

She chewed on the name, examining the sight carefully. Finally, she nodded. "My name is Nox. It's been suggested that I'm part demon. Do you think that's true?"

The hellish creation shook his head, saying, "You are no more demon than I."

She smiled kindly at its statement, leaning into the pleasant numbness she'd found. Her heart was capable of no more pain. Her eyes could produce no more tears. Fear was a concept, a distant memory.

"That's not quite the reassurance you think it is."

Ash motioned for her to take the blanket Zaccai had provided for the camp, and she wrapped it around her shoulders, grateful. The forest may not have been the best place for the silky fabrics of a seductress. One more ag'imni—an identical demon who had been cautiously loitering in the shadows—came out from where it had been hiding. The monster called Zaccai introduced the other as Uriah, though Nox mused that she wouldn't be able to tell them apart.

Nox smiled and tore a silken strand from the tatters of her black dress. Approaching the demon, she wrapped the soft fabric around his wrist.

"Now I know you are Zaccai." She offered the monster a sad, distant smile. He was terrible and dark and horrifying to behold. But as ugly as he appeared on the outside, it was nothing compared to how she felt on the inside. While he had the gnashing teeth of the ag'imni, she had the beauty and allure of a goddess. Her soul had been one of murder and deceit; her bed had been a graveyard. Any gargoyle that would offer help and warmth to a stranger was surely kinder and better than she could hope to be.

With Nox's help in translation, the reevers were able to explain what had happened in the throne room with Queen Moirai. The beautiful newcomer was just as baffled as Uriah and Zaccai to learn that Moirai was a witch. The ag'imni had let out sounds of true, unadulterated anger that even Nox shrank from when they learned the queen was the reason for the curse.

The ag'imni did not stay with them that night. They'd excused themselves, telling Nox they needed to return to Raascot, where there was much to be discussed with their king.

"If Amaris is heading north toward Sulgrave, she'll look for the answers to this curse. A priestess told her to look for an orb."

"Orb?" Nox asked. They took a moment to catch her up on the events that had occurred at the temple. It was clear from Nox's face that she needed a little more background. They began to explain Amaris's role as a reever and her status within the keep.

Once they finished their explanation, Malik asked, "If she's looking for the orb, what are we to do?"

"What would Samael want us to do?"

He frowned in response. "There's no peace or balance while Queen Moirai rules with her phantom prince in Farehold."

"My thoughts exactly."

A mixture of resolve and purpose tugged the corners of Nox's mouth upward. Decades of injustice roiled through her. She thought of Millicent and the death powers of witches. She thought of Farleigh and the laws of Farehold that would allow for children to be bought and sold like cattle. She thought of her evil power, one she would never have discovered had she not been forced into a life of servitude in the lands of this southern kingdom. She thought of the royal woman who had ordered the execution of Amaris and would never allow the moonlit girl another moment's peace while she lived.

Nox clapped her hands together, drawing their attention with her smile. "Great—we'll kill the queen. When would you like to get started?"

Epilogue

THE PLAN WAS NEITHER INTELLIGENT NOR ELEGANT, BUT that seemed to be a common theme with many of the strategies that Amaris was a part of. Careful execution had never been a luxury afforded her. She'd suspected for a long time that Gadriel had been in pain, but it wasn't until he groaned from the hours of exertion that her suspicions were confirmed. Soon Gadriel would be too tired to grip the beast's spine.

With little room for argument, he told Amaris that next time the beast dove for the tree line, they'd have to jump.

"Are you mad?" Amaris shouted over the wind and wings into the bronzed face of the general, who held her tightly while his own strength drained.

"Almost definitely."

Face plastered in shock, she asked, "What if we don't survive the fall?"

"Then let's hope the tumble doesn't smash up that pretty face of yours when we land, so you can display you on your funeral pyre."

The ag'drurath had been flying for nearly eight hours, according to the path of the sun, as it descended to their left, over the sea, still discernible even behind the clustering clouds. For some time, Amaris had felt the temperature get colder. Her muscles tensed and her teeth chattered against the frigid air. She warmed inexplicably hours into the flight and wasn't sure if it was because her cells had grown numb or if the dragon was giving off some unknowable heat, but it comforted her. She'd allowed herself to relax, unclenching her muscles for what remained of their flight.

It seemed impossible that they'd stayed in the air as long as they had, but it had become clear that they couldn't wait forever for the beast to land. How could the monster not have wanted to stop after all this time? Black blood had left acrid trails for miles upon miles until there was no blood left to be seen. While neither could swear it to be true, there seemed to be a fibrous, skin-like sack covering the wound on its amputated leg.

Perhaps flinging themselves from the animal truly was the better choice. If they waited for it to touch down, the ag'drurath would be tired and hungry. They were undoubtedly too exhausted to run any farther from the serpent. It would be a sorry end to their tale if they escaped its jaws in the coliseum only for it to eat them in a forest. Gadriel was right. Their safest bet was to leap as soon as they dipped into the tree line.

The reptilian monster was losing elevation, however gradually. What had once been dots and smudges below them colored into the shapes of distantly scattered farmhouses, trees, and cattle. The appearance of livestock piqued the demon's interest, and it began to lower its flight path, keeping its blackened eyes open for any sheep, cows, or shepherds that had the misfortune of being outside this late into this most unfortunate, fateful evening.

The clear, blue day had grown chillier and gloomier

the farther north they traveled. Clouds encroached until the sky overhead was caked in thick, gray waves. The ag'drurath flew lower and lower, slowing with a backward beat of its wings. Amaris peered up from the gap between the creature's back and Gadriel's tattered, sheltering wings. His protective body and blood-slick feathers were the only thing that seemed to be helping her cling to any body heat at this height. Amaris dared to lift her head enough to peer into the distance, spying where the dragon seemed to be angling. A clearing on a nearby mountainside was dotted with sheep.

"It's going for that flock." She pressed into his body, shouting into his ear.

He nodded and braved a look over the edge of the dragon to the fast-moving earth below. Gadriel's face was set. A muscle in his jaw throbbed with his decision. His mouth was hard and his gaze determined as he looked at her.

"When I tell you to, you need to let go of the spine and cling only to me, okay?"

Amaris didn't have the energy to argue. If they were going to die, she'd rather Gadriel be responsible for their demise. She nodded. The plan sounded insane, but so did becoming a reever, seeing demons, betraying a queen, and riding a dragon.

She didn't want to let go, but she knew they couldn't stay on its back. They could take their chances with gravity, or they could battle the serpent for a second time.

It wasn't long before the general was ready to plunge to the earth.

"Are you ready?" he shouted.

"I'll never be ready," she said as she gritted her teeth. "Just do it!"

He chuckled darkly. "You're brave, witchling. Let's go!"

The ag'drurath gave another backward beat of its wings, but it seemed Gadriel wanted to leap from its spine before the creature began to circle the upcoming sheep. He didn't want a reason to put the two of them in the demon's line of vision. It was now or never.

"Now!"

She released the grip on the black spike and wrapped her arms around the fae's torso, pressing herself into him while he allowed them to roll off the monster. They tumbled free, falling like dead weight toward the ground. Her stomach flew into her mouth as they blindly obeyed the laws of gravity, descending to the earth with the speed and force of two creatures prepared to die.

Gadriel opened his wings, and though they were shredded too greatly to allow him to take flight, the updraft caught the expanse just enough to slow their downward dive. "Hold on to me!" he commanded.

His wings closed as they hit the first tree, cocooning Amaris while they absorbed the impact of its branches. Her eyes were shut tight as her body was tossed and battered in the dark, her head tucked under his chin, against his chest as she bit her tongue to keep from crying out. She felt the brunt of the tree's trunk, then a limb, then another, then another, before the thud of the ground sent her ears ringing, wind knocked from her lungs.

His wings unfurled, and she rolled from him into the trunk of a nearby tree. The base of the tree stopped her by knocking the wind from her lungs, crunching her torso against its unmoving form. Her eyes swam as she twisted her body to see Gadriel. His crumpled body had collided into a lichen-covered boulder. He was not moving. She wheezed, unable to find air. She clawed at her chest, but air would not come. Stars spotted her vision, joining the gray clouds and swing of the overhanging canopy.

She forced herself to relax, remembering several times during her first year at the reev that she had been kicked or thrown in the sparring ring and undergone the same frantic thrash for air; each time Ash would bend over her and calm her, telling her to breathe.

The air was there. It would come.

She could almost hear his voice as it echoed its command through her memory with such familiarity. "Breathe, Ayla."

Amaris closed her eyes. She calmed herself, and though it took several minutes, she worked through the initial panic and willed herself to breathe normally once more. She remained lying on her back, staring up at the space between the tops of trees, watching the gray clouds roll by as she focused on her breath. She heard the distant screech as a demon devoured nearby sheep. The calming techniques had worked. The high-pitched ringing had faded well enough for her to hear. She could breathe. She could see the trees for what they were. Amaris rolled her head to the side to look for Gadriel. The general still had not moved.

Amaris found the strength in herself to crawl to him, shaking his limp body with her scraped, bloodied hands. She lowered her cheek to his mouth and felt the barely present heat of his breath. He was alive.

"Come on, demon. Don't you die on me."

Amaris didn't know what to do. She had been trained as a field medic at the reev for wounds, but he did not appear to be bleeding. His spine could be broken. His wings had already been irreparably cut to ribbons. He could be bleeding internally for all she knew. Amaris couldn't let herself believe any of it. She wouldn't allow herself to be consumed with such hopelessness. They'd escaped a goddess-damned ag'drurath; they weren't going to die now alone in the woods with only pine needles and moss to keep them company.

"No," she argued against the empty quiet. "You aren't allowed." Amaris curled herself around him, resting her back against the rock. "You don't have permission. You can't die now. You fucking can't. Wake up, Gadriel. Wake up."

He did not.

She sat beside him well into the night, wishing they'd kept a weapon. This forest did not seem to be the ominous, beseul-filled woods near Farleigh, nor did it have the signs or sounds of vageth anywhere in sight. Then again, nothing ever seemed treacherous until it was too late—that was the trick of treachery. She wondered absently if the ag'drurath was the worst thing ever to happen to the nearby people and felt a faint scratch of remorse for unleashing hell upon them.

It wasn't a very peaceful thought, but she couldn't bring herself to care for the greater good. If she and the fae were to die alone amongst the trees and shadows in the cold night, maybe they'd take a few sheep and villagers with them.

Amaris pulled Gadriel's head onto her lap, shuffling herself underneath him. She found her hands moving against his hair the way Nox had done for her so many times. She felt something hot and looked down at her fingers, wet with blood as they moved through his hair. A song from Farleigh wafted through her memory, one of the lullabies the matrons used to sing. It was a haunting song about the All Mother's grace. Its slow, minor key was intended as an ominous melody to be wary of crossing the goddess's goodness. It didn't seem appropriate, but she had no powers of healing or anything she could do to carry Gadriel to safety. She was too weak, and he was too heavy. All she could do was sing verse after verse of the soulful, eerie song while she touched the hair of the man who had used his body, his life, to shield her. The song stretched and swelled until it broke against a choke of her sorrow's helplessness, its ghostly melody carrying her through her memories into her current, poignant pain.

Her singing came to a halt when she heard a twig snap. It was a footstep.

She looked up, gaze darting through the forest, but there was no moonlight. It was a cloudy night with no way to see what dangers lurked in the rocks and trees. Her gift for sight did nothing for her in the dark.

Amaris had no weapon and no way to fight. She was helpless, exhausted, and defeated. If a vageth was going to eat them, perhaps it was best she alert it to her presence so it could hurry up and get on with it. She couldn't fight. Instead, she let out a pathetic "Hello?"

After a moment, Amaris heard a quiet exchange of words. A blue lantern was lit, glowing into the faces of two or three people. Humans? Fae? She couldn't tell from where she sat on the forest floor. She wasn't sure if she should be getting up to flee. Even if she had to run, she wouldn't abandon Gadriel.

If they were going to die, they'd do it now, together.

Now facing the looming figures that glowed bluish with their lantern, she tried again. "Hello?"

The sight was jarring. The shapes appeared to be nudging one another. It was a childish gesture, the elbows of jostling teenagers. The act disarmed her completely.

"We saw the ag'drurath and came to watch it hunt," said a distinctly female voice.

"I'm sorry—we didn't mean to spy. It's just… It's so rare to see a dragon, and…"

Amaris could not see the girl. She was hooded, her

shape barely lit by the blue lantern. It was a youthful voice that seemed to carry the animation of someone several years younger than Amaris.

"I'm taking a course in draconology," said another voice in the cadence of a young man.

"A course?" Amaris repeated dumbly. What was this?

"It's technically a study of the bestiary, but I'm doing my focus in draconology. Seeing the ag'drurath was a blessing from the goddess."

The girl who'd spoken seemed to be scolding him. There was a quiet eruption as if they argued amongst each other, but she couldn't hear any of what was being said. Draconology? Course? She tried to force her mind to work as she looked at the dull gloom of the blue fae light.

Amaris was too numb from the cold, the fall, the forest to appreciate the information. Her brain worked around what they had shared.

"You're students?"

They nudged each other again, and the hooded cloaks advanced. "We're not supposed to be out here." The female bravely approached and knelt near Nox and Gadriel, pulling back her hood. She looked to be barely sixteen. "We heard you singing while we were watching the ag'drurath hunt and wanted to come and see what was happening. But then when we saw you were with an ag'imni—"

The boy hushed her, his sound urgent and low.

It was too much. Amaris didn't care if they were students or farmers or priestesses or the evil queen's goddess-damned armed guardsmen. "Please," she said. "My friend is hurt."

"It—"

"Please help us" was all Amaris said.

They exchanged looks, barely daring to look at the ag'imni in her lap. Perhaps they'd taken the time to absorb the oddity of her circumstance while they had watched her sing, for they did not seem afraid.

The girl spoke again, her voice hushed with urgency as she said, "Wait here."

And so she did.

Amaris, along with Gadriel's unconscious form, waited through the coldest parts of the night when her muscles became spasmed with frost, twitching and clenching against the chill. Her teeth chattered; her lips turned blue. She clung to Gadriel, who still hadn't stirred in her lap. They waited as an owl hooted, and a distant coyote seemed to call for its scavenging pack, possibly elated to find the scattered carrion of sheep left behind by the ag'drurath. She waited until the dark night began to color into an equally cold, gray morning, her fingers fading from the red of early frostbite to the unfeeling death of chill. When Amaris felt herself slipping, releasing herself to the cold, she found herself muttering a long-forgotten prayer to the goddess for both her and the fae in her lap. It was imperceptible, inaudible. She wasn't sure if she believed half of what she said. Her hands were a deathly shade of blue.

Her eyes saw nothing as she was loaded onto a cart, unknown hands carefully placing both her and Gadriel on a flat-bed wagon behind a horse. Her ears heard nothing as the group of people hissed at one another, one a matronly, scolding voice. She perceived nothing as the lights of the forest and its clouds changed to unnaturally bright overhead lights of looming, lamplike structures, casting burning light greater than day into her unseeing eyes as she was carried into the university.

Read on for a sneak peek at
the next book in the series,
The Sun and Its Stars

CINNAMON, CARDAMOM, PEPPER." AMARIS MUMBLED the words quietly. "And plums. Always plums."

The way she inhaled was like sipping wine, as if she were savoring each delicate scent. Amaris had always said that Nox smelled like dark spices and the sweet, ripe fruit they'd had the chance to try on rare occasions. She'd also stated more than once that it was the best smell in the world, better than baked bread or perfume or chocolate.

She cuddled into Nox, sleepily muttering something about comfort, safety, and home.

Nox tucked Amaris in closely, using a single finger to trace a line down her spine.

"How do you always smell so good?" Amaris asked.

Nox smiled at that, closing her eyes. Amaris was the one with the clean scent of melting snow and freshly cut juniper. Nox relaxed her face against the top of Amaris's head. Her smile didn't last long. Her lips tugged down at the edges when the familiar feeling dampened her spirit like a wet quilt over their bubble of warmth and safety. Whether a gift or a curse, Nox had always been able to tell when she was dreaming.

Dreams were cruelties. They were painful reminders

of what wasn't and what would never be. They weren't memories, or truths, or even hopes. They were reminders of all the things that hadn't, or couldn't, come to pass.

If she were to conjure a fiction, it should have been somewhere lavish. A beach, a meadow, a star-soaked sky with the girls' feet dangling off the cliffs would have been more appropriate. She wished they rested against the cushion of a bed or the comfort of a pillow. Such an intimate occasion deserved the privacy of silks and comforters and gaudy curtains.

Instead, the room in her dream was dark, with the earthy scent of root vegetables. Their backs were pressed into the dirty stones of an all-too-familiar pantry. One small window was cut into the top of the pantry, sunlight shining through the floating specks of dust. They were in the kitchens at Farleigh. It hadn't been a place she'd hoped to return, but with Amaris, she'd go anywhere.

"I wish you were here," Nox said quietly, running her fingers through silken, pearly strands of hair. Her heart wanted to swell with its fullness at the girl's presence, but instead, it squeezed, strangled with the knowledge that Amaris was little more than a phantom. She'd been so desperate to hold her again. Seeing the rippling corners of consciousness that presented themselves only in dreams, she couldn't bring herself to soak in the joy she'd wanted so badly to feel.

Amaris unraveled herself from the hug to look up into Nox's face, the violet of her eyes catching against the filtered light. Shadows obscured her lovely features ever so slightly. Her white brows stitched together in the middle with a tinge of confusion as she looked up at her.

"Why are you sad?" she asked.

The question was as light as falling snowflakes. Each word landed in a silvery staccato as she frowned.

She continued looking with the kind of innocence that reminded Nox that none of this was real. Amaris was no longer the tender, gentle child who needed protection. She wasn't a vulnerable asset destined to line the Matron's pockets. Amaris had become so much more than Nox had ever imagined.

Her dreams had etched a few new details into her mind's eye, showcasing the bright-pink scars of Amaris's long-healed wounds, the curve of her hips, and the muscles she'd developed in their years apart. Their reunion in the dungeon hadn't been long, but Nox clung to every moment, every word, every feature.

When Nox said nothing, Amaris tried again. The frown stayed on her face as she answered Nox's quiet statement.

"I am here."

"Yes." Nox pulled her back into the hug, and Amaris folded herself in once more. Nox felt the sting of tears and knew she was about to cry. She did what she'd always done and shielded Amaris from the darkness and unpleasantness of the world. Nox murmured, "For now, you are. Right now, that's all that matters."

"I don't want to do this without you," Amaris said quietly against the skin of her neck.

"You have me," she promised.

"It hurts."

"What hurts?" Nox asked.

"Everything. It's all so much harder than I could have imagined. I know we thought Farleigh was bad, but at least there, we had each other. But out here…"

Nox's heart cracked at the speech, knowing her subconscious supplied her with what she wanted to hear. She was confident this couldn't be real, but goddess, she wanted it to be.

"You didn't die. I know you're alive. Wherever you are, you're alive."

"How do you know?"

"I would feel it," she whispered.

"I am," Amaris said with low, sleepy certainty.

"You are what?"

"I'm okay. I survived."

How wicked was she to conjure a healthy, loving Amaris when, for all she knew, the girl had tumbled to the jagged cliffs and lay comatose after falling from the back of a dragon? She wished it were true. All Nox had wanted was to keep her safe. She'd done all she could to help the snowflake, too small, too delicate for the cruelties of the world as she'd been dragged into the coliseum. Had it been enough?

But...Amaris hadn't been fragile. She hadn't been powerless or defenseless. She was nothing like the snowflake Nox had known and loved in Farleigh. She had been capable and quick and strong. She'd been agile and brave. She was someone Nox didn't know. Not anymore.

And so Nox had used her gifts and curses. She'd sent the guard to his death to face the ag'drurath. She'd picked the locks and unshackled the jailed reevers. She had fled the castle with a human and faeling in tow. She had watched the blackened shape of the winged serpent dart against the horizon as Amaris clung to its spine.

"You don't know how badly I wish this were real." It was so soft, she could barely hear her own voice.

She wasn't meant to feel this way, not unless this was a nightmare. Not now, not while she slept. Dreams weren't for remembering. Dreams were intended for rest, for fantasy, for freedom.

She didn't want danger or adventure or trials. She didn't want dragons or dungeons or assassins. She hated